Her Quiet War

Travis A. Seabrook

Contents

PROLOGUE

The world is massive. However, my mind is the universe. I breathe and feel every plant and animal around me. My soul recharges with the energy from the air, the trees, and the water. Being reincarnated time and time again is a blessing that no one should take for granted. It's being cherished and nurtured as if it were a newborn or a tiny seed, buried deep in the soil, slowly unfurling its roots and anchoring itself to the earth. With time, it grows, stretching skyward; its trunk thickens, and its branches reach out like ancient arms. With every breath of life comes death, and with every seed comes a saw cutting through it for unnecessary needs. When we breathe, we must listen to the beat of our own hearts and the beats of others. We must be in tune with all around us.

Chapter 1

For years, I've mastered what it means to be a true child of the universe. I have spread unconditional love through famine, war, and genocide. I have seen happiness and grief from many walks of life, and I was tired. It almost exhausted me to continue to come back and relive it all over again, but I did.

And I did it for love.

Some souls are born into the universe alone and live countless lives. Whether those lives were meaningful, they lived them. Sadly, for them, they weren't soul-tied. Being soul-tied was a blessing from the universe because you didn't have to go through a lifetime alone. You could experience and create stronger bonds with the one you love.

Being soul-tied meant adventures and excitement. It was a vow between two souls to love one another for eternity—a contract bound by something more potent than blood, but your soul. It was your duty to protect your soul tie as long as they lived in every life they experienced.

Every time I die and speak to the universe, I become a wealth of knowledge. I could then take that information, relive another timeline, and be a better me. It was a blessing to remember every life you have ever lived from the moment you were born into the universe.

With that knowledge, I could live a life with no regret because, in the end, I could do it all over again. I had the chance to come back and the choice to be better or worse. I could live a modest life or one marked by struggle. I could write my destiny.

I was many species and lived on various planets. Even within one lifetime, I could leave my body and travel to another, experiencing worlds like no other. I've lived countless lives, embodying beings of all forms—once a fierce lioness prowling the wild, then a disciplined Marine navigating the chaos of war. I've soared as a butterfly, delicate yet free, swam as a fish carried by the currents, stood tall, mighty, and heightened as a Troke, and even rooted myself deep into the earth as a towering tree. Each existence shaped me, and each experience left its mark, yet I was still searching for the ultimate truth of who I was. Life breathed energy into everything throughout the universe, down to the rocks we walked on.

My favorite moments of being reborn again were the talks with the universe. It was also the love that my soul tie and I shared. Oh, how powerful our love was—so strong and breathtakingly beautiful that it bound me to the cycle of life itself. Whenever we were born into the world, he would always like to take the form of a male, and I would take the form of a female. Regardless of the species we tried next, he was comfortable in a male role. My soul tie was extraordinary—his passion, his will to live, and his devotion were the essence of love more powerful than any bond I have ever felt in the hundreds of years I've lived. I've created bonds with others, but they were relationships that ceased to exist when I perished.

"Hello, my beautiful child." It was that familiar voice I yearned to hear.

The universe had spoken.

I deeply inhaled as I stood in this vast space beyond the realm of man and time. Stars, suns, and darkness floated around me, soothing my inner being. My aura was warm, and my body figure changed into beings as I understood what was happening.

Typically, I'm only here when I or my soul tie dies, where I can hear the whispered secrets of the universe. At other times, I can visit this space through meditation to gather my thoughts and seek answers, even when I cannot converse with the all-mighty.

I closed my eyes and continued to center my thoughts while controlling my breathing. A small smile crept onto my face. I've missed that voice.

There was no confusion because I knew I didn't break my soul contract, and the last thing I remembered was that I was with my soul tie, and he was dying. So, this meeting between the universe and me happened because of a broken cosmic stipulation.

"Universe, I have missed your voice," I called out finally.

"As I have yours, Imani." The universe responded.

There were soul contracts that we had with the universe, as well as cosmic stipulations. From my many talks with the universe, I gained vast knowledge. I knew and remembered every fact, life, and memory the universe gave me. The universe created only a few beings bound by the Recollection Soul Contract. This ancient, sacred agreement allows them to recall past and present lives after being reborn into another form.

When you die and visit the universe, it maps out the basics of your life, minus free will. Certain things you decide with the universe will happen in your next lifetime. Usually, you choose what kind of being you will be and how many seeds you will sow. There were other minor details, such as how you would look and whether you wanted a challenging or easy life. However, the most significant rule of the Recollection Soul Contract was the duration of your life, bound by fate to live out every moment, every challenge, and every experience, no matter how difficult. You could not escape the cycle until your time had fully passed. No matter how fleeting or eternal, you must live your life in its entirety. Only then can you transcend to the next phase of existence and remember.

You have vowed to honor the universe's order from beginning to end. If you did not live out the entirety of your life because of a fault of your own, you will not remember. You will have no recollection of the previous lives you've lived.

In my many talks with the universe, I've asked why it was such a significant contract for those handfuls of souls it created to sign. The answer was that life was precious, and it was our duty not to take it for granted, as some wait forever to be reborn again, if at all. Not only do they get the privilege of living multiple lives, but remembering all of them is also an honor.

Life is all around us in the universe. Souls are dancing around like giant illuminated bursts of energy, floating off into space. The souls that were not a part of the Recollection Contract were not reborn as often. Sometimes, they float in peace beyond the stars, awaiting a life to call their own again. Tucked off in a magical realm crafted by imagination and a little slice of heaven. Living and breathing in a reality as real as it was impossible, a dreamlike world, where life never passed on, but transitioned into another reality.

I was lucky, even though my life was often cut short by my cosmic stipulations.

Besides soul contracts, we who are soul-tied to another being have cosmic stipulations. Meaning there were rules tethered to us across vast timelines that bound us. Our cosmic stipulation was a sync death. If one of us were to die, we would both be reborn simultaneously. Once we were reborn again, it could be us in the same timeline or a different one.

The good thing about our cosmic stipulation is that if one of us ended life short, it didn't break the initial soul contract for the other being. The soul contract only falls on whoever is the catalyst.

"I assume Mahant is dead?" I asked the universe.

It was quiet for a moment, then the stars and life illuminated off into the distance.

Finally, the universe responded, "Yes."

I nodded and inhaled deeply, inhaling the crisp, cold air around me. "I, of course, want to go back. Whatever

Mahant chooses this time, I will be the same. I need to go back, find him, and help restore his mind. Did he choose to be human again?"

The human form was our favorite form. We have been human beings for most of our lives, so I figured that's what Mahant would return to again. Being human was the most rewarding because they were among the universe's highest forms of intelligent life. Humans were highly advanced in technology and space, and were dominant over many other species. However, free will makes my life even more compelling, which can appeal to someone as old as I am.

The universe spoke again. "He chose humans, yes. He was also pleased with his last body. I sent him back with no memories of his past. But as you know, as part of the Recollection Soul Contract, there are three rules."

"Yes, I remember, universe. One, I must finish my entire life, or I will have no memories of any lives I've lived. Second, a soul tie can restore memories if one has forgotten them. And three, I can jump if we don't end up in the same timeline. But please, Universe, can we both be in the same timeline this time? I beg of you. I want to be with Mahant for as long as possible in his same timeline." I said, my voice cutting through the vast space, sharp and unwavering, as if I had always known how to demand the universe's favor.

Again, it got quiet around me and lasted longer this time. I waited patiently for a response from the universe without saying another word.

Finally, the universe spoke again. "I will make you a deal since you have been such a blessing, my child. I will grant you any wish once you restore Mahant and fix him for good. If you want to add another cosmic stipulation to you both, then that stipulation will be freedom of choice to be in whatever timeline Mahant is in."

A huge smile formed on my face because this was exciting news. We have had no cosmic stipulations added to us for hundreds of years. My aura started glowing around me, and I knew I had to make this time different. I had to fix Mahant's mind.

"Well, since he went back to his previous look. I guess I should as well." I shrugged. Imani's last human body was not bad at all. It was indeed one of my favorites.

The surrounding universe vibrated as it spoke, "If I wanted, I could create infinite timelines almost identical to the one you were previously in. You can live hundreds of lives with the same body simultaneously."

"I want to get this right, and I feel as though I'm getting closer to mending this wound. Maybe the familiarity is helping Mahant's memory, too."

"I agree. For the past few lifetimes, you've made progress with Mahant. I'm hoping to see good results." The universe responded graciously.

There were a lot of thoughts rushing through my mind with that last response. The universe had never said this to me before. Although we took one step backward, the previous two lives were promising. I was excited to be reborn again so I could find Mahant.

My devotion to Mahant was beyond words—an unshakable pledge transcending time. My love for him was powerful, unwavering, and unconditional. Through lifetimes spanning centuries, I had lived it all—deep friendships, passionate love, the fleeting highs of wealth, the crushing lows of sickness, and every joy and sorrow in between. Yet, no matter how many times I was reborn or how many realities I experienced, my soul always found its way back to him. What kept me going was this burning desire to heal and love Mahant. Every life with him was different, but also beautifully the same. His devotion and love for me were unlike anything I had ever known.

Even though I had just seen him before he went back to the hospital, I was already missing him. It was hard letting him go back to Lauren, but there was no way I would be selfish and keep him to myself. He will probably never see the people in that timeline again. If one thing the universe has taught me is that every single life is precious, that everything around us has a purpose, and that love is the highest frequency we can embody.

It was always hard for me when I found out Mahant had passed. It only meant that I would have to find him all over again. Initially, it was tough to find him, but over the years, I've grown stronger, and our love has deepened. Finding his energy in the universe was easier for me, even if he was in another timeline.

However, it would have been much more convenient if I hadn't had to jump around different timelines, and we both were in the same one. I wasn't sure if the universe would allow us to be in the same timeline this time or if I had to find him first, and fix him, and then, in the next life, we'd be in the same timeline. But I was done asking questions.

I was ready to be reborn again so I could get out there and find Mahant. Being reborn had its challenges. Imagine being a newborn with memories of countless previous lives. You, of course, don't want to scare your parents to death, so it's a secret you must keep. It gets better when you get to a certain age and can manage things independently. In some lives, I've had to dumb myself down as if I didn't know better when I did. In other lives, they considered me an advanced, brilliant child.

Either way, you build connections with your family and love them until the end—at least I did.

As the universe and I concluded our conversation, I felt my energy shifting, pulsating in rhythmic waves around me. The immense gravitational pull of a nearby black hole began drawing me in, its depths endless and consuming. I surrendered to its force, drifting effortlessly into the abyss. Yet, a radiant light emerged beyond the darkness—warm, golden, and inviting. It beckoned me forward, filling me with unexplainable peace. I embraced the light without hesitation, allowing it to envelop me completely.

And at that moment, I was reborn.

CHAPTER 2

Act I – The Past Timeline

My first timeline.

You would think that it all started at the beginning of time. But for me and Mahant, it was way after that. Technology controlled the world, robots were superior, and humans quickly died from the brunt of it all. The year was 3541, and I was a Graingar on Planet 662. There were four branches of the Congolo military.

The four branches were the Mortel, the Hostep, the Triot, and the Graingar. First, you became a Mortel and took control of the ground siege. The ground siege was a war between the humans backing the bots and the Congolo Military. It was an easier battle to fight because flesh and blood were easier to kill.

Once you ranked up, you became a Hostep next. The Hostep oversaw the seizure and capture of all technology that would better aid in the war effort. There were guns, bombs, and chemical warfare that spread like famine throughout the world.

The Triot and Graingar were constantly striving to reach the top of the Congolo military. The Triot was to recruit warriors, fighters, and vigilantes to join the cause. They picked the best of the best for battle, so they always thought they controlled the Graingar. However, the Graingar military killed off the robots and was the highest-ranking branch.

This timeline was the worst timeline I had ever been in. It was my first experience in a physical life form, and I had no recollection of what life was all about. There was no reference to help me understand this cruel world. It was all about the killing and survival of my life, the will to live. Even though I never understood why anyone would like to live in a timeline of such destruction, only one person made me understand.

His name was Bayzo, and he was a handsome man who had recently been promoted from the Hostep to the Triot branch. Bayzo was tall and dark-skinned. He always wore his all-black army gear, complete with a weighted vest around him and black boots. Bayzo always had a black bandana folded and wrapped around his head. He would walk around with a toothpick in his mouth and remain quiet. There was also a scar right above his eyebrow. Bayzo was a fine soldier; however, a reserved and peaceful guy. He said little when we first met, but we often saw each other around our base.

He would always stare at me, his gaze holding an unspoken gravity, a force stronger than words. There was a cosmic pull in his eyes, something ancient and magnetic that called out to me. Bayzo felt familiar—like a forgotten melody, a dream I had lived before but couldn't quite place.

I sat in my quarters, put on my brown combat boots, and prepared for my day. We've just received some intel on robots targeting Votel, our army base. We fought different robots—manufactured AIH and the CAI, which were more dangerous. AIH stood for Almost Intelligent Humans, which were physical robots. A computer generated the CAI, or Computer Artificial Intelligence. They would hack into our systems, spread viruses through our networks, cut off our supplies, and dry us out.

The robots zoning in on Votel were the AIH, accompanied by humans, meaning not only were the Mortel going to fight, but the Graingar as well.

I stood from my bed and walked towards my mirror. As I stared into the mirror, I put on my gun holster and checked my clips to ensure they were loaded. I also loaded my AIHB, which stood for Almost Intelligent Human Bombs. These bombs could wipe out thousands of AIH in a matter of seconds. They were small and round, and I only had space for three of them, so I had to use them wisely as the AIH gathered in numbers—hundreds of thousands of them in a single battle.

After getting ready, I headed to the top deck and checked out reports. Once I reached the top deck, there I saw Bayzo. He was standing at ease with his hands behind his back. He looked over at me as I approached him.

I stood beside him, put my hands behind my back, and looked toward the enormous screens across from us, which displayed reports.

"Hey, Bayzo," I spoke, trying not to blush.

Bayzo, with a serious tone, responded. "Bailey."

I was much shorter than he was. I had a nice build, but he was much bigger and probably stronger than I was. I tied my dark black hair in a slicked-back bun today to stay out of my face. I was also a lighter tone than his, more mocha than his deep, dark complexion. We were both impeccably groomed, our appearances untouched by body art, tribal markings, or piercings.

I looked over at him, and he looked back at me, so I smiled. He smiled at me, leaned towards me, and bumped me with his shoulder.

"I don't like these reports. They're closing in on Votel, and we know what that means." Bayzo finally let out.

I nodded. "Mmm, yeah, it means I get to kick some ass."

"I don't like that for you, Bailey," Bayzo admitted involuntarily.

I continue to look deep into his beautiful, dark brown eyes. Why would he say that? Everyone knew it was a duty to fight if you were a Graingar. The Graingar held an unwavering belief in destiny. Long before we took our first breaths, we sealed our fates and were the planet's protectors. It was not just a duty but an inescapable calling. To fight with unwavering courage, to sacrifice without hesitation, and to die with honor.

We typically rank up fast, but unfortunately, you can't go from a Triot to a Graingar. You move from a Hostep to a Triot or a Hostep to a Graingar.

"I was born to fight," I replied instinctually as I reached down, held onto my holster with both hands, and looked forward again.

"I didn't mean to offend you. I just wish I could trade places with you so you wouldn't have to fight. So that you could scout and be safe." Bayzo admitted.

"We are never safe, Bayzo. Nobody is." I sighed as I spoke, then continued, "That's what the Graingar is for. To protect people until this war is over, and—"

"This war will never be over, Bailey." Bayzo interrupted. "It's the way of the world. This is how we live."

I can see Bayzo still looking at me out of the corner of my eye. I sighed and closed my eyes to clear away the deep-rooted intrusive thoughts to report him. What he said was punishable, and I, as his top-ranking officer, couldn't help but separate my feelings from his truths.

I turned and looked at him again. "What's this hero complex you have? You don't even know me."

"I feel like I know you. I feel this energy that's drawn to you that's inexplicable. I know you feel it, too." Bayzo admitted with a sense of vulnerability, a quiet longing that neither of us could ignore. His eyes searched mine, desperate for confirmation.

My chest rose and quickly fell as Bayzo moved closer to me. He stood before me and stared me down, locking his eyes on mine.

He was right that we had this inexplicable connection, even though we barely knew each other. Even with unspoken words, I could feel the energy surrounding him, and I did not understand it. I always crossed paths with him. Taking the longer route to the top deck on certain days because I knew his quarters were in that direction. We smiled whenever we made eye contact, but we were typically more serious when we were apart.

Even though this was only our second real conversation beyond our initial meeting, it felt like we had been friends for a lifetime. I looked up at him, struggling to steady my breath. He made my heart race and my mind go blank, leaving me unable to process my thoughts. Yet, despite the overwhelming rush of emotions, I wanted to be honest with him—to be vulnerable in a way I had never been before.

"I feel the same. I don't understand it, but I also feel as though I know you." I finally responded to him.

Bayzo smiled, grabbed my hand, and led me down the hall. I laughed as I followed quickly behind him.

"Where are we going?" I asked.

He turned around and looked back at me as he walked through the halls. "I want to show you something."

As we continued our walk, I noticed we were heading towards his sleeping quarters. I stopped and pulled away from him. He stopped as well and turned around to look at me.

"Are you okay?" He asked me, concerned.

I became nervous and wondered about his intentions. I've never been in a man's room before. I stepped back a bit and tried to compose myself.

"Yeah, I'm fine. I just..." I stopped myself and looked around to see if anyone was around, but the hallways were clear of people. I'm sure everyone was preparing for battle or checking reports at their stations.

Bayzo came closer and gently grabbed my hand, placing it on his chest. "I promise I got you. C'mon." He reassured me.

The heat from his body against my hand was overwhelming me. I could feel him even stronger now. We stood there momentarily, and a strong impulse took over me—I flattened my hand against his chest, right up against his heart, and softly rubbed it. I wanted to reassure myself and him that everything was okay. I trusted him.

Bayzo smiled and turned around with my hand still in his hand. Then he continued to walk to his room. Once we reached it, he waved his hand over his print pad, which unlocked his door. We walked inside, and instantly, I was captivated by his space.

Huge pieces of paper were hanging up on one side of the wall. On the paper were sketches of different images. There was also an easel in Bayzo's room with a canvas sitting on it that turned away from me. What captivated me was a mural on another wall that reminded me of Zion, a paradise that did not exist in this world. I walked around his room slowly, taking everything in.

I traced my fingers along the wall of the mural. There was green grass and clouds, water as blue and clear as the sky. A small, cute little house sat off the lake and mountains in the distance.

"You painted all this?" I finally let out. I turned and looked at Bayzo, who was standing beside me, holding his vest. He nodded slowly.

He walked over to the easel, picked up the canvas, and held it close as he examined it. I watched him as he looked it over, wondering what he was thinking.

"I have these visions when I sleep. And before I came to Votel, I saw this woman in one, so I had to draw her. She was so beautiful and a beacon of happiness for me." Bayzo paused and then sighed deeply. He turned the canvas around, and on the canvas was me. It took me by surprise, but it was such a beautiful painting. It was in color, which was a beauty because everything in Votel was dark and gloomy.

I walked to Bayzo slowly and took the canvas from him while I continued to look it over. I loved it so much.

Bayzo spoke quietly, "I had a feeling that one day I would finally meet you, Bailey. So, you could imagine when I first saw you here at Votel, I was surprised."

I broke my focus, mesmerized by the painting, and looked back at Bayzo with a smile. "This is beautiful, Bayzo. It's extraordinary. I love it."

I tried to hand the canvas back to Bayzo, but he shook his head no. "You keep it. I want you to have it."

I smirked at him and then turned to walk towards a nearby chair. I sat and crossed my legs, still looking over the beautiful painting. Bayzo sat down on his bed, and his knee grazed mine as he sat there. The room grew more intense as we sat quietly in each other's presence.

"I wish I were a Graingar. Instead of a Triot." Bayzo admitted.

I rested my hand on his knee and rubbed it gently. He bounced it, and I could feel nervous energy coming from him. "You should be proud to be a Triot. It's fine work. Hard work."

Bayzo nodded and tilted his head. "I guess. You've fought eight times since you became a Graingar, Bailey. I'm sure it's heavy on you."

My eyebrow raised. "I see you've done your homework."

It was true. I've been in many wars since becoming a Mortel at 18. I was young when I joined the Congolo military, and I put in a lot of work to get to where I am. School was hard on me, and my parents were even harder. Unfortunately, we did not come from privilege, and my family didn't survive War X, one of the biggest battles on the ground between the Mortel and the people who protected the AIH. It was why I enlisted, became a Mortel, and advanced within the ranks.

I did fantastic work as a Mortel, and our general recognized my ability to be much more. At 20, I became a Hostep, and a year later, on my 21st birthday, I became a Graingar. Almost a year has passed since I became a Graingar, and it's been tiring work.

I broke my train of thought and looked at Bayzo staring at me, so I smiled back and spoke, "My birthday is coming up. What are you going to get me?"

"Uh, it'll be a surprise." He tilted his head. "My birthday is soon as well. I'll be 22."

"Mmm, so we're the same age. Cute."

Bayzo never stopped staring at me, and I blushed a bit.

I then turned away and cleared my throat. "So, do you have any eyes on recruits?" It was quiet, and Bayzo didn't say a word. He just continued to look at me. "What Bayzo?"

Confidently, he spoke. "You're beautiful, Bailey."

23

I got incredibly red, and then I noticed Bayzo scooting in closer to me. My entire body tensed up, and I lost my breath.

"Thank you." Words escape me. It felt like something held my tongue, and I couldn't speak.

Bayzo closed the space between us and pressed his lips against mine, kissing me. A burst of energy expelled around us and wrapped us in its embrace. Heat emitted from his lips, and his essence took over me.

I've never felt such power before. The energy surrounding us was overwhelming, but it didn't last long. After my initial reaction, a calmness swept over me. Bayzo's lips were soothing and warm against mine. My eyes closed, and I let him press his lips even deeper into them. It was a feeling like no other. A feeling I couldn't possibly explain.

Everything in me exploded. Deep in the roots of my being, the feeling of Bayzo made me lose control. I wrapped my arms around his neck and never wanted to let him go. How could someone I barely knew make me feel this way? How intense this feeling was. I felt his arms wrap around my waist, and I melted even more into his embrace. I uncontrollably felt my body shift, as I sat on top of him, straddling his lap.

We continued to kiss; the kiss deepened and grew more passionate as the tips of my fingers crept up the nape of

Bayzo's neck and played with his bandana. I've never kissed a man before, and I wondered if it was always this intense.

I moaned into his kiss. His hands reached around and unbuckled my holster belt, and he carefully dropped it to the floor. Soon after, I felt the warmth of his hands creep up the back of my shirt and rub against my back. With every touch, vibrations coursed through my body, tiny sparks of electricity radiating from my core.

I don't know what took over me.

Suddenly, I pulled away from him and looked deep into his eyes as I grabbed the hem of my shirt and pulled it above my head. I reached back and pulled off my brown boots, tossing them to the floor.

Bayzo followed suit, unbuckling his vest and pulling it off. Next, he did the same by pulling his shirt over his head and throwing it towards the room's corner. His chest was so sexy. He was muscular everywhere and covered in tiny hairs. I pressed my hands flat into his chest and rubbed them all around. While I felt him, he leaned back into me. This time, his lips found their way to my neck. He sucked against my skin, and my body froze. The feeling of his lips and tongue dancing along the curvature of my neck was too much for me. It was all so overwhelming, but in a good way.

I couldn't stop the sounds that escaped my lips because our bodies intertwined like nothing I had ever experienced.

I've never been with anyone in a sexual way at all, so this was a first.

Bayzo wrapped his arms around my waist again, lifted me, then rested me against his bed. My legs spread, and he lay in between them as he unbuttoned my pants. Once unbuttoned, he slid them over my hips and down my legs, tossing them to the side. He then did the same with his jeans. Now, in only bra and panties, and he in boxers, Bayzo lay against me while my back lay flat against the bed. We continued to kiss and explore each other's bodies.

Everything about the experience was breathtaking. Even the painful parts where I lost my virginity to a man, my inner spirit, told me I knew. The room would spin and twirl, and at some points, it was as if nothing in the room even mattered. It was just this massive universe that he and I created from the sheer force of being together. This blue glow encompassed us, the first time I've ever witnessed our auras together.

He didn't just care about his self-gratification—he cared about how I felt. He would talk and coach me through moments when I thought I couldn't take any more. When tears fell out of my eyes, he would kiss them away. He held me close as we went at it, and we mended into one being. I were experiencing not only my orgasms but his as well. It was a powerful event that I wanted to experience time and time again, and we did.

When he had me on my knees, that was my favorite. In these moments, he received complete control. I trusted him to take care of us in more ways than one. Bayzo would show me he was alpha. With his hands wrapped around the back of my neck, my face would eat the pillow, and he would have his way with me.

I was always strong-willed and able to fight my own battles. My ability to have my back was unmatched. I was a Graingar—strong, resilient, and wise. I had to always be tough, whether around women or men. But Bayzo softened me. He made me feel like I could be delicate, in my strongest state, and vulnerable.

Eventually, I had to tap out. I lay flat on my stomach, completely naked. My eyes were closed, and I was breathing heavier than I had ever done before. I thought physical training in the Congolo military was exhausting. However, that session was both exhausting and exhilarating.

Bayzo lay next to me, rubbing my back, and slowly I fell asleep.

Suddenly, I jolted awake from a blaring alarm sounding off across Votel. I looked around, unaware of how long I had slept. The room was dark, and all I could see was the red signal in the top corner of the front door.

We were under attack.

"Bayzo?!" I called out, scared. I was never scared for myself in these moments. But something was different, and I was afraid for him. I looked around the room, picked up my clothes, and put them back on.

"Bayzo!" I screamed, but he was nowhere to be found. Once I finished dressing, I realized I couldn't find my belt holster with my gun and AIHBs.

They were gone.

I panicked and looked around the entire room. In the distance, I heard gunfire and bombing, and I knew I needed to report to the top deck immediately. But how could I be unarmed? Where did my gun holster go, and where was Bayzo?

"Fuck!" I screamed out as I raced towards the door. I opened it up, and it was pure chaos. People ran through the halls, racing to get to the top deck. I diverted towards the women's quarters to get my backup gun from my room. Once I reached my room, I located my weapon, put it in the back of my pants, and grabbed another belt to secure it.

Finally, I made my way towards the top deck of Votel. Votel was a very remote military base, but it was one of the few with a civilian city nearby. Our main goal was to prevent the City of Votel from falling. It was at the edge of the desert plains, and then the city sat on a big lake behind the navy ship. The desert was massive, so I panicked when I saw the copious amounts of AIH and those who stood with them filling the horizon. There were hundreds of thousands of them marching on Votel.

I needed my AIHB, and I did not know where they were. My other Graingars were fighting, and the Mortels were already on the ground. It was a battlefield I had never seen before. I hoped that the Triot was out of harm's way and had reported back to the city as ordered by the general.

Bombs were going off left and right, and I needed to get in my cargo and do my thing. A cargo was a vehicle we used for battle that had encrypted CAI-proof security. I made my way to the cargo launch as people hauled themselves into them and rode off the top deck, plunging hundreds of feet to the ground. I found my cargo and waved my hand over the starter. As soon as it started, I had an eerie feeling and felt a tingling down my spine. Something took over me, and I felt this energy pulling me. I looked over to my right, and Bayzo was in a cargo.

Bayzo should have been on the other end of Votel, heading into the city. I immediately got out of the cargo and ran over to Bayzo. I banged on the glass, and he looked up from his lap into my eyes.

"Bayzo! Get out the cargo. What are you doing?" I screamed at him. He didn't say a word. Instead, he covered his lap to hide something. I looked down and saw my gun holster in his lap. We locked eyes again, and I shook my head. "Bayzo, why do you have my holster?"

Bayzo sighed, "Bailey, listen to me. I need you to go to the city. You'll be safe there."

"Hey, listen to me. Don't do this, Bayzo. Please, don't do this." I begged him.

Bayzo swiped his hand over the starter and gripped the wheel. "I need you to trust me. All I want to do is keep you safe."

I banged on the window and screamed. "Don't fucking do this, Bayzo. That is an order!" I continued to punch at the window as hard as I could to break it.

The cargo pulled off and left me behind. I rushed over to my cargo and took off after Bayzo. He flew off the top deck of Votel, and I followed. We both plunged to the ground, which was even more chaotic. Bayzo had the training to fight, having once been a Mortel—the clearance he did not, since he was now a Triot. I also did not want to lose him, just as he did not want to lose me. I followed him as we swerved past the Congolo military battling the AIH.

People were shooting, and small bombs were going off in the distance. As I followed Bayzo deep into enemy territory, the people and AIH began banging on our doors as we drove. Suddenly, a call came through from Bayzo.

"Stop following me, Bailey. I told you to go to the city."

"Don't be a fucking hero, Bayzo. Turn around now! Again, that is an order, soldier!" I demanded, my grip on the steering wheel tightening.

While I was losing him among all the robots we were driving through, he took one of my AIHBs and threw it out the window. I immediately stopped my vehicle and backed up, realizing I needed to get out of the area as quickly as possible. The bombs were lethal and had a wide radius. Not only did they affect AIHs, but they could kill us as well.

"Are you crazy, Bayzo!" I yelled through our communications system. He continued to drive as I turned around and headed back towards Votel. "You can't be out here if you're going to set off those bombs. That's not how we use AIHBs!"

"We should have planted more of them before they arrived. But it's too late—now somebody must do the job. Listen, Bailey, thank you for today. You gave me a reason to want to end this war. Or to help fight it—"

"Don't do this, Bayzo!" I cut him off as he spoke. "We can figure out another way. This isn't the way!"

"Look, Bailey. I'm going to spread these AIHBs across this entire fucking desert, and then I'm going to set them off. That will take out this entire herd of these assholes, and they won't even see it coming. All I need for you to do is get into the city."

I continue to drive back to Votel. Tears formed in my eyes, and I wiped them away.

"Please don't do this. I'm begging you, Bayzo."

"I'm doing this for you, for everyone. We won't stand a chance against all these bots. They will overrun the city, and we will all be dead. It's our only chance, and I'm taking it."

I finally reached the walls of Votel City and entered with my cargo. Before I get out of the cargo, I sit there and listen to Bayzo breathing. We were both quiet for a while.

"Is it possible to love someone in a short amount of time?" Bayzo asked me.

I smiled through the pain and wiped the tears from my eyes again.

"I'm sure we will see each other again, maybe in another life, if possible." Bayzo continued talking, and I sat quietly, listening. "If that is possible, I'm excited to see what's in store for us. I'm excited to love you as much as I do in this life."

"I love you too." I finally responded.

"That's all I wanted to hear, Bailey. Thank you." Bayzo ends the call, and I hop out of the cargo and race back up to the top deck of Votel.

Once I get there, I see the AIH closing in on the city limits. Suddenly, a bright flash of light appeared on the horizon. There was a powerful heat unlike anything else, and that was my last memory of Planet 662.

After the white light came the universe. It was my first experience traveling beyond time, floating into a vast, endless space.

"Hello?" I called out.

"Hello, Imani. I am the universe." The voice responded.

Bright stars and planets were orbiting around me. I sat down Indian style and looked around to see where the voice came from.

"Where am I?" I questioned the universe.

"You are in the middle of where the universe breathes. Where it whispers and creates life."

My first conversation with the universe was fascinating. I learned a great deal about soul contracts and cosmic stipulations. The universe informed me I had just been born into the cosmos and that they had placed me in this timeline to test my strength.

Our conversation was long. The universe explained that when Bayzo set off that bomb, it ultimately was the end of not just his life but mine as well. That's why it was the last memory of my first timeline.

I also learned about my soul tie to Bayzo, also known as Mahant, and my soul name, Imani.

Chapter 3

A nother timeline.

    If I had to choose my favorite timeline, this would be my first pick to stay in forever. Earth was a planet many beings wanted to be reborn into. Those born into Utopia were truly blessed. The Earth was alive and abundant, and gave back to humans as it would to the universe. Utopia was the entire planet Earth, water, forest, and land meshed with buildings, and man-made structures like bridges stretched across it.

The city that we lived in was called Seph. Seph was the biggest and most popular district on Earth. It had underground tunnels that traveled throughout the city. There were huge skyscrapers and forests. It blended a futuristic look with a twist of the jungle. The many trees provided effective air filtration, making everyone happy and improving the quality of life.

Transportation around the city was fun and very different in this timeline. The routes around the town were scenic and beautiful. It captured the essence of manufactured skyscrapers meshed with nature. It was as if man brought a giant city to the jungle and planted it in the heart of the woods. The city was constantly alive, capturing its charm by day and by night, its roaring life.

This timeline of Earth had similar governing structures to an Earth you may know. However, it was one hundred times more progressive. Everyone seemed to let people live their lives as they wanted. Same-sex marriage wasn't taboo, and women had just as many rights as men. In fact, in this timeline, a black woman was our Utopian world leader.

There was no war or famine, unlike in other timelines; cancer, blood diseases, and death ran rampant. In this world, diseases were minimal, and people lived longer. The Earth had healing properties and often reminded me a lot of Troterion. There were natural remedies from plants and animals that helped fight against sickness. Holistic and healing practices were readily available and widely shared.

There was a mix of technology and old-fashioned ways of life. Introducing Artificial Intelligence into the world was a massive pivot from how most people were used to living. Some were enthusiastic about AI, while others were not. Nobody judged anyone for their decisions to use AI, as Utopia was a place of harmony and peace. Some used both and lived a completely carefree life.

Of course, there were labels in the world to distinguish between each other. Since most of the world uses AI, they were AIPop. The people who did not use AI were called Utopia GenPop, or UGP for short.

You would usually see the UGP in the more forested areas on the city's outskirts. They would walk and ride bikes and were typically more off the grid than the others. The UGP had a rich farm life, small jobs, and its own social structures. The jobs were different and geared towards small organic businesses. They were still advanced and used manufactured technology, such as cell phones and electronics. They simply didn't use artificial intelligence.

I was a part of both populations. However, I'd identify as an AIPop since I used AI. AIPop was deeply rooted in the heart of Seph City. Most of the restaurants used an AI company called Facal. Facal was a facial recognition program that identified its customers and would pop up a floating, holographic ordering screen when you walked in. On the order screen, there would be a catered menu designed for you based on your habits, so if you ordered before, it would include your go-to items or recommendations. It would recommend meals based on allergens such as gluten, peanuts, or seafood. Now, this AI technology transfers from restaurant to restaurant and would cultivate a menu for you based on your preferences.

Many forms of advanced AI technology powered Seph. But outside of technology, the beauty of Seph was unimaginable. The buildings were tall, and the abundance of trees gave life. I loved plants and all things green and living, so Seph was refreshing.

Not only was it beautiful, but it was peaceful and fun. The nightlife was the best part of Seph. It was a city that never slept. All stores were open twenty-four hours a day, and experiencing what Seph offered was exhilarating. There was always a party at a club or someone's home as soon as the sun went down.

My name was Celeste Gold in this timeline, and I was born into a very progressive home with both parents who loved me. My mom, Sofia, worked in medicine, and my dad, Booker, owned a restaurant. He was the best chef in the city.

They were an interracial couple—my dad was black and my mom Latina, making me an Afro-Latina. I had long, wavy, dark brown hair, caramel skin, and was 5'7. My eyebrows were naturally thick, and I had full, luscious lips.

It was September 4th, 1945, and I was turning twenty-one tomorrow. All week, I was excited for my birthday that I was blowing up my best friend's phone. I was texting them the plan for my birthday, the pre-plans, and every-thing in between. I have had two friends since high school, Zoe and Imogen, who were my ride-or-dies.

Like me, Zoe was of average height and had a caramel skin tone. She was a slim girl who loved to wear crop tops whenever she could to show off her stunning body. Her hair was light brown, naturally wavy, and long. Often, we would call each other twins because we styled our hair the same way. Zoe was a super sweet girl who would give the shirt off her back to anyone in need. She possessed a genuinely nurturing spirit and had a deep love for love itself. Zoe often talked about wanting to have a big family with the man she loved and to live happily ever after. She wanted a fairytale ending, just like in the movies. Zoe's love language was physical touch, so she was always super affectionate.

Now, Imogen, she was a fierce Blasian woman. Imo-gen was short, but you'd always see her sporting a height-boosting platform boot. She always had her hair in two big puffs or long box braids. Imogen was an alt-girl who took shit from no one, always dressed in all black with many tattoos and piercings on her body.

We didn't look like we would be friends, but that was the beauty of living in Utopia that I loved. People didn't form toxic opinions about others, and opposites attract.

I sat on my bed and took out my phone to text Zoe and Imogen.

We will finally be able to get into Notch tomorrow. FI-NALLY.

I smiled as I texted the group chat, then clutched my phone. Notch was a 21-and-up club in the heart of Seph. It was a place where people frequently let loose and let their inhibitions go. You can smoke, drink, and do other recreational drugs as well. It was a place everyone born in Utopia aspired to visit. So, I was excited.

My phone dinged, and Zoe texted back.

I know you're super excited. You've only brought it up every single day.

I read the text, laughed, and then rolled my eyes. There was another ding, and it was Imogen.

Well, since we're already 21, it is huge that she's finally there. We've been planning this birthday celebration for all of us, technically.

She was right. I was the youngest of the bunch, and we all promised each other that once we reached 21, we would go to Notch. We swore to each other that nobody would go before we all reached that age. It was so ironic that I was the youngest, right?

I stood up from my bed and walked to my closet. Distracted by my phone, I replied to the group chat.

Let's go to South Point Mall and do some final shopping for tomorrow.

I open the closet door and grab a mustard-colored, long-sleeve shirt and blue denim jeans. I reached back in and grabbed some boots and a light black coat.

Zoe texted back first, then Imogen.

I'm down!

For sure, I'll meet y'all there.

My black cat Crisp snuck into my room while I was in my closet and sprawled out on my bed. I put my clothes on the bed beside him, rubbed him, and then headed to my bathroom to shower.

After showering, I applied some light makeup and got dressed. As I walked out of my bedroom, a deep thought ran through my mind.

Where was Mahant?

Just like any other timeline, I've looked for him. I've jumped through timelines and never felt his energy. Usually, when I jump and can't feel his presence, he's in the same timeline as me. But if that were the case, I should have felt him by now unless he was on the opposite side of the world. It was empty and lonely without him. So, to not get in my head too much, I tried to stay present and enjoy as much of Utopia as possible, hoping that he and I would find each other someday. This time, I was not obsessed with finding him or restoring his memories.

We had a beautiful timeline before Utopia, with him as Tony, and if there was a possibility, we would both be in the same timeline. I'd hope he'd be enjoying it, too.

I walked down the stairs and entered the kitchen.

"Morning, Lest. What are you up to today?" My father asked the moment I entered. I sat on the barstool at the kitchen island and grabbed an apple from the basket.

"Going to head to the mall with the girls and do some last-minute shopping for tomorrow." I bite the sweet, juicy, and crisp apple, then wipe my lips. My mom came into the kitchen and kissed Dad.

Dad spoke nostalgically. "Oh yeah, the birthday girl is about to be twenty-one. Ah, I remember when I turned twenty-one. Notch was the best experience ever. I'm also worried—"

"Oh, Booker, don't start. You know, it's like an initiation for young adults to go to Notch. It's a ritual." My mom interrupted as she stood beside my dad, looking at me. She gave me a wink. "Plus, Celeste is very mature for her age and she is–"

"Responsible. I know, I know." My dad finished her sentence. He was messing with the newspaper and balled it up in his hands. I could feel his nervous energy. Having parents who thought you were an innocent young being was cute.

Being hundreds of years old and reliving countless lives felt almost like role-playing to me. I played the part well.

I finished my apple and got up to throw it away. I enjoyed and loved those two. They were wholesome people.

I chuckled as I grabbed my keys off the Console and headed out the door. "I love you both. Be back later!"

I took our train system because I loved its scenic route to the inner city. Our train system was the Bolt Train, the world's fastest and most efficient. It was immaculate and elegant. Bolt had staff who would hand out cocktails, cigars, or food, regardless of the duration of your travel. There were bathrooms, bars, and sleeping quarters as well. You could even get spa treatments.

Bolt would loop around trees and over bridges of water. The train would pass by massive murals painted by the city's top artists. It was also beautiful at night when the city lit up and the fireflies came out. You could smell the distinct aromas permeating the train as it passed by various cultural culinary spots. It was always a relaxing experience.

I sat next to a nearby bar and noticed my stop was soon. I texted the group chat.

Five minutes from the mall.

Immediately after I texted, there were two more texts from Imogen, first this time, and then Zoe.

Already here.

Be there soon!

I looked around, inhaled slowly, held my breath, and exhaled through my mouth. I always loved grounding myself with a quick breathing exercise. It helped clear my mind and shake off any unnecessary excess of energy.

Finally, it was my stop. I stood up and stepped off the train, going up to the ground level of inner Seph City.

There were giant trees and buildings surrounding the exit from the Bolt Train. I took it all in, as I always do when visiting the city that never sleeps. The mall was just a block away, so I headed towards it. City vendors were selling items on the street, and cars were driving by. Because the streets were so massive, it was never congested. The roads were wide and accessible for vehicles, with overpasses allowing people to cross the street without interrupting traffic.

I saw Imogen standing outside the mall as I got closer. She was in baggy black goth pants, a black t-shirt, and black boots. I walked up to her and held out my pinky. She quickly grabbed my pinky with hers in our very own signature 'hello.'

"Hey, babes!" I greeted her.

She gave me a grin and said nothing back. Imogen was very goofy when she was completely comfortable with you, and she always was with Zoe and me. But around other people, she was silent. She sat back, observed everything, and her discernment was strong.

I looked around and put my hands in my jacket as it was colder this fall, more than usual. Finally, I see Zoe coming out of the Bolt station in the distance. Zoe quickly walked up to us as she was rubbing her hands together.

"It's cold!" She complained as she wrapped her arms around me. I hugged her back, and then we let go. She then hugged Imogen as well.

"Oh my, you both look cute today!" I excitedly complimented as I stared them both down. Imogen gave an awkward look, then smiled widely and blushed while Zoe posed cutely.

Zoe wore a loose white crop top shirt with a black puffer jacket. She had on black jeans and sneakers. She pulled her coat together and bounced a little as we stood outside.

"Let's go in!" Zoe gestured for us to move inside the mall.

We entered the mall through the main lobby, which featured various outlets. Imogen headed straight towards ALT, her favorite store.

I playfully joked with her as I grabbed her arm and pulled her back. "Absolutely not. You already own everything in that store and need nothing more."

She chuckled and then pouted. "Fine, no ALT today, let me guess, Cravitz?"

Cravitz was a popular store in the mall and throughout Utopia. It was enormous and housed a variety of items—name-brand products, off-brand products, food, and electronics. Cravitz had beauty, skincare, and even healthcare products. You could find anything and everything you ever needed. Plus, they had great discounts.

"Yes, let's check out Cravitz and see what kind of name-brand stuff they have on sale." Zoe answered.

Imogen tilted her head back and unwillingly followed us.

We already had our outfits picked out for weeks now. We were doing some last-minute shopping to make sure we had everything we needed to finish our birthday looks.

After shopping for a few hours, we got lunch at the food court. We also eventually went to ALT, of course. Once we finished shopping, we all parted ways, and I returned home. It was a bit after noon, and I continued to have this feeling that I couldn't shake. So, I decided to go up to my room and practice some breathing exercises to recenter and ground myself.

Once I made it to my room, I locked my door.

"Alex, turn on the forty-three hertz frequency on Hove," I instructed my automation system, Alex. Hove was a video platform with tons of entertainment and music.

I walked to my dresser and grabbed my lighter to light the many candles scattered throughout my room. Next, I lit my incense and tossed my lighter onto the dresser. I changed into my sports bra and boy shorts, making it easier for me to relax. I grabbed my fluffy socks and put them on, too. I sat Indian style on my favorite area rug beside my bed and rested my arms on my thighs. Closing my eyes, I center my thoughts. I focused on breathing as I slowly inhaled deeply through my nose and exhaled through my mouth.

As I meditated, I finally realized what had caused a shift in my spirit. I hated this feeling because I typically like to be grounded and at peace. However, whenever I was away from Mahant, my happiness fizzled. It dimmed my light and weakened my core. Mahant wasn't just my soulmate; he was my twin flame. He was who I was bound to for eternity. The love I have for Mahant is deeply rooted in who I am. We were one. When the universe created us, we separated into two identical forms with unique capabilities.

I could always feel energies and see auras around me, but it was different with Mahant. His feelings were my own, our essence predestined. When he remembered, his mind was beautiful and as cognizant as mine.

I missed him so much and needed him to fill this void. Whenever I thought about him and his tenacious mind, I wondered what he would be doing. Who would he be with, and what lifestyle would he have?

I continued to take deep breaths as I sat on my floor. My thoughts slowly shifted to how Mahant would touch me in every timeline when we were together. How meticulously his mouth would move against the curves of my body. The way I could not only feel when my body erupted but also feel when he would as well.

My entire body grew warm as I sat there. I could feel my heart rate increase. The feeling of my chest rising and falling faster was pure excitement, and the anticipation of finally seeing Mahant again and wrapping my arms around him made me feel alive. My thoughts were indeed wandering.

I could taste and feel these memories of us. It was both insufferable and euphoric.

I craved Mahant's presence.

My eyes opened, and I shook off all the excess energy I felt through the tips of my fingers and shoulders. I exhaled deeply and then stood up from the floor. If I continued down this path, I'd need to find someone to satisfy my needs.

I noticed a few cries from Crisp outside my door. The poor kitty must have been out there for a while, and I didn't notice. It's a good thing I had not meditated for long. Unfortunately, my thoughts were heading into a place I didn't want to reconcile tonight. I opened the door and let Crisp in. He trotted in swiftly and jumped on my bed.

Even though I didn't get stuck in my thoughts for too long, unfortunately, I ignited a craving for physical touch. I picked up my phone from my bed and went through my texts. Dare I hook up with one of my frequents tonight? I stood in the middle of my room, staring at my phone, contemplating.

I scrolled through my phone and texted Jay.

Want to link?

Jay was a guy I went to high school with. He was a loner and didn't talk to anyone but me and my girls. Initially, I thought he was gay until he confessed his feelings for me.

He was fun to talk to and knew how to engage in a genuine conversation. Jay was black and slightly taller than me, but not much. He reminded me a bit of Mahant and his reserved yet friendly personality. We never had sex before, but we hung out twice and flirted with each other. I never wanted to lead him on, but maybe, explore other options.

He immediately texted me back.

Want me to come scoop you?

I smiled at the text and waited a bit to respond. Self-gratification is selfish. However, this might benefit us both.

No need, I can walk to your house.

I went to my closet and quickly threw on some jeans and a T-shirt since he only lived right down the street from me. Then I grabbed a light jacket. I heard a ding from Jay on my phone, and he responded.

Bet.

I put on sneakers, headed back out of my room and out the front door.

Once I arrived at Jay's house, I rang the bell and waited. I heard a click, and the door must have unlocked.

"Come in!" I heard through the door.

I twisted the handle, opened the door, and then walked in. Jay walked up to me and hugged me immediately. I held onto him a bit longer than usual, enjoying his body against mine.

"Hey, Lest. Long time no see." He greeted me as we finally disengaged from each other's embrace.

I smiled and followed him as he turned around and headed to his living room. He looked handsome, as always, since his style was always on point. His go to was always a sweatshirt and jeans with high-top sneakers. Jay's hair was short, and he had a thin-trimmed beard. Both of Jay's ears were pierced, as was his nose, and he had the most perfect, straight, white teeth.

I focused and responded to him. "Yeah, it's been a while. Hasn't it? What have you been up to?"

Jay sat on the couch, reached for his remote, and leaned back as he put his foot on the coffee table.

Nonchalantly, Jay spoke. "Working mostly at the shop. Outside of that, I'm boring, Lest."

I walked over to the sofa and sat down next to him.

"Sounds less boring than me. I should work more or travel."

He looked at me and smiled. He had such a gorgeous smile. "Yeah, you've always said you've wanted to travel, even when we were in high school. You wanted to see all of Utopia across the lands." His hands animated as he moved them around in the air.

Looking at him, I hike my leg up and sit sideways on the sofa. I allow him to continue talking.

"I would love to travel, too. I'm just afraid to leave Seph. It's all I've ever known, and my parents are here."

Both of Jay's parents were in an accident and buried in a local cemetery. That's what he meant by 'my parents are here.' I could understand that sentiment, where he wouldn't want to leave the essence of them. I wish I could help him understand they are out there somewhere in the universe, thriving.

I gently touched his knee, then began rubbing it slowly. I noticed Jay looked over at my hand and tensed up. "I think you should travel and take a piece of both your mom and dad with you. It would be as if you all were traveling together."

"Yeah." He responds hesitantly, visibly uncomfortable. Jay cleared his throat and stood off the sofa with the remote still in his hand. He walked to the TV and stood in front of it. "Want to watch a movie?"

I laughed at him, and he turned around quickly.

"What?" He responded in a high-pitched voice as he cleared his throat again.

I pat the sofa next to me and shake my head. "Come sit down, Jay, and stop being scary. I literally just touched your knee."

His entire face flushed, and he looked taken aback. "Don't do that, Lest. You know how I feel about—"

I sighed and then stood off the sofa and walked over to him since he didn't come sit down. I stood in front of him and looked into his eyes. "Feel about me? Yes, I know. But you don't have to be weird about it. I like you too, Jay, and if we are going to be friends, then there shouldn't be any awkwardness when I touch you." I grabbed his hands, led him back to the sofa, and pushed him to sit down.

He looked up at me as I stood before him, his mouth slightly open. "So, what are you trying to get into?"

I smiled. "Anything you want."

His eyebrow raised, and then he adjusted himself on the sofa.

"And you promise that this won't affect our friendship?" Jay asked for clarity.

I sighed, then responded to him. "It won't if you don't let it."

I wanted him to be confident and to take charge at this moment. To grab me and pull me onto him or to stand up and kiss me. But he just sat there.

I sighed again, took off my jacket, and tossed it on the sofa arm. Jay responded by grabbing the hem of his shirt and pulling it above his head. He had a nice body, and I admired every inch of him as he undressed. Even though he was a skinnier guy, he still had some muscle to him. Since he took off his shirt, I played his game and took off mine. I gave him another naughty look and waited for him. He looked around and then reached forward to unbutton my jeans. I ran my fingers through my hair and pushed it out of my face as I looked down at him and watched him struggle.

There I stood, finally in just my bra and boy shorts, after he finally got my jeans off. Through his jeans, I could tell he was ready.

"Your body is amazing." He complimented me.

"Thank you," I responded, waiting patiently.

I could tell at that moment that I was seeking something from Jay that he couldn't provide, which was dominance. Even though that was not present, his aura burst at the seams. His energy and emotions were through the roof. A shocking, faintly pink glow surrounded his body—symbolizing a shy edge to him; he felt vulnerable. This glow also meant kindness and compassion, embodying who Jay was.

I finally sat back on the sofa and grabbed his hand. The back of my shoulders rested against the armrest as I pulled him on top of me. I let go of his hand and wrapped my arms around his neck as he lay comfortably between my thighs. Next, I leaned up and kissed his lips. Jay kissed me back, and his mouth tasted like mint, as if he had brushed his teeth right before I arrived.

It heated up as we kept making out. Jay's lips left mine and kissed my neck, finding my spot. I let out a soft moan as I grabbed the back of his head, and his lips continued to go lower and lower. Across my collarbone, between my breasts, and down my stomach, over my belly button. I bit my lip and closed my eyes as I allowed him to explore my body.

However, it wasn't the same. It wasn't Mahant. I thought about him again. He would have been much more aggressive with me if this were him. Being passionate and soft wasn't bad, but I felt Jay lacked dominance.

Thinking of Mahant helped, however.

I wanted this to be him so badly that I let out another moan as I felt Jay's lips finally reach below my waist. My panties weren't off, but they were to the side, and he was very soft and gentle. However, I wanted him to devour me.

Not even minutes passed, and Jay finished. He leaned up and pulled down his jeans, revealing himself. Then he pressed his pelvis into me as he guided himself inside.

I let out a gasp and covered my mouth as he rocked his hips back and forth. We went at it briefly, and I could tell his energy had peaked. His once softly lit pink aura was now roaring around him, even though this wasn't entirely fulfilling for me yet.

The next thing I knew, Jay was done, and I was unsatisfied. As we lay there, I stared at the ceiling, and my mind continued to wander.

I attempted to shift my thoughts to my birthday and experiencing Notch with my girls tomorrow. I was in Utopia, and even if I never found Mahant, I should be happy to be here.

Soft snores broke my train of thought, and Jay was out cold. I rolled him off me and stood up to get dressed. I looked at him and let out a short and quiet scoff of disbelief, then laughed. The poor kid couldn't even last three minutes. I sighed and walked out the front door.

Once I got home, I undressed and went into my bathroom. I pulled out a UC pill. It was a Utopia Choice pill that helped with making terrible, unprotected decisions with men. I swallowed it and then looked in the mirror.

"You will find him, Imani," I told myself.

I turned and stepped into the shower to wash off. After my shower, I got dressed in my tank top and shorts. I found my cat wandering around my bedroom as I left the bathroom. I picked up Crisp and headed to my bed to lie down. My head rested against the pillow as my eyes closed. Slowly, I stroke Crisp's fur as I drift off to sleep.

Chapter 4

Soft singing voices were off in the distance as I slowly opened my eyes. I rolled over in bed and noticed my parents creeping into my bedroom. My mom held a cake, and my dad recorded on his phone.

"Happy birthday to you." They both were singing as they got closer to me in bed. I smiled and wiped away the sleep in my eyes. Ever since I was a child, they've done this every year. It was cute.

They continued. "Happy birthday to our Lesty. Happy birthday to you." Mom and Dad stood in front of me, waiting. I sat up, looked at them, rolled my eyes playfully, and blew out the candles.

"Thanks, Mom and Dad," I said sweetly. They both hugged me and then left the room. I then noticed my phone started dinging. I reached for it on my dresser and checked the time first. I slept in late, and it was almost noon. I finally checked my group messages.

Happy birthday, bitchhh!

There was a message from Imogen, followed by another from Zoe.

Happy Birthday, bestie!

More messages started coming through from them.

Get up! We are supposed to be pre-gamming all day!

I texted back.

I'm up, I'm up.

Imogen texted again.

We're at my house. Get your ass here.

Imogen lived in the city's heart. She could afford it since her art had gone viral several years ago, and ever since, Imogen had people ordering custom-made paintings and buying her work left and right. She was very popular and well-known throughout the city.

I got out of bed and went to my closet to grab my pre-planned outfit and duffel bag. My duffel bag contained all my accessories and makeup. Everything prepared for the day. Once I gathered everything, I rushed out of the house and headed downtown. Imogen had a loft right next to South Point Mall. I arrived, and she buzzed me up. I walked to her apartment, and someone already cracked the door. I walked in and—

"Surprise!" Imogen and Zoe yelled out.

Balloons and decorations filled every corner; their black and gold hues elegantly draped throughout Imogen's loft. The space perfectly reflected her—eclectic yet inviting, a harmonious blend of chaos and charm. Whenever I visited, my thoughts instantly transported back to my timeline with Bayzo. His room carried the same artistic energy—paint buckets scattered across the floor, easels leaning against the walls, intricate designs, and thought-provoking photos adorning every surface. Imogen's space had the same magnetic pull, and I loved to immerse myself in its creative embrace.

Imogen had a bottle of champagne in her hand and popped it open.

Music was quietly playing until Imogen called out. "Alex, turn that shit up!"

The music grew louder, and Zoe danced. I approached the island as Imogen poured the champagne into the glasses. Zoe danced up next to me, then wrapped her arms around my shoulder, clinging to me.

"Happy birthday, beautiful," Zoe said, kissing my cheek.

I set my bags down on the barstool and draped my dress over them. I tried not to get emotional. "Y'all are the best."

I had the best friends ever. They truly loved me and cared about me. There was no jealousy or secret animosity. We all got along very well.

My phone dinged, and I looked down at it. It was from Jay. It vibrated again, then again.

"Who the hell is blowing you up if it's not us, birthday girl?" Imogen called out.

I unlocked my phone and read the text.

Sooo about last night.

You left. Sorry, I fell asleep.

Happy birthday.

I typed and responded to him.

Thank you for the happy birthday! xo

I then looked up at Imogen, who was curiously reading my face, and I smiled.

"Oh, it's just Jay," I finally responded, then picked up my glass and took a few sips. It was deliciously crisp and sweet, just like we all liked our champagne.

We pre-gamed and talked for hours until we finally decided it was time to get ready. It would take us a few hours to get dressed, and we wanted to be at Notch no later than ten. We all showered and got our outfits out for the big reveal.

Once we finished getting dressed, we all looked at each other and hyped one another up. Imogen wore a black, double-split halter maxi dress with long, thigh-high black boots. She had a black collar around her neck and shades to match. Her braids were down, hugging her face, and they were long past her butt. Zoe wore a short blue dress that barely covered her ass. It was sexy, the way the dress showed off her curves. The back was out, and so was her torso, revealing her stomach a bit. Her hair was down and silk-pressed. She had a gold chain around her neck and rings on her fingers. Her nails were a striking blue and black, in a long, almond-shaped style that perfectly matched her dress.

I wore a pink, body-hugging pencil skirt with an open-back crop top shirt. I had my rose quartz crystal, Eye of Horus, and Evil Eye layered necklaces on. On my fingers were normal statement rings. My nails were stiletto-shaped, and the colors were pink quartz, like the rhinestones on my necklace. Then, on my feet were silver open-toed heels. I had my hair down and in its naturally wavy state.

We were ready.

After getting dressed, we went to Imogen's kitchen island and poured a shot of dark liquor, then clinked our glasses together.

"Tonight is going to be a fun ass night. We are finally going to Notch!" Zoe yelled. She was already tipsy. We all were. Holding our shots in the air, we both looked at Imogen.

"Hey, my speech is to hopefully get laid. All of us!" Imogen yelled, adding her two cents.

We all busted out laughing.

Then I chimed in. "I'm down for that. Here's to getting laid on my birthday!"

"Cheers!" We all called out and then took our shots.

We left the loft and headed to Notch, which was only twenty minutes away, so we called a luxury ride-share service to drop us off. When we pulled up to the club, many people were outside, all trying to get in. It was challenging to gain entry unless you were someone important or if it was your birthday. Either way, either Imogen or I were getting us in. Imogen walked right up to the bouncer and cut the entire line. The bouncer instantly recognized her, looked us all over, and then gestured for us to come inside.

We entered, and music was blaring from every direction. Notch was huge, and everyone was dancing. Engulfed in darkness was the entire room, except for the pulsating lights that flickered and danced across the crowd, flashing and strobing in rhythmic bursts from the distance.

We made our way through the crowd and to the bar, where we ordered some shots. There were cages in the air with people dancing naked in them while being fed shot after shot. Instantly, the aroma was deep, musky, smoky, and nicely scented. There were multiple stages where women and men were seductively dancing on poles. The middle of the club was a free-for-all where everyone else could feel the music's rhythm and let loose. The VIP sections were packed, except for one area that stood noticeably empty yet clearly reserved. The music pulsed through the air—a hypnotic fusion of house beats and smooth R&B undertones. It was the sound that seeped into your bones, compelling you to move, sway, and lose yourself in the rhythm.

"This place is insane!" Zoe yelled at both of us. We could barely hear her. I nodded and took the shot that Imogen ordered. Zoe and Imogen followed suit by taking their shot, then Imogen turned back around and ordered another round.

Imogen then started having a full-blown conversation with the bartender while Zoe and I took in our surroundings. Zoe suddenly grabbed me, and we started dancing. She smiled at me and then backed up into Imogen, still dancing as she was between us two. Imogen's back was still facing us as she conversed with the bartender.

I smiled back when I suddenly got an overwhelmingly powerful feeling inside me. Goosebumps crept up and covered my entire body as I stood there. The hairs on the back of my neck and arms stood straight up as my heart raced and my whole demeanor changed. I knew exactly what this was.

Mahant was here.

My pulse quickened as my eyes darted through the crowd, scanning every face, every shadow. I didn't know exactly who I was searching for, but I knew without a doubt that the moment Mahant got closer, I would feel it—that undeniable pull.

The feeling intensified with each passing second, stretching time until minutes felt like hours. My surroundings blurred as my focus sharpened, everything else fading into a white noise. I barely registered Zoe saying something beside me, her words muffled and distant, lost in the static of my mind.

My gaze flickered to the entrance, then toward the dimly lit back rooms of the club—still nothing. My breath hitched as I lifted my eyes to the VIP section overlooking the dance floor.

Where was he? He had to be here.

I could feel his energy pulling me in. It was so powerful and like nothing I had ever felt before.

Everything was in slow motion for me. The lights that danced around slowed, as did the music rippling through the room. My temperature rose, and my heartbeat quickened—the pulsing in my ears was loud.

Suddenly, a man walked right up to me and stood before me. He was a tall, well-built, chocolate man with braids under a backward baseball cap. His eyes were dark brown, and he had a full beard that looked freshly trimmed. Around his neck was a gold chain, and he wore a black button-up dress shirt. His black jeans were tailored perfectly to him, slimming down to his ankles and cuffed above his black boots. I looked at him while his energy burned through me. Out of my peripheral vision, I could see both Imogen and Zoe staring as well, and then they turned around as if compelled to mind their business.

"Happy birthday, Imani." He finally said.

I stopped breathing, then asked, "Mahant?"

He smiled widely and nodded. I quickly launched forward and wrapped my arms around his neck, pulling him close. It was the tightest hug I'd given in a long time, and the warmth of his body against mine sent chills down my spine. It was him, and I was so ecstatic. The feeling of his arms wrapping around my waist melted me completely. I let out a sigh, and tears fell out of my eyes.

"I've missed you," I whispered into his chest as I hugged him, never wanting to let go.

His deep, boisterous voice responded. "I've missed you more beautiful."

As we held each other, I questioned everything. There was one thing I didn't understand. Mahant knew I was Imani. How did he remember? But then it all made sense. He didn't end his life in our previous timeline, and he finally finished it all the way through. That makes sense. However, if he remembered all his previous lives and time-lines until now, why didn't he come to find me sooner? I pull away from him and look at his gorgeous dark brown eyes.

Scolding him, I asked, "Where the hell have you been, Mahant?"

He tilted his head and then smiled more. "Exploring the beauty that is Utopia."

I scoffed, then pouted. "Without me?"

Mahant rested the side of his index finger underneath my chin and looked me deep into my eyes. His energy was so intense that it burned through me like the heat from the sun. My hands grabbed his arms as he made me look at him.

"I've come to take you with me. I'm just glad I've finally found you." He looked behind me at Zoe and Imogen, and I also turned my head slightly to look at them. They were both staring at us. The looks on their faces were both confused and intrigued.

I turned back to Mahant and chuckled. "I should probably introduce you." I wasn't sure exactly what I would say if I did.

"Absolutely, I think you should," Mahant agreed.

I grabbed his hand and pulled him to follow behind me. We walked up to Imogen and Zoe, who were whispering to each other.

I began speaking, "Zoe, Imogen, this is—"

Shit. What was Mahant's name? My eyes darted around.

"Thomas. I'm Thomas. Nice to meet you, ladies." Mahant intervened as he reached out his hand. Zoe was the first to grab his hand and greet him. Imogen looked at me as she shook his hand next.

"And you are?" Imogen asked with all the discernment in the world.

"He's a friend I've known for a while," I interrupted before Mahant could respond.

"Bullshit. We've been your friends since high school. You've never mentioned Thomas." Imogen crossed her arms, and I gave her a look, my eyes wide open.

"That's because I met him on Troli, and I thought it was embarrassing. But we've been talking forever." I say in a low whisper through my clenched teeth. I, of course, was lying.

"Girl, I use Troli all the time. That's not embarrassing!" Zoe blurted out.

Imogen added, "Yeah, it's just a dating app, so why the secrecy?"

I fluff my hair and then push it out of my face. "Anyway."

"Ladies, I got the VIP section with some friends if you want to join. It's up top." Mahant broke through the awkwardness between us all.

"Okay, Thomas, with the VIP section. I'm down." Imogen said, clutching her purse in one hand and her drink in the other. Zoe picked up her drink from the bar, took a sip, and then handed me the other drink they ordered.

Mahant signaled to the bartender, who nodded, and we followed him as he made his way through the crowd and up the stairs to the VIP section. The VIP area we went to was the section I noticed was empty when we first entered Notch. A few guys and a girl were already there as we entered the space.

Mahant walked up to them, then turned towards us and introduced us to his friends. "This is Imogen and Zoe and—"

"Celeste, or you can call me Lest." I finished. Mahant smiled at me and then cleared his throat.

"These are my boys, Jordan, Joe, and Caleb. Then there's Caleb's girl, Lani."

"Nice to meet you." We all said in sync with each other.

There were bottles on top of bottles and marijuana throughout the VIP section. Mahant sat down, and I sat in his lap, reaching my arm around the back of his neck to play with the tiny baby hair strands. Imogen, Zoe, and Lani hit it off immediately. Lani recognized Imogen and said she would love to commission a piece of art from her one day. Everyone was talking, dancing, smoking, and drinking. It was a good time, with incredible energy all around us. The VIP sections merged slightly. Zoe and Lani had friendly personalities and started talking to the people in the VIP spot next to us.

Mahant's hand rested on my thigh. His energy against mine felt nostalgic.

I looked at him and smiled widely. "So, you remember everything, huh?"

He looked at me and nodded. "Everything. It's wonderful. You and I have been together since the beginning of time. Now we get to be in the great Utopia together."

"Thomas looks good on you." I complimented, locking my eyes on his.

Mahant laughed and rubbed my thigh. "Celeste or Lest looks good on you, too, Imani. But you're always beautiful. In every timeline."

My heart fluttered, and I blushed. "Uh-huh. Trying to flatter me."

His arm around my back tightened as I continued to sit in his lap. I scratched the nape of his neck slowly. I could see our auras mending together—a bright blue in the middle of this low-lit club. I couldn't help but stare at him. He would smile, then look away, and then look back at me. I just wanted to kiss him.

"What?" I said to him in a low whisper.

"Nothing, I've just missed you, that's all. You already know that." His lips were beautiful, and I watched them as he talked to me. He continued. "I figured you would be here for your birthday. Since ours are always on the same day."

"Oh, shit! Sorry, babe! Happy birthday." I said to him, I was so distracted by his presence that I forgot it was his birthday, too. I wrapped my arms around his neck again and hugged him tight.

"Thank you, baby." He replied.

As I released him from the hug, we stared at each other more. Then Mahant finally leaned in, his lips pressing against mine with an intensity that sent a shockwave through my entire being. When our mouths met, everything inside me ignited—my blood burned hot, and a fire deep within my core roared with life.

I could feel him everywhere, as if his very essence intertwined with mine, caressing my skin and igniting every nerve ending. The warmth of his touch, the way his breath mingled with mine, set me ablaze with a passion so consuming it felt eternal.

I kissed him back deeply, my arms draping around his neck as I pulled him closer, wanting nothing more than to lose myself in the fire we had just unleashed.

His arms wrapped around me so tightly that even if I wanted to, I couldn't leave this hold he had on me. I sighed into his mouth. I wanted him to take me right here, right now. I didn't care who was around and watching. Nobody existed to me when Mahant had me engrossed. I craved his touch and wanted him to give me all of himself.

We sat there and kissed each other passionately. Time flew by, and I finally felt the urge to come up for air. He was turning me on, and I needed a second. I pulled away from him and tilted my head back, letting out a deep, agonizing groan. As I tried to catch my breath, I felt small kisses along my neck. My eyes rolled to the back of my head, and I bit my lip. He knew exactly what he was doing.

"Quit it," I said reluctantly.

Mahant doesn't stop. Instead, he pressed his lips deeper into my neck as he mumbled against my skin. "No, I don't wanna stop."

I pulled my neck away from him and looked deep into his eyes. My eyes were full of lust.

"Wanna leave?" He asked me.

"I do," I responded. "But I can't. I can't leave my girls. Notch is mediocre at best, but this means everything to them. I thought it would be crazier here. But you and I know we've seen our share of clubs way better than this."

Mahant laughed and then looked around. "I mean, there's lots of ass and tits here. Can't knock that."

I slowly nodded, pressing my thumb into his lip and wiping it gently. "True."

Imogen comes over and sits next to us, staring at Mahant.

"So, Thomas, where are you from?" She asked him. Imogen had a lollipop in her mouth, twirling it around. She took it out and held it, waiting for a response. I laughed under my breath and shook my head.

"I'm from Juro." He responded to her.

"Juro?!" She yelled. "Dude, that's like, on the other side of Utopia. The other side of the world. What the hell are you doing in Seph?"

Mahant looked at me and grinned as I looked back at him. "Came for Celeste. I know she likes to travel, and I thought we could do that together. I've been to a few places on my way here, like St. Dek and Tru'lok City. I want to take Lest to Winterdon, Treedom, and a couple of other places for her birthday."

"Oh, you got money. I see." Imogen looked at me briefly, then her eyes locked back on Mahant. "However, you guys are meeting for the first time from a dating app. I'm not letting you take my girl away from the city alone."

Imogen's discernment was strong with Mahant, which was reasonable. The story I made up about how I met Thomas wasn't as believable as it could have been. But what was I to say? I've known this man for centuries, and he's my twin flame. We have been soul-tied and reborn into different timelines. For the first time in all the years we have been alive, he could remember other timelines, and that meant the world to me.

Before I could say anything, Mahant started talking. "So come with us."

I quickly turned my head to look at him again, and then my attention went back to Imogen, who was making a thinking face.

It got remarkably quiet for a moment. Then Imogen turned and called Zoe, who was all up on Jordan. Zoe stood up, fixed her dress, walked over to us, and sat down.

Imogen used her fingers to count. "Winterdon, Treedom, and where else did you want to go, Thomas?"

"Maybe Paxton as well. Two weeks, road trip. All expenses paid by yours truly." His eyes shift back and forth between Imogen and Zoe for their approval.

"Umm, what?" Zoe asked in disbelief.

"Well, he wanted to whisk our girl away to these places, and I didn't feel comfortable with it, so he's inviting us to come with," Imogen explained to Zoe.

"Oh, absolutely, hell yes. I am down. When are we leaving?" Zoe asked excitedly.

"Tomorrow," Mahant replied.

"Damn, Thomas, you're giving us no time to pack," Imogen teased.

Mahant laughed and lowered his head, then nodded. He then looked up at me and smiled. "So, Celeste, ready to travel the world?"

"With you, I'm ready to go anywhere." I stared at him and smiled back. Zoe squealed with excitement, then got up and started dancing. I looked over at Imogen, who was still studying both of us carefully.

We only stayed for a little while longer. We were all eager to get home and start packing. Mahant gave us his address and phone number so we could meet him in the morning. I didn't want to leave him tonight because of the irrational fear that I wouldn't see him again. However, I had to trust that everything would be okay.

Once I got home, I quietly snuck through the hallways and into my bedroom, not to disturb my parents. I packed up my entire life; it seemed. I had a multitude of clothes, accessories, and skincare products to bring with me on this road trip.

I texted Mahant.

I miss you already, babe.

Mahant responded immediately.

I miss you more, beautiful.

I smiled at the text and then threw my phone onto the bed. I had finished packing and lay down to sleep. However, as soon as I did, there was another ding on my phone. I reached over, grabbed it, and it was another text from Mahant.

If you're already packed and ready to go, you can come over now and sleep here.

I knew for a fact that if I went over there, we would not sleep at all.

I grinned and texted him back.

Me come over there and sleep? Funny man.

I saw his text bubbles, and then another text from him came through.

Just sleep, I promise.

I bit my lip and thought about it.

Fine. I'll be there soon. xo

Mahant replied.

Text me your address, and I'll send a ride share.

I texted him my address and then gathered all my luggage. I dropped everything off in the kitchen and then looked for a notepad and pen. My parents would wonder where I was, so I left them a note saying I'd be back in a few weeks and that I was with Imogen, Zoe, and friends.

The ride share pulled up to the house, and I grabbed all my things, gave Crisp a small kiss, and left the house.

Chapter 5

Mahant and I barely slept last night, because we talked for hours. As I lay in the giant bed, the sun's rays snuck through the blinds. I stretched in the bed and then turned over to my side, noticing the bed was empty. I rubbed next to me and then rested my head on his pillow, smelling his lingering pheromones. Mahant walked into the bedroom wearing only sweatpants and a tank top, showing off his muscles. He had two mugs in his hand.

"Good morning," I greeted him sweetly.

He came over and leaned over the bed, kissing and greeting me back. "Good morning, beautiful. How'd you sleep?"

I closed my eyes and sighed. "Good, this bed is very comfortable. I don't want to get up."

Mahant laughed, then handed me the mug. "Well, you have to, unfortunately. Your friends will be here soon, and we gotta be on the road in a couple of hours."

I pouted and then investigated the coffee cup. Slowly, I take a sip while looking at Mahant.

"Mmm." I hummed. "Thank you."

Mahant gave me another kiss and then sipped his coffee as well. The house he was renting was huge. He was a man who liked nice things, so it made sense for him to rent out such a lavish place. I stretched one more time and then got out of bed. The hardwood floors were cold against my toes as I slowly crept to the nearby accent chair in the corner where my clothes were. I was only in a bra and panties, and my body was fighting against the cold air. I grabbed my socks, put them on, and then went to my suitcase to find clothes.

"I need to take a shower," I said out loud.

"Can I join you?" Mahant asked slyly.

I turned my body slightly and looked at him. "Then I'd never get ready before everyone got here."

He shrugged and then came up to me. He set his coffee mug on the dresser, then grabbed my wrists. Mahant pulled me into him and then leaned down and kissed my lips. My eyes closed as I kissed him back and then pulled away. He could turn me on instantly, and I didn't want to divert from the shower I needed to take.

Mahant whispered, "How long are you going to make me wait this time?"

"Until the perfect time. When our energies are so powerful and intertwined, we are one." I answered him.

I pulled a pair of blue jeans and a yellow crop top T-shirt from my luggage. The weather said it would be nice today, so I didn't have to bundle up. I grabbed some undergarments and a towel and headed to the bathroom.

"That's when it's the best, I know. I've just been craving you for years now." Mahant followed me.

"Well, then you should have found me sooner." I playfully teased him.

Out of nowhere, I feel and hear a loud smack against my ass. I turned around quickly and looked at Mahant.

"Don't be a brat." He warned me.

I squinted my eyes at him and then scoffed. "Fine."

I turned the shower on and hopped in, so I was ready when Imogen and Zoe arrived.

A couple of hours passed, and I was finally all dressed. I put on some shades and all of my statement rings, then grabbed my luggage to put it in the front hall. Mahant looked so good, wearing black jeans with a black compression shirt and a blue-and-white striped button-up shirt he kept unbuttoned. His sneakers were black as well to match. He saw me wearing sunglasses, so he took some out of his bag and threw them on.

I received texts from Imogen, and Zoe's phone, saying they were here. We exited through the side garage door and entered the spacious garage, where a sleek black truck gleamed under the overhead lights. Its futuristic design and angular edges gave it an imposing yet stylish presence, making it impossible not to admire.

"This you?" I asked as I walked around the truck, admiring it.

"Mhm," he responded. Mahant held the key fob and pressed a button. The engine started up, and then the doors opened. The garage doors rose behind us. I hopped into the passenger seat, and he entered the driver's seat, then put the car in reverse. Mahant backed the truck out of the garage and stopped in the driveway where Imogen and Zoe stood. We both jumped out of the vehicle to help them with their luggage, grab our own, and load everything in.

Jordan suddenly emerged from the house, unaware that he had been with us in the house the entire time. Good thing both Mahant and I were on our best behavior last night. Jordan had luggage with him as he rolled it to the back of the truck.

"Oh yeah, I invited Jordan as well. Figured we could use some more testosterone on this trip." Mahant joked.

Zoe blushed, then turned to look at me. Jordan was Zoe's type. He had deep, dark skin and a lean build with a hint of muscle. Like Mahant, he was also tall. Jordan was very goofy and flirty with her, and he had a short haircut. Since I met him, he has seemed to enjoy covering his head. Last night, he was wearing a snapback; today, a beanie.

I took a step closer to Zoe and whispered to her. "You arc blushing so badly, girl."

Zoe turned even more flushed, then nudged me. "Shush!"

Imogen looked at both of us and rolled her eyes playfully. She loaded her luggage and hopped into the truck's third row, spreading her legs on the seat to claim the entire row. Imogen put her earbuds in and started listening to music as she scrolled through her phone. Jordan walked up to us and immediately gave Zoe a big, very long hug. He then put his bags into the trunk before walking up to me to hug me. He pounded Mahant's fist, then hopped into the truck in the second row. I motion for Zoe to get into the car next to Jordan. Zoe, still blushing, jumped into the second row with Jordan. I got into the passenger seat again as Mahant finished loading everything into the car. Once done, he got into the driver's seat and put on his seatbelt, looking at all of us to follow suit.

We put on our seat belts as Mahant entered the resort into his navigation system, then looked at me.

I smiled at him. "So, where's the first stop?"

"Winterdon," he replied enthusiastically.

"Dude, I'm so ready for Winterdon!" Jordan said excitedly.

Winterdon was the only place in Utopia that ever saw snow. So, people who have never seen snow love to vacation there.

"Yeah, I booked three rooms at Mahogany Snow Resorts for three nights. One of the biggest luxury resorts out there," Mahant bragged.

"Zoe, have you ever been to Winterdon?" Jordan asked as he leaned closer to her.

Zoe fluffed her hair and smiled at him. "Never been before, I'm excited!"

Mahant finally backed the car out of the driveway and proceeded down the road. As soon as he got on the highway, he pressed a few buttons and let go of the wheel, and the car drove itself. He turned and looked at me, then reached across the car to place his hand on my lap. I smiled at him, then grabbed his hand, squeezing it tight.

Zoe and Jordan were in the back, talking and laughing while scrolling through Hove. Imogen was in her own world, where she thrived, so I wasn't too worried about her.

We drove for hours. The navigation system said it would take twelve hours to get to Winterdon. The only time we stopped was for restroom breaks and to refuel. We played music, sang, and talked the entire time. Even Imogen would occasionally take out her earbuds and join our conversation or games.

It got dark after a while since we left at noon. However, that only meant we were almost there. As we got closer, the temperature dropped significantly, and it became much colder. Mountains were off in the distance, and it was as if we were going into the valley. The mountains were a cool, blue, and white snowy scene. They were tall as ever, reaching the sky, cascading the skyline. The air that crept through the car's vents was crisp and sweet, tasting like blue raspberry ice pops on a hot and sunny day. I closed my eyes and breathed in all the purifying air.

Thankfully, at our last stop, before we reached Winterdon, we changed into more fitting clothes and made sure they bundled us up.

Winterdon was remarkably beautiful at night, and I could not wait to witness its beauty during the day. Finally, we arrived at the resort and hopped out of the truck. I stretched and walked around to the back of the car to help get out all our luggage. Jordan ran in, got a trolley, and brought it back so we could haul all our things onto it. I put on my backpack, and we all went inside. Mahant checked us in, and then we awkwardly stood by the elevators.

"Sooo..." Mahant said as he held the keycards.

Everyone stared at the keycards, and then I scoffed and grabbed one. "The girls can take a room, and you guys can have your own. Simple."

"Fine by me," Zoe chimed in.

Jordan shrugged, took one keycard, and Mahant put the other in his pocket.

"Cool," Mahant said. "Good thing we're all on the same floor."

The elevator opened, and we all got in with the trolley. Mahant pressed the floor number three button, and then the door closed.

Once we got off on the third floor, we walked to the rooms next to each other. I handed the keycard to Imogen, and she opened our door. Jordan went into his room, and before Mahant could go into his room across from ours, I reached out and grabbed his arm. He turned around and smiled at me, and I got on my tiptoes and kissed him.

"See you in the morning?" I asked rhetorically.

Mahant nodded his head as he licked his lips.

We went our separate ways and closed the doors.

"You two act like you have been dating for years!" Imogen yelled as soon as the door closed.

I smiled and put my stuff down on the table.

"I know, right? It's so cute. I wish I could find a guy who looks at me like Thomas looks at Lest. Did you see that look he gave her when she kissed him? Girl, you might as well go stay in the room with him at this point." Zoe added on.

"Please, stop," I demanded under my breath, in a playful tone.

Imogen continued, "No, seriously. Your connection is remarkable. I swear it's like you both have known each other longer."

"I mean, we texted and talked on the phone for a long time, like a long time." I lied. I sat down on one bed and crossed my legs.

"I noticed you were at his house when we all met up. You totally stayed at his place last night. Did y'all... You know?" Zoe asked as she sat next to me.

I shook my head. "Not yet."

"Yet! Keyword, keyword!" Imogen yelled as she laughed and plopped down on the other bed.

"Hey, enough about me," I said, trying to divert the attention from me. "Let's talk about Zoe and Jordan. You two were cozy at Notch and in the car. What's going on?"

Zoe immediately got red and blushed. "Oh my god, he's so fucking fine. I swear I want to climb on top of him and—" She then balls her fists up and then releases them. "But then I think, is it just sex I want, or do I really like this guy? We were texting all night, and he's such a sweetheart."

"He seems like he's a nice guy." I agreed.

Zoe and I both looked at Imogen, and she diverted her eyes back and forth between us.

"What?" Imogen asked.

"I know for sure you walked away with some phone numbers last night," I told her.

Imogen smirked and then scrolled through her phone. "Maybe…"

We all laughed, and then I grabbed my charger from my backpack.

"The bartender was hot. Got her number last night. Then Joe gave me his number. He's cute, but eh, not my type at all, really." Imogen continued.

I plugged my phone in and it started charging. I suddenly received a text from Mahant.

Come see me.

I smiled, then turned around and looked at Imogen and Zoe.

"Thomas wants me to come over," I told them both.

Imogen nodded her head in approval. "Oh, absolutely go, and please fuck that man up! While you do that, I'm going to catch some z's." She stood up, undressed, and walked to her suitcase to grab an oversized T-shirt.

"Umm, hell yeah. Please go, and we will ask for all the details in the morning." Zoe cosigned.

I shook my head. "You're both bad influences."

I entered the bathroom and freshened up before heading to Mahant's room.

My heart fluttered as I stood in the hallway across from our room. After waiting a few moments, I finally took a deep breath and exhaled slowly before knocking on Mahant's door. He opened the door, and I smiled at him as my eyes shifted to his muscular body. Mahant was not wearing a shirt, only boxers.

I pushed his chest and shoved him into the room as he burst out laughing.

"That's how you answer the door!" I yelled at him playfully. He continued to laugh as he backed away, and the door closed behind me.

"This body is immaculate. I did a good job with it in this timeline. I had to show it off to you."

I rolled my eyes at him and walked into the room's open space, where the bed was. He had the TV on, and a sports game was playing.

I looked around and then turned to look at him again.

"You're immaculate in every timeline we are in." I reminded him. I sat on the edge of the bed and leaned back, my palms flat against the blankets. I looked up at him as he came and stood directly before me. He looked down at me like a predator over its prey.

I could feel his energy getting stronger as he stood before me. With my eyes locked onto his, I never broke my gaze. His eyes did the same.

"Oh, if anyone asks, we have been texting and talking on the phone for months," I informed him.

He laughed, then came and sat next to me. "You'd think we have a better story to tell as often as we've done this."

"You know what..." I paused and looked over at him. "You're absolutely right."

Mahant leaned in and kissed my lips, and I kissed him back gently. My hand pressed into his chest, and I pushed him away.

Trying to distract him, I asked, "So, what's the plan for tomorrow?"

He sighed. "Snowboarding, snow angels, skiing. The usual snow stuff for Jordan, Imogen, and Zoe. Then I have an awesome surprise for us all for dinner."

I smiled at him. "That sounds fun. I can't wait!"

"Good," Mahant said as he pressed his lips into mine again, this time longer. I reached out and palmed his face, kissing him back deeply. His body grew warmer against my touch. I could feel him getting excited as he kissed me, so I pulled away again.

"Let's get ready for bed," I suggested as I stood up and took off my shirt, revealing just me in a bra. I unbuttoned my jeans and kicked off my shoes. Once my jeans were off, I tossed them on the nearby chair and then turned around to see Mahant watching my every move.

"Yeah, bed." He says, uninterested.

"Don't sound too excited," I responded playfully to him. He gave me a scolding look as he stood up and walked to the right side of the bed. I walked over to the left side, and we both pulled the blanket back. I hopped in to get out of the cold, and Mahant followed.

We both got into bed and snuggled close together to get warm. Winterdon was so cold that it made goosebumps on my delicate skin, and you could see your breath when you spoke.

As I lay on my side, I rested my hand on his chest and rubbed gently. The heat he emitted was unmatched, radiating intensely, and it felt good against my cold palms. Mahant was lying on his back, one leg raised.

"So, Imogen seems very protective of you," Mahant mentioned, randomly.

I looked up at him and bit my bottom lip. "Mmm, yeah, that's my girl. She's huge in protecting the people she loves. I know you can see the aura that surrounds her."

"Yeah, it's orange. It glows so bright whenever she's observing her surroundings, cultivating and crafting her artistic mind." Mahant delightfully spoke of her. "It's beautiful."

I nodded and then closed my eyes as I continued to rub his chest and trace my fingers along the grooves of his abdomen. Electricity would shoot from Mahant's body to the tips of my fingers and through my body with every touch. I inhaled deeply and then exhaled slowly, trying to center my thoughts and control the sensation of him being so close to me.

"And Jordan has a thing for Zoe," Mahant admitted.

I lifted my body and rested on my elbow. I looked down at Mahant as he lay there on his back.

"Oh, my god! Do you see how she blushes whenever he gets close or talks to her? She's got it bad. His aura tells me he's a good guy, but tell me more. Do you think he only wants sex?"

Mahant looked over at me. "You know I don't hang around unevolved men. Low vibrational beings, c'mon, Imani. You know me better than that. Jordan is a very good dude who takes relationships seriously. I can tell he really likes her."

I conceded, "You're right."

His phone dinged, and he ignored it. Then it goes off again.

"It's sooo far away." He complained. I rolled my eyes playfully at him and then got out of bed and grabbed his phone off the entertainment table. I ran back and jumped on him as he lay comfortably in bed. I landed right on top of him as he let out a groan, then quickly sat up and wrapped his arms around me. He gave me a big bear hug, then playfully shook me. I laughed and tried to escape his arms, but couldn't budge. He was too strong.

He finally let go and then grabbed his phone from me. He unlocked his phone and then read the messages.

"Speaking of Jordan. Looks like somebody got lost and made their way to his room." He slyly spoke.

In shock, I responded, "No fucking way!"

Mahant laughed and then showed me the text.

Yooo, Zoe is here. She said Imogen went to sleep, and she wanted some company.

I covered my mouth and then let out a laugh. "My girl, tryna get her some! Okaaaay."

Mahant shook his head and then texted Jordan back.

"At least someone is getting some tonight." He mouthed as he texted Jordan, making his dissatisfaction obvious.

I quickly grabbed the pillow next to me and swung it at him, hitting him right on the arm. He flinched and then grabbed the pillow from me.

"Listen, sir, with your track record. You've never been able to handle it without going off the deep end." I reminded him.

"It's different this time, Imani." He pleaded with me, nearly pouting.

"Is that so? How?"

Mahant continued his plea, "I remember everything this time around. I will not go off the deep end. I promise."

His eyes locked onto mine, and I couldn't help but believe him. I wanted to believe him more than anything. I also craved him. The hunger was so intense that it drove me crazy. I breathed deeply and then let out a huge sigh of frustration.

"I know you want it too." He egged me on.

I got back under the covers and scooted closer to him again. Lying back on my side, I pushed my hair out of my face and rested my head on my pillow. I closed my eyes and stayed silent. I heard Mahant reposition himself in bed and get comfortable beside me.

Finally, I spoke. "Of course, I want you, forever and always. To the universe and beyond. In this life and the next, I will always want to. I will always want you. I choose you, Mahant."

Mahant grabbed my hand and pressed his palm against mine as we held them in the air before us. More energy surged through us as our auras intertwined as one. I opened my eyes and watched as we held them in the air.

"I choose you, Imani," Mahant promised me. "You are my forever and always."

I leaned forward and kissed his lips softly. He kissed me back as I let go of his hand and pressed the palm of my hand against his cheek, holding him in place.

Whenever we touched, I could hear the universe sing. The energy and sounds around us collided in harmony and danced. Our blue auras ignited into this powerful flame that illuminated the entire room. The energy was ruthless, its presence permeating every crevice and crack. Our love was powerful. I couldn't help but continue kissing him passionately and lovingly as we mended into one. Our souls erupted, and the passion engulfed our spirits.

My breathing deepened as our kiss grew more intense within seconds. Mahant's arms wrapped around my torso, and he pulled me in closer. I loved being in his embrace, his warmth and love.

We made out for a while longer before I had to push him off me again. Our make-out session was spiraling out of control, and something inside me thought it wouldn't be a good idea. Eventually, we both fell asleep, frustrated, but in a good way.

The next day, we woke up and got ready for all the snowy adventures. I snuck out of Mahant's room and back into mine to see Imogen and Zoe getting dressed. Imogen was getting dressed on one side of the bed. Zoe was doing makeup at the TV entertainment table with her vanity mirror. They both diverted their attention towards me and had the biggest grins.

"What's up?" Zoe asked immediately.

I threw the keycard on the table and shrugged.

"We talked, we made out, we went to sleep," I responded nonchalantly.

"That's it?" Imogen asked in a disappointed tone.

"That's it. That's all." I walked to my luggage, put it on its side, and then sat Indian-style in front of it. I sorted through it, and I could feel daggers looking at me. It was quiet in the room.

"You are so lying!" Zoe yelled at me.

I looked up at them both and rolled my eyes. "I'd never. I swear. We just talked."

"Just talking is crazy. If I were that man, I'd be all over you. He didn't want to have sex?" Imogen asked curiously.

I sighed and picked up one of my long-sleeved shirts. "Trust me, he did. He was all over me, but I'm the one who decided not to move too fast."

"So let me get this straight... You finally meet up with Thomas, and he's handsome and a gentleman. He takes not just you, but all of us on a road trip. Dropping hella money on us and putting us up in a hotel. You spend the night with him and don't treat yourself?" Imogen continued.

I laughed at her as I continued to sort through my clothes. I then shook my head and looked up at her. Zoe looked at me, then Imogen, and then back at me.

"I want to treat myself, trust me. I want to pounce on him. But I'm taking it slowly. Besides, why are we so concentrated on me? Zoe snuck her ass into Jordan's suite last night!"

Imogen's eyes got big, and she quickly turned to Zoe, who instantly turned red.

"Zoe!" Imogen called out.

"What!" Zoe responded, then tossed one of her lipstick tops at me. I flinched and then laughed.

"You two are giving me heart palpitations, I swear," Imogen dramatically said as she continued to get dressed.

Zoe continued doing her makeup, then started giggling devilishly.

It got quiet in the room, except for Zoe's laugh. We all laughed under our breath until I finally broke the silence. "So, how was it, Zoe?"

"It was so good." She said, responding immediately. She leaned back in the chair and rested her head back as she closed her eyes. "He's packing. We went at it for hours. He tossed me around that hotel room like I was a raggedy doll. I loved it."

"Okaaaaay." Imogen let out as she gestured her hand above her head, rooting for Zoe.

I added to the conversation, appalled, "Damn, girl!"

"I like him a lot, and I just hope he likes me too," Zoe confessed.

I finally laid out my outfit and stood up off the floor, dusting my butt off. "Well, I think you got yourself a good one. Thomas said he's a decent guy, and he takes relationships seriously."

"They both seem like decent guys." Imogen agreed. "I still want to get to know them more, though."

"Understandable," I said as I entered the bathroom. "I'm going to shower quickly and get ready."

"Hurry up, girl!" Imogen yelled at me playfully.

After my shower, I got ready. I made sure to dress to impress but also dress to keep warm. We stood in the hotel room as we did our last finishing touches, and there was a knock on the door. Then, my phone dinged, and Mahant texted me.

Jordan and I are outside. Open up.

Imogen went over to the door, unlocked it, and opened it to let them in. We were all bundled up in hats, scarves, and gloves.

We all left the room, and our first stop was a breakfast diner in town. We ordered a bunch of different items and shared them. These were my kind of friends. Zoe, Imogen, and I would always order different appetizers and entrees whenever we went out, so we could try various dishes. So, it was nice to see Jordan adapt to it. I knew Mahant would care less.

After breakfast, we visited The Slopes. It was a ski section tucked away in the mountains. Zoe and Jordan skied, while Imogen, Mahant, and I got snowboards.

We had a blast.

We would use the ski lift to reach the top of the mountain, then ski and snowboard down. Mahant and I were naturals, while the rest kept falling. We laughed at each other whenever someone fell, all in great fun. After skiing, we discovered another part of The Slopes, where families were building snowmen and having snowball fights.

Jordan picked up some snow and turned towards Zoe, who was standing next to Imogen.

"You better not!" Imogen yelled. However, the snowball released from Jordan's grasp, heading straight towards them. Imogen jumped out of the way, and the snowball hit Zoe on her arm.

"Hey!" Zoe yelled as she leaned down and picked up some snow. Next thing you know, it was a full-blown snowball fight.

After our much-needed and very childish snowball fight, we went to the nearby shops called The Slopes Outlets, which were so cute. There were small shops and people with pop-up tents on the street. It wasn't as busy as you'd think. Only a few cars drove through the area. Everything was within walking distance, so if you needed ski gear or a hot, steamy coffee, you only had to walk.

Mahant and I walked down the cute cobblestone sidewalks, holding hands. I bumped into him and gestured for him to look at Jordan and Zoe, who were holding hands as well. Imogen was taking pictures of everything in sight as we all walked together. I'm sure she was getting a bunch of artistic inspiration. We shopped for a while, and as we finished at the outlets, we realized we had a lot of shopping bags to carry.

Mahant also announced that he had a surprise for us all.

"Hey, so we're here!" Mahant said excitedly to everyone as we stopped in front of a building. We all looked around, confused. We then turned our attention to the building's name in front of us.

"Dine on the Go?" Jordan asked as he read the name.

"Yeah, so it's a cool dining experience. A private chef will cook a three-course meal as we ride on a luxury party bus. The bus will take us sightseeing through Winterdon Lights, and then drop us off at the dock, where we can see the aurora borealis."

Zoe's jaw was on the floor as Mahant explained what was in store for us. She looked so excited. Imogen's face was genuinely impressed, and Jordan said 'wow' to it all.

We entered the storefront and a guy greeted us. "Good evening. My name is Jeff, and I'll be your host tonight. Do you have a reservation for a tour, or are you simply grabbing food today?"

Mahant spoke as he looked around, "Reservations under Thomas."

We stood in front of Jeff and looked around the store. Inside, the restaurant was very upscale and fancy. Everything was immaculately clean and white, with gold trim. Some people were sitting at tables, eating, while others were ordering. The aroma was pleasant and fresh, with hickory and spices.

"Oh! Thomas, thank you so much for being on time. Let's head out to the back so that we can get started." Jeff instructed us.

We all followed Jeff to the back of the building and down some steps. A blacked-out bus waited with its doors open. We got on the bus, and the layout matched that of a restaurant. There was a tiny luxurious kitchen at the rear and a driver in the front. The windows had good visibility, allowing us to see the scenery. Another person came out from the back, wearing a chef's jacket. She was black and of average height with the most gorgeous locs up in a messy bun. She had a septum and a labret piercing.

"Hey guys, my name is Monti and I'll be your chef for Dine!" She introduced herself.

"Hey, Monti!" We all greeted each other as we took our seats at the round table. The driver started up the bus and put on his seatbelt.

The bus took off, and Chef Monti immediately brought over a platter. On the platter was a cute assortment of hors d'oeuvres.

Monti pointed to each one of them. "This is a fig and mascarpone on a cracker with a honey drizzle and peach foam. These are smoked gorgonzola-stuffed dates with caramelized bacon jam and crushed roasted peanuts. And the last one is a salmon and cream cheese crostini with pickled onions, capers, and dill."

"Oh wow," Imogen responded as she reached for her hors d'oeuvres. "Now, this is art. So beautiful, Monti!"

"Thank you!" Monti replied. "What are all of your names, and where are you from?"

Jordon, with a full mouth, spoke up. "I'm Jordan, and I'm from Juro."

Zoe playfully nudged him and then gestured for him to chew his food.

Mahant shook his head at Jordan. "I'm from Juro as well, and my name is Thomas."

I spoke up next, "I'm Celeste, and that's Zoe and—"

"Imogen. I'm Imogen, and I'm already in love with this presentation. Nice to meet you, Monti. All three of us are from Seph City."

"Oh wow! I've always wanted to go to Seph City. I hear it's a sight to see." Monti spoke directly to Imogen.

"You should come, and I'll show you around. I live in the heart of the city." Imogen replied flirtatiously.

I looked at Mahant, and he looked at me. I couldn't help but smile.

"Well, you all enjoy your hors d'oeuvres. I'll be back shortly with your first course."

Monti walked away as Imogen took out her phone and started snapping pictures of her plate. Jordan teased Zoe as she also took photos of her food. I ate each one of the different appetizers, and they tasted so damn delicious. One of the tastiest foods I've had the pleasure of eating. The driver got on the speaker and announced that we were entering Winterdon Lights, so we all turned our attention to the windows and watched as we passed by lights strung throughout the city and homes. There were lights everywhere and on everything. It was so bright it lit up the sky, even through the sunset.

Time passed, and we finally had our main course meal, which consisted of braised short ribs over a layer of sweet potato grits. Surrounding the sweet potato grits was a hearty, dark-brown gravy. On top of the braised short rib were crunchy fried onions and curled scallions.

Monti also came out with cocktails.

"Here are your raspberry and gin cocktails in a long-stem glass. Garnished with a sugary rim, raspberry kabob, and lime." Monti explained to us as she set each glass in front of us.

"Wow," Imogen expressed with a shocked look.

She was almost speechless this time.

Monti smiled, then let out a cute laugh. "So, we have your dessert coming soon. How did you all like the braised short rib?"

"Oh, it was quite delicious. Thank you." I complimented her.

"Yeah, those sweet potato grits were amazing. I've never even heard of that before." Zoe said.

"It's a specialty of mine. I'm glad you are all enjoying everything so far. I'll be back with more." Monti promised before disappearing again.

"We're almost at the docks." The bus driver announced over his speaker as he continued to drive carefully. It was a slow ride, but sightseeing and enjoying scrumptious food made it worthwhile.

"Hey Thomas, thanks for inviting me. I'm having a blast." Jordan thanked him as he leaned back and rested his arm around Zoe's chair.

Mahant nodded, then responded, "Of course, man, you're my guy. You're always welcome."

"Thank you, Thomas, for inviting us along as well. I'm sure you just wanted some alone time with Lest, and we just rained on your parade." Imogen said with a hint of guilt in her tone.

"Nah, don't do that. I wanted to meet Celeste's friends, too. I'm glad you all came." Mahant was so loving and has always been such a sweet guy. I know he truly meant that. He was such an introverted soul, yet he loved people. We were very much alike. "Plus, I wanna be honest. I've seen your work and wondered if I could ask you a few questions. Just haven't had the courage to."

Imogen raised her eyebrow and gestured for Mahant to continue. "Ask away."

"So, what inspires you?" Mahant asked.

Imogen thought for a moment and then smiled. "My eyes."

"Your eyes?" Mahant repeated. He tilted his head slightly as he looked at Imogen. I turned my attention to her, and she pressed her phone against her lips as she looked up. She was thinking.

"Yeah, the privilege of being able to see. I'm blessed every day to see these things, and if my eyes ever fade away, I will continue to see the beauty in the world in my mind. Every single one of my drawings imprints a sketch in my mind that I will never forget. And that's why I draw." Imogen looked directly into Mahant's eyes and sighed. "Long story short, I have an irrational fear of going blind."

"Hey, listen, I love your inspiration. Your next piece should be you drawing in the dark, facing your fears, and creating a beautiful piece. Record it as you always do and put that shit on Hove. I bet you will sell it for millions. Shit, if it doesn't, I'll buy it." Mahant advised her.

She nodded her head slowly. "Not a bad idea."

I loved that they were having such a wholesome conversation. I just sat back and enjoyed my man getting along with my friends. Monti emerged from the back with another platter filled with our dessert.

"So, for our final course, we have a peach and blueberry pavlova with a rum peach glaze and crispy mint garnish," Monti explained as she set the plates down.

"This is beautiful." Imogen piped up again. She started taking pictures as soon as her plate hit the table.

We all devoured everything and complimented the chef. We arrived at the docks as soon as we finished our final course. The bus stopped, and we all got up. Our host came over and escorted us out. I overheard Imogen talking to Monti while waiting for everyone else to leave the bus, exchanging contact information. Finally, we exited and walked along a path from the parking area.

The sun had finally set, and the sounds of nature called out all around us. As soon as we got through the path, we saw a long dock that led out to the water, with an awning overhead.

Jeff instructed us, "We will have another car pick you up in an hour. Please make your way back through the path, then."

We all agreed and headed out to the dock. The lake froze over, but it was beautiful to see the aurora borealis appear in the night sky. Imogen, Zoe, and I sat on the comfortable chairs at the end of the dock, gazing up at the sky. Mahant stood behind me and grabbed my shoulders, massaging them as he watched. Jordan came up, sat next to Zoe, looked at her, and then smiled.

"We should take a picture," Imogen suggested as she held her camera out in front of us, angling it so we could all fit in the frame.

We all smiled as she started capturing multiple pictures of us doing different poses. The docks ended our spectacular night. After an hour, the car came, picked us up, and took us back to the hotel.

We did so much in one day that we were all exhausted. Imogen, Zoe, and I returned to our rooms and undressed for the night. I hopped into bed with Zoe. Imogen had her bed, and we all fell asleep.

We spent two more days in Winterdon before we hit the road. The next day, we went back to The Slopes Outlets to shop some more. We wanted to take a lot of stuff home with us to Seph City that they didn't have there. But before returning home, we were on to our next destination.

These were core memories of me in Utopia. I turned twenty-one and went to Notch. Mahant and I found each other, and he took my friends and me on adventures through Utopia. It was the highlight of a century.

I wanted to create more of these memories in my present timeline with Mahant. I craved for him to be whole again. I missed the confident and highly intelligent being that he indeed was. However, no matter the cost, I would repair his mind.

He would remember it as he did in Utopia, if it were the last thing I did. I promised myself this. Repeatedly, in every timeline, I have felt like I failed Mahant, but I won't again.

Chapter 6

Act II – The Present Timeline

It was raining outside, as it always did at the same time each day, but then the sky would open, and the day would blossom into its beauty. That is one of the things I loved most about where I lived. When the sun shone, it glistened against my beautiful chocolate skin and radiated off me. The beaches were lovely, and the city was enormous. However, what I liked the most about Bluepoint City was knowing Mahant was close. I could feel his energy coursing through my soul as if it were my own. This time, it was even more potent than any timeline we had been in together before, and I knew I just had to find him.

I stood in my penthouse on the top floor of Diamond's Landing. Overlooking the city, I wondered where he could be and how I would restore his memories. In every timeline, I typically took him to Troterion, and I wondered whether that would be successful this time around. All I knew was that Mahant would resemble his appearance when he was Lanno, since this timeline followed right after. Lanno's death in his previous timeline still took a toll on me. It was hard seeing him in his final moments, knowing even though it wasn't goodbye, it was the hardest 'see you later' we could muster up.

Now, in this present timeline, I am very fortunate, and my backstory was exceptional. My parents adopted me as a baby and named me Zya. My dad owned a popular tech company that manufactured vehicles and transportation systems. His company, Peach, is known for its focus on clean energy, so all his transportation was electric. Once I turned 18, my net worth skyrocketed to 18 billion, and it has increased substantially every year since. I have the best parents in the world. They didn't make me work unless I wanted to, and they support everything I do. I didn't have to be an overachiever, and they didn't throw money at me as love; they genuinely cared about my well-being. The Universe blessed me once again.

With all the resources at my fingertips, I did my best to find Mahant. I, however, was unsuccessful.

My candles flickered off in the distance, and I turned to find my black cat, Roo, lounging on the sofa. There were small details that I needed to tether myself to in every timeline. I loved my candles, incense, and meditation. Of course, my collection of the same three necklaces was another iconic Imani staple, and I was also a huge cat person. I believe cats are the entrance to one's soul—a powerful relic to get in every timeline to ground me into my memories. Cats are the closest to humans of all species in having multiple lives. They are also fierce, loyal, and free-spirited.

I also loved music. In every timeline, I enjoyed different artists and genres. It fascinated me how music emerged as a natural expression of the spirit, regardless of the place or time. All species, in some form or another, developed and enjoyed music, whether for ritual or entertainment; music curated joy.

Even in this present, more futuristic timeline, music still gave purpose.

It was 2249, and I was twenty-four years old. You would think that technological worlds would scare me, given my first experience in a futuristic, robot-driven world, but this one was riveting. The entire city sits in the middle of these vast commuter rails, which provide adequate transportation. You could go anywhere in the city. My dad was to thank for that, as Peach owned the commuters. Surrounding the lively city was water on all sides, with one long underground tunnel connecting us to the mainland. It was beautiful.

My family and I were not from Bluepoint City. One day, I accompanied my dad on a business trip here, and as soon as we entered the city, an intense energy took over me. I knew Mahant was here. I told my father I would stay, and since he always wanted the best for me, he set me up for success and bought me this penthouse.

My penthouse on the top floor had 360-degree views of the city, showcasing the island skyline and high-rise buildings, capturing a moment in time that felt unreal. The inside of my condo was pristine, offering luxury and comfort with updated, new appliances and décor. The floors, buffed with expensive white and gold-trimmed marble, perfectly offset the very white walls, on which I hung my favorite artwork. The living room was an open-concept space featuring a three-piece white sofa set, an accent chair, and the kitchen, which included its own island, bar, and a Sub-Zero see-through fridge. Off to one side was an electric fireplace that added coziness to the upscale, modern home, while a series of gold-trimmed chandeliers hung in the center of the space. Of course, I need plants to boost my endorphins and create an even more comforting atmosphere. So, around the condo were plants hanging, some potted against the glass to absorb the sunlight, while others greeted you when you first walked through the doors.

The natural light that crept through the windows was a treasure, but what I enjoyed the most about my home was the aroma therapy that I created by mixing my favorite scents—jasmine and vanilla. It captivated you the moment you entered, whether you were in the bedroom, the bathroom, or simply in the main living room. It was truly inviting. The final detail was my patio, which allowed me to enjoy fresh air at any time—decorated with a cute table and two chairs, orb-shaped planters, and massive monstera plants.

I walked around my apartment and then sat on the sofa. Whenever I thought of Mahant, this deep-rooted sensation took over me, and memories of us together flashed through my mind. I reached up and softly grazed my lips with my fingertips. His kisses were so powerful and very missed. I closed my eyes and continued to think about him. The way he touched me, how he smiled, or looked at me. His gaze burned a hole through my soul, filling it with his essence. Our conversations were engaging and fun, and his mind was so beautiful. I couldn't wait to find him again.

Roo walked over, stretched in front of me on the sofa, and climbed into my lap. I smiled and stroked Roo's fur, and she purred as she lay down.

Today, I had business to attend to at Blue City Mall. And by business, I mean a pamper-me day. It had been a year of living in the city and multiple unsuccessful ploys to find Mahant. I figured I'd indulge myself in some shopping at a mall I hardly ever visited.

I got up from the sofa and went into my room to get dressed for the day. As I entered my massive walk-in closet, I thought about what I should wear. I looked around at the off-white walls and the white-and-gold-trimmed cabinets. My clothes were hanging everywhere, and shoeboxes were in their rightful place. I pulled out my brown Charlotte Co. long coat and Ralph Paul black denim jeans.

I grabbed a black shirt as well and got dressed. After dressing, I grabbed my dress boots and slipped them on. Then, I headed to my closet island dresser to add some accessories. I went nowhere without the many rings I wore on my fingers, my hoop nose ring, and necklaces. My necklaces were essential to me. Whenever I was in a new timeline, I would purchase a rose quartz crystal, the Eye of Horus, and the Evil Eye, as long as the accessories were available. Sometimes, there was no such thing as spiritual practice.

Being able to feel people's energies around me was sometimes draining. You could tell when people felt low or when they were high. I could sense overstimulated people, and those who seemed to have no emotions. In most worlds, they refer to this as an empathetic ability. Wearing the Eye of Horus protected and healed me when those energies invaded my own.

Now, the Evil Eye was even more important for me to wear. In every timeline, some people are more dangerous. They would manipulate, steal, and plague the world with negative energies. This small, unassuming emblem carried immense power, warding off harmful energies sent intentionally or unintentionally by others. Whether it came as envy, malice, or even careless thoughts, the Evil Eye acted as a vigilant sentinel, deflecting those forces before they could penetrate my aura. And finally, the rose quartz was just my favorite crystal, and I always thought it complemented my complexion.

I looked into the mirror at my hair and laughed at myself. I needed to do something with this bird's nest. My hair was naturally curly—a wild expression that not everything in Zya's life was perfect. I typically get it silk-pressed so that it's nice and straight down the sides of my face, with a part in the middle.

Finally, I finished dressing, and the last touch was to spray some A'untaj Feroo perfume on me. It was my favorite scent in this timeline, with hints of vanilla, chocolate, and musk.

I decided that, instead of taking my Peach Z8 car, I would enjoy a lovely day commuting. The weather was nice, and there was no chance of rain. Still, I took my umbrella. Living in Bluepoint City, you always take your umbrella. I left my apartment and headed to my first stop: my appointment with Tasha to get my hair done.

Once I got to the shop, I stood in the waiting area for Tasha. It was a charming little shop within a shopping outlet, alongside other cute boutiques and small business-es. Inside the shop was a small space for one person, who would be Tasha. The walls were pink, and there was a washing station, a chair for clients to have their hair done, and a small waiting area with three seats in case people walked in to make appointments. The aroma smelled like fresh soaps, hair products, and coconut.

"Look at you, right on time, Zya. How are you, girl?" Tasha asked as she walked up to me and hugged me.

I smiled and hugged her back. "I'm doing great, love. How are you?"

"You know, living my best life. Getting this money." Tasha looked at me and then stepped back in awe. "You look fine, girl, and you smell good, too. I'd give anything to spend a day in your closet."

I laughed and shook my head as I followed her into the salon. "I don't know, it can get scary in there."

I took off my jacket and folded it. Tasha reached for it, grabbed it from me, and set it aside. She motioned towards the chair, and I sat down.

"Are you doing a silk press today?" Tasha reconfirmed with me.

"Mmm yes, please," I replied.

As she did my hair, I took out my phone and scrolled through my Zed account. Zed was a social media platform everyone had. Being Zya Peach, I had a huge following and had to keep appearances to a minimum. I scrolled through my notifications and tried entertaining myself until Tasha finished my hair.

My phone dinged as I scrolled through Zed. It was Kat who texted me.

Hey, babes, Dustin's having a thing tonight. Are you down?

Dustin's was a popular lounge in the heart of Bluepoint City. They've always hosted amazing events, and I've never been able to attend any of them.

Kat, whom I've known since moving to Bluepoint six years ago, was my only friend who was wise beyond her years and a natural beauty. She was a little shorter than I was, and her skin complexion was lighter as well. Both her parents were black, but very light-skinned, with caramel-colored complexions. She had long, wavy brown hair and hazel eyes. She was a thick girl, not fat or skinny, just perfect. I remember the day she admitted to me she liked women, and she cried so hard, thinking I wouldn't be her friend anymore. Little did she know I had been with women before as well. Once I told her that I was fluid, a lover of all, she felt more at ease.

I texted her back.

I'm getting my hair done. Then my nails and toes, and I was going to do a bit of shopping.

I locked my phone and bit my lip, thinking. Every weekend, I try to get out of the house with Kat and explore Bluepoint hoping to find Mahant. Unfortunately, I always come up short. What would make me think this time was different? I should stick to my plans for the day and then go home. Another ding came through on my phone.

I can meet up with you at the mall when you're finished. Then we can pregame at your pent.

I unlocked my phone and read the text. I sighed in the chair and then texted Kat back.

Not really feeling it tonight.

There was almost an immediate response from her.

Don't be like that. We go out every weekend. I need my drinking buddy!

I smiled and then shook my head.

Fine. I should be done by 5. I'll text you, and then we can skip the mall and head to my place.

Roughly two hours later, Tasha finished with my hair. I paid and tipped her, then left to get my manicure and pedicure. I had to ensure that if I ran into Mahant; I looked my best.

After wrapping up the mani-pedi, I texted Kat to tell her I was heading back to my apartment. Once I got home, I sat at my bar and grabbed my expensive bottle of Rolo. I poured some into my glass and then took a shot.

The lack of a physical and emotional connection with Mahant for years was frustrating. I craved him, and he seemed unobtainable. So, most times, I did what I had to do. And tonight, I was feeling frisky.

There was a knock on my front door, and Kat spoke through it.

"It's me." She called out.

I turned towards my COMO and spoke to it. "COMO, open the door."

"Yes, Zya." It responded to me.

COMO was an artificially intelligent system that I could command. Kat opened the door and walked through. She was wearing a burgundy red dress with black heels, and she clutched her handbag.

"Hey, babes!" She called out as she walked up to me and hugged me. I hugged her back and then reached to grab another glass. I pour some Rolo into both of our cups and wink at her.

"Oh, you are starting early, huh?" Kat took the glass from me.

"Mmm, absolutely," I responded with a devilish grin.

Kat held her glass up, and I tapped it with mine.

"Cheers!" We both take the shot, and then I reach for the alcohol bottle again and pour another one.

"So, what's happening at Dustin's tonight?" I asked Kat.

Kat sat her glass down. "Slam Jam is happening, and it's supposed to be a huge event. You're supposed to pay, but you know I know Derrick, and he will let us in."

I raised my eyebrow. "Derrick? You sure he will not want some ass for letting us in?"

"He might," Kat responded, and then she laughed.

Kat was the girl who knew everybody at the party. She loved to dress up and network with people when we went out and explored the nightlife. But outside of the nightlife, she often dressed down as a tomboy. Kat had a few tattoos in random spots and loved smoking weed. I thanked the universe that marijuana existed in this timeline. Kat had a pre-roll that she took out of her purse and lit up. She inhaled deeply, held in the smoke, and then exhaled, blowing it out. She took another puff and then passed it to me.

I smirked. "Well, Derrick is cute." I take a hit off the pre-roll and then exhale slowly. Kat gave me a look and then laughed again.

"Another one of your subjects." Kat playfully teased.

I don't respond. Instead, I took another hit off the weed and then picked up my glass, staring at Kat. I took the shot with my eyes locked on hers.

We continued to talk, drink, and smoke for a while. I got incredibly high, and I was in a good mood. Whenever I smoked, it was as if the veil lifted, and my emotions unlocked to their fullest intensity. Every feeling, every hidden corner of my mind, came rushing to the surface, raw and unfiltered. It wasn't just a heightened sense of awareness, but it was overwhelming yet profound, a reminder of the deep threads binding my existence to others.

I could also feel the energies that surrounded me, much more potent. Smoking was almost like ecstasy for me. It unlocked chambers of my mind that I didn't even know I had. My senses sharpened to where memories came alive in ways I could never have imagined. I could see the faces of people I had long forgotten, hear the echoes of laughter and voices from lifetimes ago, and even taste and smell the essence of moments long past. Each sensation was vivid, as if I were reliving those experiences rather than merely recalling them.

Mahant's presence stood at the forefront of these memories, glowing like a beacon. Every shared moment with him, every glance and word replayed in stunning detail. It made his absence and the craving for his presence harder.

I got up and turned on some music from my phone, which connected to COMO and my speakers. It was a vibe; the music was slow and inviting, and all I wanted to do was dance. I got up from the barstool and swayed back and forth with my eyes closed. Kat had another pre-roll that she lit up and then passed to me. I took another hit as I danced.

"We will never make it to Dustin's," Kat complained as she watched me dance. I laughed and looked at her, and her eyes were bloodshot red. She got up from the barstool, went to my refrigerator, and pulled out a snack.

Still swaying to the music, I spoke. "We can still go. I'm just feeling excellent right now."

All I wanted at this moment was Mahant. No matter how hard I tried, I could not shake him from my mind.

Kat ate her cheese snack and then turned to put her black heels back on.

"Let's go then!" She demanded.

I take another hit and then hand it to her. She takes a hit, puts the rest out, and then puts the half-smoked pre-roll back in a container inside her purse. I grabbed my boots, put them on, and then grabbed my brown trench coat.

I conceded, "Mmm, fine. Let's go."

We left my apartment and took a ride-share to Dustin's.

Once we arrived at Dustin's, we realized the lines to get in were extremely long. Thankfully, Derrick was standing outside the lounge, checking tickets and IDs. We approached the front of the line, cutting in ahead of everyone, and Kat waved at Derrick. Derrick was a dark-skinned Black man with a bald head who often wore beanies to cover his head. Derrick had a thick black beard, a nose stud piercing, and a tall, heavy, muscular build. Tonight, he was wearing all black, with a black sweatshirt that read "Security."

"Oh, Kat, wassup!" Derrick yelled out as soon as he saw her. Meanwhile, the other bouncer continued to check the tickets while Derrick was distracted.

"Hey Derrick, how are you?" Kat said with a flirtatious voice. I laughed under my breath and stayed quiet. I was still extremely high.

"I'm good, baby, I'm good." Derrick looked over at me, and his eyes got wide. "Is that THE Zya Peach?"

I smiled and looked up at him. "Hey, Derrick."

He stands back a bit and looks me up and down. "I'm sorry to be this forward, but you look fine as hell tonight. I can't believe you are blessing Dustin's with your presence. You got your tickets?"

I looked over at Kat, and Kat looked at me, then at Derrick.

Kat smiled and rested her hand on his arm. "So, yeah, about that. No tickets, but—"

"Oh, so you want in, baby Kat?" He asked with a smirk on his face. "I got you this time around, but you owe me one."

Kat leaned forward, wrapped her arms around him, and hugged him tightly.

"You're the best, Derrick, thank you!" Kat turned and walked towards the door. I tried to follow her, but a gentle hand grabbed my arm before I could.

"You should come see me after the lounge closes," Derrick whispered as he got close to my ear. He smelled of a deep mahogany scent—his touch was both commanding and gentle. I turned, locked my eyes on him, and smiled.

"Maybe," I responded to him. He grinned and nodded his head, then let go of me, so that I could continue following Kat into the lounge. The lounge was full of people. No seats were available, and people stood around watching all the talent perform on stage.

As soon as I entered, a rush of energy took over me. It was more potent than any energy I'd felt since coming to the city, making me realize Mahant was close.

My eyes darted around, scanning for anyone, but there were too many people. Was he truly here? Or was this overstimulation from smoking and drinking earlier? No, it couldn't be. I knew my Mahant and his energy, and I could feel him. I stood dead in one spot and continued to look around. Even though the music played in the distance, people clapping and cheering, everything around me went silent.

I couldn't pinpoint the source of the massive energy shift in the room. My chest started to rise and fall quickly as my anxiety increased. Someone grabbed my arm, and I jumped.

"Hey, babes. Are you okay?" Kat asked me as I broke focus.

I must have looked entirely disoriented—hot and flushed, my body language uncomfortable. My palms were sweaty, and my heart was racing.

Hesitantly, I responded. "Yeah, I'm good. I'm good, I'm just—"

I started looking around again, and Kat snapped her fingers at me.

"We smoked a shit ton of weed and had a lot of shots. Are you sure you're good? Do we need to go to the restroom?" She held onto my arm.

I cleared my throat and tried to compose myself. "Yeah, let me follow you."

Kat took my hand, and we beeline to the back of the lounge. I could still feel Mahant's energy pulsating around me, growing stronger with every step. I was almost nervous to see him. What would I say? What would I do?

As we almost reached the bathroom, the feeling grew more intense; I could taste Mahant and smell him.

There I stood, frozen in time, as this tall man exited the bathroom and began walking towards me. He wore a black shirt, jeans, and a loose black button-up. He also wore a long-brimmed fedora hat. He was beautiful and looked just like Lanno, but with slight differences. He had tattoos, and his hair was jet black, shorter, but still curly. I stopped again and watched as he slowly walked by me. As soon as he did, he stopped and looked around, confused. I wondered if he felt my energy as I felt his. Kat started pulling my hand to lead me to the bathroom. I didn't want to go, but what would I say to him?

All I knew was that I had just found my Mahant.

Once we got into the ladies' room, I shook off all the excess energy, vigorously shaking my hands. Kat stared at

125

me, watching as I took a deep breath in, held it, and then let it out.

"Are you okay?" She asked me, very concerned.

I responded. "Mmm I'm good, I'm good. I promise."

"You're scaring me. I've never seen you like this. Was it the weed?" Kat continued to ask questions.

I looked up at her and grabbed her hands. "No, it's not the weed. I promise I'm fine. I just saw someone that I know and—"

"Oh my God, go talk to them. Don't let me get in the way! You made me scared. I'm over here thinking you're trippin', and you're being scared because you saw some guy. I saw how you looked at him. Who is he?" She asked curiously.

I nervously laughed and shook my head. "You wouldn't believe me if I told you the truth."

"Try me." Kat challenged me. She crossed her arms and looked at me, waiting for a response.

"Let's just say—" I thought for a moment and put my fingers to my mouth. I bit my nail softly. "Let's just say that I've known him for a long time, and he's why I moved to Bluepoint City."

Kat teased, "So, you're stalking him?"

I made a face at her and then pushed her playfully. "Be serious!"

"Okay, I'm sorry. I'm sorry. I'm still a little high, and it's just a tad bit funny seeing you get all mushy over someone. I've never seen this side of you. But seriously, spill the tea?"

"This is a conversation for another day. Maybe when you are much higher than you are now." I promise her.

Kat sucked her teeth and then grabbed my hand, leading me back outside the restroom. Once we exited, I looked around again. I noticed Mahant was sitting by the bar, talking to some girl. He looked disoriented—his body language was very similar to when his memories would return. Who was this woman next to him? Thoughts started running rampant through my mind, and I got extremely nervous. If Mahant's disorientation were due to him regaining his memories, then this would have to be a soul tie, because only a soul tie could restore memories. But how was that possible? Mahant must have created a powerful connection to Lauren before he passed away in his previous timeline. My mind completely jumped the gun and plagued every single thought that raced through me.

Usually, I'm calm, cool, and collected. But this? Seeing Mahant with another woman who might be a soul tie hurt me to my core.

If this were really Lauren, I'd be devastated.

My eyes watered as I watched them together. I turned to Kat, and she looked worried as her eyes shifted focus from them to me.

Holding tears back, I speak. "I need to leave."

"Okay, I'll come with you." She assured me.

I attempted to compose myself. "No, you stay here. I need to be alone. I'm going to head home."

I hugged her and then walked away, heading back towards the entrance. I walked out and passed Derrick.

Derrick reached out and grabbed my arm. "Hey, whoa, whoa, whoa, where are you going? You just got here?"

I stopped and turned around, attempting to look away from him. Derrick stared at me and then closed the space between us as he asked. "Are you okay?"

With my mind all jumbled, I made a rash decision to invite Derrick over.

"Leave work and come with me," I demand.

Derrick looked behind him at the lounge and then back at me. "Are you dead serious?"

I nodded and grabbed his hand, pulling him away from the lounge. We make our way to the commuter and head towards my apartment. During the entire ride home, he would stand behind me and wrap his arms around my waist. I knew it was temporary, but I felt safe.

Once we arrived at my condo, I unlocked the door and walked inside. I beeline straight to my bar and took out two cups. I poured Rolo into both cups and watched Derrick stroll through my apartment, taking it all in.

"This penthouse is ridiculous." He whispered.

I walked over to him, both cups in hand, and handed him one. We toasted glasses and took the shot. I didn't say a word. I just stared at him, grabbed the glasses, and set them on my coffee table. Derrick's eyes locked onto mine, and our breathing deepened. I could see his aura glowing brightly, and his energy filled with pure excitement. I grabbed his hand and led him to my sofa, making him sit as I took off my coat and draped it over the couch's armrest, then straddled his lap and sat down.

My arms immediately draped around his neck, and I went in for a kiss. Derrick kissed me back and wrapped his arms around my waist.

I just wanted to feel anything other than what I felt about Mahant and Lauren. My feelings were irrational, and I jumped to conclusions without knowing the whole story, which led me to question everything. Could I compete? What does this mean for me?

Unfortunately, I felt nothing when I kissed Derrick. I was empty inside, and I tried to push through it. Derrick's hands reached under the hem of my shirt and pulled it over my head. He then tossed it aside. His lips pressed against my skin, and he kissed my jaw down to my neck. It wasn't the same as when Mahant kissed me there.

My eyes began to tear up again, but I tried to hold it back as much as possible. Derrick unbuttoned my jeans, and his hands slipped into them. I sighed and tried to enjoy these moments, but it wasn't working.

"Stop," I told him. We paused, and I slowly stood up from his lap and walked back over to my bar.

Derrick questioned me, "Is everything okay?"

I poured another drink. "I just need you to leave. I'm sorry."

Derrick sat quietly and then scoffed. He stood up and grabbed his things before heading towards the door. The door opened and then slammed shut.

These emotions were new to me. For the first time in centuries, my unbroken stream of thoughts faltered. I was confused and hurt. I never truly had Mahant to myself, and I've shared him across timelines with no problem. But the thought of him having another soul tie cut deeper than I expected. The idea unsettled me, forcing me to question how I could bear it if it were true. How could I reconcile sharing him with someone who might hold a part of his soul that I believed was mine alone? I pulled off my jeans and headed to my bedroom to fall asleep and think about this.

"COMO, lock the door!" I called out.

"Yes, Zya. The door is now locked. Security armed." COMO advised.

As I lay in bed, my thoughts shifted. I hated thinking negatively and needed to find more positive ground. I breathed deeply and held my breath as I counted backward. Once I got to five, I slowly exhaled until I got to one. Before I left Dustin's lounge, I noticed the woman with Mahant was wearing a Dustin's worker outfit. I should talk to her, pick her brain, and see what she's all about.

I mapped out this plan in my head as I slowly drifted off to sleep. I was relaxed now and ready to see what the future had in store for us. I'm most happy because I found him.

I found Mahant.

Chapter 7

I woke up with a sore face.

My eyes were hard to open because they were so swollen. Instantly, I remembered how I fell asleep crying. I was tossing and turning all night, plagued by thoughts that danced menacingly through my mind. I turned on my back and stared at the ceiling. I hated these newly found emotions. I've experienced happiness, love, and loss. However, these emotions felt erratic and deeply rooted within me. I got out of bed and slowly sank to the floor. The cool marble against my thighs sent chills through my body, but I didn't care. I sat on the floor and closed my eyes. I needed to center my thoughts expeditiously.

I've never awakened to so much pain coursing through my body. Emotions manifested as physical discomfort, and as I sat there meditating, I tried to shift my thoughts to more positive memories—ones with Mahant and me alone.

For a while, all I did was recollect all the good times we had spent together. Suddenly, a smile formed on my face. It made me so happy to think about the countless dates we've been on and the timelines we've been in. He was my 'always and forever'.

I meditated for a while, clearing my mind of impurities and filling it with positive affirmations.

After my meditation, I sat there and thought about the plan for the day. If the person I saw were truly Lauren, I would want to go and meet her. I didn't want to lurk or spy on her, or make it seem malicious or ill-intentioned. I also didn't know how to break the ice and tell her I was Imani. All I knew was that I needed to approach this delicately and with pure intentions.

I finally stood off the floor and stripped out of my bra and panties to shower. I had slept in, and it was much later than anticipated.

After my shower, I got out and dressed. I did not feel like dressing up at all, so I put my hair in a messy bun, then put on my joggers and a sweatshirt.

Walking out to my living room area, I noticed how messy it was. Little Roo was sleeping on the sofa that I very embarrassingly almost had sex on last night. There were glasses and bottles of alcohol everywhere.

Since it was two in the afternoon and Dustin's didn't open until four, I gave my home a much-needed deep cleaning.

"COMO, play my favorite playlist!" I called out.

COMO turned on some tunes, and I started cleaning.

Getting lost in cleaning helped to keep my mind at bay. A few hours had passed, and I finally checked the time on the clock.

I didn't feel like changing. However, there was no way I could go to Dustin's like this. I also needed to get out of this mental funk, and my choice of clothing was not helping. I went back into my room and got dressed.

I changed into a graphic crop top, a sheer beige maxi skirt, and black boy shorts. This look required heels and a leather jacket to complete the look. I took my blown-out hair out of its bun and grabbed my black handbag. I looked in my huge vanity mirror, which sat off to the side of my bedroom, and made a few poses to ensure I liked the outfit. I smiled because I looked pretty and felt a lot better mentally.

As I walked out of the house, I called out to COMO. "COMO, feed Roo. Lock the doors and set the alarm in ten seconds."

"Yes, Zya," COMO answered.

The dispenser to Roo's food went off as I closed the front door and left my apartment. I walked down the hall and to the car garage to ride in style to Dustin's.

Once I arrived at Dustin's, I parked in the back of the building and walked around the front to enter. Derrick was outside, and I came to a stop.

"Shit!" I uttered under my breath as I continued to walk towards him. I forgot my extreme lack of control last night. With my emotions heightened, I realized I was not myself at all—a typical human being's response.

There wasn't a line just yet, as it was very early. Derrick was scrolling through his phone as he sat on the railing of the stairs. I walked up slowly to the top of the step and put my hands in my jacket pockets.

Derrick looked up from his phone and stared me straight in the eyes. He scoffed and then looked back down at his phone.

"Zya Peach." He said, his tone was very short.

My body language was uneasy, my hands gripping the inside of my pockets as I responded with guilt. "Hey, Derrick."

It was quiet, and he said nothing back. I stood there awkwardly for a few seconds and then looked around.

"Sooo..."

"Yes?" He responded.

I sighed. "Can I go in?"

"You can do whatever you like. I'm sure you're used to getting your way." Derrick's tone was snippy still.

I rolled my eyes and then took my hands out of my pockets to cross my arms. "Can we not do this? I really don't want to do this."

With his eyes still locked on his phone, Derrick did not look at me; instead, he laughed. "You don't want to do a lot of things, Zya. What's crazy is the one thing you actually want to do is waste my time."

I was frustrated, even though I had no right to be, because Derrick was right. So, I apologized. "Look, I'm sorry I wasted your time. I really am. I was in a fucked-up space last night, and I used you to make myself feel better."

I knew the truth would be harsher than the lie, but I needed to be honest. I wasn't interested in Derrick, and he would have only been a placeholder until I found Mahant.

Derrick nodded his head and started rapping some lyrics. I knew he wasn't trying to hear me out. His energy was dark and cold. I cleared my throat and then walked away, entering Dustin's Lounge.

Once I entered the lounge, I looked around at the space. My eyes darted around, hoping to see Lauren, but she wasn't there. I walked up to the bar and took a seat.

The bartender immediately walked up to me. "Hey, what can I get for you?"

"I will take your lemon drop special."

He snapped his fingers and responded, "You got it."

I drank for a couple of hours, and as time passed, more people entered the lounge to hang out. There was no big event tonight, but I'm sure this place still got busy. Every few minutes, I looked around to see if Lauren had come in.

"Are you looking for someone?" The bartender asked me as he wiped down the bar.

I averted my gaze from around the bar to the bartender. I smiled, picked up my fifth lemon drop, and finished it.

"I think I may need something stronger, Rolo, please," I requested, avoiding the question.

He pulled out a bottle of Rolo and poured it into a shot glass.

"Expensive taste you have. And listen, I'm no narc, just a curious bartender trying to make conversation."

I picked up the shot and took it. "Is that right?"

"Yeah, you've been looking around this bar since you arrived. So, unless you're casing it, which I promise you don't want to rob this place. Derrick has been itching to play the hero, and you don't look the type to rob a joint. So, I'm assuming you're looking for someone."

I pressed my palms against the bar, spread out my fingers, and then slid my hands out as I looked at him. I was feeling good, but not tipsy enough.

"Okay, maybe I am," I admitted.

"Who is he? A guy you met last night." The bartender continued pressing me.

I responded without hesitation, "No, a girl, actually."

He finally stopped wiping the bar, and his eyes got big. A smirk grew on his face, but he quickly corrected his expression, and his face returned to normal.

He cleared his throat and then proceeded. "Interesting. You don't look like a—"

"A lesbian?" I laughed, cutting him off. I then sat up straight and tapped my glass. "Don't judge a book by its cover, sir."

He filled my glass up with another shot and then stood there with his eyebrow raised.

"So, what does she look like?" He continued to probe, and I loosened up.

"She's short and has beautiful, dark brown, curly hair and freckles. You know, I think she actually works here." Just as I spoke, a hand slammed onto the bar, and the bartender looked away from me to the person.

"Hey, Bobby!" a soft voice spoke to him.

Bobby, the bartender, nodded his head to gesture what's up. "Hey, Aeries."

After saying hello, he looked at me from the corner of his eye.

I looked over at her, and there she was—this had to be Lauren. She looked at me, smiled, and then looked away.

She continued her conversation with Bobby. "I had a very long, interesting night and didn't even want to come into work today. However, it's a new job, and I know I need to be here. I may check out early tonight if it doesn't get too busy. Have you seen your brother so that I can tell him?"

"Nope, I haven't seen Aaron yet. But if I do, I've got you," Bobby said back to her.

I continued to stare at her, unable to break my gaze. Aeries looked at me again.

"Hey, you're Zya Peach, right?" She tilted her head and semi-pointed at me.

I smiled back at her. "I am, and you're Laur—Aeries. You are Aeries. Cute name."

"Thank you! Zya Peach is super cute, too." She complimented me.

I could see Bobby out of the corner of my eye. He picked up a glass and started wiping it down. My heart was racing because I did not know what to say. I wanted to break the ice and tell her who I was and rip the bandage off.

"Hey, actually, can I talk to you about something?" I asked Aeries.

Her face showed shock as she looked at Bobby and then back at me. "Uh, yeah, sure."

Bobby stood there awkwardly, and I gave him a look. He cleared his throat and then walked away. My attention turned back towards Aeries, whose energy vibrated with mine. A powerful energy I've never felt before, except in Mahant. I could always feel people's energies or see their auras, but this was different.

I laced my fingers together and placed them in my lap. "So, I'm just going to go ahead and just rip it right off and get to the point."

Aeries held her hands up in front of her. "If this is about a guy, you've got the wrong girl. It sounds like you're coming to me as a woman, and I can assure you I'm not like that."

I put my finger on my lips and then tilted my head. "Kind of? But not in that sense."

Aeries shifted uncomfortably, "Okay..."

"I'm Imani. Does that ring a bell?"

Immediately, her eyes got big, and she leaned away from me. "Shut the fuck up!"

I nodded and then gently bit my nail.

Aeries, with her eyebrows raised, and a shocked expression, continued. "You're lying. You're Imani? Like Imani Imani, Mahant's Imani?"

I leaned in towards her and whispered. "Yes, and you're Lauren. Right?"

Aeries sat forward and rested her elbows on the bar, then covered her mouth. She slowly nodded her head at my question.

"This is insane, so... insane." She whispered to herself, staring straight ahead, not looking at me.

"Yeah, we are all in the same timeline," I told her. "I was here last night, and I saw you with Mahant. Where is he?"

Aeries was still looking forward, shaking her head in disbelief. She was more in shock than I was.

She cleared her throat. "Mahant is at my house right now. Last night made him extremely disoriented. I didn't know what to do, but I was afraid to leave him like that."

I was very familiar with this process and worried. I overheard Aeries say that this was a new job and that she needed to stay, but we needed to get back to Mahant.

"Hey, Aeries, look, we must get back to Mahant. Can we go check on him, or should I?" I asked her.

She finally turned towards me. Her eyes were red, as if she were on the verge of tears. "This is a lot for me. Since

I was reborn again, it's like I can feel everything, and it's overwhelming."

I reach forward and rub her arm softly to help calm her down.

Aeries sighed and then looked across the bar. "Bobby, I need to run. I'm so sorry. Tell Aaron I'll pick up anyone's shift next weekend."

Bobby gave her a nod and waved his wash towel as we both left the bar and rushed to her home. As I followed her in my car, I couldn't help but lose myself in my thoughts, hoping Mahant was okay, and after about a fifteen-minute drive, we approached her home. She had a cute little townhouse on the outskirts of the city, nestled in Shockoe Court—a rougher neighborhood where crime seemed more prevalent. I parked the car, and we both got out and walked to her front door. Aeries unlocked the front door, and we both entered her cozy home.

Inside was homier than the outside and the area where the home was situated. The first thing you notice upon entering the house is how small and comforting the space is. The hardwood floor stretched to the back of the home, but on one side, the wood met carpet that opened into a warm, naturally lit living room. She had one small sofa in front of a fireplace and a fish tank that nestled between her windows. On her mantle were pictures of her and her family, presumably from this timeline. She also had many paintings, most depicting the solar system, along with one distinct crescent-moon painting. The second almost immediate introduction was the sweet islander aroma—coconut infused with warmed citrus, a scent close to how she smelled at Dustin's, just more robust.

After taking in my surroundings, my eyes began searching for Mahant.

"Brandon?" Aeries called out.

I looked at her and then around the room. I heard footsteps approach, and Mahant entered the room.

I could feel my entire aura radiating around me as I got excited to see him. Mahant's aura was dim, but it slowly deepened and glowed as brightly as the stars in the universe.

"Imani?" He called out.

I rushed over to him, wrapped my arms around his neck, and pulled him into my body. His arms wrapped around my waist, and he held me close. I sighed into his embrace and hugged him as tightly as I could. I never wanted to let him go.

"Hey, baby, I've missed you so much," I told him.

I pulled away from him and looked up into his eyes as he looked down at me.

"It's coming in as bits and pieces all at once. I remember so much, but it's challenging to process everything. What's happening?" Mahant whispered.

This time, I wanted to be completely transparent and give him all the answers he needed. I took his hand, led him to the nearby sofa, and sat down. Aeries entered the kitchen, grabbed water for us all, and then returned to the living room. She set the glasses on the coffee table and sat on the other side of Mahant.

"You can only remember all your memories when a soul tie finds you and helps you remember." I looked at Aeries, pointing at her as I explained. "Aeries, I believe, is your soul tie now, so she's helped to restore some of your memories. There are other methods to get them all back."

Aeries rested her hand on his arm and began rubbing it gently. I adjusted myself uncomfortably next to him. It was difficult for me to accept even my own words that Aeries was now his soul tie. Even though the only proper way to confirm if they were soul-tied was to ask the universe, there was no doubt in my mind that they were, because I had not contacted Mahant, and his memories were restored. Not only was it hard for me to admit that truth, but it was now hard for me to see physical contact between them. We had explored relationships and connections with other people—sometimes separately, other times together. We agreed upon it, something that had always worked for us. Together, we experienced the beauty of sharing intimacy with others, allowing our bond to grow through trust and freedom.

But this felt different, and I couldn't quite explain why.

Every time I saw them together, every time the thought of them crossed my mind, something inside me twisted, sharp, and unrelenting. It was jealousy in its purest form.

The emotions I felt were ones I had never felt in my hundreds of years of walking this universe.

Mahant spoke softly, "Aeries told me what happened when I was Lanno, and that's why I couldn't remember until now."

I looked at Aeries, and she shrugged sheepishly.

"Well, you have a habit of hurting yourself, and if you end your life, you won't remember the next. So, let's set a ground rule: don't hurt yourself." I explained to Mahant.

I stood up from the sofa and walked around the coffee table. I needed a moment to think. I didn't want to overload Mahant with information too soon, but I wanted to be as transparent as possible. Unfortunately for my game plan, Aeries already told him quite a lot.

I turned around and looked at them both. Aeries was caressing Mahant's cheek, and her other hand held onto his forearm. The jealousy remained unmatched and fueled by emotions and resentment. Just the way she was touching him sent my mind down a rabbit hole.

Mahant lowered his head and grabbed it, then started bouncing his knee. Aeries wrapped her arm around his head and pulled him in close.

"Hey, it's okay. We will get through this." She reassured him as she kissed the side of his head sweetly. Her hand left his head, and she started rubbing his back gently. I could feel Mahant calming down with every touch as he looked over at her. She kissed his cheek, then his lips, and he kissed her back.

I sighed and closed my eyes, trying to center my thoughts again. Seeing the kiss sent a nauseating feeling through me.

"Okayyy," I piped up, feeling defeated.

I just wanted to leave and address my emotions. I opened my eyes, and thankfully, they weren't kissing anymore. They were both looking at me.

"Mahant..." I spoke, and then I noticed his eyes widening.

Aeries intervened. "Yeah, that's been happening. So, I've been calling him Brandon."

Mahant stood up and walked over to me. "Whenever I hear Mahant, flashes of memories rush over me. But they're with you, Imani. I feel this powerful desire and energy bursting at its seams. It's like I don't understand it, but I do at the same time. We have been down this road so many times."

"Hey," I said with a calmness to my voice as I reached out and palmed his face. "Listen to me, this will all make sense, and you will be your old self again. If you'd like, we could meditate at my place."

"Can Aeries come?" Mahant asked.

I nodded my head reluctantly and then looked around him at Aeries. "Absolutely."

"Oh no, it's okay. I had him last night, and maybe if you take him tonight, we can bring him up to speed." Aeries said. "He's all yours."

Mahant looked at Aeries, then approached her and kissed her. Once again, I felt this weird sensation take over; this time, it was more than nauseating—it was anger.

Mahant and I left Aeries' home and quickly drove to mine. We parked the car in the garage and took the elevator to my floor. Once we got into the condo, he looked around.

"Can't believe Zya Peach is my Imani." He said, poised.

I turned around and looked at him as I blushed. "Oh, yeah?"

Mahant smiled. It was almost as if he were a different person from when we were at Aeries' place. His aura was brighter, and he sounded more confident.

"This place is really nice. You've done well for yourself." He complimented me.

I walked to my bar and started pouring drinks for myself and Mahant.

"I don't drink. And it's a good thing that I don't. All the memories that rushed back with Lauren and my drinking habits were maddening. I was in bad shape in that time-line, but I promise I will do better." Mahant promised, acknowledging his faults.

"It's good that you're remembering things so efficiently. It all feels different, promising." I walked up to him with my drink. "I wonder if that has anything to do with Aeries."

Mahant smirked at me as I stood inches away from his chest. "I can't believe I have two soul ties."

"Yeah, so how is that possible, Mahant? Or should I call you Brandon like Aeries?" I rolled my eyes and then gave him a look, then mockingly said, "That's why I've been calling him Brandon."

"Don't be like that, Imani." He said, staring at me. "How is she my soul tie? I asked the universe for her to be, that I remember vividly."

I took the shot and then locked my eyes on him, glaring.

"Well, that was very selfish of you." I expressed my emotions openly, sharing how I was feeling.

Mahant closed the space between us, and as I held the glass in my hand, I looked him over. Even though I was upset with him, I couldn't help but admire him; he was even more handsome than I remembered from his previous timeline. His arms naturally wrapped around my waist, and my eyes moved to his chest. My hand peeled back the open button-up shirt slightly to take in all his tattoos. They covered him, which was different. I examined him from head to toe as he embraced me. Next, my hand went to his full beard, and I played with it, twirling it between my fingers. Mahant then tried to lean down and kiss me, but I pulled away slightly.

"Tell me, when you kiss her, do you feel the energy surging from her and entering your soul?" I stared at his lips and kept playing with his beard.

His voice was low and heavy, he responded. "Do you really want to know?"

"Yes," I responded immediately.

Mahant sighed and then continued to stare at me. I made sure not to look up into his eyes, knowing it would weaken me. My heart fluttered, and there were butterflies in my stomach. He still made me melt whenever he was near or touching me.

I was upset with the universe and knew it would take me some time to adjust. As emotionally evolved as I thought I was, this was hard for me. Without him responding, I already knew the answer. Even more, his silence was a response. I knew he loved Lauren so much in his previous life that the universe was bound to tether them together. I was naïve.

I changed the subject. "How much do you remember?"

"A lot. More than Lanno ever did."

"I guess we have Aeries to thank for that." My tone was sarcastic and short.

Mahant gently grabbed my jaw and made me look at him. "Hey, you know when you called me Mahant earlier, I gained a lot more memories from you and me. You are helping me remember, too, Imani."

I looked into his eyes and felt my eyes water.

"Call me Mahant again." He demanded. "Tell me you love me."

A tear fell out of my eye, so I closed my eyes. "I love you, Mahant. Always and forever."

I opened my eyes again and saw his aura glowing even brighter. Mahant's eyes closed, and he inhaled deeply, then exhaled.

His lips finally pressed against mine. As always, it felt familiar and epic, instantly turning me into a puddle. My arm draped around his neck, and I pulled him into me. I couldn't help but kiss him back, even though I was frustrated. Suddenly, I pulled away and got out of his grasp. I wiped my tears away and put my glass on my kitchen island.

"You're frustrated with me. I can tell." Mahant sighed, defeatedly.

"I am frustrated with you, Mahant. All of this is new for me. You know me, I've never been the jealous type. We've always been very open with our relationship. You've let me do my thing, and you do yours. But this is different for me." I explained as I tried to compose myself. I sat at my island table, gazing at him as he stood there.

"Are you going to make me choose?" He asked me.

I gave him a look. "Are you serious? Did you seriously ask me that? Do I look like Lauren to you?"

Mahant walked up to me, but I held my hand out. "Don't." More tears fell from my eyes.

Mahant continued, "I've never seen you like this. I'm sorry. How can I fix this?"

"This can't be fixed, Mahant. The universe did its big one for you. You wanted this! It's never been about what I want. It's what Mahant wants. Let's grant his every wish." My energy shifted significantly, and I became angry.

I was never angry, and I hated crying.

I wiped more tears and looked away from Mahant while he quietly stood there.

"I love you, Imani. That will never, ever change. I promise you that sincerely, from the bottom of my heart. My connection to you is so powerful it's beyond the clutches of the universe. It's stronger than any soul tie I can form with anybody. You're my twin flame, and we are one. You're my other half." Mahant closed more space between us and stood before me as I sat on the barstool.

"Don't do that. Don't minimize your love for Aeries, Mahant. I don't want that. That's not what I'm asking for. I need you to understand that this will be hard for me, no matter how long it takes. It might just be tonight. It might be tomorrow or a year from now. Shit, it might be for centuries. I'm upset that you're no longer just mine. I have to share you now, someone I have devoted my life to. In every timeline, in every lifetime, for eternity!" I yelled, my voice elevated, shaking with every word spoken.

I continued, "I can feel her, too, Mahant. Did you know that? I can feel Aeries. Is she my soul tie, too? Is she included in my stipulations? What the hell does that mean for me?" I paused for a second, completely exhausted, then continued. "I have so many questions, and I'm so confused. For the first time in my life, I feel icky. I feel so gross not being able to manage my emotions. But one thing I have accepted is that no matter how much I bitch or moan, I'm stuck with this. So no, I won't make you choose. I can't." I caught my breath and looked up at him, and he stared back at me.

"I selfishly asked for another soul tie without truly considering how you would feel. I'm such a dumbass, and I fucked up." Mahant admitted as he rested his hand on mine.

I looked at him and then shook my head. He rested his forehead against mine and let out a deep sigh, so I sighed in return with him.

I was glad I could get all of that off my chest. I've always been honest, open, and transparent with Mahant. However, this was the most vulnerable I had ever been with him.

As frustrated as I was, I wanted to be in Mahant's arms. I knew he could tell. Mahant reached down and picked me up, lifting me into the air. I wrapped my legs around his waist and my arms around his neck as my face buried into his chest. Mahant held me tight as he walked through my apartment and entered my bedroom. He rested me on the bed and then took off his shirt. As he undressed, I followed suit. Mahant was in his boxers with no shirt on, and I was in my bra and panties. He got into bed with me under the blankets. All Mahant did was hold me for the rest of the night. There were no words, pressure, or expectations. He didn't coax me into conversation or attempt to start anything more. He was a steady, quiet presence I desperately needed but couldn't bring myself to ask for.

We lay there in the stillness, his arms wrapped around me like a shield against the world. Occasionally, he would shift slightly, rubbing slow circles on my back or gently massaging my shoulders. His touch was soft, comforting, and unspoken in its intent. When he finished, he would pull me closer, tucking me into his chest as though he could keep the storm within me at bay.

And for that moment, it worked.

I needed this more than I could have ever admitted. In my current mental state, I felt weakened, fractured, and hopeless, as though the weight of my thoughts might crush me completely. But in his arms, I found something I hadn't felt in what seemed like an eternity. I found peace.

We didn't even get to meditate. However, as the minutes bled into hours, my breathing slowed, syncing with the steady rhythm of Mahant's heartbeat. My thoughts grew dim, and I felt a sense of relaxation. Being in his arms, us in sync, was the meditation we both needed. Slowly, my eyes grew heavier now that my mind was at ease. The tears that had once streaked my cheeks in anguish had dried, their presence now a quiet testament to the release I hadn't realized I needed. And as my consciousness faded, a faint sense of hope lingered—a whisper that maybe tomorrow would be a better day.

Chapter 8

When I woke up, my bed was empty. Mahant must have woken up before me and was in the living room. I could hear people talking outside my bedroom, so I got out of bed and threw on my robe to investigate. Mahant was in a costly pajama suit outside my room, and Kat was there as well.

"Hey," I said softly to them both. Kat was sitting on my sofa, and Mahant sat on the barstool at the kitchen island.

"Good morning, beautiful," Mahant greeted me.

Kat looked at Mahant, then turned her attention back to me.

"Good morning, babes," Kat said as she stood and walked towards me. "I was coming to check up on you, but it looks like you're in good hands."

I smiled as I held the robe around me, then grabbed the straps and tied them around my waist. Kat looked at me, and then her face grew concerned.

"Are you okay?" She whispered as she reached out and grabbed my arm. She rubbed it gently up and down.

"Yeah, I'm okay. Just tired." I lied. In reality, I was exhausted and defeated, having spent the entire night crying on and off, which had taken a toll on my composure.

Kat looked straight through me. "Then why does it look like you've been crying all night?"

I sighed. "It's a long story, but I promise you, I'm fine. We will talk about it soon."

I walked past her and up to Mahant. He had a glass of orange juice in his hand. He lifted the glass to his lips and took a sip.

"Good morning. I see you found the Brandon section in my closet." I whispered. He smiled, looked down at his clothes, and then nodded. "I see you two also met."

Kat walked back to the sofa and sat down. I opened the fridge and grabbed a bottle of water, twisted the cap, drank some, then walked to my teapot and turned it on.

"Mhm, Brandon and I have met. He's been telling me a little about himself. I'm curious how you two met, though." Kat announced.

I grabbed a coffee mug from the cabinet and set it beside my teapot.

"Remember, I told you that you wouldn't believe me if I told you the truth?" I reminded Kat.

"And I told you to try me."

I continued to fix my tea, grabbing some honey and a stress-relief tea packet from its box. I unpackaged it, put the tea bag in the cup, and poured the steaming hot water into the mug. Next, I added my honey.

"I need lemon," I said to myself out loud.

Mahant got up from the barstool and walked to my refrigerator to grab my container full of lemon slices. He then walked over to me and handed me the container.

"Thank you," I said sweetly, then palmed his face and caressed it.

"You two are so cute. It's giving energy. It's giving soul-mates. You two move in sync, in harmony." Kat said, gesturing expressively with her hands.

I smiled and looked at Mahant, who looked back at me and laughed under his breath. I knew I could tell Kat the truth. She connected with her higher self. To her, everything wasn't just a metaphysical world, but much more profound and powerful than it seemed. Our conversations always centered on whether there was a higher power that controlled the universe. Her mind didn't just live in the present; it transcended beyond what most people could comprehend. She had a deep passion for astrology and meditation, immersing herself in the mysteries of the cosmos and the art of inner peace. Kat reminded me a lot of myself.

"He is my soulmate." I finally relinquished it. "My twin flame."

Mahant sat back on the barstool and drank more orange juice, marveling at my words.

"How long have you known each other?" Kat asked.

I paused and thought for a moment. "Nine hundred and seventy-six years?"

I looked at Mahant, and he was thinking, too. "Yeah, it's been nine hundred and seventy-six years."

Kat squinted at us. "That's so damn specific. What does that even mean?"

I walked across the other side of the island and stood between Mahant's legs, my back against his chest. I held my tea in both hands.

"It means that I have known him for multiple lifetimes. That reincarnation is real. We have been together for a very long time." This time, my tone was more serious.

Her mouth dropped open slightly, and then she nodded her head slowly. "Impossible. Reincarnation? I have so many questions."

I laughed and then looked back at Mahant. "It's understandable. It's a lot to process, but in all seriousness, it's the truth. His soul's name is Mahant, and mine is Imani. There are different timelines out there with endless lives and possibilities."

"Am I reincarnated?" Kat asked, intrigued.

Mahant nodded and then joined the conversation. "More than likely, you have been. You probably also have other timelines of you living different lives."

"If that's true, then why don't I remember any of my past lives?" Kat continued to ask more questions. She was very interested in how it all worked. Her yellow aura vibrated with each question.

"You may not be a part of a specific contract that would allow you to remember," I explained to her.

"Interesting." She responded, then grew extremely quiet. "And you're not pulling my leg? Reincarnation is real?"

"I would never do that to you. I know how your mind works. I can feel your energy and understand how important this can be to you." I promised her.

Mahant's phone dinged as text messages came through.

"It's Aeries. She wants to know if she can stop by," Mahant informed me.

I sighed. "Why not? The more the merrier."

Mahant texted her back and then put his phone down.

"Aeries?" Kat asked.

I laughed. "Oh, yeah, Mahant created another soul tie from his previous life. So now we're a thruple. Hence why it looks like I've been crying. It's been a lot to take in."

Kat's face was confused. "I don't even understand what you just said, Zya—Imani? Whatever. However, it doesn't sound good. Mahant, what did you do?"

Mahant did a big sigh. "I let my heart guide me to a rash decision without Imani's consideration, and now I will spend the rest of eternity making it right."

Kat shook her head in disapproval, then crossed her legs.

We talked for a bit more before Aeries arrived. Kat had so many questions, and even when she said she wouldn't ask anymore, she'd ask three more questions. We shared a lot with her, telling her about our past and favorite memories. We discussed the possibility of jumping into other timelines while in a meditative state. I even told her about soul contracts and cosmic stipulations.

There was a knock on my door, and I moved from Mahant. Aeries had finally arrived.

"I'm going to go get dressed in something more appropriate. COMO, open the door and let Aeries in." I called out.

COMO unlatched the door. "Come in, Aeries."

I went into my room and removed my robe, replacing it with leggings and a tank top. After getting dressed, I left my bedroom and saw Aeries standing beside Mahant at the kitchen island. Kat continued to sit on the sofa, playing with Roo.

"Hey, Imani." Aeries greeted me.

"Hey Aeries, how are you?" I asked her.

Aeries smiled and then sat on the barstool. "I'm good. You have a beautiful condo. I love the open space and the natural light coming through. Plus, all the plants and art are stunning."

Aeries was so sweet, and her compliments made me smile. She was such a beautiful woman, short and petite, with the most gorgeous brown curls and brown eyes. Her freckles painted a unique portrait on her face, dancing in the natural light that crept through my windows. Aeries also had a faintly glowing red aura surrounding her.

"Thank you," I responded sweetly, giving her a friendly smile. "Aeries, did you meet my friend Kat?"

Aeries shook her head. "No, I haven't."

"Well, Aeries, this is my home girl, Kat, my bestie. Kat, this is Aeries. The other soul tie to Mahant we were telling you about." I introduced them to each other.

Aeries' eyes got big as she looked at me. "You told her? Isn't that, like, against the rules?"

I laughed. "Rules? No, it's not against the rules, and yes, I told her."

Aeries looked at Mahant and then back at me. "Also, can we talk about the elephant in the room, please? That's why I came over."

I looked at Mahant, and he shrugged, then spoke. "What, or who, is the elephant?"

"The elephant is our relationship with Mahant. We're both technically dating him, and he's dating us," Aeries blurted out.

"Dating is an interesting choice of words," I replied under my breath, unfriendly and short.

Kat sat back on the sofa, and I could tell she was enjoying the awkward conversation that had started.

Aeries crossed her arms and continued to go back and forth with me. "Well, Imani, we are both dating him. At least I'm dating him. Soul tied to him, whatever you wanna call it. And I know we're both feeling some type of way."

I sighed, walked over to the sofa, and sat beside Kat. Roo left her immediately and came to sit on my lap. "It's bigger than dating; your souls are intertwined for eternity. You will never be free of him."

Aeries responded, "You mean you'll never be free of us because I can feel you, too, Imani. It's weird, but your energy flows through me and is overwhelming. It's the same sensation I feel when I can feel Mahant."

I stared at her, stunned. Her energy was magnetic, unlike anything I had ever felt—powerful, consuming, and impossible to ignore. It drew me in effortlessly, as if the universe had conspired to connect us. The only explanation that made sense was that when the universe created Mahant's soul tie to Aeries, it entangled me with them and connected us in ways I was only beginning to understand, ways I didn't know were possible.

"The only explanation is that we are all soul-tied together." Mahant finally engaged in the conversation.

"This is some crazy ass shit!" Kat yelled as she looked at all of us, her eyes darting all over the place.

"How is that even possible? I do not know. I assumed I would have been made aware that I had another soul tie. However, I was not." I chimed in, not excited about any of this. "This is unreal."

"What's the problem?" Aeries challenged me.

I gave her a look and then shook my head. "That's a loaded question with a loose trigger."

Aeries scoffed and continued to question me. "Why the animosity? I didn't do anything wrong here. I didn't ask for any of this. I didn't ask to be soul-tied to you!"

"You're right. Mahant did!" I replied quickly, glaring at him.

Everyone looked at Mahant, and I could feel his energy shift. I could tell he was embarrassed. Kat adjusted herself on the sofa, and I saw her looking at me from the corner of my eye. I was getting those uncontrollably annoying emotions again. Anger was peaking inside of me.

"Look, I'm sorry to both of you. Lauren and I had such a strong connection. I didn't think it would be such a big deal because Imani was so cool about Lauren. I didn't think this through, and I didn't know my decision to create another soul tie would link you two together as well." Mahant admitted.

I butted in, "Of course, I was super chill about it because I didn't think you would actually make another soul tie. I remember the conversation in our last timeline. You were worried I was going to freak out because you were fucking Lauren. I was cool about it. Then, after we had sex, you asked about teaching her how to jump. I didn't realize you would create a link to her, Mahant!"

Aeries' eyes widened from what I said, "Wait, you two had sex in our previous timeline when you were with me, Mahant?"

Mahant turned to look at me, his eyes locking onto mine with an intensity that sent a shiver down my spine. In that instant, the room seemed to fall into an unnatural silence, as if the air held its breath. The faint hum of conversations all of it disappeared, leaving only the weight of his gaze. It was as if time had paused, and the energy in the room shifted.

I felt uncomfortable in my home after admitting to sensitive information that I hadn't realized Aeries wasn't aware of. Her eyes instantly watered as she stared Mahant down, and Mahant's eyes were closed, taking in the moment. The room was silent, yet it blared with energy so intense that a plastic knife could cut through with ease.

Finally, Aeries crossed her arms and spoke. "Right, the morning you decided to crash out, then decided to drink and hit your head. The day that I will never forget."

Mahant nodded his head slowly, and when his eyes opened, the fire in them locked onto mine as if I had been the one to cause everyone such pain, as if the turmoil that was locked away in a safe had released because of me. It wasn't fair that I held the brunt of it all, carrying the weight of not only my emotions but everyone in the room. That, at least, is how it felt.

"Hey, don't look at me like that." My tone was exasperated. "You did what you wanted to do with me. I'm not the one who created this messy situation, Mahant."

Mahant sighed. His demeanor softened, and he rubbed his head to release stress. "You're right, I'm sorry."

Aeries laughed under her breath in disbelief and shook her head, as if trying to regain the strength to continue the conversation. She then played with her fingers as she looked down at them.

"I should leave. I feel like coming here was a mistake," Aeries admitted, finally getting a word out during the silence between us all.

A part of me felt bad, but I also didn't want to prevent Aeries from leaving. This situation was a huge change for me. To understand the precipice of what was happening is to know how the universe works. Even if we all tried to stay away from each other, the power of the universe would not allow us to. Mahant and I's bond transcended beyond the forces of love and creation, linking us together forever. Now that Aeries was an addition to this cosmic bond, there was no escaping the inevitable. Even though I knew deep down in my heart, I would have to tolerate Aeries, I would not give in so easily from the start. Even if this seemed stubborn of me, I stood my ground.

Aeries walked towards the door, and Mahant followed her.

"Wait, Aeries... We need to find some common ground." Mahant called out, grabbing her arm to prevent her from leaving.

I rolled my eyes at his attempt to make her stay. Aeries stopped in her place and turned around, looking Mahant in his eyes.

"I will let you and Imani have your day, and I'll be at the bar down the street. I need a moment to think about everything that is happening." Aeries pulled away from Mahant and left the condo.

Mahant sighed, turned around, and looked at me and Kat.

Kat made a face of discomfort. "Yeah, I think I should go." She turned to me, hugged me, and then got up off the sofa to exit as well.

Once again, it was quiet in the home. Mahant walked over to the couch and sat next to me.

"You remember our second timeline?" He asked randomly.

I thought for a moment and then nodded. "Yes, I will never forget our second timeline. It was a complete mind fuck. Being born into a universe with all my memories and navigating through life, not understanding why everything seemed so familiar and vivid."

Mahant added on to what I was saying. "Or why our emotions were heightened, and we could see other people's auras and feel their emotions."

Our second timeline was intense. Growing up was difficult because I was aware of my past timeline, and my parents thought something was wrong with me. There was a gravitational pull towards something more profound, a presence only Mahant and I could feel. That feeling was finding and locating each other. We both felt it throughout our childhood and into adulthood, until we finally located one another, and I helped him regain his memory of us as Bayzo and Bailey. We would have conversations about how strange it was to recall a previous lifetime and wonder whether this was normal for all species. Emotions were overwhelming and uncontrollable; the universe would explain to us they were a thousand times harder to manage than those of a normal human being. Thus, the reason Mahant would self-destruct every time he regained consciousness. These emotions are so powerful that only the most awakened beings can control them.

We took on and bore the beauty the universe gave us. It was a beautiful symphony of magic and honor, but also a relentless curse.

"Aeries told me this was her second timeline. She spoke to the universe, and the universe birthed her as Lauren for the first time. So, she has been navigating this world, our current timeline, by herself. At least we had each other." Mahant explained, his voice calming and gentle, his posture firm and deliberate.

Instantly, I felt even more guilt in my heart. To navigate a world alone, after just being reborn into the universe, is a mission I wouldn't want anyone to experience by themselves. Even though Mahant forced us all into this situation, I needed him to be the man that I loved in this moment. I needed him to go after Aeries.

I turned to him and sighed, "So, go get her, Mahant."

Mahant looked at me, "I can't lose you again, Imani."

I shook my head and spoke calmly. "Listen, I know we have had relationships with other people. Sometimes it's another guy, sometimes it's another girl. We are both fluid and open. But I need you to understand that this is so very different, Mahant."

"I know it is." Mahant took my hands and placed them in his lap. His grasp squeezed gently as we locked eyes with each other.

"I don't think you do," I admitted, swallowing a huge lump caught in my throat. "We have been able to experience people together and then leave them in our past. This time, you can't leave Aeries in your past; she is with you for eternity."

"Hmm." Mahant cleared his throat and looked away slightly.

"Going back to what she said about being able to feel me. How is that even possible, Mahant?" I shifted onto the sofa uncomfortably. "How could the universe tie us all together without me agreeing to any of it. None of this seems right. You and I are twin flames, now what are we?"

Mahant's face was just as stunned as mine. His body language was disoriented, and I could tell he was trying to push through it. To be the calm of my storm, my confidant of the turmoil that was brewing within me.

"Well... we can only get answers from the universe. Until then, we will manage." Mahant turned slightly as well and faced me. He leaned in and pressed his lips into mine, giving me a sweet, short kiss before pulling away. Mahant then stood up and went into the bedroom. I sat there, my lips still tingling from the lingering kiss. As much as I wanted him to stay with me, I needed him to go to Aeries and help her. I also realized that if anyone could help her get through this world, it would be me.

Mahant eventually came out of the room after taking a shower, dressed and ready to leave. As he approached the door, I called out, "Hey, I love you."

He turned around and smiled at me. "I love you more, beautiful."

He exits the front door, leaving me on the sofa, to the array of thoughts that swarm me.

Chapter 9

After Mahant spoke with Aeries, he came home, and we spent the day lounging on the sofa, talking about our current timeline and all things Brandon and Zya Peach. We talked about everything from him being an orphan at a very young age to how well-rounded he turned out to be. With my back against his chest, leaning into him as we sat comfortably on the sofa, nothing else mattered in the world. As long as I was in his arms, I was at peace, I was safe. All my worries washed away, and my love for Mahant melted into the very fabric of my existence.

One of the most important conversations we had was us discussing how he had to keep wraps on his mental state and not crash out in this timeline and hurt himself. Mahant promised he would try everything in his power not to self-destruct and that one of the hardest parts about being Lanno was the fact that he couldn't be with me.

Now that we ended up in the same timeline, that helped to keep his stressors in check.

Mahant and I talked about his conversation with Aeries and how she wanted to spend some time alone with me to get to know me better. He gave me her number, and as we sat on the sofa and talked the day away, I sent her a text to start the conversation about when and where we could meet up and talk.

I wanted to treat my relationship with Aeries with care. I knew this meant a lot to Mahant, and it obviously would not be a hook-up like Mahant and I had with others in the past. If Aeries were going to be a part of our lives for the rest of eternity, I wanted to build a strong foundation for our friendship. I wanted to get to know her and what she stood for, see past what Mahant saw, and dig deeper into who Aeries was. Even though I was with Mahant and nothing else mattered, in this moment, Aeries was still always present in my mind now.

Mahant laced his fingers with mine and then kissed the back of my hand as we sat on the couch. I squeezed his hand and then snuggled into his chest.

"I learned something new during my time here in Blue-point City." I broke the silence between us and felt Mahant adjust his posture behind me.

Mahant sighed, then spoke. "Oh, really? What's that?"

"The Collection," I spoke vaguely, trying to find the words I wanted to say.

Mahant quickly responded, "The Collection? What is that?"

I thought for a moment before speaking and took Mahant's arms, wrapping them around me tighter.

"Have you ever wondered who else was a part of the Recollections Contract? Who could remember their previous lives outside of us?" I asked Mahant, then waited for his response.

He thought for a moment, then finally responded. "Yeah, all the time, actually. We've never really had a conversation about it."

I nodded my head slowly, "Well, The Collection is an organization of people who proclaim that someone has reincarnated them and can remember their past lives. I had gone down a rabbit hole a couple of months ago when I was looking for you, and came across them."

"Well, that's interesting. So, did you reach out to them or see what they were about?"

I shake my head no, "I was too nervous about it. My gut told me to stay away from it, but..." I get up and make my way to my bedroom to grab my laptop. I came back into the living room and sat back against Mahant. I opened my computer and typed in the webpage I came across so I could show it to Mahant.

"They apparently have secret meet-ups. We would have to email the website to get the details. My guess is that you get vetted and then get the location because there is no info on their site about any meet-ups, but they talk about them a lot." I bite the tip of my nail as I explain everything to Mahant. He leaned forward and scrolled on the mouse pad, looking over the website.

"We should email them and get the deets." Mahant encouraged me.

I look back at him, eyebrows raised with excitement. I scrolled to the bottom of their website and clicked on the email button. I then typed up the email and hit send.

"Done! Now we wait." Bursting at the seams, I rock back and forth while against Mahant. I feel his lips press against my cheek softly.

While we waited for an email response, we kept talking the day away. Eventually, I made us egg salad sandwiches, and we listened to our favorite playlists, sharing artists we found enjoyable with each other during this timeline. A few hours later, I received a notification on my phone about a new email in my inbox. To my surprise, it was from The Collection. I grabbed Mahant's arm and pulled him back to the sofa. We both plopped down and grabbed my laptop to open up my email.

"I'm so excited!" I yelled as I opened the email. Mahant and I had our eyes glued to the screen as I opened it.

Mahant read aloud as I followed the words on the screen. "The Collection invites you to meet us at 65 Sycamore Street, tonight at 8 pm. Be there, as this will be your only invitation." I grabbed my phone, and it was already 6 pm.

"Ah! Let me get dressed." I squealed as I jumped up from the couch and ran into my bedroom. I heard Mahant chuckle, and eventually, we both made it into my walk-in closet. I sorted through my clothes as I felt Mahant's eyes on the back of my head.

"They didn't even ask us questions. They're just like... meet us here. Is that not odd?" Mahant asked hesitantly.

I opened one of my drawers and pulled out my taser. "We will be safe. I'll bring the taser in case we run into any crazies."

Mahant shook his head at me and then walked over to his section of the closet, picking up De jour–a cologne I had bought him with notes of some of his favorite scents, cedarwood and vanilla. "It's like you know me. Look at all these beautiful black clothes. You even have my favorite scents."

I smiled as I pulled down a white crop top and a red button-up shirt. With this outfit, I grabbed some high-waisted denim shorts and some tennis shoes. I wanted to be comfortable yet presentable for this meeting. Mahant, in his true fashion, grabbed a black pocketed shirt and black jeans to match. After we finished getting dressed and accessorizing, we quickly left the condo to head to our meet-up location. I let Mahant drive my car as I sat in the passenger seat, and the navigation system told us Sycamore Street was a 20-minute drive from my home.

Upon arriving at the address, we noticed it was an abandoned factory. There were no lights on, and all the windows had wooden boards covering them. Mahant and I stayed in the car for a while, scoped out the area, and told ourselves it was sketchy.

"Yeah, I don't like how this looks. There's nobody around." Mahant expressed as we sat in the car across the street from the building. "I should have brought my gun."

I looked out the window and into the alley next to the building to see if I saw anyone, but no one was there. It was five minutes before 8 pm, and I finally looked at Mahant and scrunched my face. I opened the passenger door and stepped out of the car. Mahant got out of the driver's seat, and we crossed the empty street, walking towards the building. I had my hand in my tote bag, on my taser, ready for anything. Mahant pressed the lock button on the key fob, and I jumped as the sound of my car locking scared me.

"Babe!" I yelled, and Mahant laughed as we continued to cross the street.

"I'm sorry. I didn't think your own car would scare you." Mahant bumped into me, and I rolled my eyes at him, then pushed him away. We finally stood in front of the building and tried to look inside, but nothing was visible.

Everything was quiet. No cars were driving on the street or at the intersection, and all the shops around looked closed down or abandoned. Sycamore Street was on the outskirts of the city, not in the best location. But as sketchy as it was, there were no homeless people or addicts on the street.

We waited until it was 8 pm, and then Mahant and I looked at each other.

"Maybe the website is a joke? To see what weirdos are out in the world thinking reincarnation is real." I hopelessly admitted.

Mahant shrugged and stood on the sidewalk. "Maybe… I just can't believe we came all the way out here and it's a hoax."

A random, low voice came from the alley next to the building. "A hoax? Never."

Mahant and I both turned towards the alley. My hand went back into my bag, and I scooted closer to Mahant as a person emerged from the shadows. She was my height, on the taller side, and had two side ponytails in poofs, with gold charms in her hair. She was wearing a green one-piece jumpsuit and matching gold sandals. On her hip was a holster and a gun inside it. Mahant and I immediately took a step back from her presence. Her aura was roaring with energy out of this world. It wasn't a dangerous energy, which was good, but its power was intense.

"No need for whatever it is you have in that bag. I'm not here to hurt you." She whispered carefully as she held her hands up and away from her weapon. "I'm guessing one of you sent the letter to The Collection? Well, my name is Sasha and I'm the second in command. I rarely do these meet-ups, but I was in the area."

Mahant and I look at each other. "Second in command? What exactly does that mean?" I asked nervously, but curiosity piqued as well.

"I can explain everything, but it's best to do it if you follow me." Sasha turned around and disappeared back into the alley. Mahant and I exchanged looks again, and I started walking towards the alley. Mahant grabbed my arm and pulled me back towards him.

"Imani, I don't like this," he admitted, worried.

"It's fine. Her energy has good intent. Let's do this."

Mahant shook his head and followed me as I followed Sasha. Once we entered the alley, there was a single light on a door, and we entered it. As we entered the massive abandoned building, the scent of cinnamon and honey filled the air. We entered the dimly lit conference room with a large oval table surrounded by chairs. Sasha sat down at the head of the table, and we joined her. I looked around and took in my surroundings, noticing a giant chandelier that sat at the focal point of the room, above the table. There was also a coffee bar by another entrance to the building, next to the one we entered. The walls were a deep forest green, with black trim and natural finishes.

As I looked around, my eyes finally met Sasha's, who was studying me. We briefly made eye contact before she spoke.

"The Recollections Contract. What do you know about it?" She asked, her tone serious and precise.

Mahant and I looked at each other. If we were thinking the same thing, we both knew already that she was the real deal.

"The Recollections Contract is a contract for certain beings that will remember their previous lives," I answered quickly and effectively. I placed my hands in my lap and locked my eyes on Sasha.

Sasha's eyes darted from me to Mahant, then back to me quickly. Soon after, a grin appeared on her face. It was an inquisitive smirk—she knew we knew our stuff.

"I'm two thousand, five hundred and six years old, or twenty-two in this timeline. How old are you both?" Sasha continued drilling us to see if we'd waver in response to her questions.

Mahant spoke up this time, "Twenty-four in human years, nine hundred and seventy-six in soul years, both of us. You've almost tripled us in years. How..." He pauses, then continues, "fascinating."

Sasha gave us a warm smile and then stood up. She walked over to the coffee bar and started making herself a drink. I looked at Mahant, and he stared back at me, then reached his hand over and grabbed mine.

"I'm one of the oldest beings I know for sure, yes. Definitely not as old as Sage." Sasha opens a tea bag, drops it into a cup, then grabs the kettle and pours hot water over it.

"Who is Sage?" Mahant asked curiously.

Sasha walked back over to us. "She is the founder of The Collection." Sasha sat back down in the chair, holding her cup in both hands and looking down, examining the steam rising from it. "I'm just second in command. I haven't been in the field in some time. Usually, we have other members who meet and vet people, but like I said, I was in the area and wanted to see if you all were truly gifts from the universe."

"We are." I finally speak. "We have had our share of talks with the universe. We have visited our share of different worlds and timelines together."

"Twin flames are beautiful. I can see you both glowing and mending as one together. It's a sight to see," Sasha complimented us.

Her knowledge was vast. I was impressed. Without having to ask the many questions that ran through my mind, Sasha delivered answers. It didn't feel like we were speaking in code; we were talking like people who understood the universe and how it worked. Her beautiful purple aura glowed and vibrated around her, effortlessly shimmering with the beauty she exuded. Sasha was gorgeous and had an incredibly warm demeanor. Even though she appeared mysterious, you could tell she was a loving, caring, and empathetic being.

"So, what was your favorite timeline?" Sasha asked as she lifted her cup and sipped slowly.

Mahant and I both looked at each other and smiled.

"Utopia," we both said together, then directed our gaze back to Sasha.

Sasha smiled, "Ahh, Winterdon and Treedom were so beautiful. Utopia was great."

I perked up. "This is so awesome! I can't believe we actually found another person involved in the Recollections Contract. And you seem wise beyond your years. Thank you so much for meeting up with us."

Sasha rested her cup back on the table, still with a smile on her face. She nodded and continued speaking. "There are so many others out there. In this timeline, in other timelines. We can reach the highest form of meditation and transition to other timelines. Some of us even have gifts or special powers. Do any of you have these?"

"Well, we can see Auras. Like seeing colors around people and understanding intent." I informed her, expressively speaking with my hands.

Sasha nodded. "That, my friend, is a gift."

Mahant held out his hand. "Wait, do you have a gift?"

"I do. Most of us do." She smirked again and then placed both hands flat on the table. "I can shape-shift into any being I have ever reincarnated into."

"No way!" I yelled, overly excited.

Sasha nodded again and then leaned back into her chair.

She explained that after discovering her ability to shift; she spent most of her life reincarnated into species that could be of use to her. Sasha told us she had been other intelligent beings, like birds or water mammals, and whenever she wanted to escape being human, she would shape-shift. She said it's almost like a cloak to get away from the world, and a blessing the universe has only given her. Sasha explained that many people had unique gifts. She explained mediums were usually part of the Recollections Contract and that some people could even wield magic.

It was fascinating to learn that there were more powers and special people out there who were just like us. There were so many questions brewing in my mind, and I didn't know where to start. For a while, we just let Sasha talk about all the possibilities of the world. We spent hours talking about The Collection. Sasha informed us they have meet-ups with other people every Friday, which means the next meet-up will be in five days. She gave us a card that was completely black on one side and a galaxy with a person in a mudra pose on the other and then mentioned that she wanted to see us there. She informed us that this timeline had the most people from The Collection present, and that it would be good to connect and network with others.

"Will Sage be there?" Mahant asked as he looked at the card Sasha gave to us.

Sasha made an uneasy facial expression, "Sage? I doubt it, but you never know with that one. The Collection is still fairly new, so she might make an appearance."

Sasha stood up to get ready to leave, so Mahant and I got up as well and adjusted ourselves.

I held my hand out and shook Sasha's hand as I spoke. "It was nice meeting you, Sasha, thank you so much for the opportunity, and I can't wait to see you Friday."

We all walked towards the entrance we had come in through, and Sasha leaned in to open the door. "Of course, it's been a pleasure to get back out there and recruit people again. Also, keep that card stored in a safe 'cold' place."

I raised my eyebrow and then looked at Mahant, who squinted at what she said.

Sasha laughed and then threw her hands up. "Well, we have to keep this a secret. So hide the card in your freezer, promise you, you will understand when you do."

We all left the abandoned building, and Mahant and I got into the car. Mahant handed me the card and then started up the car. As he drove back to my house, I flipped the card between my fingers, examining it. There was nothing on the card except for the small meditating person. No information was available regarding the meetup's location or time. The ride home was quiet; both of our minds were undoubtedly racing from the conversation we had with Sasha—at least mine was. I was curious about the meetup later this week and all the people we would connect with.

We finally reached the condo, parked in the garage, and hopped out of the car to head to the top floor. Mahant tossed the keys onto the counter once we entered. I kicked off my sneakers and then went into the kitchen to place the card in the freezer as instructed by Sasha.

So much energy had built up from the encounter that I needed to release some of it from me. So, I meditated.

"COMO, play my meditation playlist. 43 hertz please," I called out as I grabbed my yoga mat from the closet and spread it out across the floor. "Babe, your mat is in the closet, too, if you'd like to join me."

Mahant walked to the closet, grabbed his mat, and then walked in front of me, setting his mat on the floor as well.

COMO played the playlist as I walked around my condo, lighting the candles that spread throughout the home. I needed to create a calm, serene atmosphere around me to help center my mind and reconnect with my current timeline. As I lit some incense and candles, Mahant kicked off his shoes and then sat in his mudra pose on his yoga mat. I walked back to my mat, sat in front of him, and then smiled. He glanced back at me, smiled, and then reached to grab my hands.

With unspoken words, we both closed our eyes and began our breathing exercises. Mahant's mind was stronger than ever before, and I didn't have to walk him through our breathing exercises, he simply remembered. It was a sharp contrast to the previous timelines we had been in, where he struggled to remember his past. I didn't understand why his mind was strong, but I definitely questioned it. This phenomenon had Aeries written all over it; she was the only thing that was different in the constant that was me and Mahant. Self-doubt crept into my mind more than ever now. The countless years spent trying to mend his broken mind, then out of nowhere, Aeries' presence fixed him.

I pulled my hands out of Mahant's grasp and rested them on my knees as I continued to ground myself and shrink these polluted thoughts that ran rampant through my mind. I told myself to focus, manifest a better reality, and disengage from the jealous thoughts that trickled in.

Was it jealousy, or my reality? Either way, it was present in my mind like a storm brewing off the coast, ready to slam into an already eroded shore. Would this affect the relationship I wanted to build with Aeries? These thoughts clouded my mind, igniting a restlessness inside me that slowly crept up on me. Feelings I couldn't dodge or shake, relentlessly beating against me like a chaotic rhythm. I need a release, badly.

So I screamed out loud, loud and unforgivingly. Mahant's eyes opened instantly, and he grabbed my hands.

"What's wrong? Are you okay?" Fueled with concern, his voice was deep, vibrating into me to realign me.

I shake my hands from out of his, trying to rid the bad energy and stifling thoughts. "I'm so sorry. I don't know what came over me."

Mahant rested his hands on my lap and then scooted closer. "Today has been a lot. Maybe we should skip meditation and get some rest."

I sighed and then locked my eyes on Mahant's beautiful, dark brown eyes. How comforting and trusting they were. His aura melted into mine and wrapped me in its warm embrace as we both sat in front of each other on the floor. Trapped between wanting to be consumed by him and wanting to knock his head off for creating another soul tie. Caught between telling him how I truly felt every time he and Aeries crossed my mind, or just accepting my fate. However, no words would escape me at that moment.

His hands moved swiftly to my thighs as he pulled me closer into him while we sat there. My legs draped around his waist, and he rested his forehead into mine.

"Talk to me," he whispered, his arms now wrapped around my waist, hugging me.

He was more intuitive than I gave him credit for. Mahant knew I was off, and I knew he could tell my energy had shifted tremendously. I was not ready to talk about how I felt just yet. I needed more time for everything to marinate. To collect my thoughts about Aeries and decide how I wanted to address this newly found change to our dynamic.

I reached up and pressed my hand against Mahant's chest, rubbing it gently. Then, I leaned in and kissed his lips softly. "I'm alright, I promise. Just a lot of pent-up energy that needs a good release."

Mahant gave me a devilish grin and then kissed me again.

"Not that kind of release." I laughed and then pushed him away playfully. Mahant laughed with me and then leaned back into me. "I think I just need some sleep, like you said. Today has been a lot."

Mahant stood up quickly, then held out his hand. I reached up and grabbed it, then he gently pulled me to my feet.

"I'll put the mats away, you can go get ready for bed." Mahant crouched and began rolling the mats up. I gave him a nod and then turned towards the bedroom to retire.

"COMO, lock the doors and arm security," I called out.

COMO responded instantly, "Yes, Zya. Security armed."

I undressed and climbed into bed, under the blankets, snuggling in. Mahant soon entered the bedroom after putting the mats away. He undressed as well and then climbed into the bed, spooning me. His arms around me were home, undeniably my favorite place to be. Just his touch, his presence grounded me in ways I could not explain, in ways I sometimes couldn't even fathom. His ability to calm me was a superpower, like a drug crafted by the universe itself to wash away the storm. I could be on the verge of exploding or losing control, and all Mahant would have to do was be present. I sighed into his embrace and closed my eyes. He was my peace, no matter the chaos created around us.

Slowly, I drifted off, my energy calm, my heart relaxed, my mind at ease.

Chapter 10

I opened the freezer, reached in, and pulled out the card that Sasha had given to Mahant and me. To my surprise, there was writing all over the back of the card.

"Oh wow, babe, look!" I called out to Mahant as I stood there examining the card. Mahant ran over to me, looked at the small card, and started whispering as he read the details. On it was information regarding Friday's meet up. On the card were the address, time, and attire requirements, which were slowly fading because we had left it outside the freezer. This temperature-sensitive card displayed information when it was cold, and when it was warm, the information disappeared. Before the message on the card disappeared, I ran to my desk, grabbed my phone, and snapped a picture.

"So the attire is nude colors, and the meetup, of course, is this Friday at 8 pm. There's even an address on here, perfect." I placed my phone back down on the desk and turned to Mahant, who was standing by the kitchen island.

Mahant raised his eyebrow while he texted on his phone. "I don't think I have anything nude."

"We will have to go shopping for you, then. We can go to the mall tomorrow. I can meet you there after you get off from work." I walked up to Mahant and stood before him. He nodded his head as he looked up from his phone, locking his eyes onto mine. Mahant then leaned forward and pressed his lips into mine, kissing me deeply.

"When are you leaving?" He asked as I walked back to the desk to grab my phone, then into my bedroom, so that I could stand in front of my gigantic vanity mirror that stretched along the wall.

As I was checking myself out in the mirror, I called out to Mahant, "In about five minutes. Aeries said she wanted to hang out and grab lunch around noon."

I noticed Mahant entered the room from the mirror. He stood behind me, checking me out. It was a beautiful summer day, mid-June, and my outfit screamed happy, sunny vibes. I wore an orange spaghetti-strapped crop top with high-waisted, mustard-yellow palazzo pants. To finish the look, I had orange heels on and my blue oversized tote. I accessorized with all my jewelry, my statement rings, my layered necklaces, nose ring, and earrings. Thankfully, I recently got my nails done in an almond shape with 3D rose gold abstract designs on matte black nail polish.

"You look sexy," Mahant complimented me as I posed in the mirror. I smiled at his reflection and then angled my phone to grab a picture for my Zed account.

"Thank you, baby!" I made a cute squeal as I responded to him and snapped pictures at the same time. Mahant walked up next to me and posed in the photo with me for a few shots. "Okay, I'm going to go meet up with Aeries. I'll see you later, babe."

I turned and patted his chest, then walked out of the bedroom, grabbed my tote and keys, and headed out the door. As I made my way down to the garage, I texted Aeries I was on my way. I figured we could carpool together and head to lunch. I put her address into my navigational system and drove off.

Once I reached her home, I parked in the driveway and texted her.

I'm outside, ready when you are.

Aeries immediately texted me back.

Coming!

Her front door opened, and out came Aeries looking stunning as ever. Her outfit also embodied the essence of summer. Aeries wore an emerald-green button-up shirt that tucked halfway into her denim shorts. Her naturally curly hair, now straightened, was pulled back into a bun, and she wore black knee-length riding boots. As she walked to the car, I noticed she was carrying a matching emerald-green handbag and wearing a crescent moon necklace around her neck.

Aeries got to the car, opened up the passenger door, and climbed in.

"Hey!" She greeted me, then went in for a hug.

"Oh, hey!" I hugged her back and then looked her up and down. "You look gorgeous. Love the fit!"

Aeries looked down at her outfit and adjusted herself in the seat. "Thank you! You look beautiful. Your closet must be amazing."

I laughed, "Everyone always thinks that. It's an okay closet."

"So modest, Ms. Peach." Aeries chuckled with me and then fastened her seatbelt. "So, where are we heading?"

I put the car in reverse, backed out of the driveway, and then continued down the street. "So, I want to take you to one of my favorite places here in this timeline. The food is excellent, and the customer service is superb. Have you ever been to Chalet?"

"Oh, my gosh! I've heard of Chalet. That's super fancy." Aeries turned in her seat, looking at me, and out of the corner of my eye, I could see the excitement on her face. "But no, I've never been. I'm super excited though!"

"Good, I'm glad you're excited. I think one of my favorite things about being reborn is all the culinary geniuses you meet. All the delicious food and culture you get to indulge in. It makes living in certain timelines worth it." I turned and looked at Aeries for a moment, seeing her beautiful red aura glowing. She was hanging onto each word I said with curiosity and admiration.

"So, what was your most favorite dish you've ever had?" Aeries asked curiously.

I smiled big as I continued the drive. "Oh wow, that's a hard question. Do you know how much food I've eaten in the nine hundred and seventy-six years of living?" I thought for a while, and Aeries patiently waited for my response.

"So, this timeline was unique because it wasn't Earth or anything you'd ever imagine. This realm was a completely different planet with different animals, species, and social constructs." I painted the picture to imprint itself onto the blank canvas that was Aeries' mind. "It was this animal called the Chickopae, and the way it marinated in the natural spices that spread across the lands was out of this world. It was rich, creamy, and had the right amount of spice. The presentation wasn't the most appealing, but the taste is what I remember. The taste of heaven graciously frolicking on your taste buds."

Aeries' mouth was slightly open. "What was the dish called?"

"Nakdulocta Enris la tru. Qu pa tu lo?" I said in a different language.

Aeries tilted her head and scrunched her face. "What in the world did you just say?"

"That was the language of the Bochan people, and I said, animal of the forest. Would you eat it? It's one of the most fascinating languages I've ever learned, outside of Trosthu."

"Do you remember every language you ever spoke? And what is Trosthu?"

I laughed at all her questions. "Trosthu is the language of the Troke people from the planet Troterion. It's another timeline that I can jump to. And yeah, kind of. I remember the languages, but after a while, they all blur together."

"Jump to another timeline? Is that what Lanno was doing in our last timeline?" Aeries continued to ask me question after question, and it was admirable. She was genuinely interested in my past and what I've experienced. I had to remember that this was all new to her and that it was only her second timeline, her first time being reborn.

"I keep forgetting that you are literally so new to all of this." I expressed as I turned into the parking lot of Chalet. I parked the car, and we both exited the vehicle and walked to the front doors as I continued to explain all the many possibilities of the universe to Aeries.

"Once you get to a certain point of enlightenment and your consciousness is at its highest form, the universe will create a Troke of you and place it on Troterion," I explained as I held the door open for her, and she walked in, with me following her. "Your Troke is dormant in that timeline forever, and you can jump to it and enjoy Troterion; you can technically stay there too in between timelines until you are ready for a new timeline. Think of it like heaven."

"Hi! Welcome to Chalet." The server greeted us. "Do you have reservations?"

I turned towards the host. "Hi, for Zya Peach, please."

"Oh! Sorry, I'm new here, Ms. Peach. Your table is ready for you. Follow me."

I smiled at him, then Aeries and I followed behind him as he led us to a private section in the restaurant. The energy in the restaurant was perfect for a midday lunch. There was soft jazz music playing, and a soft haze of lights streaming across the ceiling to curate a relaxing, dimmed atmosphere. The finishes were upscale and luxurious, with chandeliers and expensive wooden trim on the posts that structured the building. The aroma was splendid, bursting with savory and sweet flavors from the mix of entrees to decadent desserts. What I loved the most about Chalet was the pungent smell of garlic that emanated from the restaurant as if they were baking their own bread, growing their own garlic, and combining the two behind the staff-only door that led straight to the kitchen.

We sat down at our table, and our server filled our glasses with water. He handed us digital pads to scroll through the menu, then walked away.

Aeries scrolled through the pad, "So are the timelines very similar? For instance, this timeline in Bluepoint City reminds me a lot of my previous timeline as Lauren. We're on a planet called Earth; there are still nine planets. Same kind of government and social constructs."

"Mmm," I nodded my head at her question, then said, "No, not every timeline is the same. Trust me, some timelines are so different you'll go crazy because it takes time getting used to different ways of living. Mahant chose this timeline first, and we followed him. So, he likes familiar timelines, and he enjoys being human."

"Ahh, so the universe granted his request to be in a timeline that was familiar to the one before." Aeries looked up at me and smiled. "Makes sense."

I smiled at her and then continued to scroll through the menu. "Yeah, think about it like this. Timelines can be identical or slightly different. There are billions of different realities out there that the universe has crafted. Sometimes a timeline can even branch off and continue from another one. For instance, if Mahant wanted to go back to the Spalling District, he technically could have asked. It may have just been a later decade."

Talking to Aeries seemed more seamless than I ever could have imagined. She was easy to talk to, and our conversations were fun. I loved how she stayed curious and questioned everything. I loved how beautiful her inquisitiveness was. It made me want to show her the universe and all it offered.

The server came back with a bottle of wine. "Hi, this imported wine is from Downing, and it's one of the oldest wines in history. Crafted from the Witcher family, the first to sell wine. It's on the sweeter side since it was a simple fermentation process. Nothing like what's on the shelves today. Would you like to try?"

I looked at Aeries and raised my eyebrow, then turned my attention back towards the server. "Yes, we would love to try."

He uncorked the bottle, then poured some into two new wine glasses he had, and then slid them over to us.

I picked up my glass, watching Aeries as she swirled hers around, then sipped. I swirled the wine in the glass as well, then drank from it.

"Oh, this is beautiful." I complimented the drink. "I'm sorry. What's your name?"

Aeries' eyes closed, and she leaned back against the chair. "Ugh, that is so good."

The server smiled, "Oh, my name is Link."

"Link, thank you so much for the recommendation. You can leave the entire bottle."

"Of course, Ms. Peach." He set the bottle on the table and then pulled out his digital pad. "Are you ready to put in your order?"

Aeries cleared her throat. "Yeah, I will take the Chicken Flower Au gratin."

"And I will take my usual, the Flight and Fig," I ordered, and Link punched in both our orders into his system, then looked at us to see if we wanted anything else. "That will be all, thank you, Link!"

"You're very welcome. I will be back with your entrée shortly." He promised, before walking away from the table to help other guests.

I looked over at Aeries, and she glanced at me. Her eyes caught a nearby light, and for a quick second, they sparkled against it. Our eyes meet, and I smile at her warmly. She returned a warm smile to me, then leaned forward and laced her fingers together.

"I can see your blue aura, and Mahant's blue aura. Mine is red, but it's so colorful in this new timeline because I can see everyone's aura. Sometimes I can turn it off, but often I cannot." Aeries explained, almost as if she were concerned.

"Empathetic energy. You can see and feel others; it's a gift the universe has given you. Sometimes it's amazing, other times it can be extremely overwhelming." I explained to her as I picked up the bottle of wine and poured us some more.

"This might be too much information, but like... when I'm with Mahant, I feel this ravenous hunger. I want to devour him, as if I have no self-control." Aeries blushed as she explained, her freckles glowing against her light caramel skin.

I chuckled, "You will get used to that as well. It never goes away, but it gets easier to be around him."

This energy she was feeling, I've felt as well whenever I was around Mahant. He also feels it when he's around us. It's our cosmic bond and overstimulation of being able to feel energies. I explained to Aeries that the connection between soul ties is powerful, unlike anything in the universe. I told her that together they are bound by the force of the universe, a bond that is beyond human comprehension. We could sense and feel the energies of others, but when we connected with each other, it was an overwhelming sensation of love and devotion.

Aeries played with her fingers as she looked down at them nervously. Her energy shifted, and I tried to read her as much as I could. I can tell she was holding back and wanted to say something.

"Hey, talk to me. You soon will learn that I don't judge and I'm one of the easiest people to talk to." I encouraged Aeries to speak up.

Aeries looked up at me, her eyes locked on mine. "How do we navigate each other? I can feel your energy, too. You intrigue me, but I don't want to force it because of the universe's will. I want us to be friends of our own volition."

I was really enjoying Aeries' company and conversation. However, she was right. How did we know if we were choosing our own paths? Was this our own free will? Or the coercion of the universe tethering us together.

"The universe is not the bad guy. I believe we have free will. Let's go at our own pace, get to know each other, and see how this goes." I hoped Aeries would hear me out. I waited patiently while sipping more of my wine.

Aeries laughed and grabbed her glass of wine, sipping it, then setting it back down. "I feel like we are on a speed date."

I laughed then cleared my throat, "You're not so bad for a speed date."

Aeries raised her eyebrows and then shook her head as she blushed.

"So, tell me. How was your first talk with the universe?" I curiously asked Aeries as I sat back and laced my fingers together, folding my hands into my lap.

"Oh, it was interesting. Strange but interesting." Aeries scrunched her face. "At first, I was like, am I dead? What is this? Then, when I heard the voice but didn't see a face, I started trippin."

"Girl! When I first heard the voice, I thought I was dreaming something crazy."

We both laughed, and then Aeries continued, "Yeah, the universe told me I could ask them questions, and I swear the first thing I asked was about Lanno. Ugh, we are suckers for that man."

I rolled my eyes and laughed. "Tell me about it. I have followed this man across the universe for hundreds of years. Falling in love with him repeatedly."

"When the universe told me he was safe, tucked away in the heart of Bluepoint City, I immediately asked if it was possible to be together again. The answer was a yes, and that's all I wanted to hear. I was happy. I don't know, the short time we were together felt like years of us loving each other. We have had our ups and downs but his love stayed with me forever."

I smiled with good intentions. Hearing how Aeries talked about her and Mahant at this moment did not bother me. Their love story and how it blossomed actually warmed my heart. She told me about how they first met as Lanno and Lauren, all the things they got into while dating. We had meaningful conversations about our shared experiences with Mahant, noting how similar they were to our feelings about him.

Soon our food came out. My beautifully crafted flight featured a crispy duck breast in the center of the plate, atop savory mashed potatoes and chives, with a hearty maple fig compote on top. Decorating the plate were asparagus tips and whole figs. Aeries plate looked appetizing as well, with a crunchy quarter leg of chicken, thinly sliced potatoes decorated in a flower pattern, and a cheesy gravy on top. We wasted no time and dug into our dishes, eating until the final bite was gone.

When we finished eating, we conversed for a bit more. Finally, the check came, I paid, and we left the restaurant. As we headed back to Aeries' home, we continued to talk about so many things. Aeries wondered if she could ever jump to Troterion, and if so, would I teach her how someday. I promised her we would meditate and try to jump to Troterion, and see if the universe blessed her with her very own Troke.

I dropped her off at her townhome and then drove back to my condo.

Once I arrived home, I noticed Mahant was lying on the sofa watching TV. I kicked off my heels and walked over to him, and stood in front of him.

"So, how did it go?" He asked, smiling proudly, as if he already knew it had gone well.

I smiled at him as he sat up and wrapped his arms around my waist as I stood there. "I like Aeries a lot. I can see why you love her. She's so sweet."

Mahant's grin got even wider, and he nodded his head, "Yeah, Aeries is amazing. Just as amazing as you are."

"I don't know Mahant... I might have to steal her from you." I looked down at him and rested my hands on his cheeks, playing with the curls of his beard.

"I wouldn't mind as long as you give her back sometime."

"Uh-huh," I whispered.

Mahant reached up and pulled me down. I bent over and pressed my lips into his, kissing him deeply. I could feel his excitement burning through me. I wanted more of him, but I was still nervous about being physical, given his track record.

I sit down in his lap and straddle him, his arms immediately wrapped around my waist, holding me tightly. The hunger, the ravenous. I craved him in every way as if something came over me. Our kisses were raw, fueled by an itch we both needed to scratch. The way he held me and kissed me, letting me know how much we wanted me, made a shiver trickle down my spine. I draped my arms around his neck, closed my eyes, and enjoyed the moment we transcended into.

As our session heated up, I pulled away and stood up from Mahant. I cleared my throat and ran my fingers through my long, silk-pressed hair.

"I've got to do a few things for my dad and Peach Motors. I can't get too distracted." I grabbed my laptop and sat down on the sofa next to Mahant. Out of my peripheral vision, I could sense his discomfort. We both wanted each other, but my PTSD wouldn't allow it.

"I can handle it, Imani. I promise," Mahant said convincingly, sighing and resting back against the couch cushions.

With my laptop in my lap, I turned and looked at him, biting my bottom lip. "I'm so afraid that you won't be able to handle it, and something will happen to you where you hurt yourself."

"I know, and you have every right to be fearful that I'd hurt myself because of how I acted as Lanno. But I promise you, I know my mind, and I get it now. I know what I'm supposed to do in every timeline. I must live it through."

I reached out and palmed his cheek. "Are you sure?"

Mahant nodded and then leaned forward, pressing his lips into mine. He had the most amazing, passionate kisses that I adored. My eyes closed, and I held the back of his head as I felt his hand touch my stomach and grip my waist. His body weight pressed against me, pushing me back into the armrest of my sofa. I grabbed my laptop and set it aside on the coffee table, holding onto him as he positioned himself over me. Immediately, our energies collided, and an overwhelming sensation rushed over me. Our auras mending into each other was such a powerful force that my eyes welled up and a tear fell. It was always this electrifying whenever Mahant and I got physical. Our intimate connection was sometimes hard even for me to manage.

I couldn't help but cave into what seemed like a forbidden desire. I wanted Mahant in every way so much that my legs eagerly spread open for him, and he lay in between them. The feeling of his weight on me as our kissing intensified felt out of this world. Like a distant memory, I wished to experience it repeatedly.

Our kisses got deeper, and soft pants escaped both of our lips. I grabbed the hem of Mahant's shirt and pulled it above his head, revealing his perfectly in shape body. My hands touched the contour of his muscles, pulling him into me as I wiggled underneath him. His lips left mine and kissed against my jaw, hungrily, moving at a steady pace. Just how I liked it.

We ripped each other's clothes off. The room spun, and our energies glowed even brighter, showcasing our love. Swiftly, Mahant pulled down my palazzo pants and tossed them to the side before comfortably repositioning his body between my legs.

The rest of the night was a whirlwind—a passionate showcase of how much we loved each other, how much we missed each other, and connected on a deeper level. Every emotion that rippled through Mahant crept through and awakened every single current in my body. My favorite part was being able to experience how he felt, as I enjoyed my own emotions and physical energy. Every orgasm I had, I knew rippled through him because he would lose control, then let go inside of me, then I'd feel his pleasure as well. We were in sync, a perfect harmony mixed with a quiet fear that traveled through my mind. Would Mahant keep his promise and live through this entire timeline? All I could hope was that the words he spoke were true.

Mahant even got rough with me, which I thoroughly enjoyed. The way he would wrap his hands around my neck and squeeze, pinning me to the couch. My knees to my chest, having nowhere to go. There was no escaping the clenches of this man, not that I'd even want to. I loved every moment.

We stayed on the sofa the entire time, breaking it in since I never got the chance to do so with anyone else before finding Mahant.

As the night grew later, we finally finished and were exhausted. Mahant fell asleep, and before I could doze off, my mind wandered. I had a good day with Aeries and was more hopeful than before. I was happy and couldn't wait to have more connections with her, like today. I wondered what was in store for the three of us and how the relationship would develop over the next few timelines.

Would it blossom fast? Or would it be a slow burn? Either way, I told myself to welcome this change with an open mind and a kind heart, no matter what.

Chapter 11

I woke up to the sound of my phone buzzing. Quickly, I grabbed it off the coffee table and answered the phone.

"Hey…" My voice was raspy and full of sleep.

It was Mahant on the other line. "Sounds like you slept in. I'm at work, but I'm getting off early. You promised me we would do some shopping today."

My eyes were closed as I lay on the sofa and talked to Mahant. "I'm so sleepy. What time is it?"

"It's noon. I get off at two."

I dozed off again and then heard Mahant clear his throat. "Imani, wake up, sleepy head."

"I'm up. I'll meet you at the mall at two." I promised Mahant.

"Bet, I'll see you then." Mahant hung up the phone, and I sat up on the sofa. My entire body felt sluggish and sore. I stretched and then looked around my apartment, noticing Roo lying in front of the windowsill, basking in the sun.

"COMO, is the auto feeder on for Roo?" I called out sleepily.

COMO responded. "Yes, Zya, preset one is available for Roo to eat in the morning and in the evening."

"Good, thank you, COMO."

I stood up, completely naked, and walked into the bedroom to grab my cardigan. I put it on, then wrapped the open seams around me. The need for coffee was strong, but I barely had the energy to take a shower, let alone make coffee. So, I got into the shower and told myself that I could grab a coffee at Blue City Mall.

After I washed up, I went into my closet and got dressed. Today I wore a yellow maxi skirt with a thigh-high split and a white graphic crop top. I grabbed my black satchel, put on my sandals, and then applied some makeup. I, of course, accessorized with all my everyday jewelry before heading out of the condo and into the garage.

Once I reached the mall, I found a parking space in the food court parking lot. I exited the car and went into the mall, making my way to Mahant.

I texted him as I walked through the mall.

Hey, so where exactly do you work?

Mahant texted me back.

I work at QT Beauty.

I texted Mahant back that I would be on my way, but first, I wanted to stop for coffee. My usual go to was matcha, but I needed something with a little more kick. So, I ordered a cold brew of iced coffee with white chocolate cold foam on top. After I got my coffee, I made my way to Mahant. When I approached QT Beauty, there I saw Mahant looking more handsome than ever in his security gear.

"Hey, gorgeous," He greeted me, wrapping his arms around me, giving me the warmest bear hug.

I hugged him back tightly. "Hey, handsome. You look so good."

Mahant was wearing all black with a bulletproof vest, and his holster belt was on his belt buckle with a gun on his right hip. He had boots on and stood taller than usual, making him look gigantic.

"People still steal from you looking like that?" I asked, then laughed.

Mahant grinned as he grabbed my coffee and took a sip. "Not since they hired me. Stealing has been at an all-time low."

"Well, that's good!" I responded, taking my coffee back from him and drinking it. I take out my phone and look. "It's five before two, so you will be off soon, right?"

"Oh, yeah. Actually, let me clock out." Mahant turned around and entered the store as I waited there for him to return.

When Mahant returned, he grabbed my hand and laced his fingers with mine as we walked through the mall. He looked at me as I looked at him, and we both smiled.

"You're glowing," I nudged Mahant as I whispered to him.

He smiled even wider and then tried to rid his excitement by neutralizing his expression.

Looking at him, I continued. "Aw, come on, it's a good thing. I'm glad I can still make you glow."

"Well, you're glowing too." Mahant nudged me back, and I winced playfully.

"I'm also very sore. I feel like I'm out of shape, and you wrecked me last night."

Mahant raised his eyebrows, "Wrecked, huh?"

"Uh, huh." I squeezed his hand, then gently swung it.

He laughed again and then looked forward. "So, where are we shopping today?"

I thought for a moment, putting my nails to my teeth and biting the tip of one. "Mmm, we could go to Charlotte Co."

"Charlotte Co. is mad expensive. You think my security job can pay for anything in there?" Mahant wavered at the thought of that store.

We stopped walking, and I looked at him. "I'm clearly treating you today. What's mine is yours. I got you, babe!"

Mahant and I entered Charlotte Co., which was an upscale business casual store. From suits to formal wear, they had it all. It was absolutely on the pricier side, but the quality of the clothes was excellent, and only the most prestigious influencers or famous people shopped here. When we entered, we immediately met with a floor representative.

"Hello, Ms. Peach, nice to see you back at Charlotte Co. Haven't seen you in a while," Preston greeted me. "Are you looking for anything specific?"

I smiled at Preston, "I love, love, love your nude section. My favorite jacket is from here. So we are going to browse there for a bit, thank you."

Preston nodded and gestured with his hands toward the nude clothing. "Of course, Ms. Peach. If you need me for anything, please find me."

Mahant and I walked away, heading towards my favorite section of the store.

"He knows you by name. That's impressive." Mahant gloated as we entered what was called The Tavern, where they kept the nude apparel.

"I get that often, familiar face. I blame my dad." I winked at Mahant.

Mahant went to the men's section and picked up a nude-brown turtleneck shirt, then held it up against his frame.

"Oh my, that would look damn good on you." I instantly fell in love with the shirt, and Mahant smiled at me.

"Yeah, I can see myself in this, with a belt and some pants to match." Mahant agreed. He looked at the price tag on the shirt, and his eyes grew big. "This shirt is one hundred and ninety-nine bucks!"

I laughed under my breath, then grabbed the shirt from him. "I told you, I got this. Don't look at any of the price tags here."

Mahant did not listen at all. He flipped through more shirts in the cupboards and on the racks, looking at the prices. Every time he looked at a new item, his face grew more shocked. I couldn't help but shake my head at him.

"Four hundred bucks for this?!" He yelled obnoxiously loud.

I snatched another shirt from him and put it back. "Hey, stop it!" I laughed and then grabbed his arm, pulling him away from the shirts and to the pants.

"It's been a while since I've had such a lavish taste. Thomas was the last time I spent money frivolously. Sorry, these prices are insane."

I flipped through some nude-brown pants and then pulled out Mahant's size. "I know. I'm going to add you to my bank account, by the way. So that you can have access to unlimited funds and buy what you want."

Holding the pants up to Mahant, I shook my head and then put them back, "Not these. Maybe a skinnier leg with that turtleneck."

I grabbed another pair and held them up to Mahant.

"I like this one." Mahant grabbed the pants from me and examined the quality. "I'm not even going to look at the price tag."

We left The Tavern, checked out, paid for the clothes, and left the store. Mahant and I headed towards Valeco, a formalwear and shoe store.

As soon as we entered, Mahant gave me a look. "Are these shoes expensive, too?"

"They can be, depending on what you're looking for."

Mahant beeline towards the boot section, his favorite. "I think a dress boot would look good."

"I agree." I followed behind him.

He picked up a brown boot, looked at it, and then set it back down. We both search for the right shoe, and then finally we come across one that fits his outfit perfectly.

"Yeah, I might cuff the pants or tuck them with these boots. I like 'em." Mahant held the dress boots in his hands. We then took it to the front counter and handed it to an employee. They went into the back room, located Mahant's size, and then brought a box out to the front.

We were all finished shopping for Mahant, concluding our day. I had a bunch of nude clothing at home, so there was no need for me to buy anything. Mahant and I walked around the mall for a bit, holding hands, before getting ready to head out.

"Did you eat?" Mahant asked as we walked through the food court on our way out of the mall.

I shook my head, "No, I actually did not eat yet today."

"Want some mall food? Tuskin's burgers are actually pretty decent."

I thought for a moment and then nodded my head. "Yeah, let's grab a bite to eat."

I got a double-stack burger and some fries, and Mahant got a jalapeno cheese mushroom burger. We sat down in the food court and ate our food while we conversed.

"Are you excited about Friday?" I asked Mahant in be-tween bites of my burger.

Mahant nodded his head and chewed his food, "I am. I'm excited to meet new people."

"Me too! And people with powers? It feels like I'm living in a movie." I picked up a fry and stuffed it into my mouth.

"Hey, can you drop me off at Aeries when we leave? I wanted to check in and see how she's been holding up." Mahant seemed nervous to ask, his voice a little shaky, as if trying to avoid any unwarranted tension.

I smiled, "Yeah, that's no problem. I feel like I kidnapped you for a while, anyway. I'll drop you off over there."

Mahant smiled at me and then finished his last bite of his burger and the remaining fries. After we finished eating, we left the mall and walked to my car.

I threw my keys at Mahant. "I like it when you drive."

Mahant caught the key fob, unlocked the doors, and climbed inside. I got into the passenger seat and we made our way to Aeries' home.

Aeries didn't live too far from the mall, so we arrived relatively quickly. Mahant pulled into the driveway and took his phone out of his jeans. He started texting on it while he sat there.

"Hey, so... don't mention The Collection to Aeries just yet. Let's figure all of this out together before we bring her into it."

Mahant looked at me when I said that and nodded his head. "That's fine. It will be our thing for now."

I reached and touched his face, "Thank you, baby."

I turned to see Aeries open her front door and walk out. She strolled up to the passenger side, and I opened the door and got out.

"Hey, babes!" I greeted her with a hug, and she returned it.

"Hey, Imani. How are you, gorgeous?" Aeries asked, letting me go from her warm embrace.

It was sunnier out now, so I grabbed my shades from the passenger seat and put them on. "Oh, I'm doing great!"

Aeries winked at me. "I can tell you're glowing."

I did a cute pose and then giggled at her remark. "Thank you!"

Mahant got out of the driver's seat and walked over to us both. He wrapped his arm around Aeries, and she hugged him back.

"Hey, baby!" She cheerfully greeted him.

Mahant kissed the top of her head and then leaned in and kissed her lips.

"I need him back in roughly three days," I warned as I walked around to the driver's seat and got back into the car.

"I'll be back by Friday, promise," Mahant told me as they walked towards the front door of Aeries' townhome.

I put the car in reverse, backed it up, and then drove off, heading back to my condo. On the way back home, stagnant thoughts ran through my mind. I knew the next few days I was going to be lonely without Mahant. Sharing him was never the hard part for me after all these years; it was missing him that was tough. Anyway, I figured I could have some girl time with Kat or catch up on some work for Peach Motors. All I needed to do was keep myself and my mind busy from any negative thoughts that tried to enter.

As soon as I got home, I hung up Mahant's new outfit in the closet and then sat on the sofa, staring off into space.

I grabbed my phone from my pocket and texted Kat.

Hey girly, what's up?

I locked my phone and waited for a response. A few minutes passed, and Kat texted back.

Nothing much, working. I get off in an hour.

I texted her back

Swing by.

Kat responded she would swing by after work, and while I waited, I turned on my TV and watched one of my favorite shows.

An hour and a half later, there was a knock on my front door and a voice called out.

"It's Kat. Tell COMO's ass to let me in!"

I laughed and stood up from the sofa, then walked to the front door to open it. Kat walked in and went straight to Roo.

"I don't need COMO for everything."

Kat laughed dramatically. "Girl, COMO is your best friend, not me."

I rolled my eyes playfully and sat back on the sofa. Kat started petting Roo and baby-talking to her.

"Hello to you, too," I said, pretending to be jealous that Roo got attention first.

Kat walked over to the sofa, leaned over, and wrapped her arms around me, squeezing me as tight as she could, not letting go. "I love you toooo, Zya."

I let out a suffocating noise as she bear-hugged me, and then she chuckled. "Uh, huh."

Kat finally let go of me and sat down on the sofa, almost instantly opening her bookbag and taking out some weed. "So, tell me, how did that whole Aeries and Mahant thing go after I left?"

I sighed. "It's been eventful, really. I actually hung out with Aeries yesterday and got to know her."

"Well, that's good." Kat lit up the pre-roll in her hand and took a puff. "Aeries is cute. She has this innocence to her that is intriguing."

I eyed Kat, "Uh huh, cute, is she?"

Kat gave me a look and then handed me the pre-roll. "Not like that. Can't a girl compliment another girl without it being like I'm tryna get at her?"

I took the pre-roll from Kat and put it to my lips, inhaling it deeply. I held in the puff and then exhaled slowly. "Yes, you can compliment her. I'm just teasing."

Kat continued to side-eye me. "Do you think she's cute?"

"She's adorable, but I don't know. I'm still feeling her out." I admitted to Kat. "I get jealous when they kiss, as if I've never seen Mahant kiss another person in front of me."

"So what exactly is the difference, then?" Kat leaned back against the sofa.

I sighed and then took another puff of the weed. "I don't know..."

Kat became quiet, and I handed her the pre-roll back. She inhaled and smoked it, allowing me to gather my thoughts and continue talking.

"It's hard to even process my feelings about Aeries. Can you believe Mahant and I just had sex yesterday, and then I dropped him off at her house today, his soul tie, like it was nothing?"

"You're better than me." Kat handed me the pre-roll. "I couldn't share."

I shrugged. "Well, sharing is not the problem. Mahant and I have shared both men and women for ages."

"Mahant likes men? And if you have shared before, again, what's the hesitation with Aeries?" Kat asked as she rocked back and forth.

"Mahant is fluid. That man loves everybody. I wouldn't know how to label him." I answered the first part of her question, and even though I knew how to respond to the second part, I gave myself time to think.

For me, the problem was not sharing Mahant with Aeries. The problem was that, despite trying to fix Mahant's broken mind in many timelines, I couldn't until Aeries came into the picture. It made me feel useless and powerless. I was utterly jealous of the fact that his fractured mind was no more, and I felt as though I didn't have a hand in it at all. What also upset me was that Mahant created a soul tie without discussing it with me first.

There had been plenty of people I had connected with during my many lives, and I would have never made such a rash decision without discussing it with Mahant first. I explained all of this to her.

Kat was quiet, then finally asked, "But how do you know you didn't help fix Mahant? You both were at Dustin's, right?"

I nodded, "Yes, but she contacted him first, and since then, he's been more than the Mahant that I've known for lifetimes over. There are no missing links; he's healed and remembers everything. That has never happened before this timeline."

"Hmm," Kat raised her eyebrow. "I don't know, babes, I think you're not giving yourself enough credit and dwelling on something you don't know if it's factual or not. But listen, I get the whole creating another soul tie bit. That is really selfish of him."

"It is selfish of him. I can feel resentment building up inside of me, and for the first time in hundreds of years, I don't know how to handle it." I continued to let it all out.

It was easier to talk to Kat about the thoughts that ran wild through my mind than it was to speak with Mahant. Our love was me constantly trying to protect him, to where it sometimes seemed like I wasn't protecting myself. As if I put myself on the back burner and loved him unconditionally, no matter how much it hurt me.

A part of me felt as though there was nothing else I could do but love Mahant. The pull to him felt stronger than a current, a powerful reminder that plagued me to feel I had no free will. My gut told me that the universe's blessing was a curse, because I couldn't break away from the clutches Mahant had on me, if I wanted to. But did I truly want to?

It became quiet in the room, and I was feeling extremely high. I took out my phone and texted Aeries.

Hey! We should hang out again when you're free, if you're down.

I saw typing bubbles and then Aeries replied.

I'm free this weekend! I would love to.

Kat stood up and went to my kitchen to grab some snacks.

"Hey, can you grab me a bottle of water? My mouth is so dry." I asked as she rummaged through my pantry. Kat walked back over to the sofa with a bag of chips, some grapes, and two bottles of water. She handed me a bottle, then plopped back down, crossing her legs under her.

We spent the rest of the evening watching a comedy show together and laughing all the way through. After a few hours, it started getting late, so Kat collected her things and headed home.

I undressed and got ready for bed, tucking myself in and snuggling my pillow. There was a ding on my phone, and I looked at it to see a text message from Mahant.

I love you and miss you.

A smile formed on my face as I read the text message. It was the last message I read before I drifted off to sleep. I allowed the text message to put my mind at ease so that I could have sweet dreams. Not the festering thoughts that fueled a quiet war and depression within me.

Chapter 12

It was finally Friday, and the excitement in the air was through the roof. I spent the entire day preparing for an eventful night with Mahant. However, it was getting closer to 8 pm, and Mahant was not home yet.

I texted him.

Where are you?

I did some light cleaning around the house, took a shower, and had a meditation session to clear any negative energy. I got dressed, did my makeup, and sat on the sofa, waiting for Mahant to text me back. The outfit I wore for the night was a nude beige, crop top, tucked into my nude beige high-waisted trousers. To complete my look, I wore a long, nude beige cardigan. My belt from Charlotte Co. had a massive CC on the buckle, and I wore stiletto pumps.

Suddenly, Mahant walked through the front door with a few bags in his hands.

"Hey, I texted you," I told him as I gripped my phone.

Mahant dropped the bags by the front door and looked at me. "Yeah, sorry. I've been running around all day. I had to grab a few things from my place. My boy KJ has had Stacy over for the past couple of days, so I've been trying to give them space."

"Well, you are always welcome to move your stuff here, Mahant." I walked up to him, and he leaned in and kissed me. "Hurry and get dressed. We have to leave in about an hour."

Mahant nodded his head and went into the bedroom. I followed him into the bedroom to put on the last finishing touches of jewelry and some perfume. As soon as I finished, I went into the closet and leaned against the wall frame. Mahant was changing into his turtleneck and pants.

"Did you have a good time with Aeries?" I asked curiously.

Mahant adjusted the turtleneck collar, put on a gold chain, then took off his jeans and switched into his other ones. "Yeah, we had a good time. I think she needs some help to meditate, though. We, or you, should show her how to."

I nodded my head in approval. "For sure, we're hanging out this weekend, so I will run it past her. But why do you think she needs to meditate?"

"Just to help manage her emotions. Wash away the stress, you know..." Mahant pulled up his pants, tucked his shirt in, and then buttoned them.

"Is she stressed? And what about?"

Mahant looked at me, then walked over. "Life. She doesn't have many friends. She has an overwhelming amount of feelings about being reborn again. Like anxious energy. Asking a lot of questions. I just figured meditation would help ground her."

I pressed my hand into Mahant's chest and rubbed gently. "I'll try to help her."

Mahant finished getting dressed. He grabbed his dress boots and put them on, then took his deodorant and applied some. His cologne was the last finishing touch before he looked at me, eager and ready to go.

"You look amazing." He complimented me as we headed towards the door. I grabbed my handbag, and he grabbed my keys.

"Thank you! You look pretty handsome yourself."

We head out the door and make our way to the car. Mahant enters the address into the navigational system, and we buckle up and drive to our destination. On our way to the address on the card, Mahant and I talked about what might be in store for us.

"What powers do you think some people in The Collection have?" Mahant asked as he loosely clutched the steering wheel and leaned back.

"Mmm, maybe someone can fly."

Mahant laughed, "Fly? Well, don't you have a wild imagination?"

I giggled and then looked out the window. It was a forty-five-minute drive to Huntington, which was well outside Bluepoint City's city limits and past the underwater tunnel that connected us to the mainland. It was a thriving town, filled with little to no crime. The homes were massive, expensive, and modern compared to the homes on the outskirts of Bluepoint City. Mansions and trees stretched down every road. There were parks for children to play in, and cozy cul-de-sacs that made the town feel welcoming. As we got closer to Huntington, I noticed more luxurious cars driving by, mostly Peach models. We entered the Kyro Strip—a street that stretched for miles, having the best restaurants, casinos, and clothing stores you could find. There were clubs and lounges as well, with lines of people looking to get in. We finally pulled up to a red-brick building with the address from the card on it. There was a sign that said off-street parking in the back, so

Mahant drove down the alley to the back of the building. We parked and then walked back around to the front.

It was twelve minutes past 8 pm, so we were fashionably late. Once we got back to the front of the building, a guy was standing in front in a full black suit, blocking the entrance.

As soon as we walked up to him, he spoke, "Name, please."

I responded to him sweetly, "Mahant and Imani."

He immediately checked his digital pad and then stepped to the side without saying a word. Mahant and I entered the building. It was a giant ballroom with a massive crystal chandelier hanging in its center. They painted the walls cream, with a bar to the far left and, on the opposite side, a band playing live music. The floors were exceptionally clean, with fresh wax, and the aroma smelled like cinnamon and honey once again. There was a massive staircase leading up to the second floor, with 360-degree railings overlooking the ballroom. The moment we stepped into the space, we noticed many people sitting at beautifully crafted round tables spread throughout, each with a decorated centerpiece. We were ready to take our seats, so Mahant and I found a table with friendly faces.

"Are these seats taken?" Mahant asked before sitting down.

Two people were sitting at the table, a woman and a man. The man looked androgenous—his hair was long and flowed beautifully against his face in waves. He was Asian, with black eyeliner and pink lips. He wore a purple nude vest, his arms bare, and his muscles giving his look an extra pop. What completed his unique look were his stunning hazel eyes and flawless makeup. The woman sitting next to him was black, with not a single follicle of hair on her head. She wore a salmon colored bodycon dress that did right by her slim-thick figure. Both of their auras were welcoming, hers yellow and his green.

"Oh, of course, babes. Please take a seat. Aren't you stunning?" The man said. Even his voice was delicate and sweet, matching his presence. "My name is Kye. Please tell us your names."

Mahant and I sat down at the table and looked at each other with smiles. We then refocused our attention on our company.

"I'm Imani. Nice to meet you, Kye." I introduced myself.

Mahant, continuing his smile, spoke, "And I'm Mahant."

Kye had a fan in his hand and was fanning himself. He shifted in his seat and did a pose. "Imani and Mahant, cute. I love your soul names. This is my friend Omari."

Omari waved at us, and we smiled and waved back.

"Nice to meet you, Omari. Have you been to one of these meetups before?" I curiously asked as I crossed my legs and rested my phone on the table.

"Oh, we've been to plenty. Never seen either of you. At least not in this timeline." Kye raised his hand, and someone from the wait staff rushed over to our table.

"Hi, here are some menus. Everything is complimentary. It's open bar, and all you can eat." The server handed out menus to all of us and then patiently waited. I looked around and saw many staff members at the tables, taking orders and then rushing through the double doors into the kitchen.

On the menu were four dishes which were spaghetti, lasagna, beef wellington, and lobster ravioli.

We ordered our food and continued conversing. I noticed during our conversation that Kye was the talker and Omari was not.

"So, I'm curious. Do you wield any special abilities?" Kye asked with no filter, getting straight to the point.

"Well, we can see auras and feel energies around us," Mahant spoke up as he sipped some water that was on the table in front of him.

"Ooo! That's so cool. So what's my aura?" Kye asked curiously.

"Green," both Mahant and I said in sync, then I continued, "Green is a beautiful aura. It means you've had a lot of spiritual growth and love with all that you are."

Kye smiled. "Sounds like me. I'm a true, hopeless romantic. Oh my gosh, speaking of hopeless romance, are you two soul-tied?"

I looked at Mahant. "We are. We're actually twin flames."

"Oh! That is so damn sweet!" Kye said enthusiastically. "I wish I were twin-flamed or at the least soul-tied. I keep asking the universe, but they have other plans for me."

I shifted in my seat. "So, what are your special abilities?"

"I'm a prophet." Omari finally spoke up, her tone melodic and precise.

"Interesting..." Mahant responded as he leaned back and then tapped his fingers on the table. "Care to explain how that works?"

Omari smirked. "Well, when I dream, I have visions, and those visions come true. I have a one hundred percent accuracy rate, but I don't have visions all the time. Sometimes I can actually go hundreds of years without one."

"That's awesome," I complimented her. "And you, Kye?"

"Oh, honey, the power of persuasion." He made a face and pushed his hair behind his ear, showing off. "I know.

It's a true gift. Manipulation, all that good stuff. I've had my share of abusing my power, but now I use it sparingly."

Mahant was in awe, completely as fascinated as I was. His mouth was slightly open as he listened to Kye speak.

"So, how does it work, Kye?" Mahant asked.

"I must touch someone physically, lock eyes with them, and then dilate my pupils to reach their inner mind. Your eyes are the gateway to your soul, and if you can get in, mmm, you've got yourself someone who will bend to your every will." Kye explained carefully, so that we understood how powerful his ability was.

"So, no touching Kye." Omari snickered, warning us.

"Noted." Mahant nodded and then smiled.

"Yeah, I hate when people touch me, anyway." Kye stood up and pushed his chair in. "I'm going to go mingle. I'll be back once our food arrives." Omari stands up, too, and they both head to the bar where other people are sitting, talking, and ordering drinks.

I looked over at Mahant, noticing both of our auras glowing brighter than ever. "Wow, I can't believe we're meeting people like us in a way. I want to ask how old they are when they return."

Mahant grabbed my hand and laced his fingers with mine, then kissed the back of my hand. "I want to just go up to everyone and ask them all the questions."

We both laughed at what Mahant said. I definitely related to how he felt. It was fascinating to be in a room full of people, a part of The Recollections Contract. Suddenly, someone sat down in the extra seat that was next to Mahant. It was Sasha.

"Oh my gosh, hey Sasha!" I greeted her as soon as she sat down.

She smiled and waved at both of us. "Hey, I'm so glad you both could make it. Have you made any friends yet?"

"Yeah, we just got here. We met Omari and Kye." Mahant informed her.

Out of my peripheral vision, I noticed all eyes were now on us. I didn't understand why, but I uncomfortably shifted in my seat. "Um, so... everyone is looking at us."

Sasha laughed, "Sorry, that's my fault. People know who I am, and it's a big deal, apparently."

Kye and Omari rushed back to the table and hurried to sit down again.

"Oh my gosh, you're Sasha. The second in command, the shapeshifter, Sage's right hand!" Kye was almost yelling, visibly excited.

Sasha, continuing her smile, directed her eyes towards Kye. "I am. And you're Kye, and you're Omari, I assume. Nice to meet you both."

Omari tugged on Kye's vest and gave him a look. "Relax," she whispered.

"Yes, I'm Kye and that's Omari. I'm so sorry. Not every timeline you get to run into Sasha, Sage, or Julio." Kye attempted to calm down, but was on the edge of his seat. "I'm a huge fan."

Mahant and I looked at each other. "Julio?" I asked.

Kye continued talking without hesitation. "Julio and Sage are soul-tied like you and Mahant. They all started The Collection."

Sasha raised her hand slightly. "Well, they started it. I only helped. We have recruiters that do most of the heavy lifting."

"I would love to one day become a recruiter; it actually sounds quite fun." Kye finally returned to a calming nature, his aura not blaring as much as before.

"Maybe one day," Sasha replied sweetly.

Our server returned with our food and set down the plates in front of each one of us. Sasha eventually left, and I noticed she made her way to a table with two other people and two empty seats. Our food tasted remarkably divine, the flavors harmonizing and complementing each other perfectly. You could easily tell they made it from scratch, using fresh produce, spices, and other high-quality ingredients.

An hour had passed, and we had finished eating our food. More people had entered the building, and the glow of colors refracting from everyone was a sight to see. If there were an end to the rainbow, it would be in this room full of eclectic people. The presence of everyone was inviting, warm, and friendly. It felt familiar, like the feeling you get when you pass over, ending a life and leaving it, drifting through space before you meet the universe. This feeling felt peaceful, like heaven beyond the stars, across the galaxy, in a realm where happiness lived. Mahant and I were with our people.

We walked around the ballroom, fingers laced and locked together. Gripping each other gently as we walked past people, trying to find the perfect person to converse with.

Mahant suddenly tapped my shoulder and pointed out into the crowd of people, off towards the dance-floor. I looked to where he had pointed and saw a side profile of a very familiar face. Her hair was styled in long braids that hung past her waist. She wore a nude brown mid-waist crop top, high-waisted nude brown linen lounge pants, and a matching loose, long-sleeve linen jacket. Even though her style was different in this timeline, her beautiful orange aura and energy were easily recognizable, and her face was unchanged. I knew exactly who this woman was. I immediately lit up with excitement, and with Mahant's hand in mine, I dragged him right up to her and stood next to her.

She slowly turned her body towards us and looked at me. "Hi!" She greeted us excitedly.

My eyes glistened, my eyebrows raised, a name on the forefront of my mind and the tip of my tongue, and I finally said her name. "Imogen?"

Her aura, already glowing with tremendous light, lit up even more brightly.

"Well, that's a name I haven't heard in centuries." She laughed. "And you are?"

I pointed at myself, "It's Celeste!" Then I pointed at Mahant, "And Thomas. Do you remember us?"

Her eyes widened as her gaze moved from me to Mahant, then back to me. "Oh, my gosh! Celeste? Thomas? No way!"

"Way!" I yelled with pure joy, matching the warmth in my heart. Mahant waved and said hi. Even Mahant had a massive smile on his face. Imogen lunged forward and wrapped her arms around me, embracing and hugging me as tightly as possible. I hugged her back, and we squeezed each other as we rocked back and forth.

It was a reunion almost as big as when I would find Mahant in every timeline. I was thrilled to see her. I couldn't believe that not only was she part of The Recollections Contract but also in this timeline, happily part of The Collection.

"You are so gorgeous in this timeline!" She compliment-ed me, finally pulling away from our embrace. "So, what are your soul names? I'm dying to know."

I smiled and looked at Mahant. "Well, I'm Imani, and this is Mahant. What about you?"

"Soja!" she quickly yelled out. "I love the name Imani. It suits you. Did you choose the name for this timeline?"

I shook my head, smiling, "No, I'm Zya Peach."

Once again, Soja's eyes grew bigger, and her facial ex-pression was thoroughly impressed. "I knew you looked familiar! Peach Motors, you are the it-girl of our timeline!"

I laughed and then blushed a bit. "Yes, my dad is—"

"Jonathon Peach." She cut me off. "Yes, I know. I have a Model T car."

A Model T car is a luxury model at Peach Motors. Many people bought this model for its affordability, and it also added a touch of glamour to their lifestyles. It was actually one of my favorite cars, aside from the Z8 model that I currently own.

Soja was cute. I couldn't tell if she was more excited to see me because I was Celeste or because I was Zya Peach. We sat down and talked about how her timelines have been. She explained she had been doing a lot of soul-searching, understanding the fundamentals of being part of The Recollections Contract and how she could become a better person in each timeline. She even explained how lately she's been wanting to retire to Planet Troterion for a bit and enjoy one timeline for all of eternity, in peace. She inquired about us, asking how long we had been soul-tied. We explained to her how long we had been in the universe. I even let her know about the trials and tribulations we faced with Mahant's inability to remember, and how, in most timelines, I had to help him. Soja, on the other hand, had no soul ties and was a free spirit.

"So, what was your favorite being?" I was curious and had so many questions, just like she did, I'm sure. "And do you have a special power?"

Soja smiled. "Being human will always be my favorite, this body exactly. Also, I'm a root worker. I quietly cure people with home remedies using roots, spices, and herbs from whatever planet I'm on. I test myself first. It's difficult to explain, but I have a tolerance for a lot of toxins that most people would die from. I thank the universe for that."

"That's amazing, truly amazing." I smiled back. "That makes sense. I wish you had still been around as Imogen when Thomas got sick. Sounds like you're very successful at what you do."

"Yeah, very successful in most diseases that ravage our land. Sometimes it's scary, though. I remember one time-line where the pharmaceutical industry was corrupt, and they wanted people to be sick so that they could profit from manufactured medicines and hospitals. So, when I started curing cancers, autoimmune diseases, etc., oh, the government didn't like that at all. I had to go into hiding and do it secretly. Those timelines were scary, and unfor-tunately, there are a lot of those." Soja crossed her legs as she explained, and Mahant and I listened intently.

Many timelines refer to Soja's work by various names. They were root workers, Hoodoo practitioners, or Con-jurers. Sometimes it came from a specific group of peo-ple where the majority were of melanated descent, their pigment darker than other beings on the planet. Root workers were spiritual workers who treated their bodies, minds, and souls as their temple, allowing their practices to elevate and help them grow while also helping others. It was a magical tradition; these were the magicians of the world through the normal-looking eye. In some timelines, people didn't like the idea of conjuring magic. However, they failed to understand that root workers used only the naturally abundant resources of their world and the power of the tongue. They believed affirmations were powerful, so if you say them out loud, they will come to fruition. They were herbalists, spiritual guides, and self-empowered people.

All of this fit perfectly into who Soja was as a person. She was eclectic and wise beyond her years, even when I knew her as Imogen. She always had the power of discernment and was quiet, but when you truly knew her, she was an intelligent being with a complex nature.

"So, what are your powers?" Soja asked as she grabbed her drink and took a sip.

Mahant and I looked at each other and smiled. Mahant looked at Soja and said, "Well, we can see auras and feel others' energies."

"Oh, lovely, empathic abilities. That sounds like it can be stressful." Soja set her drink back down.

"It can be stressful. Right now, though, in this room full of people, it feels amazing, soothing almost. When the surrounding energy is good, it's like a tingling sensation that moves through you. Almost like the feeling you get right before you're about to kiss someone for the first time." I looked at Mahant as I explained that last part and smiled before giving him a sweet kiss.

"You two are so cute." Soja smiled, then smirked. "It also sounds very euphoric."

I nodded and then waved down a staff member to order a drink. A server rushed over to our table and took our order. I got a sangria, and Mahant asked for a soda.

We talked some more, and the night grew later. Eventually, the server returned with our drinks as we continued speaking with Soja about anything and everything. After about forty-five minutes of talking, I diverted my attention to the second floor, across from where we were sitting, and saw someone standing behind the railing. I squinted as the lights dimmed, wondering who the person was.

As I watched them come down the steps, their presence awed me. She was astonishing, with straight, white hair and perfectly manicured eyebrows that were as white as snow as well. Her jaw was defined, her cheekbones high, and she had sleepy, almond-shaped eyes and full lips. She was tall, around 5'10, and very slender. I took one look at her skin and noticed different shades of chocolate brown, with pigment loss that let some white through. She wore a long necklace, and it was an evil eye necklace, resembling mine. Her attire was all white linen trousers and a white tank top with white shoes. Around her arm was a golden arm cuff, and she wore statement rings on each of her fingers, along with long white acrylic stiletto nails.

She looked ethereal, her presence almost otherworldly—impossible to fully grasp. Yet she carried a familiar energy that instantly filled the room, stirring something deep within me until tears welled in my eyes. It was a warmth, an invitation, laced with a timeless wisdom that felt older than humanity itself.

I immediately knew that this had to be Sage. The entire room fell into an eerily quiet abyss, and now all eyes were on her. There was a platform where the DJ was, and she made her way over to it. She stood on the platform, turned around, and faced the entire room.

"Good evening, everyone. I am Sage, and I'm so happy to see all of your beautiful faces tonight." Her hands stayed in a mudra pose in front of her as she spoke. Her eyes glanced around the room. Her smile was warm and inviting, and her voice was calm and soothing.

"Hi, Sage." Everyone in the room said back in unison.

Sage continued to smile as she spoke. "I want you all to meet each other and grow connections. That's what this meetup is all about. Building bonds, creating relationships, and loving what the universe offers. Thank you all for being here."

Sage stepped down from the platform and sat at the table with Sasha, and then a gentleman joined them.

"Wow, Sage is beautiful," I whispered under my breath.

"She is stunning, isn't she?" Soja agreed. "Do you know she has the power of spiritual location?"

I turned my gaze back to Soja and squinted. "What do you mean?"

"Her power? She can find anyone a part of The Recollections Contract, no matter the timeline." Soja explained as she leaned back in her chair and sighed, "That's how she's found most of us."

"That's pretty dope," Mahant admitted as we looked at each other.

I nodded my head and then looked back towards Sage and Sasha.

We stayed a little longer than we initially planned, then finally decided it was time for us to head back home. I got Soja's number so that we could hang out later this week. As we headed towards the entrance, Sasha and I made eye contact, and before we could exit, she motioned for us to come over. Mahant and I walked over to their table and stood before it.

"Leaving?" Sasha asked us.

We both nodded and then smiled at her. "Thank you so much for inviting us. This was great." I thanked her.

"Of course, gorgeous. Oh, I'd like for you both to meet Sage and Julio."

I smiled big as Sage turned her head and looked at me and Mahant. Sage nodded at us and then gave us a warm smile.

"It's a pleasure to meet you both," Mahant greeted them as I wrapped my hands around his arm and held him close.

Julio was a Latino man dressed in a cream-colored suit. He had a long mustache and beard, with kind hazel eyes. On his head was a cowboy hat, completing his outfit.

"Nice to meet you as well." Sage greeted us back. "Hope you enjoyed yourself tonight."

"We did!" I responded cheerfully.

Julio held out his hand and greeted Mahant with a handshake, then tipped his cowboy hat at him.

It was a quick meet-and-greet. Sasha stood up, hugged us before we left, and then gave me her phone number. Once outside, we got into the car and drove back to Diamond's Landing.

When we arrived home, I quickly kicked my shoes off and headed to the bedroom so that I could undress and get into bed. I was feeling good and on a high, but my energy was exhausted. Overall, I was in a good state; my body just needed to decompress from all the different energies I had felt tonight.

After we both undressed, I put on my robe, went to the fridge to grab some water, and then came back to the bedroom to find Mahant comfortably in bed. I got into bed with him and snuggled in close.

"Tonight was fun." Mahant's voice was low and soft. I could tell he was tired, too.

I turned and looked at him. "It was a lot of fun. I'm looking forward to the next one. Maybe we can bring Aeries along."

Mahant smiled, then closed his eyes. "I'd like that. I'm sure she will as well."

I wrapped my arms around his waist and rested my head on his chest as I closed my eyes.

"Goodnight, babe."

Mahant sighed, "Goodnight, beautiful."

CHAPTER 13

The plan for the day was to hang out with Aeries again. It was Saturday, and we both promised to get together this weekend. It was almost noon, and Mahant was at work as I prepared for Aeries to come over. I told her we would have a meditation session today at my place to help ground her.

I got dressed in some yoga pants, a tank top, and thick white socks. I threw my hair into a messy bun and then went into my living room to straighten up. Today was beautiful outside, so I opened the blinds to all my windows, allowing the sun to cast a haze into the open condo. As soon as I opened the blinds, Roo trotted over to her cat tree next to the window and looked out. A smile formed on my face as I stroked her fur, and she purred softly.

I then walked around the apartment, lit some candles, and used incense to set the mood.

"COMO, can you turn on my meditation playlist, please?"

"Yes, Zya, turning on your meditation playlist now."

There was a knock at the front door, so I made my way over to it and opened it.

"Hey babes!" I greeted Aeries.

Aeries smiled at me, "Hey!"

I opened the door wider, allowing her to enter my space. Aeries walked through the door and stood in front of the coffee table.

"I bought my yoga mat." Aeries hugged her mat as she stood there.

I chuckled. "You're so cute. You could have used Mahant's." I went to my closet and pulled out my pink yoga mat. Aeries lay her mat down in the space behind the sofa, and I joined her, sitting in front of her.

"Okay, first things first... finding your mudra pose," I explained as I crossed my legs and rested my hands on my knees.

"Mudra pose?" Aeries questioned me as she watched, mimicking my movements.

I inhaled deeply and then exhaled. "Yes, your mudra pose will help the energy flow through your body. It's a hand position or gesture to help ground you, enhancing concentration and focus. I usually hold my hands like this."

I showed her how I gesture with my hands, connecting my thumb to my ring finger.

I then continued to explain, "This mudra is called many things in many timelines, but it's the same universally. In this timeline, it's called the Rafti Mudra. I've heard of it in many other timelines, such as the Prithvi Mudra."

Aeries' eyes glistened with wonder as she performed the Rafti Mudra.

"Mahant enjoys the Yoni Mudra pose. I'm sure you've often seen him do it just out of the blue." I gestured with my hands, placing my thumbs and pointer fingers together, then allowing the rest of my fingers to press inward against each other, pointing towards me. "He also likes to place his hands together in prayer; we call that the Prayer Mudra."

Aeries followed each mudra pose as I showed her, attentively hanging onto every word I spoke. I place my hands back into the Rafti Mudra and rest my hands on my knees. Aeries does the same.

I continued, "There are so many poses. I'm sure you will find one that resonates more with you, but for now, we will stick with the Rafti Mudra pose. Now, we are going to do breathing exercises. Breathing exercises help

create a calm baseline in the body and mind, clear away impurities, and foster stability. So, box breathing, using the
four-eight-four-second method. Inhaling through your
nose for four seconds, exhaling eight seconds through your
mouth, and then inhaling again for four seconds."

We both began practicing our breathing exercises as we
sat facing each other. After five minutes had passed, I gathered Aeries was ready for her next lesson.

"Now, when I meditate, I do two things. I focus on
where my breath goes on specific body points and release
tension through breathing. Then I repeatedly speak positive affirmations in my head, which are called mantras."

"What's your favorite mantra?" Aeries asked as she continued her breathing exercises.

"I am free. I am love. I am power. I am omnipotent." I
softly chanted. "That's one of my many mantras. You ba-
sically want to send out to the universe what you want and
what you already know. For instance, if I wanted abundance, I'd say something like, I have abundance, I have
wealth, I am successful, and repeat. You want to claim that
energy." I kept my eyes shut as I walked Aeries through the
motions. "What are you looking to gain or release?"

"I've been feeling stressed about remembering everything and being so alone through this entire ordeal. Losing
Mahant in my first timeline really put a lot of emotional

stress on me, which has resurfaced." Aeries sighed deeply, so I opened my eyes and looked at her.

"Hey, look at me." I encouraged her. Her eyes opened, and a tear fell from them. I leaned forward, wiped away her tears, and smiled at her. "Mmm, so maybe say... I am here, I am now, present in this space. I am free of the burdens before me."

Aeries sighed again and then closed her eyes. Her energy was low, and her aura was shrinking. I could tell she was sad and holding onto a lot of pain from her previous timeline. "I am here, I am now, present in this space. I am free of the burdens before me."

"Again. Repeat it." I guided her through her affirmations.

Aeries chanted before me. "I am here, I am now, present in this space. I am free of the burdens before me."

I closed my eyes and focused on my breathing. "Now internalize those words, say them in your head, and go back to focusing on your breathing exercises. Think about where the tension lives in your body and then let it flow through you, into your hands and out. If you need to shake it off, do it."

I could feel everything she was feeling and more; even my eyes watered. She was hurting and carrying around this weight that was heavy to bear. I was happy that we were doing this together, that I could help her get through the trauma.

Out of nowhere, the energy in the room shifted, and Aeries burst into tears. I opened my eyes, noticing tears were streaming from her closed eyes, and her hand was holding her chest. She inhaled, or tried to, but couldn't catch her breath. I quickly scooted closer to her and pressed my hand into her chest.

"Hey, I need you to breathe. Catch your breath." I attempted to console her. Both her hands clamped onto each of my shoulders as she hunched over and bellowed out a cry while hyperventilating. "It's okay, let it out."

"I'm so sorry!" Aeries cried out in between her uneven breaths and tears.

"It will all be okay, I promise." I consoled her.

Aeries wrapped her arms around my torso and pulled me in, catching me off guard.

Our auras merged , and I could feel her more than ever. It was a beautiful sight, my blue aura blending with her red aura to create a mesmerizing purple haze. Although I felt a glimpse of discomfort, there was a slight feeling of joy. Aeries' arms felt amazing around me, and I didn't know how to admit it. I tensed up in the moment and then gradually melted into her embrace, finally hugging her back and holding her close. As if this were Mahant,

I could feel everything—her energy, love, and sorrow. At that moment, I just wanted to be there for her, support her, and care for her as though it destined me to. Slowly, she calmed down, her breathing evening out with every second that passed.

We stayed in this embrace for a while as her body regained its composure. Finally, she pulled away from me slowly and gazed into my eyes. I looked back at her, and we locked eyes. The tension was thick, however; I raised my hand and wiped away her tears as we looked at each other. I could feel her heartbeat quicken against mine as I wiped away.

Aeries finally pulled away from our embrace and cleared her throat. "I am so sorry." She composed herself as she sat on the yoga mat and looked away from me. I could sense embarrassment, not just from her body language, but also from her aura changing.

I leaned back, pressing my hands flat behind me and holding myself up on them. "It's okay, really. That happens. It's completely normal."

Aeries didn't say a word; she just stood up and walked around my condo as I watched her. She went over to my gigantic bay window and stood before it, quietly. I wondered what was running through her mind.

The room was so quiet you could hear a pin drop. I didn't know what to say or do, so I just sat there and calmed my racing heart. The feeling I had for Aeries during our gaze felt similar to how I'd feel right before kissing Mahant to console him—our hesitation made me question it all. Was Aeries feeling the same way I was feeling?

"Are you okay?" I finally spoke quietly, just enough for my voice to reach her.

Aeries sighed and continued to look out the window. She then turned her attention towards Roo and petted her. "I'm okay. That was just a lot. My emotions are all over the place. I feel so embarrassed."

"Don't, babes, you're fine," I promised Aeries as I stood up and walked to my bar. I grabbed two glasses and poured Rolo into them. I picked up each glass, walked over to Aeries by the window, and handed her the glass. "Think about it. You're conjuring so many emotions from your past. All of it was brewing inside of you, and you needed to release it. I'm glad I could help you do that. Hopefully, you're feeling better."

Aeries took the glass from me and took the shot to the head. I sipped mine as I watched her inquisitively.

"I definitely needed that cry. I do feel better; I need to learn to control my emotions more. I feel so hard about everything." Aeries looked into her empty glass.

I laughed, grabbed the glass from her, and then handed her mine. She took the glass and then took a sip from my glass. I knew she needed it more than I did.

"Well, if you can see and feel auras, you are definitely an empath. So, not only are you experiencing your empathic abilities, but you're also dealing with a new world while remembering your old one. I don't blame you for feeling on edge. You need a release, I promise." I walked back to the bar, filled her glass, and then approached her, trading glasses and taking mine back.

"Thank you," she said, taking the glass and sipping from hers. We both left the window and went to sit on the sofa. Aeries took her shoes off, propped her feet up, and hugged them while sitting on the couch. I sat next to her, crossing my legs as I watched her.

"We can try again in a bit if you want to. Or we could order lunch and do whatever." I gave Aeries some options, and she took a moment to consider them.

"Food sounds great. I need a break from all the energy." Aeries looked at me and rested her head on her hand that sat on top of her knees.

I smiled at her. "That sounds like a great plan. What are you in the mood for?"

Aeries laughed. "I could eat anything, truly."

"Burgers?" I grabbed my phone and started scrolling through our delivery app called On the Go. "There's a really great burger spot called Smashed BC Burgers."

Aeries lit up and smiled. "Oh, I loved Smashed Bluepoint City Burgers. They're so amazing. Let's do it."

I handed Aeries my phone so she could add her burger to the cart, then I scrolled through to add mine. I paid for the burgers, and we waited patiently for them to come. As we waited, I reached forward and grabbed the remote, turning on my TV.

"Have you ever watched Profile Match?" I looked at Aeries, and she smiled. Profile Match was a reality dating show that was very popular in this timeline. The show was about people dating each other based on their online dating profiles. Each person had to create a profile, but the challenge was that they couldn't add a picture of themselves. They would date blindly based on the profiles they see, and then once they matched, they would meet in the real world.

"I love Profile Match." Aeries rolled her eyes to the back of her head and then laughed. "I'm obsessed with that show. I have not seen the new season yet, though."

I used the arrows on the remote to select Profile Match, then pressed enter. "Let's watch it!"

"My favorite couple from Profile Match are Trey and Dominique. They are so cute! And they are still together." Aeries expressed, excitedly.

"Oh my gosh, Trey and Domo are the best. I love them so much!"

The show played, and we both got quiet as we watched the introduction. Soon, our food arrived, and we continued watching Profile Match as we ate our enormous burgers and tasty fries. Profile Match had us completely lost in the show, and we lost track of time as we binged-watched it. Soon, the hour went by, and the sun went down. We got through eight episodes, eight hours straight of yelling at the TV, drinking Rolo, and laughing with each other.

Suddenly, the front door opened, and Mahant walked through. He saw both of us cozied up on the sofa and smiled at us.

"Hey, babe, I didn't think you'd still be here," Mahant spoke to Aeries as he walked over and kissed her.

Aeries kissed him back and smiled, "Yeah, we're watching Profile Match. This season is so messy and full of drama. Love it."

Mahant then stood before me, and I looked up at him. "How was work?"

"It was good, beautiful." He leaned down and kissed me, and I kissed him back, tasting the lingering traces of coconut and citrus on his lips. I looked over at Aeries, and she looked at me and smiled. It was still strange, us both kissing Mahant, sharing him. Even more bizarre to taste the remnant of Aeries on his lips. Mahant walked into the bedroom, removed his holster, and immediately put his gun into his safe. He returned to the living room and went to the kitchen to grab water from the refrigerator.

Aeries picked up her phone from the coffee table and checked the time. "It's getting late. I should go."

Impulsively, I blurted out. "It's really late, and we've been drinking too much for you to drive home. You can crash on the couch."

Aeries looked at Mahant and then looked at me. "Are you sure?"

I smiled. "Yeah, for sure. I don't mind."

Aeries stretched and then leaned back onto the sofa. With playful banter, she spoke. "This couch is comfortable."

Mahant walked back in front of us with his bottle of water. He took off his black t-shirt, revealing his toned body. Out of the corner of my eye, I saw how Aeries looked at him and bit her bottom lip. I stood up, went to my laundry room to grab an extra blanket for Aeries, and then walked back to her to hand it over. She took the blanket, unfolded it, and wrapped it around her body.

"Thank you." Aeries spoke softly as she lay on the sofa, getting comfortable.

I stretched and watched Mahant as he walked around shirtless, in just his black jeans and socks. Mahant disappeared into the bedroom, and I heard him groan as if he had just gotten into bed.

"I guess I'll get ready for bed. See you in the morning, Aeries." I grabbed my phone and headed towards the bedroom.

"Goodnight, Imani." Aeries called out.

I started speaking to COMO. "COMO, it's bedtime. Time to lock up."

"Yes, Zya, locking the doors and arming the security. Goodnight, Zya." COMO robotically said.

I went into the bedroom and closed the door halfway. Mahant was in bed, and I went to shower before joining him. After my shower, in only a bra and panties, I joined Mahant in bed. Aeries continued to watch TV for a while as Mahant and I lay in bed, scrolling on our phones.

I finally turned and looked at Mahant, whispering. "You two haven't had sex yet, have you?"

Mahant slowly turned his head and looked at me. "That was such a random question." He then laughed and continued scrolling through his Zed account. It was quiet for a moment before he finally responded. "No, we haven't."

"I can tell." I continued to whisper. "I see how she looks at you. Also, she's super tense. She needs a release."

Mahant's facial expression lightened, and his eyebrow raised. "How'd the meditation session go, anyway?"

I froze and thought for a moment before answering Mahant's question. The moment between me and Aeries still lingered in the back of my mind—traces of her embrace still lingering on me like fresh paint. Something I could not wash off, even with a hundred showers before bed. How she looked at me and clung to me, the tension in the air thick like cement right before it hardens. Was it only me who felt the energy between us?

I could see Mahant staring at me out of the corner of my eye. My head tilted side to side as I continued to think long and hard about his question.

"It was... a lot." I finally spoke. "She has a lot going on in that beautiful mind of hers."

"Yeah, I told you. If you two continue your meditation sessions, it will get better for Aeries." Mahant placed his phone on his nightstand and then rested his head on his hands as they crossed behind his head. His eyes closed, and he sighed deeply.

I nodded without saying a word and then closed my eyes. It was time to sleep and let the thoughts in my head escape me as I drifted into the dream world.

The next morning, I woke up around noon to cook a late breakfast. Neither Mahant nor Aeries had worked today, so I surprised them with brunch.

As I started cooking in the kitchen—bacon, eggs, and pancakes—Aeries slept peacefully. However, it was not long before she sat up and stretched, then looked at me in the kitchen. Immediately, I smiled at her sweetly as I cooked, and she returned the sentiment with a smile.

"Good morning," I called out over the sizzling and crackling of the bacon. Two pancakes were cooking in the pan, so I turned around and grabbed the spatula to flip them.

Then I went to the refrigerator and grabbed the carton of eggs. "How do you like your eggs?"

Aeries yawned. "Scrambled with cheese, please."

I also took out some cheese and then grabbed a bowl from the cupboard.

"It smells so delicious in here." Aeries complimented as she stood up and walked to the island counter. "Did you need help?"

I cracked the egg and then mixed shredded cheese into the bowl. Before I could answer, Aeries continued to enter the kitchen. As I made my way to the stove to pour the egg mixture into the pan, Aeries stood beside me, grabbed the fork, and flipped the bacon before it could burn.

I looked at her. "Thank you!"

While Aeries continued to tend to the bacon, I called COMO to play my chill playlist. COMO turned the TV on, and a DJ set started playing. Aeries and I swayed our hips as we cooked and listened to the tunes played throughout the house. I turned to the cupboard and grabbed plates and some glasses for us to eat.

"Ooo, I forgot I have blueberries!" I yelled, my voice laced with excitement. "Do you like blueberry pancakes?"

Aeries tilted her head back, and her eyes fell to the back of her head in her cute, animated fashion. "Yesss, I love blueberry pancakes, chocolate chip pancakes. I love it all."

I went to the fridge, grabbed the blueberries, and then went to the sink to rinse them. After I rinsed them off, I made some blueberry compote to put on top of the pancakes and then added whole blueberries to the pancake mix.

Aeries helped with the eggs while I worked on the pancakes. Then, from the bedroom, I heard Mahant groan and stretch. A few minutes later, he appeared from the bedroom, wearing sweatpants, socks, and no shirt.

We finished breakfast and set the dining room table in the condo's corner, off to the side of the home. I grabbed some orange juice from the refrigerator and put it on the table.

"You're right on time, babe," I told Mahant as he walked up to me. I rested my hand on his chest as he leaned in and kissed my lips. "Good morning, handsome."

"Good morning, beautiful." He greeted me back, then went to Aeries and gave her love as well. Mahant then sat at the table and looked at all the delicious food we had made. "I could get used to this."

"Uh huh, I'm sure." I rolled my eyes and joined him at the table, as did Aeries.

We wasted no time digging into the food and fixing our plates. Everything looked scrumptious, and it smelled heavenly.

"So, what's the plan for the day?" I asked them both as we ate.

Aeries shrugged and then picked up her bacon. Holding it in her hand, her eyes shifted from me to Mahant as she took a bite. "I want to just relax, honestly. If I'm being real, I need to look for a new job."

"A new job? Not feeling Dustin's anymore?" I asked, curiously.

Aeries shook her head, "It's okay. I need something more serious, steady, with good benefits."

I nodded and then chewed the rest of the pancakes in my mouth before speaking again. "I could get you something at Peach Motors. Good hours, amazing benefits, all that good stuff."

"Shit, get me one of those, too." Mahant blurted out as he took a sip of his orange juice.

"Trust me, we will be okay in this timeline. I got y'all." I laughed, placing my hand on Mahant's knee and looking at Aeries. "I will talk to a few people at work, and we will get you in."

"That would be amazing." Aeries smiled graciously at me and then continued eating.

"I need to grab some more things from my place and bring them here," Mahant added to the conversation.

"What if..." I started, then paused. "What if you move in? We can get movers to go get your things."

Mahant nodded in approval. "Yeah, that's cool. That would probably be a lot easier. I just need to talk to KJ."

I grabbed my phone and started looking through my search engine for the moving company I used when I moved into my current home. "The Moving Brothers is who I used. They're excellent with raving reviews."

I went onto their website, looked at their scheduling, and then I texted Mahant.

Hey, let's bring up The Collection to Aeries.

I look over at Mahant, and his phone dings. He grabbed his phone, read the text, looked at me, and then replied.

Sure thing.

I turned my attention towards Aeries. "Hey, so there is something we want to talk to you about."

Aeries looked very curious, her eyes shifting between me and Mahant. I knew she had noticed us texting and possibly felt left out at the moment.

"Hopefully it's good news. What's up?" Aeries questioned.

"Yeah, it's nothing bad," Mahant interjected. "We just found like-minded people like us. People who remember their past lives. Folks a part of The Recollections Contract."

Aeries' eyes widened, and her jaw dropped slightly. "No way!"

I nodded as Mahant and I explained all our recent adventures. We discussed looking up the website, and I even showed it to her on my phone. Mahant dramatically explained our first interaction with Sasha at the abandoned warehouse. I told her about the second meetup, where we met Kye, Omari, and a few others with special abilities. Everything we were telling her, fascinated Aeries. She paused from eating momentarily, leaned into the conversation, and was so intrigued when we discussed the special abilities.

As we continued to tell her everything we knew about The Collection, there was a knock on my door. I turned to look at the front door, then back at Mahant.

"I'm not expecting anyone or a package, you?" I questioned him. Mahant shook his head. So I called out to COMO. "COMO, who's at the front door?"

COMO responded. "It looks like a package from Bluepoint City Postal. It's a huge box that was left for you, Zya."

I stood up, went to the door, opened it, and grabbed the box from outside. Nobody was around when I looked, so I closed the door and returned to the dining room table. The box was massive, but not as heavy as it looked. I placcd it on the chair and then opened it. Once the box was open, I immediately knew who it was from. Coincidentally, we were talking about The Collection, and I received a package from someone from there. I knew because the first thing I saw in the box was another temperature-sensitive, color-changing card. I took the card out of the box and looked at it.

Mahant leaned forward and grabbed the card out of my hand. "Another one?"

As he examined the card, I returned to see what else was in the box. In the box was clothing and a letter that I read out loud.

Mahant and Imani,

Thank you so much for attending our ballroom event and being your authentic selves. Not every day do we get to meet twin flames and have them be a part of an extraordinary organization. We have selected two timeless pieces for you both to show our appreciation. I hope you enjoy these, and until next time,

-Sasha.

I pulled out the first outfit, which was for Mahant. It was a suit from Kal & Bliss, one of the world's most prestigious fashion designers.

"Wow, Kal & Bliss? This is crazy money." Sasha truly surprised Mahant as he held out his suit and then picked up his cuff links. "This navy color is super deep, and these cufflinks are gold. Is this real gold?"

I reached back into the box and pulled out a stunning floor-length lamé golden gown. The dress material draped over the shoulders, with the sides open, connecting to the mid-waist with a golden clamp that extended more material, flowing like a side cape. It was breathtaking, a true high-fashion dress. I couldn't believe my eyes as I held it in the air and pressed it against my body—a perfect fit.

"That is gorgeous!" Aeries stood up and walked around to inspect as I held it up. "Girl, your body is going to eat this dress up!"

I smiled so hard and then looked at Aeries. "You're cute."

Aeries reached and grabbed the tag, "Oh my gosh! Do you see the price on this thing?"

"My suit is in the thousands. This is too much." Mahant whispered as he folded the suit back up carefully and placed it in the box. I followed him, put the dress back into the box, and shook my head in disbelief. I grabbed my phone and texted Sasha.

Just received the gift. This is way too much.

A few minutes passed, and Sasha texted me back.

Oh, it's a small gesture. Hopefully, you enjoy it! See you soon.

Mahant jogged over to the freezer and placed his hand inside while he held the card.

"Is that the color-changing card?" Aeries asked as she followed Mahant over to the fridge. "I wanna see!"

I laughed and texted Sasha back.

Hey, so... we told someone about The Collection. She's also a part of The Recollections Contract and was hoping we could bring her to the next meetup.

I squeezed my phone as I waited for a response and walked over to them. They were pressed against each other, peering into the freezer, waiting for the card to change.

"This is so cool! Look, it's changing!" Aeries yelled. "What does it say?"

Mahant laughed and looked at her as she held onto his arm in the freezer.

Aeries began reading the text while I stood behind them. "The next meet-up will be at 424 Ballow Way in Bluepoint City. It's at 8 pm this coming Friday."

"I wonder if these meetups happen every week." I crossed my arms and then turned around to go back to the table so that I could straighten up.

Mahant turned around, handed the card to Aeries, then walked to the table where I stood. "I got it, babe. You two cooked. I can clean and load the dishwasher."

I touched his face and nodded. "Thank you."

A ding sounded off on my phone; it was from Sasha.

She will need something for the meetup this week. I can vet her an hour before, and then we can all ride there if you like.

I smiled at the text message and then texted Sasha back.

I'll get her an outfit. Sounds good to me. Thanks!

I walked up to Aeries, clutching my phone. "Good news. You're coming with us! Now we have to go shopping for an outfit."

"Oh my gosh, oh my gosh, yes!" Aeries squealed and jumped as she clung to me. I laughed at her excitement.

"If you want, we could go now before you head home. I have an extra toothbrush if you want to freshen up, and then we can head out?" I offered to Aeries.

Aeries finally let go of me. "Let's do it!"

I walked into my bedroom, and Aeries followed me. Mahant continued to clean up as we got ready to head out. He joined us after finishing cleaning the kitchen, so he got ready as well. Once we finished getting ready, we left in our cars and headed to Lucille Mall. Lucille Mall had more high-end clothing stores than Blue City Mall and was in Huntington.

It was a unique mall, with shops both outside and inside a structured building. There was a massive overpass for a train to transport you from one end of the mall to the other. Lucille Mall was the largest mall on the East Coast, featuring the best clothing stores and restaurants. Attached to the mall was a casino and hotel for people to stay at if they traveled from outside the region. We entered the mall on the left wing, where Carters, a store that held many fashionable gowns and suits, was located. It wasn't our first stop, as we entered many other stores first, but it was our last.

Aeries strolled around, looking for the perfect outfit once we finally entered Carters. As she looked, I could see her facial expression change as she noticed the price tags.

I walked up to her and whispered in her ear. "This is my treat. So don't look at the tags; look at what stands out to you."

Aeries' eyebrows arched, then she visibly forced a smile onto her face. "Are you sure?"

"Positive." I touched her arm and immediately felt the warmth of her energy. I pulled away and then distracted myself with the clothing.

"Oh wow, look at this," Aeries called out to us. Mahant and I found her a few sections away and headed in her direction. She was standing in front of an emerald green satin, crisscross-tied back bodycon dress with a mid-thigh split.

"That's a stunning dress and would look amazing on you," I complimented, as she grabbed it from the shelf and pressed it against her body. "Talk about me. Your body would eat up that dress too."

Aeries blushed and then looked at Mahant. "What do you think? Do you like it?"

Mahant placed his hands together, like a prayer mudra, and pressed the tips of his fingers against his lips. "Please, get the dress. I need to see you in it."

Aeries rolled her eyes and then took the dress to try it on. We went to the dressing rooms, and the dress was the perfect fit. She decided this was the dress for her, and now we needed to get some shoes. So we stopped by another store, grabbed some shoes for everyone to complete their look, and then walked around the mall for some more light window shopping.

The day was getting late, and we wrapped up our adventures and headed back home. We parted ways from the mall, and then Mahant and I went back to our condo.

We arrived home and got ready for the week ahead. It excited me for what was in store for us and was happy that Aeries was a part of it. Spending more time with her felt great, and I noticed I hadn't been in my head for the last few days, which was a positive sign; that was progress. She was growing on me in the best ways possible, and day by day, I wasn't as mad at Mahant as I initially was.

I wanted to rid myself of it all, let all the animosity be done and gone, but unfortunately, I could admit that some resentment remained.

At the end of the day, this was everything he wanted. However, what did I want? That question lingered in my mind like a cold sore festering and brewing within me.

Chapter 14

I t was Wednesday, and the week had gone by rapidly so far. Mahant had talked to KJ about moving out, and KJ was completely fine with it, now that he had Stacy, who seemed to always be at his place. So, it was officially move-out day for Mahant. We took my car to his place to load up some little things and allowed the movers to handle the rest. Aeries offered to help, so she tagged along. When we arrived at Mahant's apartment, we exited the car and walked inside to the second level. Once in the apartment, KJ and Stacy walked up to greet us.

"KJ, this is Zya and Aeries. Ladies, this is KJ." Mahant introduced us, and we held out our hands to shake his hand.

KJ shook my hand first, then Aeries. "Nice to meet you, ladies."

KJ then turned to Stacy and introduced her. We all greeted each other and then entered Mahant's room to retrieve a few items he didn't want to put in the moving truck.

"Your room is such a bachelor's pad." I snickered as soon as we entered his space.

Aeries chuckled and looked around the room curiously. We loaded Aeries' car or my car with Mahant's things. After we finished, we drove back to my place and unloaded the cars.

I plopped down on my sofa after unloading everything and sighed deeply. "The movers are going to put most of your things in storage, and then they will bring the rest here."

"Yeah, it's mostly clothes they're bringing here," Mahant responded as he sat beside me. "Should be a quick-moving process."

Aeries walked over to the sofa and sat on my other side. "Even though we did little, I'm tired!"

I laughed, looking at her. "Too much manual labor for us. Glad we got the movers."

Aeries nodded and then laughed as well.

"I'm going to get ready. I'm hanging with Soja today!" I stood up from the sofa and turned around to look at Aeries and Mahant. "Aeries, you are more than welcome to hang here."

Aeries smiled. "I actually need some food. Let's go get some food, babe." She turned and looked at Mahant, who then looked at her. They both stood up and got ready to head out the door as I left the living room and entered my bedroom. I heard the door open, then close, and then they left the house.

"Mmm, what to wear today?" I said out loud to myself as I walked into my closet. It was beautiful out—a lovely, sunny, hot summer day. Soja and I decided we would grab some lunch and then head to Ryan's Rage Room. So, I wanted to make sure whatever I wore, I would be most comfortable in. My outfit of the day consisted of a black men's button-up shirt with orange tropical leaves, a leopard print sports bra, and black Palazzo pants. I took a shower and then got dressed in the outfit I had picked out. Standing in front of my vanity mirror, I looked over the outfit to make sure it looked good. I wore cream heels, but I also packed more comfortable shoes for after we ate.

Before leaving my home, I patted Roo on her head and told COMO to lock up once I was gone. I turned to grab my fanny pack satchel from the coat rack and put it on. I left the condo, got into my Z8 from the car deck, and drove to Splitz to meet up with Soja. Once I got there, I parked the car and hopped out. I locked the doors and then entered the restaurant. As I looked around the restaurant, she was nowhere in sight, so I took out my phone and texted her.

Hey, girly, I'm here. Where are you?

A few minutes passed, and then there was a ding on my phone from Soja.

Pulling in now.

I stood and waited to be seated, and a server approached me.

"How many are in your party?" She asked.

I put up two fingers and smiled. "I'm just waiting for her to get here."

The server smiled, grabbed two menus and two sets of cutlery, and waited. Soja came through the door, and her energy was unaltered. She was vibrant and glowing with a powerful force—her aura more potent than mine. Soja was wearing a black skirt, a cream sweater, a white button-up shirt, and a black leather jacket. She has black buckled boots on her feet and fishnet stockings on. On her head was a beanie, and sprawling out of it were her long braids. Soja, without hesitation, comes up to me and gives me the biggest hug. We followed the server to our booth and took a seat.

The server set down the menus, and then walked away, almost instantly coming back with two glasses of water for us. I smiled at her and grabbed the drink menu to check out their specials.

"Can I grab you ladies a drink?" The server took out her COMO pad.

Soja looked through her menu, and we carefully decided what to start with.

"I'll take a Rolo, please and thank you." I pointed at the menu as I placed my order. "And let's order the bleu cheese crispy wings for an appetizer. Keep it simple for now."

"Yesss, girl, I'll take a Rolo as well," Soja ordered right after me. "We're sharing, right? Like old times?"

I grinned happily. "Oh, absolutely."

"That will be all for now." Soja looked up at the server and smiled.

The server walked away, and we sat silently looking over the menus to decide on our entrees.

Soja finally broke the silence. "You do not know how much I've missed you. We grew so old together, and when I was gone, I wished there was a way I'd be able to see you again. The universe is highly in my favor."

She spoke so highly of our relationship that it brought tears to my eyes. The memories of Utopia came rushing back to me. Magical memories of Zoe and Imogen. They were my girls. The best friends a girl could ever ask for.

"I've missed you, too. I still can't believe we could be in two timelines together." I sipped my water and then placed it back down on the table.

Soja laughed, "There's gotta be a reason. The universe is mysterious like that."

"True. I also miss Zoe," I admitted.

"Me too, still so very sad how young she passed away." Soja was evoking distant memories that I had long since locked away. "Ugh, that was hard and still haunts me. Her car accident was tough for all of us to get through. Especially Jordan, poor kid. I hope that somehow, the universe created a tie between them."

"Same," I agreed, trying to hold back tears from the past. "So, what do you think about The Collection?"

Soja picked up her water, took a sip, and then set the glass on the table. "Awesome organization. I actually discovered them in Utopia and have been a part of it since."

"I can't believe I'm just now finding out about them!" I excitedly yelled across the table. "Wait, how old are you?"

"I'm one thousand and twenty-four years old, but yeah, girl, they exist in every single timeline. It's just about seeking them out and finding them so that you can connect with people who are like you, ya know." Soja raised her eyebrow as she explained. "Oh, did you get invited to the annual gala?"

"This Friday? Is that what that is?" I continued to look through the menu as we talked, deciding what I wanted to eat. Soja did the same.

"Oh, yes. Every year, The Collection goes all out. If you think their meetups are extravagant, wait until you go to the Gala."

I smiled and closed the menu, finally knowing exactly what I wanted to order. "I'm so excited, I can't wait. Mahant and I will bring Aeries."

Soja's eyebrow raised, and she peered up at me. "Aeries? Who's that?"

I cleared my throat and scrunched my face. "So, long story short... Mahant created another soul tie, and somehow she's tethered to me as well."

"Pause, wait." Soja gestured with her hands, holding her hand up to halt me from speaking. "He created a soul tie. Did you know he was going to?"

"I had no idea, none. I found Mahant in this timeline, like a couple weeks ago, and she had already refreshed his memories since he lost every single one due to him not living out his life in full in his previous timeline." I explained, spilling everything.

"Yeah, I remember you telling me the other night. It's still so bizarre. I've met no one who actually broke The Recollections Contract and lost their memories."

I nodded my head and continued explaining. "Mmm, yeah... well, Mahant has only been able to remember once, and that was in Utopia as Thomas."

"This is so crazy! So wait, back to him creating a soul tie without your consent." Soja placed her hands on the table, leaned in, and whispered. "What the fuck?"

"I'm still trying to work through that. Don't get me wrong, Aeries is a sweetheart. She's so very, very sweet and kind, and gorgeous, but what an asshole move Mahant pulled."

The server returned with our Rolos, placed them on the table, then grabbed her COMO pad and looked at us. "Are you ready to place your entrees?"

"Oh, yes! I will have the lemongrass fish, please." I ordered and then handed over my menu.

Soja glanced over the menu to take one more look before placing her order. "I'll take the lamb tziki burger!"

"Sure thing!" The server keyed in Soja's order and then grabbed the menu from her, quietly leaving our table.

I sighed and looked at Soja, and Soja shook her head and sighed with me.

"It's only been us together for over nine hundred years; now it will be a major change with Aeries."

"Navigating through those emotions has to be tough for you." Soja sat back and crossed her arms.

Her disappointment was just as present as mine, and she wasn't even the person going through it; yet, she understood.

As close as Aeries and I have gotten in such a short time, my anger was still very present. My anger wasn't towards her at all, but geared towards Mahant. If anything, jealousy was the emotion I felt towards Aeries. I was upset that she now had a piece of him. Would that even be jealousy?

"I'm trying to. It's a weird ass poly thing, and even though we have navigated through this before, if any issues had ever arisen, it was easy to sever ties with the third party. It's not so easy to do that with a soul tie." I explained carefully, and my words were precise and anchored with clarity.

"Of course not. A soul tie is a part of who you are forever. It's not a simple evolution for a normal being when life ends. Our lives continue, and so does that soul tie." Soja continued to talk expressively with her hands. "I get the magnitude of it. I don't think Mahant does, for that matter, it seems like he acted so impulsively."

It felt good to get this off my chest and talk it out. I wanted to dig deeper and put how I felt all on the table. It's almost as if I were practicing to address this with Mahant.

"Another thing that's bothering me is that every time I have restored Mahant's memories, they are never restored all the way. There were always gaps, blanks he couldn't remember. However, Aeries comes along and restores his memories, and he's got them all back." I explained, tilting my head slightly. The weight of my words escaping my lips and carrying over to Soja's ears made me reflect on the magnitude of my reality. I slowly sank into a state of heartache and insecurity over this ordeal. It didn't feel good.

"Oh no, bitch!" Soja yelled. "The nerve of whoever's doing that was."

"The universe?" It was a very defeated question. "I mean, maybe the universe gave her more power over restoring the brokenness in his mind."

"Yeah, oh, the many questions I'd ask when I pass over." Soja shook her head and picked up her Rolo, sipping it quickly.

"Trust me, I'll be asking..." I picked up my Rolo as well and had a drink.

A few moments passed of us talking, me getting off my chest everything I've been feeling lately to Soja. It was a great release and was very much needed. The server came over, set down the chicken wings for us to indulge in, and informed us that our food would be out momentarily.

"Mmm, these are so delicious." I hummed as I took a bite of the chicken wing after dipping it into a house-made sauce.

Soja picked up a wing and bit into it. "Ooh! That's very good. I love these."

We ate, ordered more drinks, and connected as if time had never been a factor since our last encounter. Our food finally arrived, and we dove into the delicious plates cooked to perfection. We even let each other taste what we had ordered, sharing our meals like we used to back in Utopia.

About an hour and a half later, we paid for our food and headed out to the rage room. We followed each other as we drove in separate cars, and once we parked, I changed shoes and got out of the vehicle. Soja got out of her car, and we walked into the building.

A guy stood by the counter. "Hey! My name's Rich. Welcome to Triple R. Have y'all been here before?"

Soja looked at me and smiled, then looked back at Rich. "I have been. She has not. We will do the road rage room and the lovers' quarrels room. Which I wish y'all would have kept as the domestic violence room."

Rich laughed and then pressed some buttons on his COMO pad. "Yeah, many people thought domestic violence was a little too vulgar."

Soja laughed as well. "I loved that name."

"That will be sixty-two bucks," Rich announced as he did some final calculations on this COMO pad.

Soja paid, and then we followed Rich through a door that led to the back of the building. He opened another door, revealing a truck and a car inside.

"You're in luck. We just cleaned up this room and replaced the vehicles, so you two will be the first to do some damage to these." Rich explained as he walked to a nearby wall.

Paint buckets, bats, sledgehammers, and crowbars were on the wall. It looked like a mad mechanic's dream house.

Rich walked over to us and showed us the COMO pad. "Just need both your signatures here. It's just a safety waiver. We are not responsible for any injuries that may occur. We just asked that you be careful and stay five feet apart. Also, you will need to wear protective goggles. They are hanging up over there on the rack."

I took Rich's COMO pen, signed it, and then handed it to Soja. She signed as well and then handed the pen back to him. I walk over to the shelf full of weapons and take a moment to decide which to grab. Soja went straight for the sledgehammer and put it on her shoulder.

Rich went to the door. "When finished and ready to move to the lovers' quarrels room, just press this button here, and I'll come grab ya."

"Ten-four!" Soja yelled as he exited the room.

Soja and I put on a pair of protective goggles. I stared at the objects on the wall, and finally, I reached and grabbed the bat.

Soja huffed. "Great choice."

I winked at her. "I probably should have dressed better for this." I drop the bat, remove my button-up shirt, and tie it around my waist.

Soja laughed, "Oh, you're fine. You look the part."

I picked up the bat and walked to the car, sighing deeply.

"Just imagine, the car is the negative energy that lives inside you. You hate it and want to get rid of it. That energy has manifested as self-doubt, jealousy, and all those icky insecurities. The only way to eliminate this bad juju is by smashing it to pieces." Soja swung the sledgehammer beside her, her voice calm and serene as she spoke to me.

I closed my eyes and listened to her as I cleared my thoughts. I breathed in deep and then exhaled slowly. I gripped the bat and then heaved it up on my shoulders.

Soja continued, "This blockage stops you from making a decision that benefits you, Imani. It's the weight you carry, the guilt that wraps around you like a chain, keeping you tethered to everything but yourself. But you must see it for what it is—an illusion, a distraction. It's holding you back from making a decision that actually benefits you. You're stepping into the era of putting yourself first."

I let out a loud, gut-wrenching scream as I swung the bat and connected with the window on the driver's side. With all the force within me, the glass shattered into pieces. However, I didn't stop there. I continued to scream and let out all the air inside my lungs as I swung countlessly against the car. The car dented as I made my way to the front, slamming the bat down on the windshield.

"That's my girl! Let that shit out!" Soja cheered me on.

I continued to swing repeatedly. Soja finally joined me, taking out the headlights on each side and then moving to the side mirrors. We thoroughly destroyed the car, and after I felt the bat wasn't doing me much justice, I grabbed the paint bucket. Different paint buckets and colors made it even more fun. I threw paint on the car, and it splashed everywhere. Soja laughed and backed away as paint splattered on her clothes.

"I'm so sorry!" I yelled out as I dropped the bucket.

She used her hands to wipe the paint off, making a bigger mess. "It's just clothes! It's fine."

I looked down and noticed my outfit had paint all over it. I shrugged it off, grabbed the crowbar, and moved to the truck to destroy it.

The energy escaped me, and excitement crept in. Releasing all this energy was a different but very effective form of meditation I needed. I had a blockage that I wasn't even aware of, and Soja was helping me clear it away.

Finally, I reached the door and pressed the button so Rich could come and get us. It wasn't long before he entered the room.

He took one look at us, covered in paint, and laughed. "I see you two are having fun so far."

"Oh, absolutely!" I laughed and looked at myself again, covered in paint.

We followed him into the next room, a bedroom filled with dressers, lamps, TVs, mirrors, and fragile decor. Without hesitation, we unleashed chaos. Lamps were thrown across the room, shattering into pieces as they slammed against the wall. Our rage was unrecognizable as we ripped the sheets, jumped on the bed, and painted the room like a mosaic of beautiful colors. In many timelines, breaking a mirror was bad luck. However, we didn't care—we needed the release, and we did exactly that. We left the room in shambles, a reminder that our release was successful.

Soja and I exited the rage room building in complete laughter. She bumped into me. "You went in on those rooms! How are you feeling?"

I cleared my throat from laughing so hard. "I feel great. Thank you so much for bringing me here."

We stood in front of our cars, and Soja had one more thing to say. "Of course, you're very welcome. Thanks for hanging out with me today. You seem lighter and more sure of yourself. I hope you continue working on that blockage and decide what's best for you, Imani. You deserve the world and nothing less. You're an amazing being, and I'm proud to call you my soul sister." Soja winked at me, and then we wrapped our pinkies around each others, linking them together, smiling. Finally, we let go, and Soja got into her car and drove off.

I got into my car and drove back home. Once I got home, I parked my car on the parking deck and took the elevator to my condo. Once inside, I saw Aeries and Mahant watching a movie and cuddling on the sofa.

"Hey, babes!" Aeries greeted me as I entered.

"Hey, baby." Mahant greeted me as well. "Whoa! Look at you covered in paint."

Mahant laughed as he stood from the sofa and walked over to me. I looked down at my outfit and smiled. I had dried paint everywhere. Mahant wrapped his arms around my waist and pulled me into his chest. He hugged me tightly and then pressed his lips into mine. I kissed him back deeply as my eyes closed.

Mahant pulled away and looked me over again. "You look like you had fun."

I smiled, "I did!" I untied my shirt from around my waist and went to the kitchen, tossing it into the trash. "I'm going to shower and wash this paint off of me."

Aeries nodded, and Mahant sat back on the sofa. I made my way into my bedroom's bathroom and stripped down to take a shower. After showering, I put on one of Mahant's t-shirts, a pair of my boy shorts, and sat on the edge of the bed.

As I sat on the bed, Soja's voice danced around my mind like sheep before sleep, in a relentless loop. She brought forward the same questions that had brewed deep within me, the same questions I had been asking myself since knowing the situation I was in.

I lay on my back and stared at the ceiling as I whispered to myself, "What do you want, Imani?"

Chapter 15

F riday finally arrived, and the excitement between Mahant and me was electrifying. I knew as soon as Aeries arrived, the enthusiasm would intensify. I sat on the sofa with my laptop in my lap, reviewing all my work emails.

"Oh, look, babe! I got an email back from my dad. He said you both would be a good fit for marketing concepts, and you should have both received an email for your offer letter." I called out to Mahant while he was in the bedroom.

Mahant ran into the living room and slid onto the sofa. "Oh? Explain exactly what marketing concepts are in this timeline, please."

"It's probably one of the most fun, easiest job titles I've ever had. I'll show you both the ropes, but you will promote Peach Motors on social media. In your offer letter, you will receive your pick of one of the Peach models, and all you have to do is post a feature of the car once a week." I scrolled on my phone and showed Mahant one of my posts with me holding a coffee in my hand in my Z8. "Something like this."

Mahant scratched his head. "I don't even have a following for this."

"It's okay, you will get one as soon as you post more about Peach Motors. Trust me, as the director of marketing concepts, people love to keep up with content creators."

There was a knock on the front door, and COMO turned on. "Aeries is at the door. Shall I let her in?"

"Yes, COMO, let Aeries in," I called out while I replied to my dad in the email as the front door opened and Aeries walked through.

"Heyyy!" Aeries greeted us both. She had her duffel and heels in her hand, then placed them on the floor near the coffee table.

I looked up at Aeries and smiled. "Hey Aeries! I was just telling Mahant that you both got invited to be marketing concept content creators for Peach Motors. Congratulations! Check your email."

Aeries' eyes widened, and she pulled her phone out of her back pocket. "Oh my gosh, no way!"

I assumed she was scrolling through her email to find the one from Peach onboarding. She read quietly, her mouth moving slightly. "Congratulations, here is your offer letter. Imani, this is so amazing!"

Mahant grabbed his phone, and I leaned on him as he scrolled through his email and opened the one from Peach onboarding.

"Whoa, a six-figure salary is... insane." Mahant looked at me and then kissed my forehead.

"You're welcome," I whispered, then rubbed his arm.

"Thank you so much, Imani. I really appreciate you." Aeries walked over to me and hugged me gently. I hugged her back, and we lingered for a moment before letting go.

It was later in the day, and we decided it was time to prepare for the Gala. Aeries had already showered before she came over, so Mahant and I took turns in the shower. After I got out of the shower, I did my makeup, rubbed body oil all over, and then got dressed.

We stood in front of my mirror once we were all done getting dressed and adding on our last finishing touches. I took out my phone, captured pictures of us, and then uploaded them to my Zed account. As I uploaded the photo, a text came through from Sasha saying she was here. Then there was a knock at the front door. We all left my bedroom and entered the living room. Mahant went to the front door and opened it.

"Hey, Sasha," Mahant greeted as he opened the door wider so she could enter. Sasha wore a strapless, floor-length gown with black and white abstract patterns. The fabric was sheer on each side, and she wore a matching floor-length cape blazer.

Sasha nodded at Mahant and entered. "Mahant, don't you look nice?"

"Thanks to you," Mahant shot back quickly, stepping to the side.

Sasha's eyes traveled around the room, taking in my apartment. "You have such a lovely home, Imani. It's stunning."

"Thank you, Sasha." I smiled and hugged her, then gestured my hand towards Aeries. "This is Aeries. Aeries, this is Sasha."

Aeries held out her hand for Sasha to shake. Sasha took her hand and smiled. "Nice to meet you, Aeries. So tell me, is Aeries your soul or your birth name?"

I had a shocked look on my face, never thinking to ask Aeries that question myself. I looked at Aeries, and then at Mahant, who also had a curious expression.

"Oh, my name is Parish Grant. That's my birth name, or the name given by my parents. My soul name is Aeries, and most people call me Aeries, thinking it's a nickname." Aeries explained as she clutched her handbag.

Sasha smiled at Aeries. "Both are beautiful names. Thank you for sharing."

We stood and chatted for a while. Sasha asked Aeries a series of questions, and then she had regular conversations with all of us.

"So, how did you all meet?" Sasha's eyes bounced off each of us as she asked that question.

The room became uneasy as Aeries, Mahant, and I attempted to find the words to describe our dynamic.

I was the first to break the silence. "We are all soul-tied."

Sasha's facial expression changed into an inquisitive one. "Oh?"

"Mahant and I were soul-tied first, and he then asked the universe if he could be soul-tied to Aeries, and the universe granted him his wish. However, I can feel a tethered string to her as well. We are still trying to wrap our heads around it." I shifted uncomfortably as I explained to Sasha.

"That's very different. Usually, there's only a tie to the one who asked." Sasha looked at me, then Aeries, and then slowly turned to look at Mahant. "Hmm…"

Mahant's aura dimmed, and he looked extremely uncomfortable. Sasha's gaze alone was humbling.

"Well, let's head to the Gala. I have a limo waiting downstairs for us." Sasha was done questioning Aeries and gave her a friendly nod.

As we left the condo, I told COMO to lock up. We went down to the front of Diamond's Landing and got into Sasha's limo. It was a nice limousine—freshly washed and waxed on the outside, with a cream-colored interior. We piled in, and she immediately grabbed a bottle of wine, popped it open, and poured it into four glasses.

"Oh, I don't drink," Mahant whispered when she tried to hand him the glass.

She poured his drink into her glass and then smiled at him. "More for me." Sasha then took out her cell phone and sent a text to someone.

We drank as we headed to the Gala and continued to converse in the car. The drive wasn't that long, and we pulled up to the building in about fifteen minutes. It was celebrity status—tons of other limousines, some peach model cars, and other luxury vehicles filled the space, lined up, ready for people to exit and walk a red carpet that led into the building. People gathered outside the building, waiting to see who would exit the cars and bless them with their presence. I'm sure they wondered what was happening and who was attending.

My eyes grew wide with wonder as I peered out the car window. "This seems overwhelming and very extravagant not to be televised."

"It's in a different spot every year, every timeline. As much as we try to keep it hush-hush, people find out and wonder what the Gala is about. Some people go as far as trying to sneak in, but security is tight." Sasha explained as we looked out the window together. "So no, it's not televised, but unfortunately, we can't keep it a secret. We hand out a lot of non-disclosure agreements to anyone staffed to work or performers, but that goes so far."

"I feel like I've seen videos of a gala like this last year. It was very private, and some people on Zed had posted about it. Was your last Gala last year in... Shit." Aeries piped up, then snapped her fingers as she tried to think. She closed her eyes for a brief second, then opened and pointed. "Stanford, it was in Stanford last year!"

Sasha nodded her head and smiled. "That was us, yes."

Aeries, with excitement, spoke. "I knew it! It went viral that nobody knew what was happening, and that it was a private event."

"Yeah, so I'll let you in on a little secret. Sage will be here tonight to make a big announcement. It's concerning the Galas and meetups." Sasha adjusted herself in her dress as we approached the entrance, ready to get out of the car.

Mahant looked at Sasha. "Well, now I'm curious about what that announcement will be."

Sasha looked at Mahant. "You will soon find out."

We finally pulled up to the drop-off zone. Sasha's driver got out of the car and walked to the back, opening the door to let us all out. Sasha exited the vehicle first, followed by Aeries, Mahant, and me. We walked down the red carpet and into the building as people took photos of us, screamed, and waved to get our attention. I was mesmerized by the breathtaking decorations as soon as we entered the building. The focal point was a massive stage at the back of the building, featuring flashing lights, speakers, and large-screen TVs on either side. On the main floor were round tables, each with a white cloth. There had to have been at least fifty tables, placed strategically to the left and right of the building, with a marble walkway leading to the stage. Staff topped the tables with expensive cutlery and a floral arrangement, and there were beautiful circular light fixtures above each table. People were already seated at their designated spots as we made our way to the front with Sasha.

"You all will sit with us." Sasha waved her hand to continue following us as we navigated through the crowd. Although it was early, many people were already present. Music was playing overhead, and the aroma was decadent, with notes of chocolate and amber. Everything was mint—clean, shiny, and polished to perfection. They draped curtains throughout the space, elegantly, and in deep burgundy. We finally sat down at our table, our names clearly written on a folded plaque so we knew where to sit. I sat next to Sasha, and Mahant was between me and Aeries, leaving a space on the other side of Sasha. Our table could easily seat six people, leaving extra space for two more.

A server walked over to our table and set down champagne glasses in front of each of us, except for Mahant, who had sparkling cider. As if they already knew of his dietary restrictions.

Mahant looked at Sasha, and she raised her glass. "I texted the catering company's manager about your consumption restrictions."

"Thank you," Mahant responded, raising his glass back. "I really appreciate that."

We all picked up our glasses and sipped away as more people entered the venue and took seats. In the distance, I noticed Kye and Omari a few seats away. Our eyes met, and they instantly made their way over to our table.

"Oh my gosh, hunny, you look absolutely stunning. You are working that dress." Kye expressively moved his hands around, touched my shoulder, and then leaned back dramatically to get a better look at me.

I blushed hard and smiled. "Thank you Kye. You look stunning as well, as always."

Kye was wearing a lime-green sequin suit, and his face was done up to match his look—highlighted with green eyeshadow and blush. Kye then waved at Mahant, Aeries, and Sasha.

"Oh, Kye, this is our soul tie, Aeries. Aeries, this is Kye and Omari." I introduced them all to each other.

Kye looked at Aeries and rested his hands on his heart. "Ugh, all of you are so stunning. Such a beautiful couple. Nice to meet you, Aeries, you're gorgeous, girl."

Aeries smiled at the compliment and greeted both Kye and Omari.

"Well, let us get back to our seats. This Gala is about to start at any moment," Omari announced as she turned around and headed towards their seats. Kye waved goodbye and then followed Omari.

Eventually, the Gala started, the lights dimmed, and the music faded as two people walked onto the stage before us. It was Sage and Julio.

Julio touched the mic stand and spoke with a thick country accent. "Good evening, and welcome everyone. So glad to see all your beautiful faces. Some familiar, some new. Tonight we celebrate the beauty of life—We will drink, dance, and watch some amazing performers."

Julio stopped speaking and turned his attention towards Sage. They both looked stunning—Julio wore an all-white suit with his collar and the hems of his jacket trimmed in black. He wore a cowboy hat, boots, and a costly-looking, shiny watch to complete his look. He looked like a million bucks. Sage wore a stunning, high-split, all-black dress with sparkling gold accents. Built into the dress were gloves that fit her skin perfectly, leaving no wrinkles or imperfections. Around her waist was a high-waisted statement belt, designed like ribbons of gold. Her hair was slicked back into a bun, and she wore golden hair pieces, golden curved earrings, and gold heels to match. She stood tall and unmoving, almost like a mannequin, looking out at the crowd.

She leaned into the mic. "Our first performance is by a six-time Prestige Award winner. I welcome you to the stage, Adam Logger."

Mahant and I both looked at each other, surprised and excited. The Prestige Award was the highest musical award any musician could win for a released single. Adam Logger was one of our favorite singers of this time; his music was a powerful symphony, a cross between spiritual and R&B. Where most artists sang about money, drugs, and sex, Adam Logger sang beautifully written songs about aligning with your inner being, loving a higher power, and being divinely spirited. With his deep, raspy voice, he captivated and awed the audience whenever he sang. It thrilled me he was performing and wondered how The Collection had secured such an iconic figure for their event. I even wondered if Adam Logger was a part of The Collection and Recollections Contract.

Adam finally came out and put on the performance of his lifetime. We sang, stood up, and danced at our tables to him on stage. A few minutes into his performance, I noticed Sage and Julio closing in on our table from the side steps that led from the stage. They approached the table, pulled out the chairs, and sat down. Sage sat next to Sasha, and Julio sat in the last chair between Sage and Aeries. They both quietly waved and greeted everyone so as not to disturb the performance, then enjoyed watching.

Artists, comedians, magicians, and other speakers took to the stage throughout the night, introducing themselves to the audience and then introducing the next performer to treat us to another visual. So many famous musicians were here tonight, some of whom I followed, and they even followed me back on Zed. It was a sight to witness, an enclave of culture and joy.

The servers served food while we watched another performer, Escor, dramatically take the stage. Lights flashed, fireworks sparkled, and the dance crew performed their popular viral dance routine.

After a couple of hours, the performances stopped, allowing people to get up, walk around, and mingle with others. While we sat at the table, so many people approached Sasha, Julio, and Sage to talk to them and compliment their looks. Eventually, it died down, allowing us to converse with Julio and Sage.

"This is such a beautiful Gala, thank you so much for inviting us." Aeries reached out, shook Julio's hand, and then leaned in, doing the same with Sage.

"You are very welcome. It's a pleasure having you all here." Julio sweetly said back, drawing his attention to me, Mahant, and Aeries. "Now I'm very familiar with Zya Peach, but I'm curious about you two."

I was shocked and wasn't aware that Julio knew who I was; I should have known better. Mahant and Aeries looked at each other and then back at Julio.

"Well, my name is Brandon, but you can call me my soul name, Mahant." Mahant introduced himself. "I used to be a security officer at Blue City Mall, but now I'm marketing for Peach Motors."

"As am I. We both recently got employed with Peach." Aeries added as she rested her hand on Mahant's leg, rubbing his thigh.

"Oh, congratulations." Julio nodded at them, then picked up his fork and ate some of his food. "Tell me more."

Mahant cleared his voice, then continued. "Well, I'm nine hundred and seventy-six, but only twenty-four in this timeline. We are all twenty-four. Aeries is younger in soul years."

"I have no idea how old I am. I just know I'm twenty-four now and in my previous life I passed away at the age of eighty-four." Aeries shrugged and then chuckled; nervousness was in her voice.

Sage turned her head, as if she were done listening in and wanted to partake in the conversation. "It's simple. You add your previous years to your current years. So, my dear, you would be one hundred and eight. You're a baby. Is this your second timeline?"

Aeries blushed as all eyes were on her. "Yes, it is my second timeline."

"Oh, I remember my second timeline. It was a shit show, and I hated it. You feel you never died, and you just woke up in another body. It's crazy!" Julio bit into some crunchy celery and started chewing. "Luckily, I had Sage to help soften some of the stir crazy. She found me, jumped to my timeline, and has been my rock since."

"Wait, were you able to stay in his timeline?" Mahant asked curiously, crossing and balling up his fingers, placing them in front of him.

Sage looked at Mahant. "I can find anybody in the universe. I can jump to their timeline and stay there, yes."

"Wow." Mahant's jaw dropped. "That's an amazing gift."

Sage smiled and then sipped her champagne. I looked at Julio, whose eyes were locked on her, his gaze fueled by love and admiration.

I crossed my legs and picked up my soup spoon to eat the gnocchi soup before me. "So, what's your special ability, Julio?"

Julio shrugged. "I have empathic abilities. I can control energies and moods, but I only like to improve people's moods, not make them worse." He points his finger at us to make sure we understand he means business.

"That's awesome!" Aeries yelled excitedly.

"It's okay, nothing too crazy. It suits me because I'm such a happy little man." Julio smiled and swayed in his seat, looking very goofy.

As the night progressed, we talked, ate, drank, and enjoyed the continuation of the performances. Sage and Julio excused themselves to walk around and say hello to the people they had not seen tonight, leaving us to enjoy each other's company.

Four hours had passed since we arrived, and the Gala was wrapping up. Sage and Julio returned on stage to wrap up the ceremony.

"Thank you all for coming out and enjoying this fantastic night with us! It has been an honor and a pleasure to host such amazing events with such amazing people. As this night ends, we must remember and cherish all the incredible celebrations thus far. Now, we have an announcement to make." Julio looked over at Sage after he finished talking so she could take over.

Sage touched Julio's face and then turned her attention towards the crowd. "As some of you know, we recently started The Collection a few hundred years ago, in Utopia. It's been an honor to meet so many amazing people. Unfortunately, all the events we have been hosting have generated too much publicity. There are listening ears in every timeline threatening to hurt or expose individuals of The Collection." Sasha paused as the whispers and commotion in the crowd grew louder. "Listen, I know you want these events to continue, but my priority is keeping the universe's beings safe. All I ever wanted was for us to come together on common ground and not feel alone. However, until it is safe for us to congregate, we will halt meetups in every timeline."

I looked at Mahant and Aeries with a worried expression, as they looked back at me the same. My eyes redirected to Sasha, who was staring me dead in the eye. Her eyebrows arched, and then she nodded to confirm everything Sage said.

Sage continued speaking to the crowd. "I'm not saying there will never again be a meetup. Just for now, we must lie low. Once we are in the clear, we will return as if we never left, stronger than ever before. Thank you." She stepped off the stage and made her way out the back, disappearing.

"So that was the big announcement, wow! We just found out about The Collection and now it's gone." Mahant sadly muttered, rubbing the back of his head nervously.

Sasha leaned around me to look at Mahant. "Well, you guys still have me. Hope that amounts to something."

"Of course it does," I assured her.

The Gala was over, and as we walked out of the front entrance, a hand touched my shoulder. I turned around, and it was Soja.

"Hey girly!" I yelled as I leaned in and hugged her. Soja hugged me back and then pulled away.

She looked at Mahant and smiled. "Hey, Mahant."

"Sup Soja!" Mahant called out.

I turned and looked at Aeries, reached out, grabbed her, and pulled her closer, wrapping my arms around her arm. "Soja, this is Aeries. Aeries, this is Soja."

"Hey, Soja!" Aeries greeted me sweetly.

Soja made a devilish grin and then smiled back. "Nice to meet you, Aeries." Soja then looked at Mahant and chuckled.

"What's so funny?" Mahant looked at Soja and raised his eyebrow.

"You're funny, Mahant." Soja slyly responded, with no filter and no remorse.

I gave Soja a look, and she cleared her throat and walked away.

"I'll catch ya later, Imani!" she yelled as she exited the building and got into her personal car.

Mahant gave me a look, and I sank into myself, a little embarrassed by the awkward encounter and introduction to Aeries. We piled back into Sasha's car, and Sasha stayed outside the car.

"I'll send y'all back to Imani's. I'm going to chat with Sage and Julio. Thanks for coming out tonight, and hopefully we will hang out soon." Sasha closed the door after she informed us she was not coming with us. The driver then drove off, heading towards Diamond's Landing.

Mahant was quiet the entire ride home, and it was tense between us all.

Once we arrived, we got out of the car and went up to the top floor. We entered the condo, and I started undressing from all the formal wear.

"So, what the hell was that about? How am I funny?" Mahant asked, taking off his cufflinks and then his jacket.

"I don't know what she meant by that, Mahant." I rolled my eyes and then entered the bedroom. "Did you hear her elaborate?"

Mahant followed me into the bedroom. "Well, it sounded like she had a problem with me or something. What did I do?"

"Let's not turn a good night into a bad one." I unzipped my dress and pulled it off, hanging it in my walk-in closet. I then grabbed a long t-shirt and threw it on. "Plus, if you can't see the magnitude of what you did, what's the point of talking about it?"

Mahant hung up his jacket as well. "Stop speaking in code and just say what's on your mind."

Aeries was standing in the doorway. "Hey, I'm going to head out. Thank you so much for tonight. It was fun."

I walked up to Aeries and hugged her, and she hugged me back. "Thank you for coming. Let's hang out soon?"

"For sure." She whispered, and then we let go of each other. As Aeries left the condo, I entered the living room and sat on the sofa. "You sure you don't wanna leave with Aeries?"

Mahant continued to follow me. He stood next to the sofa as I sat there. "What the hell is going on? Why are you being weird?"

I crossed my legs and looked up at Mahant. "Listen, Mahant, I still have some animosity. I told you that all of this would take some time. I vented to Soja about our relationship, and she has her own opinions about it."

"So, Soja hates me now?" Mahant scoffed and shook his head, then rubbed the back of his head.

"I wouldn't say hate, but you know how she is. Her discernment is strong, and she gives a shit about me."

"I give a shit about you, Imani!" Mahant yelled, completely frustrated.

I squinted my eyes and tilted my head. "Do you, Mahant? Like, do you honestly care?"

Mahant scolded me. "How could you say that to me?"

I lifted my hands expressively, then shrugged. "Umm, I don't know... maybe because you created a soul tie without even running it past me. If you knew you would ask the universe to soul tie you to Aeries, why didn't you tell me you were going to when you were on your deathbed as Lanno?"

"I told you, Imani. I didn't think you would be this upset about it."

I rolled my eyes, then took off my rings and put them on the coffee table. "If you truly think that, then all these hundreds of years are a waste, and you really don't know me. Maybe I need to stop being so damn chill about all the dumb shit you do and be more serious with you."

Mahant raised both of his eyebrows. "All the dumb shit I do. Wow..."

I sighed and then looked up at Mahant. "Maybe that was a little too harsh, but—"

"Nah, you got it, Imani." Mahant walked away into the kitchen to grab a bottle of water.

"Do you hear me, Mahant? Are you listening?" I calmly asked as he drank his water. "I'm really trying to get over all of this, but I fear it will not be as easy as you want it to be."

"I got it," Mahant's tone was short, and then he left the kitchen and entered the bedroom.

"Mahant," I called out.

He entered the living room again and stared at the floor. "What?"

"I need you to go stay with Aeries for a bit. I need space right now."

Mahant sighed and left the living room again, returning dressed in black jeans and a graphic t-shirt. He put on his boots and then left the apartment.

I sat on the sofa in deep thought. Such a beautiful night, ending in shambles. With hearts broken on the floor and new obstacles to overcome. Control was what I needed in these moments. To take back my power and stand independently. Mahant made his bed; now it's time he lay in it. That didn't mean I couldn't be happy, that I couldn't live my life.

Maybe this was the perfect time to find my voice, create my path, and define my fate. Just because we were soul-tied didn't mean he had to be the bane of my existence. I didn't want my entire existence to be the Mahant show any longer. What did Imani want? It used to be about happiness with Mahant. Now it's just happiness with myself. I want to experiment and live life to the fullest. I wanted to explore and indulge in the riches of the world.

Reconciling that this was a new dawn for me was rejuvenating. As I sat there on the sofa, sadness bloomed over me. But just as the storm ended, and the sky opened to better, brighter days, I realized it was a symbol of me closing a chapter and entering a new era.

CHAPTER 16

A eries and I planned to hang out today. It had been a few weeks since I saw Mahant, and I was planning a trip to get out of the city for a while. The last few weeks were a mental fog for me. For the most part, I ate little, wasn't taking showers, and my mind replayed the torturous thoughts of Mahant creating a soul tie repeatedly. My mind was a war zone, self-doubt had crept in, and I could no longer look in the mirror because I didn't know whose reflection was on the other end. It wasn't me, but a perpetrator playing with my spirit, making me believe I was powerless and that Mahant didn't need me, especially since Aeries alone restored his memories. Even though these thoughts ran rampant through my mind, I didn't lose focus on building a relationship with Aeries. Instead of taking it out on her, I continued to push forward, because at the end of the day, it was of no fault of her own.

I met Aeries at Bradley's, a local coffee shop right around the corner from my home. My phone dinged as I sat in the coffee shop on my laptop, waiting for Aeries. It was from Mahant.

I want to give you space, but I also want you to know I'm here when you're ready to talk.

I read the text message and then replied to him.

Thank you, we will talk soon. xo

I set my phone down on the table and noticed Aeries walking into the coffee shop. She made her way over and then sat down in front of me.

"Hey!" She greeted me.

I smiled at her, then pointed to the cup next to mine. "I ordered that for you." A strawberry matcha with white chocolate cold foam was sitting in front of Aeries. Her face lit up with pure excitement as she clamped the cup, leaned in, and sucked from the straw, her eyes closing as she enjoyed it. I continued, "We are a matcha family around here."

"Thanks, babes! Don't think I've ever had matcha before." Aeries admitted once she stopped drinking the cold drink. She pointed to the cup and nodded her head in approval. "Oh, this is so delicious."

I returned my focus to my laptop, looking up all-inclusive resorts and tickets out of Bluepoint City.

Aeries scooted closer and looked at my screen. "So, what ya doing?"

Flipping through my open tabs, I responded. "I'm considering buying this ticket to Senne Island for a few days."

Aeries continued to sip her strawberry matcha. "Ooh, never been, but I've heard great things."

I stopped on a tab and showed Aeries what I was looking at, pointing at the pictures on their site. "So, Bovine Hotel and Resort is all-inclusive. It's got raving reviews. Look at Kisona Beach; the water is so blue. The hotel sits right on the beachfront, with many amenities."

"Oh yeah, it's gorgeous. It looks relaxing and fun. I think you should do it." Aeries encouraged me, placing her hand on my laptop's mouse pad as she looked through all the photos.

As I watched her, my intrusive thoughts took over, and I made a suggestion impulsively. "You should come with me."

Aeries stopped scrolling on the laptop and then looked at me. Her mouth opened, and her eyes widened. "Stop it. You're joking."

I laughed and rolled my eyes at her. "I'm not. You should come. We'll turn it into a girls' trip. Just you and me."

Aeries scoffed and then cleared her throat. "I don't even know how I'd fund this, plus—"

"Plus, nothing," I cut her off. "I wanted to give you a congratulatory gift on securing a job at Peach, anyway. You can use those funds to enjoy a few days on Senne Island with me." I took out my phone and opened my money exchange app called PayBud, typed in Aeries' number, and sent her a nice chunk of money.

Aeries playfully tried to grab my phone as she saw what I was doing. "No, no, no, stop that!"

"Too late, already sent. Congratulations, now, let me buy these tickets," I returned to the flight reservation site and typed in Aeries' information on the boarding tickets.

"Imani, this is so crazy. I've never even been out of Blue-point City." Aeries confessed as she began playing with her fingers.

"Exactly, so this vacation will show you the sky's the limit. There is so much more out there in the world, and you are going to start living." I purchased the tickets and looked at Aeries. "Besides, you don't start work until Monday, and we will be back on Sunday. That gives us almost a week to catch some rays and relax."

Aeries wrapped her arms around me and hugged me tightly. I hugged her back and smiled. Even though I had been questioning my very existence, what I wanted in the moment was to continue building a relationship with Aeries, without pressure from Mahant or the universe. In my free will, I tried to connect with her and grow a relationship. Aeries finally pulled away from me after clinging to me for what seemed like forever.

I closed my laptop and turned my head to look at Aeries. "Now, let's go shopping since we leave tomorrow morning!"

Aeries jumped out of her seat, grabbed her bag, keys, and matcha, and headed towards the door. I stood up and followed her, making our way to Blue City Mall. Once we arrived at the mall, we parked next to each other and got out of the cars. The first store we entered specialized in all things beach-related. We purchased brand-new bathing suits, some fresh towels, and SPF. After we finished shopping there, we headed to the next store to pick up a few cute outfits. A few stores came after that, and we turned a quick shopping trip into a shopping spree.

When we arrived back at my condo, there were so many bags on the floor. Aeries and I both laughed as we sat on the sofa and looked at all our purchases. We had everything we ever needed and even bought a suitcase for Aeries. Since she never traveled, she never had one. We went all out—from cute sandals to sunglasses—we were extra prepared.

"Obviously you're crashing here tonight, right?" I asked Aeries as I lugged my suitcase from my closet and dragged it into the living room so that we could pack together.

Aeries was texting on her phone. "Absolutely, if that's cool with you. Just telling Mahant I won't be home until Sunday. He's asking where I'm going."

"Mmm, I bet." I unzipped my suitcase and started filling it with folded clothes.

I noticed Aeries had looked up from her phone and were staring at me. "He misses you. The past few weeks, he's been his moody self and won't talk to me. I'm here if any of you need to vent."

I stopped folding my clothes and looked at Aeries. "I may take you up on that, just... not tonight."

Aeries set her phone on the coffee table and started packing. "I should straighten my hair for this trip."

"Oh, I have a straightener you can use; it's in the bathroom."

Aeries nodded, "Thank you!"

It was getting late, and our flight was scheduled to depart early. I walked into my bathroom to take a shower and shave, then put on a t-shirt and boy shorts before getting into bed. Aeries came into the room and went to the bathroom to shower, shave, and straighten her hair. I scrolled through my Zed account while she was in there until my eyes grew heavier, and it was time for sleep.

I awakened to no sun, and it was very dark, which almost made me fall right back asleep. However, I knew I needed to get up and get us to the airport. I sat up in bed, stretched, and then got up, pressing my feet flat against the cold hardwood floor. The coldness of the floor woke me up, sending shockwaves through my body. I tiptoed into the living room and shook Aeries gently, not to startle her but to wake her up. Aeries' eyes opened slowly, and she stretched as she sat up on the sofa. We gathered our luggage, ensuring we forgot nothing. I checked Roo's auto feeder to make sure both her kibbles and water were full before leaving. Instead of driving to the airport, we ordered a ride-share to pick us up and drop us off. I was still half asleep, but on autopilot as we walked through the airport to our terminal.

Aeries was perky, looking at everything in amazement. "I've never been to an airport, and I've never flown in an airplane."

I turned and looked at her. "Not even in your previous timeline?"

"Nope, never." Aeries laughed as we strolled along and then boarded the plane.

She was adorable and oblivious to the world around her and to all that the universe offered. I was excited to spend time on Senne Island with Aeries, creating new memories for both of us. I thought about myself in these moments, and my second timeline. If I had someone to help guide me, I'd not pass that offer for a second. I'd grab onto it and take full advantage of someone showing me the ropes. Instead, I focused on finding Mahant and healing him so I could have a glimmer of familiarity. Sometimes, in this moment, I feel as though I was to blame for setting this loop into motion for Mahant. Resentment was building, and I needed to get rid of it.

We took our seats on the airplane. I allowed Aeries the window seat so she could enjoy the whole flying experience. I told her it was the best seat on the plane, watching it take off, soar through the sky, then land. Senne Island was on the other side of the country, on the west coast islands. The flight was approximately thirteen hours long, with a two-hour layover. On our layover, we grabbed some food at this cute burger restaurant in the airport, taking note that burgers were our thing, then boarded the plane once again to make it to our final destination.

Aeries was kind enough to let me have the window seat this time so I could enjoy the takeoff and descent.

We finally arrived on Senne Island, and it was scorching hot. Thankfully, we were both wearing shorts and T-shirts with sandals. I immediately took out my sunglasses as we waited for our ride-share to take us to the resort.

"Oh my gosh, I'm dying. It's so hot out here!" Aeries screamed, then laughed, as she climbed into the SUV. I followed her as the driver loaded our luggage into his trunk. The AC was blasting in the car, and I was thankful because I was about to melt into a puddle of chocolate.

"It's so hot. We need a beach or a pool, something." I agreed with Aeries as I closed the door and put on my seatbelt.

The driver got into the car and drove off toward our destination. As we drove around the island, my surroundings captivated me. There were mountains in the distance, followed by a cloudy haze that looked even better than the pictures from the many sites I visited. You could see the ocean in the distance, and all the freshly green palm trees that lined the roads. As we drove, the sea got closer, and when we finally reached the resort, our jaws dropped at how massive it was. The first thing you noticed was the enormous building that seemed to sit right on the ocean. Water surrounded it, meshing the ocean water with the infinity pool water, which was genius, as if it flowed together in unison. Their entrance was grand, with steps leading from the circular valet parking into the main lobby. The driver parked, then got out to open the door for us.

"Thank you, sir. Oh, you're getting a great review!" I snapped my fingers in approval as we got out of the car, and the driver blushed, thanking us for our generosity. He rushed to the back of his car, took out all our luggage, and handed it to the concierge.

"Hello, my name is Devon. Can I have your name, please?" The concierge asked, as he took the luggage from our driver.

"I'm Zya Peach, and this is Aeries. Reservations should be under Peach." I stood before Devon as he took out his COMO pad and scrolled through his check-in sheet.

"Got you here, Miss Peach. Follow me to your room." He turned around and walked up the steps and into the main lobby. "You booked the ocean side suite. Thank you so much. This luxury suite has access from both the outside and the lobby. I will take you through the lobby."

I looked at Aeries as we followed him, and a bellhop strolled beside us, up the ramp with our luggage.

"Everything here is included in your stay, our spa, a private restaurant and bar for our guests, infinity pools with swim-up bars, and hot tubs. We have jet skis, day cruises, and snorkeling. All you have to do is sign up; times are on a first-come, first-served basis." Devon stopped and turned around to look at us. "But I promise you, there are many slots that are available, and we have activities accessible for all our guests. Now your room is on the first floor." He walked to room one-fifteen and then handed me a COMO fob.

"Oh, these are so cool, and new... I haven't gotten the chance to purchase one yet." I said as both Aeries and I took our own fobs. "How does it work?"

"It uses your fingerprint to open the door. To activate the fob please press your thumb down on the fob, near the door." Devon instructed us.

Aeries and I did as he said, and then the door opened. Immediately, we were both speechless as we entered the room.

Devon continued to talk. "Here is your private suite with two queen-sized beds. The bathroom is located here and has its very own jacuzzi tub."

The room was very modern and chic, with brand-new finishing touches, fresh marbled wax flooring, and clean linen. As we walked through the room, a delicious scent filled the air with intense notes of apple crisp and honey, and the AC was already on to prepare for our arrival. There was mesmerizing art décor throughout the room. Strategically placed paintings and small decorative items were next to the TV and on the console tables.

"Here is your small kitchenette, with your microwave and fridge. Just in case you leave the resort and bring things back, we want to ensure we can accommodate all your needs. If you follow me this way, you will see this door. This door leads to a patio and ocean view." Devon opened the back door and walked through it as we followed him. The patio was cute and small, with a table and two chairs decorating it. Large plants on the ground and bushes, with a pathway between them, led to the beach. "There is always a lifeguard on duty."

We all walked back into the hotel, and before Devon left, I thanked him for everything, sent him a tip through PayBud, and waved goodbye. As soon as he left, Aeries stood in front of her bed and fell on it onto her back. She sighed deeply and then let out a loud squeal. I laughed at her and sat on my bed, running my fingers through my hair.

"Everything has been so amazing so far!" Aeries finally let out as she kicked her feet. "Thank you so much again for bringing me along."

"Of course! We're going to have so much fun. I know it's late and we're pretty jetlagged, but did you want to do anything?" I asked as I stood from the bed and grabbed the COMO pad from the kitchen counter. "We could always go to the pool and grab a few drinks."

"I'm down!" Aeries got off the bed, grabbed her luggage, dragged it to the bed, and then sat in front of it. She unzipped her suitcase and took out her bathing suit.

I did the same—grabbed my luggage and looked through it for my bathing suit. After we got dressed and applied SPF, we tied sarongs around our waists and put on our brand-new sandals. Aeries grabbed her waterproof fanny pack and put her COMO fob in it. I grabbed my shades, and we left the room, making our way to the infinity pool and swim-up bar. There were quite a few people at the resort, but not enough to make it seem crowded. It was the perfect number of people to enjoy all the amenities still. We entered the pool, and it was refreshing against the blazing sun. Aeries and I walked over to the swim-up bar, and there was a cute Senne Island native serving up cocktails. I nudged Aeries to look, and she blushed and smiled, then quickly tried to compose herself.

"Hey, ladies!" He greeted us, walking through the water from the other end of the bar to where we were. "My name is Tuto. What can I get for you?"

"Well, Tuto, surprise me." I flirted as I sat on the barstool in the water. Aeries sat next to me and looked at Tuto as he winked at me and started fixing up his special.

He did a few bar tricks to show off, and once finished, he finally slid two drinks over to me and Aeries. "I call this Tuto's Dare."

I peered into the glass and raised one eyebrow. "What's in it?"

"It's a secret, but I dare you to drink it." Tuto crossed his arms, his eyes shifting from me to Aeries, waiting for us to take the shot.

I shrugged, picked up the drink, and took the shot. Aeries followed behind me, and we scrunched our faces after drinking it. It was both sour and sweet, with a fruity flavor. It was delicious, reminiscent of a lemon drop, only bubblier.

"That was delicious. We will take two more and keep our tab open." I looked at Aeries and winked.

Shot after shot of Tuto's Dare came, and soon Aeries was drunk. I, on the other hand, was tipsy, but she was gone entirely. She can hold her liquor well and is not a sloppy drunk. However, she became increasingly giggly and flirty as the night progressed.

"So, Tuto, where are the parties around here?" Aeries picked up her seventh shot and took it, then placed the glass back down on the bar.

Tuto smirked at Aeries and then grabbed a dry towel to wipe away some water from the bar. "We call those cabahnos, and we have them all the time. There's actually a big one on the beach tomorrow. You two should come."

Aeries leaned on me, then closed her eyes and mumbled. "That sounds like fun. We will be there."

Tuto and I both laughed at Aeries, and then I wrapped my arm around her waist. "Time to get this one home."

I paid the tab and then walked Aeries back to the hotel room. I placed her on her bed, and she closed her eyes and drifted off. I went out to the patio and sat in the chair as the sun set across the water. The beautiful golden haze set the sky ablaze, and birds flew home before darkness crept in. I then noticed dolphins breaching the water in harmony off into the distance, while boats and jet skis floated by. I took out my phone and snapped a picture to post on my Zed account, captioning it "paradise in a photograph."

Once the sun had set, I returned to the hotel room. I took a quick shower, climbed into my bed, and rested my head on my pillow. I heard Aeries shift, then stand, making her way to the bathroom. After she used the bathroom, she drunkenly made her way to my bed and plopped down on it.

I peeked from under the covers as she sat there.

"You're not mad at Mahant because of me, are you?" Aeries rubbed her arm as if she were cold as she asked that question, still visibly drunk.

I sighed and grabbed her arm, pulling her back so that she could lie down. She got underneath my covers and scooted in close, facing me. Her eyes were still closed as she waited for an answer.

The truth was yes, but it was way deeper than Aeries's surface-level question. I tried to take a moment and think about what to say without making it appear it was her fault. Because at the end of the day, it wasn't Aeries' fault, it was Mahant's.

"I'm sorry I came between you and Mahant." Aeries continued before I could get a word out.

I sighed and then closed my eyes as well. "Listen, you didn't choose this just as much as I didn't choose. None of this is your fault; at all. I want you to get that out of your head."

"But now you two are fighting because of me." A single tear fell from her eyes as she kept them closed.

"We are not fighting because of you. We are fighting because of Mahant and me." I promised her as I wiped away her tears.

It grew quiet between us, and eventually, Aeries fell asleep in my bed. My mind drifted, thinking about how I'd fix things with Mahant. I then tried to clear those pressing thoughts so I could enjoy my time here on Senne Island without the weight of it all crushing me. My eyes got heavy, and before I drifted off to sleep, Aeries wrapped her arm around my torso, hugging me while she slept. It took me by surprise, but slowly I succumbed to her embrace. I had mixed feelings about it all. Sometimes it appeared I wanted to be alone, and other times I dreaded it. It was scary to envision my life without Mahant, and slowly, I could tell that the same sentiment for Aeries was becoming inevitable.

She was growing on me like wildflowers in a field of meadows. I enjoyed spending time with her and having her around. Is this how Mahant felt when he was Lanno? She's easy to love, like a helpless baby needing guidance. And I so desperately wanted to help guide her.

I reached up and pushed her hair out of her face to get a look at her as she slept. I smiled, then shut my eyes for a final time, drifting peacefully off to sleep.

Chapter 17

The next day, I woke up, still in Aeries' arms, since we fell asleep in the same bed together. Aeries was sleeping peacefully, and I didn't want to disturb her, so I lay there for a while. As my body shifted, Aeries grunted and stretched, her eyes opening slowly before she rubbed them.

She looked around and noticed she was in my bed. She sighed as I lay on my side, leaning on my arm, looking at her.

"I fell asleep in your bed?" Aeries' muffled voice was a cute, sleepy voice I could barely hear.

I nodded at her, then smiled. "You did, but it's okay."

Aeries sat up, got out of bed, and I did the same. She stretched again, then went to her suitcase to take out her toothbrush so she could brush her teeth. While she was in the bathroom, I went to my luggage and began taking out clothes so I could get ready for the day. Before sitting in front of my suitcase, I grabbed the COMO pad off the console.

My finger scrolled through the touchscreen, checking all the activities available for the day. "Hey, so that boat cruise looks like they have available space today. Wanna do it?"

Aeries stuck her head out of the bathroom as she brushed her teeth and looked at me. "Sounds fun!"

"We can get some breakfast first, then go for the 10 am to 2 pm ride." I clicked on the cruise package, selected the time, and entered Aeries' and my names for the trip. "I'm excited!"

I put the COMO pad down and then went through my things to figure out what I wanted to wear. I wore black spandex biker shorts, a tight-fitting black t-shirt, and sandals. On top of my shirt, I wore a white short-sleeve button-up shirt and tied a knot in the front. Before getting dressed, I brushed my teeth, washed my face, and did some light makeup. Aeries had finished brushing her teeth and got dressed. Her outfit was almost identical to mine, consisting of brown biker shorts and a brown t-shirt with white writing on the front. On her feet were cute white shoes with white socks. We both grabbed a book to read on the yacht, along with our shades, satchels, and key fobs, and then left the room to eat breakfast.

We noticed the array of food on the countertops when we reached the lobby. The food looked catered—elegantly placed pancakes and waffles were on white plates, freshly scrambled eggs in bowls, and they presented various breakfast meats in containers. The hotel crafted the beautiful setup, and miniature fire pits were next to some dishes, accompanied by a smoker system that created a magical visual to delight the eyes. The hotel also strategically placed bouquets between the plates, sitting next to a giant charcuterie board of fruits, nuts, cheeses, and more. There was a wide variety of foods, ranging from sausage and gravy to shrimp and grits. Mimosas were even on the counter with the food.

Aeries and I walked around and got some food, grabbing a mimosa to kick off our day. We sat down at a nearby table and ate all the delicious food.

"I can't believe I'm drinking this early after how much I drank last night." Aeries shamelessly sipped her mimosa, looking at me as she drank it.

I chuckled. "Yeah, you were so drunk last night, but at least you enjoyed yourself."

"I did! And I don't even have that bad of a hangover." Aeries forked some of her cheesy eggs and ate them.

After finishing our food, we cleaned up our table and headed to the port to board our yacht. The yacht was magnificent, towering over the other boats docked at the port. Sleek and luxurious, it exuded elegance with its pristine white exterior and polished finishes. Boldly displayed on the boat was its name, *Sea Ya*. A playful yet fitting touch for such a grand vessel.

"Charming name," I mentioned to Aeries.

She whispered the name under her breath as she read it from the side of the boat, then giggled. "Sea Ya. Very cute."

Someone was standing right outside the boarding steps. He was a Senne Island native in white shorts and a tropical floral shirt.

"Hello, ladies. My name is Zander, and I'll be your host. May I have your names?" He asked as he scrolled through his COMO pad.

"I'm Zya Peach, and this is Aeries."

"Oh! Zya Peach, I'm familiar with the name. It's a pleasure to have you on board with us today. Thanks for choosing Sea Ya for your sea travel pleasures." Zander pleasantly smiled as he gestured for us to board the yacht.

"Thank you!" We both said as we walked past him and got on the boat.

The yacht was stunning. The center was the main cabin, which featured seating and a bar. There was a bartender in the cabin serving drinks. The interior featured teal trimming against the white finishes, and everything sparkled in the sunlight. Then, on the cabin's perimeter, you could walk around and look at the water, watch as the waves hit the boat, and rock it steadily. The front had more seating that surrounded a heated saltwater pool. Aeries and I walked towards the back, where a DJ and another bar were. There was also a dance floor in the back, where the DJ played his tunes. Some stairs led to the second floor, where a mini golf course was. The boat has tons of off-white seating that looks as soft and pillowy as the clouds above. There was even a small kitchen right off the seating area, with its own private chef.

"This yacht is absolutely stunning, Imani!" Aeries' eyes filled with wonder; she was as mesmerized by the yacht's beauty as I was.

We explored the entire yacht before returning to the rear, where the DJ was. Other people were enjoying cocktails and dancing to the music. A server approached Aeries and me with a platter full of various drinks. He explained them to us as we eyeballed them. I took what he called 'Sea Ya on the other side,' and Aeries grabbed the 'Why Not.' The 'Sea Ya on the other side' had Rolo, strawberries, and pineapple. It looked tropical and tasted delicious. The 'Why Not' was a play on a Caribbean drink with red, yellow, and green colors. The drink included coconut rum, pineapple juice, strawberries, and green simple syrup.

We swapped drinks and tasted each other's drinks, and both drinks were scrumptious. A loud horn sounded, so I assumed that was the boat's signal to get ready to sail away. The yacht had finally left the dock, and we were now deep out in the middle of the ocean. Aeries and I were on the dance floor dancing together with our drinks in our hands. The music was incredible, and the breeze felt soothing against my skin. It was a hot day, and the sun was doing its job, firing up our melanin.

Hours passed, and we made our way to the front of the yacht, where the pool was. Aeries and I sat on the beach chairs and read our books as the sun's rays kissed our skin. We were on our fourth drink and third shot, feeling nice. The boat was turning around, returning to the docks for our 2 pm load off.

I turned to Aeries. "How are you feeling?"

"Tipsy, but I'm good." She smiled at me as she broke her reading to look at me.

I scrolled through the Bovine site on my phone to see what we could get into once we docked. The spa looked like a decent adventure.

"We should go to the spa and get a massage," I said aloud as I scrolled through my phone.

"Ooh, that sounds relaxing. Listen, I'm down for whatever, say it, and we can do it." Aeries continued to read as she responded. I looked at her and smiled, then booked a spa session for 2:15 pm.

We continued to relax, order drinks, and read our books as the yacht returned to shore. Once we docked, we got off the boat and walked back to the resort to head to the spa. On the way to the spa, we ran into Tuto, who looked to be getting off his shift.

"Hey Tuto!" Aeries waved him down. He smiled, and then walked up to us.

Tuto crossed his arms as he stood in front of me and Aeries. "Hey ladies! Still coming to the cabahnos tonight?"

Aeries and I looked at each other.

"Absolutely. You should text me the details." I gave Tuto my number, and then he also took down Aeries' number.

"It should be a lot of fun. It starts a little before sundown, so around 8 pm." Tuto looked away, saw one of his friends, and then jogged away. "I'll see you two later!"

We continued walking back inside Bovine to the spa area. As we entered, spa music played softly in the background, and people walked around. Aeries and I walked up to the front desk with huge smiles laced with pure excitement.

"Hey! Welcome to the Bovine Spa. My name is Lola." She spoke enthusiastically as she flipped through her COMO pad. "When is your reservation?"

I placed my hands on the counter and leaned in. "It's at 2:15 pm, for Peach."

"Oh, perfect! You are right on time then. I see you booked the double massage bed room, no gender preferred." Lola stands up and motions for us to follow her. "You'll be in this room right here. Micah and Benson will be with you soon." She opened the door and let us in.

The dimly lit room, with purple and white tree lights hung throughout, created a calm, serene space. Two spa beds sat parallel to each other, and a diffuser was pumping out scented eucalyptus smoke. On the far right was a cute little sink, next to some products on the shelves and freshly stacked towels. To the right were more shelves, decorated with candles, transparent bottles, and spiritual décor, and on the last wall was a vanity mirror.

"This is so cute!" Aeries perked up as our eyes danced around the room, taking it all in.

"I love this room the most. You ladies are lucky. Get ready. You can rest your tops on this shelf. Micah and Benson will be in shortly." Lola instructed before she left the room and closed the door.

Aeries and I both undressed, covering ourselves a bit before we lay down on the massage tables. I got comfortable on my bed and then closed my eyes.

"My body is going to love this," Aeries whispered as she got comfortable as well.

I laughed softly. "Yeah, mine too. Haven't gotten a massage in forever."

"Do you think Benson and Micah are guys?"

I thought for a moment. "Mmm, not sure. I don't mind either guy, girl, etcetera."

"Oh! Me either. I don't mind either." Aeries nervously muttered under her breath.

A few minutes later, the door opened, then closed, and footsteps approached the tables.

"Hey, ladies! I'm Micah." A girly voice escaped and rang throughout the room.

A raspier voice greeted us next. "And I'm Benson. I use they and them pronouns. Thank you for booking with Bovine Spa."

Benson and Micah went through the motions of performing our massage. They were delicate yet firm, attentive, and personable. A deep tissue massage was exactly what I needed to work out the tension in my body. Their hands massaged all over our backs, and they even used hot stones to relieve tight muscles and improve blood circulation. It was extensive, alongside their great conversation; they were very sweet. Micah explained they were both native to Senne Island. Benson also opened up by saying that even though the island was beautiful, it still needed to be more progressive.

"I actually had to leave the island to receive top surgery because no doctors here would do it. So I flew to a city on the mainland and the doctor took my breast right off." Benson continued their plight.

"Ugh, that sucks so bad. I wish people were more open to others different from them." Aeries huffed in response to what Benson had said.

I smiled, knowing that a more progressive timeline existed somewhere out there. "Well, I'm sure we will make strides to be decent human beings soon."

"I hope so!" Micah added her two cents as they wrapped up the massage. "You both are done. We will allow you to get dressed and hope you enjoy the rest of your stay."

"Thank you so much." I sat up, covered myself, and took a peek to see what Micah and Benson looked like. Micah had curly, dark hair—it was so thick and naturally beautiful. She was a short, thick girl, dressed in white shorts and shoes, wearing a floral button-up shirt. Benson was extremely handsome, with a buzz cut, perfectly high cheekbones, and a slender build. They wore a floral shirt, white shorts, and sneakers as well.

Benson smiled at me before they exited the room. I got off the massage table, grabbed my shirts, and put them back on. Aeries did the same.

After our massage, Aeries and I walked the beach for a bit and soak up the sun for a few hours before the cabahnos tonight. Tuto had texted us the details, but there wasn't an address, more so directions on how to get there from Bovine Resort. It felt almost like a treasure map.

It was getting late as we sat on the beach, talking—almost time for us to head to the cabahnos. The sun was setting, and the sky looked breathtaking, almost surreal—painted in orange, blue, and red hues.

I turned my head and looked at Aeries, who was also staring out towards the ocean, mesmerized and engulfed in the sunset. "It's 8 pm, ready?"

Aeries looked over at me and nodded. "I'm ready."

We stood up from the sand, and I took out my phone to get Tuto's directions. We started walking in the direction Tuto told us to go from the hotel. It was about a fifteen-minute walk before we started seeing a crowd gathered on a beach around a massive bonfire. The sounds of the waves crashing against the shore, mixed with the crackling of the fire, sent chills down my spine. The sun was finally gone, and above, the stars twinkled in the distance, reminding me of the universe's vastness. There was an enormous house up the hill. All the lights were on, showing off its grandness in the darkness. Music played in the distance, and as we got closer, we realized it was Senne's traditional music. Senne Island natives danced in a ritual tribal dance, and then we saw Tuto.

He grabbed the music speaker and took out his phone. "Okay, okay, enough showing off! Let's party!" Tuto played hit music on his phone, and everyone cheered and danced. I laughed and shook my head at Tuto as Aeries and I swayed our hips.

You could overhear Tuto yelling at people to grab drinks from the coolers or go to their bar if they wanted something harder to drink. There was a bar stand in front of the stairs that led up to the house on the hill. I grabbed Aeries' hand, and we made our way over to the bar, and to my surprise, Benson was the bartender.

I laughed and then smiled at Benson. "How many jobs do you have?"

Benson looked up from making a cocktail. "Oh, hey!" they screamed, coming around the bar to hug both of us.

Aeries hugged Benson after me. "Hey Benson. How are you?"

"I'm good—chillin' and enjoying the vibes. How are you and this goddess doing?" Benson looked me up and down.

I shook my head slightly and rolled my eyes. "We're good, thank you."

Benson went back behind the bar. "It's Zya and Aeries, right?"

I pointed to myself. "Yes, I'm Zya." Then pointed to Aeries. "And this is Aeries."

"Are y'all together... or?" Benson hesitated when asking, but spat the words out while mixing drinks and watching their hands meticulously.

I looked at Aeries, and we both smiled at each other. It had been a question neither of us had been asked before, and I didn't think we knew how to answer it. What exactly were Aeries and I? We obviously were soul-tied, as we knew, but beyond that, how could we possibly explain our relationship to others?

"We are really great friends." I finally allowed the words to escape my lips.

"Oh, so I have a shot then?" Benson smiled, finished making a drink, and then handed it to someone standing next to us.

I blushed, smiled slightly, and then shook my head. "What makes you think there isn't someone back home?"

"Is there?" Benson was coming on strong, and I was not mad at it one bit. I loved the game because they knew exactly what they wanted and went for it. There was no hesitation in any response; it was pure confidence, and I loved confidence.

"Can I get a drink, please?" I laughed and attempted to change the subject.

"For sure, for sure." Benson nodded and rubbed their nose. "What can I get for you?"

"I take it there's no Rolo?" I looked around at the bottles available.

"Expensive taste, I like it. Nah, we have cheap shit. Oh, and I even know how to make Tuto's Dare if that's what you're into." Benson looked at me, another flirtatious gesture to see what my type was.

Before I could speak up and tell them that was more of Aeries' type of drink, Aeries perked up and stepped forward and said, "I will take a shot of Tuto's Dare, please and thank you."

Benson made Tuto's Dare for Aeries, looking up at me briefly here and there and smiling. Benson had the most gorgeous smile, with the straightest, whitest teeth. They had changed since I saw them earlier and were now wearing a sleeveless tank top, beach shorts, and sandals. On their head was a backward-snapback hat.

"Look, I'll make you a Benson Dare, if that's more your style." Benson handed Aeries the shot and locked eyes with me.

"Benson Dare?" I laughed. "Did you just make that up?"

Benson laughed and nodded their head. "I did, I did. But what do you say?"

"I'd like a Benson Dare, please." I winked at Benson, and then they made my drink. I eventually gave Benson my number and told them to find me later. Aeries and I went back near the bonfire and started dancing. Tuto eventually took over the bar, and Benson went to hang out with friends on the other side of the beach. Shot after shot came and again, Aeries and I were drinking like there was no tomorrow, exceeding the amount we drank the night prior. I was moving past my state of being tipsy, and I knew if I was at that point, Aeries had to be way further gone than I was.

The dancing kept us alive; we moved our hips and danced on each other all night long. It became a blur. A whirlwind of emotions took over as the alcohol infused with my bloodstream, and Aeries was all over me. Our auras heightened, and she was emitting a heat out of this world, an energy so profound that it lit up like stars around us. Her hands were on me, and mine were on hers as we moved in sync to the music, gliding down each other's arms, then wrapping around the waist, pulling ourselves into one another. Everything felt slower; our dynamic, the music, and even the sounds around us fell into a low hum.

I placed my forehead against Aeries' head and closed my eyes as we danced. It was as if I needed her to hold me up just as much as she needed me to do the same for her. Our energies fused, creating a beautiful purple aura around us. I could feel her more than ever now, and it was only the beginning. The stars danced all around, encompassing us in their realm as if we were the only ones on the beach—it was truly divine how amazing she felt against me.

My breathing deepened, my heart quickened, and before I could stop myself, my hand lifted to play with the tiny strands of the ends of her hair. I could feel everything—her heart was racing as fast as mine, and I was locked in so much that I heard her sigh break through the surrounding noise. Aeries looked up at me, her eyes glistening, latching onto mine. Curiosity had peaked, and neither of us knew what to do about it.

We both leaned into each other, and then, before we could seal our fates, Benson walked up and interrupted the entire exchange. Aeries and I pulled away from each other and composed ourselves.

I cleared my throat and ran my fingers through my hair. "Benson, hey!"

Benson smirked and looked at both of us. "I was just coming to say goodnight. I just got a call at the hospital to cover someone's overnight shift. But we should link up tomorrow, if you'd like. I'm off work the entire day."

I wiped my face, still trying to catch my breath and get it together. "You work at the hospital too?"

"I'm a nurse, yeah. Everything else I do for fun. I guess I'm a jack of all trades." Benson shrugged and then looked down at their feet, awkwardly.

"Yeah, I'll um... I'll text you. We're not here for long, so if I'm free, we can connect." I looked back at Aeries, who immediately looked away from me and towards the ocean.

Benson nodded and then walked away, exiting the beach. I slowly turned around to look at Aeries, who was still avoiding eye contact with me.

I took out my phone and checked the time, not realizing how much time had passed. It was already after midnight. "Hey, so it's getting pretty late. Wanna head back to the room?"

Aeries turned towards me, but still didn't look at me. "Mhm," she mumbled.

I sighed and then walked down the beach as she followed me. Once we returned to the hotel room, Aeries beeline straight into the bathroom to get ready for bed. I took off my clothes, put on my nighttime clothes, and then sat on my bed, waiting for her to exit.

Eventually, she came out, and before she could continue avoiding eye contact with me, I spoke up.

"So, are you okay?" I asked her, placing my hands in my lap.

Aeries folded her clothes and put them next to her suitcase, still not looking at me. "Yeah, I'm good."

"Then why can't you look me in the eye?"

Aeries stood up from bending over, sighed, and finally looked at me. "Can we talk about this another time? I am so extremely inebriated and tired."

I stood up from my bed. "That's fine, Aeries. Whenever you're ready to talk, we'll talk." I walked into the bathroom to wash up. I brushed my teeth, wrapped my hair in my bonnet, and exited the bathroom. Aeries was dead asleep when I entered the room, so I went to bed and got under the blankets.

My mind ran rampant, and I couldn't settle the chaos in my head as I tried to fall asleep. I hope I didn't mess up what Aeries and I were building. Unfortunately, it was now hard to deny the pull she had on me. It wasn't just when we drank that enhanced our cosmic bond; I've been able to feel Aeries since the moment we met at Dustin's.

Now she's sticking to me like glue, and it's harder to pull her away from the deepest parts of my core with every second of us being together.

Hopefully, tonight wasn't a mistake, but only another door opening to what might be.

Chapter 18

A eries was still sleeping when I woke up the next morning. I sat up in bed and looked at her, my mind hazy, recollecting the night before. A part of me felt embarrassed; the other part accepted that I was only human. I got out of bed and made my way to the bathroom to take a shower. After my shower, I exited the bathroom with only a towel, and Aeries sat on her bed.

"Hey good morning." I greeted Aeries, trying not to be weird about last night.

Aeries replied in her sleepy voice. "Good morning."

I grabbed my body oil, sat on the bed, and oiled my body from head to toe.

"Benson was all over you last night. Are you two going to hang out today?" Aeries asked as she stood from her bed and grabbed some clothes from her suitcase.

I tilted my head and thought for a moment. "Not sure. I mostly want to hang out with you."

Aeries smiled. "Aww, you're so sweet, but don't let me stop you from enjoying yourself."

I nodded, then heard a ding on my phone. It was from Benson.

Wanna grab some coffee?

"Speaking of Benson, they are texting me to grab coffee." I paused before texting back and looked at Aeries.

Aeries, with her clothes in her hands, laughed. "Hey, that's all on you. What do you want to do?"

I shrugged my shoulders. "I'm not sure. What do you think about Benson?"

Aeries sighed and then sat on her bed adjacent to mine, facing me. "Benson is handsome, has many great careers, it sounds like."

I laughed and rolled my eyes., "Oh my gosh, I'm not going to marry Benson, it's just us hanging out, if not just that, a small hook up."

Aeries laughed, then stood up and walked away. "Everyone is getting play but me. What do you think my opinion is going to be?" She was being playfully serious, her voice monotone as she walked into the bathroom, putting her clothes on the ledge to shower.

"Um, yeah, let's talk about that, actually. Why are you and Mahant not, you know?" I pressed her to see if she would open up about their intimacy.

"It's embarrassing." Aeries returned from the bathroom and stood in the doorway, looking at me pitifully. "We tried to be intimate, but I got too excited and couldn't handle it. It was overwhelming and like nothing I have ever experienced, so we stopped."

"Mmm, yes... that is normal, and will never go away. You're going to have to jump into it." I influenced Aeries as I texted Benson.

Aeries' face lit up, her eyebrows raised as she looked at me. "It never goes away?!"

I made a face, holding back laughter. "No, in fact, it only grows stronger. Yeah, sorry, girl."

"Ugh!" Aeries tilted her head back, walked back into the bathroom, and turned on the shower. "I'll be back."

The feeling of two soul ties being intimate was like two stars colliding, a force few people experience in their lifetimes. It's not just about being physically intimate with someone, but about connecting with them on a deeper, more spiritual level. Your essence combines as one, fusing like nucleotides, creating the perfect DNA. It was a science that only the universe could understand and explain, and an event only soul ties could fathom.

Last night was the perfect example of what Aeries, and Mahant were experiencing. Aeries got extremely overwhelmed afterward and didn't even want to talk about our moment on the beach. Thankfully, we weren't weird towards each other anymore.

While Aeries took her shower, I told Benson that I could not meet up with them today, but hopefully I would get to see them around the resort before Aeries and I left. We also exchanged Zed accounts and followed each other.

Today was another relaxing day for me and Aeries. After getting dressed, we left the hotel room and got manicures, pedicures, and facials. After finishing breakfast, which was another amazing spread, we headed back to the spa for our booked appointment.

It was another fun and pampered day. The next few days were the same; we would book different activities—exploring the island on a tour bus, snorkeling with tropical fish, or flirting with different men at the bar. Aeries and I had fun. Unfortunately, we never discussed the moment we shared. Our time on Senne Island had ended, so we packed up all our belongings and some souvenirs before boarding the plane and heading back to Bluepoint City.

I awakened Aeries from the flight home. We got off the plane, exited the airport, and got into our ride-share. We arrived at Diamond's Landing, and the ride-share pulled up behind Aeries' car.

Before we got out of the car, I reached over and placed my hand on top of hers. "Thank you so much for coming with me. I had so much fun, and I hope you did as well."

Aeries smiled at me, then leaned in and hugged me. We embraced for a while, not letting go of each other. She was warm and comforting. "Thanks for inviting me. Words can't express how much this trip has meant to me, and I had so much fun."

We both exited the vehicle. Aeries got into her car, and I headed upstairs to my condo.

As much as I enjoyed myself, it felt good being back in my home. When I arrived inside, Roo raced over to me and rubbed all against my legs, purring her heart out. I leaned down, picked her up, and gave her lots of hugs and kisses.

Suddenly, Mahant appeared from the bedroom, scaring me.

I jumped and stepped back. "Mahant! What the hell are you doing here?"

He was wearing sweatpants and a t-shirt as he walked up to me. "Hey, sorry."

"I thought you would be at Aeries' house." I pressed my hand over my heart to help myself calm down.

"I came over a couple of days ago to grab some stuff and just stayed, my bad." Mahant's voice was low and soft; it sounded as though he had just woken up.

He continued to walk up to me as I rolled my luggage in and then pushed it against the wall, out of the way. We hugged each other, and Mahant wouldn't let go. It felt so good to be in his arms again.

"I've missed you." He confessed, gripping me tighter.

I ran my fingers across the nape of his neck, then up through his hair, twirling my fingers between his curls. "I've missed you, too."

He pulled back some and pressed his lips into mine. I kissed him back and closed my eyes, feeling the heat of the moment. All the built-up tension I had crashed down on me, forgetting that he and I ever got into a spat. Mahant's hands went to my waist, and he lifted me off the floor. My legs wrapped around him, and he carried me into the bedroom.

He undressed me and allowed me to get some very much needed sleep.

The next morning, I woke up and found Mahant gone. I assumed he was off to work, since it was now Monday.

I lay in bed and looked at the ceiling for a while. I then looked over to my nightstand and grabbed my phone. While scrolling through my Zed account, I saw pictures

Aeries had posted of us and posted some of my own, tagging her. Finally, I got out of bed and walked into the living room. I grabbed my laptop and worked on it for most of the day before setting it aside and getting lost in some TV.

I rotted on the sofa for the rest of the day until Mahant came home. He walked through the door looking handsome as ever.

"Mmm, look at you, sir." I lifted my legs and crossed them under me, Indian-style, as I sat on the sofa. Mahant was wearing an all-black suit with black dress shoes. I didn't realize it last night, but he even got a fresh cut and lineup.

Mahant cracked a smile and then set down his expensive briefcase. He trots over to me and leans over to kiss me.

"Mmm, you even smell good, baby." I kissed him back softly and got even more excited. "So, how was your first day? Did you enjoy orientation?"

Mahant walked away into the kitchen to grab some apple juice. "It was good, baby. I enjoyed it. Everyone was so nice and accommodating. They even ordered us a nice, expensive lunch."

"That's good!" I rubbed my legs as I watched him walk back towards me and sit on the sofa. "Ooo! Did you pick out your car?"

Mahant stopped drinking his juice, set it on the coffee table, and then looked at me. "Hell yeah! I went for the prototype wagon. That truck is beautiful. They will customize it for me, and I should get it within six to eight weeks."

"The brand new P Wagon S Class is a choice. It definitely screams you. I'm sure you choose a matte black exterior and burgundy interior, huh?"

Mahant slowly turned his head and looked at me. "You don't know me!"

"Mmm, I know you." I laughed as Mahant grabbed one of the throw pillows and hit me with it. I leaned away from him as he continued to hit me with it playfully. He then leaned over and tickled me as I attempted to push him away. "No, stop it. Stop!"

Mahant eventually stopped as my screams got louder and stood up from the sofa. He stretched and began undressing. I observed him, biting the tip of my fingernail between my teeth.

"Take it off!" I yelled flirtatiously.

Mahant laughed and shook his head as he entered the bedroom. He returned with sweatpants and a t-shirt, then sat on the coffee table in front of me. His demeanor changed, and he became more serious.

"Ahh." He exerted as he leaned forward and rested his hands on my thighs. "Let's talk."

I squinted at him and then raised my eyebrow. "Talk about what?"

"Our fight before you left for Senne Island." Mahant locked eyes with me and rubbed my thighs. "We have to talk about it, babe. You always want to talk things out. It's not really like you not to talk about it and then dip out on holiday."

He was right, and I knew that eventually I would have to face the beast—the elephant in the room—my emotion over Mahant's decisions. Usually, I'm ready to talk and hash things out, but this time it was different. I even questioned why I didn't want to discuss my feelings with Mahant. Maybe it was because I didn't fully understand what I was going through myself. All I knew was that behind this smiling face was depression chipping away at my inner core. No matter how hard I tried to overcome Mahant's creation of a soul tie or Aeries' ability to restore his memories, I simply could not. I continued to push it to the back of my mind, allowing it to lie dormant inside of me, brewing like a kettle on the scorching sun.

"What do you want, Mahant?" I finally asked, breaking my silence and looking into his eyes.

He tilted his head and then grabbed my hands. "I want us all to co-exist. I want you to be happy, I want to be happy, and I want Aeries happy as well."

"And the decision you made. Do you think that makes me happy?"

"I know for sure it does not, and I'm so sorry, baby. I want you to forgive me so badly." Mahant gripped my hands tighter.

"You really fucked up, Mahant. Even though you fucked up, I am trying." I sighed and pulled my hands away, placing them on my chest as I continued to speak. "I am trying so damn hard to be okay with all of this." I tilted my head back as my eyes watered, and tears fell. I tried to remember the last timeline when I cried this much over something Mahant did, and I couldn't.

"Please forgive me, Imani," Mahant begged for my forgiveness, his voice cracking under the pressure of my refusal to accept his pleading or apology.

The tears flowed down even harder, and I didn't hold back any longer. My cries echoed throughout the condo, finally releasing the weight that pressed down on me relentlessly. I didn't hold back because I needed to let go and try to move forward from this. This was the tipping point for me, the point of no return. That resilience in me had broken. The woman who for centuries always kept it together for everyone around her, especially Mahant, was crumbling.

I was ugly, crying, releasing all the energy within me as Mahant attempted to console me.

"Baby, please tell me what I can do to fix this," Mahant continued, grabbing my hands again and holding them.

I finally looked at him. "That's the problem, Mahant. You can't fix this. What's done is done, and we must live with your decision."

"I wish I could take it back."

"But you can't, Mahant! Don't you see the magnitude of this? You can't take it back, even if you really wanted to! And you don't, Mahant, you don't want to take it back." I yelled at him, pointing my finger in his face. I pulled my other hand away from him and wiped my face, trying to rid all the tears.

This tension between us was hard for me because Mahant and I never fought. The tension between us was the worst it's ever been throughout the hundreds of years we have lived as beings.

"I really would not have done this if I knew this is how we'd be." Mahant sighed and continued to focus on me.

"It is what it is. Like I said, Mahant, I will hopefully move past this. Thankfully, Aeries is actually growing on me. I like her, Mahant. I really do. Ugh!" I cleared my throat and started my breathing exercises to calm myself down, then continued, "Aeries is no longer the problem."

Mahant's eyes watered. "Then what's the problem?"

Without hesitation and very short, I responded. "You."

Mahant hesitated, and tears finally fell from his eyes. "So then, now what, Imani? What happens to us?"

I breathed in deeply and then exhaled with the same breath. "I love you, Mahant. That's all that matters. I need time. I keep telling you this."

"But is love enough to get us through this?" Mahant's question even made me ponder the reality of it all.

I leaned forward and palmed his cheek, wiping away his tears. "We will have to see."

I stood up and walked away from him, entering my bedroom so that I could lie down. Mentally, I was exhausted and just needed to sleep.

I lie in bed and wrap my arms around my pillow, tears streaming down my face. Hours passed by before I finally fell asleep, my pillow stained with the trail of dry tears, and my heart feeling broken all over again. I couldn't see a way out or a resolution to this problem between Mahant and me. The conversation was the same every time, and I would no longer talk about it. I just wanted to move on and continue figuring out what exactly I wanted.

My dreams were more peaceful than my reality. And as I dreamt, a solution came to me. Before I was born into this timeline, I talked with the universe, and the universe stated it would grant me a wish. The wish originally was for me to be in any timeline as Mahant when reborn, if I could fix his broken mind. Now that his mind is no longer broken, I shall claim my wish, but ask for something different.

In this timeline, I would continue down the road I was on, the one I wanted to pave for myself, and build my relationship with Aeries.

Then I would ask the universe for my wish.

CHAPTER 19

Act III – The Future Timeline

Aeries and I had been spending a lot more time together and were becoming inseparable. There had been many inexplicable moments between us, fueled by tension and a hunger that burned through us for each other that neither of us dared to explore. However, every time we were around each other, our temperatures flared, our auras radiated and merged into one in a powerful reality neither of us wanted to admit was there.

A few months had passed, and we were getting ready for a winter party and the new year. Mahant and I had a party at our place and invited all our friends. Aeries came over early and helped me direct where the caterers' food went and where to put all the decorations. She also showed the DJ where he could set up.

In this timeline, like many others, religion was a thing. Sometimes, it was different people they believed in, or science, that created the world. In this timeline, people believed in a higher power named Jesus Christ, and in celebration of him, we had Christmas. The story of Jesus Christ was like another timeline Mahant, and I experienced many years ago, involving a man who had great wisdom and communicated with the Gods. Although I never believed it, I celebrated in spirit to appear normal in that timeline. We knew who the true higher power was: the universe—an expansive energy that creates all life. Not some man or prophet who broke bread, but an all-encompassing source with no face. The power around us, living and breathing in the air, trees, and water. So, we called this spiritualism—believing that a higher power exists, but it may not conform to normal, practical beliefs.

Christmas was a fun holiday to celebrate. Even though it was in commemoration of Christ, people truly celebrated it for the copious amounts of food and gifts. On the last day of the year, people who celebrated would cook an abundance of food, drink a lot of alcohol, and exchange gifts. It was about giving in all the best ways.

We had decorators come in and put up blue, silver, and white balloons throughout the house, in arches, across the ceiling, and some on the floor. The caterers prepared an array of appetizers and cocktails and placed them on the kitchen island.

Next to the window were presents stacked high underneath a Christmas tree for all my guests to enjoy. Since all our friends would be here, Aeries, Mahant, and I shopped for everyone to make them feel special.

Before everyone arrived, Aeries and I got dressed in my bedroom. Mahant was already dressed and assisting the crew with last-minute finishing touches. Aeries and I thought it would be cute to match, so we wore a satin high-waisted mini skirt, a long-sleeved black shirt, and knee-high black boots. The only difference was that my skirt was red, and hers was green. I had my hair freshly silk-pressed, and Aeries had her hair back in a bun. We accessorized with earrings and rings to complete the look.

We stood in front of my vanity mirror and took some sexy photos together, and then a couple of silly ones. Aeries and Mahant's following on Zed grew substantially since they started working for Peach. So, as soon as she posted the pictures and tagged me, her notifications blew up. We turned to look at each other, and I pushed a tiny strand that wasn't secure in her bun out of her face, then smiled.

"You look stunning." I complimented her.

Aeries wiped something off my shirt and then looked at me. "Thank you. You look gorgeous yourself."

After complimenting each other, we joined Mahant in the living room. He looked sharp—wearing a burgundy long-sleeved sweater, black slacks, and white sneakers. His belt was showing and fitting his waist perfectly, and his watch was sparkling on his wrist. He took one look at us and his jaw dropped.

Mahant stopped what he was doing and walked up to us. "Wow."

I blushed and did a hair flip. "Do we look good?"

"You both look beautiful." Mahant complimented us as he leaned into me and hugged me. He hugged Aeries next and then looked behind him at someone calling his attention. "Okay, let me finish helping these people."

I walked to the charcuterie board on the island and picked up a grape. Aeries followed and stood next to me as I turned and fed her the grape.

Her eyes closed as she let out a hungry moan, "Mmm, that was a crunchy grape. It tasted delicious."

I winked at her and then smiled.

Finally, guests arrived, with Kat being the first. We greeted each other and caught up briefly before she made it to Roo to pet her. Next to arrive was Soja, followed by Stacy and KJ. Every time someone entered, they would go to the tree to drop off their gifts and then grab some food from the island. While people mingled, Kat walked over and stood awkwardly by me.

I slowly turned my head and looked at her, knowing exactly where this was heading. "Yes, my love?"

"Soja looks so damn sexy tonight. I can't stand it." Kat sipped her cocktail as she eyed Soja from afar.

I gestured with my hands. "So, go talk to her, silly."

Kat whined, "I can't, I'm too nervous!"

I rolled my eyes and crossed my arms, looking at her. "Since when do you get nervous about talking to someone or flirting? You're you, you're Kat."

"I knowww. I feel this connection with her. Like, I know she's my wife already, and we were meant to be together. We're soulmates."

I scolded her. "Kat, Soja has been around for months now, and you've barely said two words to her. Just go talk to her and stop being scary. Make Christmas night the night."

Kat froze in place and continued to stare at her like a creep.

I rolled my eyes again, sucked my teeth, and then waved my arm in the air at Soja. "Soja! Come here, babes."

Kat turned to me, her eyes widened. "Oh my God, what are you doing?!"

Soja heard me and saw me motion my hand. She was speaking with Stacy and KJ by the window. She excused herself and approached Kat and me, standing next to the bar.

Kat awkwardly waved at Soja as she stood before us, then spoke softly. "Hey, Soja."

"Hey, what's up?" Soja looked at Kat and then at me, holding a drink.

"Oh, nothing." I had a massive smirk on my face as I swayed from side to side. "Actually, you two should talk. I forgot I had to tell Mahant something about the catering. Silly me."

As I walked away, Kat tried to reach out and grab my arm, but I weaseled away. I went to Mahant and Aeries, who were talking to KJ and Stacy.

"Hey, guys!" I interrupted. "Hopefully, everyone is enjoying themselves."

"Oh, absolutely, and your place is beautiful, Imani. Thank you so much for the invite." Stacy smiled at me and then looked at KJ.

KJ spoke, "Yeah, stunning condo. Hopefully, with this new streaming gig I have, we can move into something as nice as this."

TRAVIS A. SEABROOK

I nodded and smiled at them both, then looked back at Kat and Soja, talking. I could tell Kat was flirting because she would place her hand on Soja and laugh now and then.

The DJ was spinning great tunes, so I grabbed Aeries' hand. "Excuse us!" I pulled her away, and we stood behind the sofa where there was space to dance. We danced together to the beat of the music.

"Having fun?" Aeries asked as we danced.

"Mmm, I always have fun when you're around." I smiled at Aeries. "So, yeah, I am."

Aeries blushed and then looked away. "Good, I'm glad."

We danced briefly, and then it was time for everyone to open their gifts. There were so many presents under the tree for everybody; we went all out this year. We gave each other gifts and opened them, thanking the person who got them. After we opened all the presents, we continued drinking and eating until midnight, when the new year began. We even played a few board games; some were drinking games, while others were games from our childhood.

Once the clock struck midnight, we popped a bottle of champagne and celebrated the power of friendships and family. Everyone hugged and loved one another, and eventually, as the night wore on, the party died down, and people left. KJ and Stacy were the first to go. Soja and Kat left together, very drunk, and Mahant, Aeries, and I made our way to my patio, looking out at the city and watching the fireworks.

With a soda in his hand, Mahant stood in the middle of us against the railing. He sipped it and then sighed. "What a successful, fun night."

"Mmm, yes, it was. I had so much fun." I rested my head on Mahant's arm and kept watching the sky.

Aeries leaned against him as well. "I had fun!"

Mahant then leaned down and kissed the top of my head. I looked up at him, and then he pressed his lips into mine. We kissed passionately, then pulled away to catch our breath.

"It's a new year, new us." Mahant looked at me as I locked my eyes on him.

I nodded my head in approval. He then turned to Aeries and kissed her lips as well.

It was normal for Mahant to kiss us both now, without me feeling awkward or like the other woman. Before, it was hard for me to kiss him after tasting the lingering remnant of Aeries on his lips. The torturous thoughts of feeling like they could replace me were no longer present. I was completely used to it and accepted our lifestyle. After they finished, Aeries and I gazed at each other and smiled. Mahant took a step back, and Aeries and I closed the space between us.

"Thank you so much for helping me meditate and navigate this new world, Imani. I can't express how much it all means to me. You have been a constant in my life, my true rock lately." Aeries spoke beautifully, warming my heart.

I leaned forward and wrapped my arms around her, squeezing her tightly. "You are so very welcome, my love."

We pulled away from each other and locked eyes. Our auras fused once again, beaming brighter, louder, and more explosive. Our connection was fierce, radiating and bursting at the seams, screaming for me to make a move—to just... do it.

So, I did.

I leaned forward and pressed my lips into Aeries' lips, then quickly pulled away, awaiting her reaction. Aeries' eyes closed, and she sighed deeply, not saying anything. I kissed her again, and this time, before I could pull away, she grabbed my arms and made me stay. The tension that had grown over the past few months made this moment feel unbreakable, as if no one could pull us away from the inevitable. It was a moment in time that felt surreal and planned, with fireworks in the background lighting up the night sky as we kissed for the first time. She tasted like sweet coconut and fresh-squeezed orange juice. Her body heat warmed me through the brisk night air. My hands grabbed a hold of her face, pulling her deeper into the kiss as our moment heated even more. Her arms wrapped around my waist, holding me close as we became one.

Everything up to this point—the longing gazes we've given each other, the lingering hugs. All the affection and love between us made this kiss the most powerful kiss I have ever had with anyone outside of Mahant. I didn't want to stop kissing her or let go. I didn't want this moment to end, and I don't think she did either. Our kiss grew more passionate, with a deeper hunger and intent. Eventually, we had to come up for air, and out of the corner of my eyes, I noticed Mahant, and he was back inside. I knew he wanted us to have our moment uninterrupted. My eyes panned back over to Aeries, whose aura radiated like wildfire.

I wiped her bottom lip gently. "Remember your breathing exercises. In through your nose and out through your mouth."

Aeries listened to my words, then began her breathing exercises. I grabbed her hand, and we went back inside to escape the cold. Mahant was straightening up before he went to bed.

"I should call a ride-share since I've been drinking." Aeries grabbed her handbag to get ready to leave.

I took her clutch from her. "Don't be silly. You can crash here tonight." I let go of her hand and then went into the bedroom to change into something more comfortable. "Did you need something to sleep in?"

"Yes, please!" Aeries followed me into the walk-in closet, and I handed her some nighttime clothes to sleep in. She changed and then exited the closet, and Mahant grabbed her and tackled her onto the bed. "Oh my gosh, babe!" Aeries screamed as they wrestled around.

I laughed and stood at the foot of the bed. Mahant then jumped to his knees, leaned over, grabbed my arm, and pulled me into bed as well. Aeries and I doubled-team him, playfully fighting and beating him up.

Aeries playfully punched him while I grabbed the pillow and started swinging it at him.

"Okay, okay!" Mahant was laughing so hard that he fell to his stomach and lay there as if he were dead. Aeries lay next to him on one side, and I was on the other. We were breathing deeply, Aeries and I staring at the ceiling.

Mahant then rolled out of bed and onto his knees, leaning over the side of the bed. "I'm going to undress and get ready for bed." He lifted himself in one swift movement and began taking off his clothes.

Aeries watched him as he undressed, and I watched Aeries. Mahant took off his shirt, threw it into his laundry basket, and exited the room to tell COMO to lock up.

"Still haven't?" I asked curiously.

Aeries bit her bottom lip and shook her head as she looked at me. "Soon, I'm sure."

After Mahant finished in the living room, he walked back into the bedroom and lay down between us. We talked for a while, and eventually I fell asleep before Mahant and Aeries.

The next morning, I woke up, Mahant was gone, and Aeries was sleeping peacefully in bed. Since it was the Christmas holiday, we were all off for the week and could spend time together. I scooted closer to Aeries as soon as she woke up, facing her. She smiled at me and then yawned.

I gave her a warm and friendly smile back. "Good morning. How did you sleep?"

"Your bed is heaven. So very comfortable." Aeries wrapped her arm around my waist and pulled me in closer. "Also, now that I'm sober, I want to do this again so that you know I meant it last night."

Aeries leaned forward and pressed her lips into mine. I was shocked for a moment, but then I instantly melted into her. I was happy with this sentiment; it meant she was okay with what happened last night in a drunken state. Once again, I leaned forward, pressed my lips into hers, and kissed her. She kissed me back and let out a sigh of relief. My hands reached up and palmed her face gently as we kissed with our eyes closed.

Her touch was everything—soft, delicately humming through me like a melodic tone, and I didn't want her to stop. It was, however, very different from Mahant, where Mahant was dominant and took charge whenever we were intimate. Aeries and I were more sensual.

It's been sensual with Mahant, but not like this. Yes, I wanted to devour her, but in the most passionate way. I wanted to touch and kiss every inch of her body, to explore every curve and imperfection from head to toe. This time, I felt as though I was in charge, though. I couldn't fathom being in charge when it came to Mahant; I didn't want to be. However, with Aeries, I craved to be.

Instantly, we melted in each other's embrace, and the room danced around us. Aeries' aura grew significantly and illuminated around her as it merged with mine. And even though I have seen the beautiful purple as they combined, it was still a sight to see.

The way her hands gripped me, pulling me into her kiss, turned me on. My hands were on her waist now, creeping up her shirt. Her skin was impossibly soft, warm, and unbearably smooth beneath my fingertips. With every touch, I felt the subtle tremors of excitement ripple through her body, a silent plea for more. Her responses intrigued me, drawing me in deeper, so I let my hands explore more—gliding along the curve of her back, tracing the contours of her spine. Each kiss intensified the moment, our bodies melting into the rhythm of our desire.

Finally, with introducing Aeries' tongue, our kiss got nastier. Aeries moaned into my mouth, and I slid my nails down her back gently. Her back arched in, and I could feel the chills that tingled down her spine.

I could feel everything. A powerful force shook me to my core and awakened a hunger I didn't know I had.

There was no doubt in my mind that our souls were a thread to each other because I could also feel my emotions and hers. It was an intense connection that intensified even further during intimate exchanges.

Aeries finally pulled away from me, and we both could come up for air. It was only momentarily before I leaned forward and pressed my lips against her jaw. I kissed along Aeries' jawline as my hands were still underneath her shirt. As I kissed her, I inhaled her warm coconut and citrus scent, filling my nose and wrapping around my brain. The tips of my fingers were rolling across her back and then to her sides. I would squeeze her sides and then caress them softly, pulling her deeper into me.

"Shit. This feels so amazing." Aeries whispered as she tilted her head to the side.

My lips moved to her neck, and I kissed against her soft, moisturized skin. Aeries' hand cradled my head again as I kissed her. With ease, those kisses turned into firm suctions against her skin. Her breathing got deeper, and more moans escaped her mouth.

The energy in the room was electric, humming with an unspoken tension that wrapped around us like a tight embrace. Every glance, every touch, and every movement carried weight, amplifying the charged atmosphere. It was as if the very air vibrated with anticipation, thick with something unexplainable yet undeniable. As I kissed Aeries' neck, my hands grabbed the hem of her shirt and lifted it above her head, tossing it to the side.

My lips continued to explore her body sensually, leaving her neck and traveling across her collarbone slowly and passionately, while small expels of air left Aeries' lips.

I could feel the tiny bumps rising across her skin, a visible reaction to the electricity between us. How her body responded sent a thrill through me—once smooth skin now tingled under my plump lips. I watched as shivers rippled down her arms, the faintest tremble in her breath betraying the effect I had on her. It was intoxicating, her body's silent language more honest than any words ever could be. I backed up a bit as I got lower and lower, running the palm of my hand up her belly and resting it on her chest.

"Focus your breathing. In and out slowly." I remind her of our meditation and breathing exercises we had been practicing for months.

She began breathing harder, her panting intensifying as she tried to control herself, unable to listen to my command. My hands gripped her thighs and positioned them before me, so that I could comfortably lie on the bed. I looked up at her as my face hovered between her legs. Our silent communication made her eyes roll to the back of her head.

For Aeries' first time, she handled it very well. She allowed me to explore her body, trusting me to take care of her physically and emotionally. The room pulsed with an almost tangible intensity, a charged energy weaving between us, binding us together in perfect sync. It was unlike anything I had ever experienced—overwhelming yet exhilarating, lost in a current too powerful to resist. The air crackled with bursts of energy, igniting with every moan and whimper that filled the space.

My favorite part was when Aeries was on the verge of losing it, and I didn't let up as she released these raw, honest emotions. She lay on the blankets, defeated and out of breath.

She didn't allow me to please her without giving in return. For the first time, Aeries explored a woman's body, and it honored me that it was mine. She was soft and gentle, touching me in ways only a woman would know how—with ease and perfection. Like an unspoken code, it was as if she knew what I liked and how I liked it.

Aeries was... great. The best woman I have ever been with.

We explored each other further and had multiple sessions that lasted until late in the afternoon. It was around 2 pm, and we lay completely naked in my bed, breathing deeply.

"I feel... amazing." Aeries whispered, her voice breaking as she focused on her breathing.

We lay beside each other—sweaty and damp, out of breath and on cloud nine. The covers tangled up around us as we, in sync, breathed through the rippling orgasms. Aeries let out a deep, euphoric groan as she turned onto her side, facing me so that she could wrap her arm around my torso.

I smiled and bit my bottom lip, then turned and looked at her, whispering, "I'm exhausted."

Aeries giggles and then rubs my stomach. "Same." She yawned and then closed her eyes.

The silence between us was reassuring, showing that we were both comfortable and ready to drift off into an afternoon slumber. Aeries was the first to fall asleep, and as I watched her, I couldn't help but smile and be grateful we could share a space. My love for her grew deeper as time went on, and we spent more time together. Moments like these had a lingering effect on me, allowing me to push the thought of Mahant's fuck up to the back of my mind.

I slowly drifted off to sleep as my mind was in a calm, quiet peace, all because of Aeries.

Chapter 20

A eries' first time with one of her soul ties was with me. Our intimate session catapulted our friendship, and our relationship has strengthened ever since. We had already been inseparable, but we were together even more, and spending time together. Aeries would come over after work, hang out on weekends, and eventually start sleeping over regularly. A few more months had passed, and it was now late spring. The rain returned to Bluepoint City, marking the beginning of our normal hurricane season period. For weeks, it would rain, pouring down like a faucet let loose from above.

Kat and Soja invited me and Aeries out for an all-girls' dinner date at a fancy restaurant called the Mixer. I arrived at the restaurant and entered a relaxing, inviting ambiance—an elegant enclave where everyone dressed in formal wear from head to toe. I wore a white unitard, tucked into cream high-waisted pants with a CC belt. On top of the unitard, I wore a cream cropped sweater and tan heels to match. I accessorized with a watch, bangles, and a wide-brimmed fedora.

A hostess stopped me in my place and smiled. "Evening, do you have reservations?"

"Yes, my party stated they were already here. The reservation should be under Kat." I clutched my creamed colored bag by the handle as I waited patiently as they scrolled through the COMO pad.

"Ah, yes, follow me, please." The server finally said, then turned and walked towards the back of the restaurant.

She brought me to the correct table, where Kat and Soja were sitting down. Immediately, they both stood up and hugged me. I hugged them both, and then we all sat down at the table.

The restaurant smelled divine, gently permeating my nose with fresh garlic, spices, and a sweet touch of cinnamon. A live musician was playing music on stage, tucked off into a corner, but loud enough to fall on all ears around. Every staff member and server was in sync—dressed in perfectly clean, ironed uniforms that boasted consistency and professionalism. They polished all the decorations, empty chairs, and cutlery to perfection. The atmosphere set the mood right, not lacking in any capacity.

As soon as I sat down, I grabbed my cutlery, unfolded it, placed the cloth in my lap, and smoothed it out. I then picked up the menu and looked it over. Soja and Kat were sitting close as they looked at the menu together, and then Kat turned her attention towards me.

"So, where's Aeries?" Kat asked as I looked at her.

I took my phone out and saw a message from Aeries that said she was almost here. "She's almost here. She went into the office today for work, so she's heading here straight from there."

Soja set the menu down and placed her hands in her lap, "So, how are things going with you and Aeries? You and Mahant? I feel like we haven't had time to really talk in a while."

"Honestly, we are all good," I admitted, looking at both of them as they glared at me. "Aeries and I are closer than ever. Mahant has been giving me the time I need to adjust without pressuring me to forgive him. Things are looking up."

It wasn't the whole truth.

Inside, there was still turmoil, rough and jagged, heavy like rocks falling from a cliff. However, the mask I had on masked the reality of how I truly felt inside. I was still hurting, still depressed, and forcing myself to adjust to a reality I didn't want. The good news was that Aeries wasn't my problem, and I clung to her for stability and love. It was Mahant whom I'd grown to resent over the course of the last few months.

It was a strange phenomenon, though, because I still loved Mahant; I just hated what he did. So whenever he was around, I was okay and happy, and I could forgive him in those fleeting moments when we made love or conversed in the early hours of the night. But when I was alone in my thoughts or forced to question how I truly felt, I loathed him.

"Well, that's good!" Kat excitedly chimed in and touched my shoulder. "I'm happy for you, because I really like Aeries. She's a sweetheart. At first, I was like this bitch tryna steal my best friend's man, but once I got to know her, I realized she's really awesome."

I agreed, "She is amazing."

Soja added, "I'm glad because Mahant was really going to get an ass kicking from me. I'm glad we can forgive him now."

I laughed as I rolled my eyes and shook my head. My attention went back to the menu, and then a familiar hand touched my shoulder. I turned, and it was Aeries, who finally arrived.

"Hey babes!" I called out excitedly. I stood up, hugged her, and Soja and Kat did the same.

Aeries then sat down, "Hey, everyone, this place is so fancy."

"I know, right? I've always wanted to try them." Kat agreed.

A server finally came over with water for the table, set them down, and then pulled out his COMO pad. "Hi, I'm Mel. Would you ladies like to put in an order for anything?"

Aeries picked up the food menu and reviewed it. Kat and Soja went back to looking over their menu, and I had the drink menu in my hand.

"Can we get a bottle of the Tabernaet?" I smiled at Mel as he punched it in on the pad, then looked around. I spoke up again, "I think we all need a few more minutes. Thank you."

Mel nodded and then walked away.

I set the drink menu down and turned my attention towards Aeries, gazing into her beautiful brown eyes. "So how was work, my love?"

Aeries smiled and looked at me, "It was good. We had a short training session today that was very informative about marketing strategies. How was everyone else's day?"

"My day was great, just spent it with Soja. We actually went flower picking earlier, and have a nice bouquet sitting on our dining room table," Kat announced, then picked up her water and sipped it.

Mel returned with a basket of bread and our wine, set it on the table, and then walked away to buy us more time. Kat reached for the bread, spread some butter on it, and fed it to Soja, who ate it happily.

I reached for the wine. "Pause, our dining room table?" I asked, looking for more clarity.

Kat turned red, and Soja looked at her as she tried to hold back laughter.

"Yeah, so Kat moved in." Soja shrugged as she spoke, as if it were no big deal.

Aerics covered her mouth, "Congratulations!"

"Hello?!" I yelled. "That's a huge deal! Congrats, you two."

"Thank you, thank you," Soja couldn't conceal the smile on her face. She looked at Kat, and Kat leaned in and kissed her.

I looked at Aeries again, who looked at me, then rested her hand on my thigh for comfort.

Kat stopped kissing Soja and looked at us, gazing into each other's eyes. "You two look as in love as we are. What's tea?"

My eyes widened, and I turned my attention back towards Soja and Kat. "Nothing's tea. We are all simply happy."

Mel finally returned and took out his COMO pad again. "What can I get for you?"

Everyone ordered their food and drinks, and Mel took our requests and then left once again. The bread was delicious, with perfectly crispy edges and a soft, pillowy interior. Even the butter tasted freshly churned in-house, salted to perfection, with a slight drizzle of honey for sweetness. Eventually, our food came out, and the plating was superb. I ordered the balsamic honey-glazed lamb chops over a bed of yellow rice, topped with pineapple chutney, crispy onions, and twirled scallions. Aeries ordered mussels in a creamy garlic parmesan sauce over a bed of pasta. Soja had the red curry wonton soup, with a side of white rice, and Kat had honey-lemon garlic chicken over risotto. Thankfully, the Tabernaet paired perfectly with each one of our dishes as we feasted on the delicious meals before us. I ordered another bottle for the table as we ate and conversed the night away.

"This food is orgasmic," Aeries murmured as she covered her mouth and chewed the last bit of food.

"Mhm," Soja added as she nodded her head with food in her mouth as well.

I smiled, enjoying the company of my girls, then picked up my glass and took a sip of wine. "We need more days like these."

"I agree! Date night at least once a week or month, whatever works." Kat piggybacked on the conversation, adding her two cents. "Oh, remember when we drove to Almeida's and my mom freaked out?"

My face lit up at what Kat said, and I burst out laughing. "Oh my gosh, yes! Your mom did not want you at Almeida's at night. That club is a wasteland, plus, you had a curfew."

"Curfew at eighteen is insane." Kat mocked and laughed even harder.

"Ugh, yes. That was when we first met, and you were such a badass, Kat." I smirked at her.

"Yeah, I was out there. Almeida's was so fun that night. Dancing with all the guys, drinking, and smoking so much weed. No wonder my mom had such a strong grasp on me; I was always a wild child."

"Wait! You weren't eighteen, you were seventeen with a fake ID!" I yelled and pointed at her from across the table while laughing.

Kat covered her face, embarrassed. "Oh shit, you're right. Because that was the night they raided Almeida's, and we all ran out of that place so fast."

Soja looked at Kat with the most surprised face she could muster up. "Oh, you were so wild back then, huh?"

"She was," I told on Kat before she could object. Kat looked at me with her mouth open and grunted.

"Almeida's is so sketchy, you probably didn't even truly need a fake ID to get in there. Especially if you're a young, vulnerable female." Aeries piped up and joined the conversation.

"Exactly why her mother flipped out," I added as I looked at Aeries. "She had every right and thought I was a bad influence until she met me. Then she was like, no, it's just Kat."

Everyone at the table laughed, and Kat continued to hide her face behind her napkin.

"You're not the only bad one, my love." Soja consoled Kat playfully, wrapping her arm around her and pulling her close. "Imani's hook-up game is real. In Utopia, there was this kid named Jay and—"

"Hey!" I yelled, cutting off Soja as she spoke. "Do not bring up Jay."

Soja laughed as I pointed my finger at her playfully, warning her. Aeries looked at me again and smiled, then turned her attention back to Soja and Kat.

"Oh, I must hear about Jay now." Aeries encouraged Soja as I sank into my seat.

Soja continued, "Jay was obsessed with her! For years, he tried to get with her, and she denied him, and didn't want to ruin their friendship."

"Oh my gosh, please stop," I begged, embarrassed.

"What? It just goes to show you that you have the goods." Soja inappropriately hinted at my undeniably good game. "She gave him some nookie, lasted all but a minute, and he stalked her so badly that Mahant had to press the poor guy."

I closed my eyes and sighed deeply. "I feel so bad about that entire ordeal, you know. Like, I can honestly say that the situation has never happened to me before. I've never had someone stalk me that badly. He would show up at my parents' house. Even after I moved out, he found where Mahant and I lived. He would text me, buy me flowers. I had to turn him down, block him, but he was still very persistent."

Aeries and Kat both had shocked expressions.

"I don't know, Imani, you have the juice. Hopefully, I won't become obsessed now, too." Aeries quietly spoke, admitting the now obvious connection between us two.

Kat's eyes got even wider, and her jaw dropped. "You two hooked up?!"

I clapped my hands together. "So why are we talking about my sex life right now?"

"Because it's so interesting, it's very fascinating, Zya Peach." Kat playfully said, then laughed.

I laughed and then sipped more of my wine. "Anyway, Imogen was the one with the harem of women, not I."

Kat quickly turned to Soja, "Is that right, babe?"

Soja nodded. "Utopia was intense for me, I'll admit. Utopia was fun altogether."

Aeries picked up her water and sipped it. "I would love to experience Utopia."

"You will." I grabbed Aeries' hand and squeezed it as I gazed at her.

We finished eating and then ordered dessert. Mixers' dessert menu was just as delicious as their dinner menu, showcasing an 18-layer chocolate ganache cake and a fruit-shaped mango pastry. The pastry was a cake with mango compote and a white chocolate, mango stained shell, which Aeries and I shared, while Kat and Soja had the cake. Soon after finishing dinner and paying for our food, we exited Mixers and stood outside the building.

"I had fun! Who's picking our next dinner location?" Kat asked all of us.

Soja looked at Aeries. "Aeries can pick the next spot we go to."

Aeries smiled, "Sure, I don't mind. I will have to do some research."

We all said our goodbyes, then Kat and Soja walked to their vehicle. I grabbed Aeries' hand and laced my fingers with hers, then swung them as we walked towards our cars. I noticed she had parked next to the charging station, next to my vehicle. She unlocked her car and climbed in. I stood next to her door and looked at her.

"So, can you stop by tomorrow?" I asked Aeries as I rested my hand on her shoulder. She started up her car, then turned and looked at me.

"Yeah, I'm free. What time did you want me over?"

I thought for a moment, "For dinner. So, let's say, 6 pm?"

"That works for me! I will see you then, love."

I smiled and backed away so that Aeries could shut her door. Once she drove away, I headed to my car, took the charger out and hung it up, then climbed inside.

I arrived home and went into my apartment to see Mahant asleep on the sofa. As soon as the door shut, it startled him awake, so he sat up on the couch.

Mahant stretched and then rubbed his sleepy eyes. "Hey, babe. How was dinner with the girls?"

I placed my key fob on the console and walked to the sofa. "It was good! Very much needed."

Mahant yawned while speaking, "Good, very good." He patted the sofa next to him, gesturing for me to join him.

I got closer and sat down on the couch, then crossed my legs and looked at him.

"How was work?" I asked him as I placed my hand on his knee.

Mahant sighed, "It was great. Aeries and I had that training today. That went really well. I'm happy with the marketing ideas. It was a long day, though. I'm tired."

I lifted my hand and palmed his face, rubbing it gently. "Aww, my baby." Using my other hand, I took my phone out of my pocket and checked the time. "You can call it an early night. We have somewhat of a big day tomorrow."

"Somewhat?" Mahant sarcastically said. "No, we have a big day tomorrow. Especially with what you're planning."

"True. So let's call it an early night and go cuddle." I stood up from the sofa and started stripping out of my clothes while making my way into the bedroom. Mahant followed behind me, entering the bedroom with me and climbing into the bed. I threw my clothes into the laundry basket and then climbed into bed with Mahant.

As he lay on his back, I wrapped my arms around his torso and placed my head on his chest, closing my eyes. His body heat warmed me up in all the best possible ways. I felt his hand on my back, rubbing gently as I allowed my mind to relax and mellow out.

My feelings remained conflicted toward Mahant. Even though he was home, he was also what fueled the fire brewing within me—still a weird conundrum of emotions wreaking havoc on my mind, body, and soul.

I waged a quiet war in my mind, wondering how long I would wear this mask. Knowing precisely what the answer was.

Chapter 21

It was Saturday, and I had a surprise for Aeries, so I woke up to get things moving for the day. Mahant helped me straighten up the house, then we went grocery shopping to cook dinner tonight.

I wanted to cook lasagna with garlic bread and a Caesar salad from scratch tonight. As Mahant and I were shopping in the store, Aeries texted me.

Still on for tonight, right?

I read the text message and then sent her one back.

Absolutely! xo

I locked my phone and held it while pushing the cart through the store.

Mahant walked over with a box of pasta and placed it in the cart. "Are you excited about tonight?"

As I pushed the cart to the pasta sauce, I smiled at him. "Mmm, yes I am. Also, nervous."

Mahant placed his hand on my back and rubbed it. "You'll do fine."

We grabbed the rest of the ingredients, checked out, and headed to our next destination to pick up a gift for Aeries. Once we finished our errands, we returned to Diamond's Landing and up to the top floor.

I grabbed the bottle of wine I'd bought at the store and placed it in the fridge to chill before Aeries arrived, then started working on the meat sauce. It didn't take too long before I had finished assembling the lasagna in the baking dish and popped it into the oven. Then, I started working on the garlic bread and salad. I danced around the kitchen as I cooked, while Mahant set up Aeries' gift in the bedroom.

An hour later, the food was ready, and I set the table by 6 pm. Aeries had arrived and knocked on the door.

"COMO, let Aeries in!" I called out from the kitchen as I grabbed the bowl of salad and garlic bread, placing them on the table. The door unlocked, and Aeries walked in. I ran up to Aeries as she entered and wrapped my arms around her, hugging her tightly. Aeries embraced me, hugging me back.

Aeries pulled away, and her eyes instantly rolled to the back of her head. "It smells soooo amazing in here. Oh my gosh!"

"Mmm, yes. Dinner is actually ready. I made lasagna, garlic bread, and salad."

Mahant exited the bedroom and walked up to Aeries, giving her some love. We then all walked to the dining room table and took a seat. I fixed everyone a plate with a little of everything, and we ate and conversed until our plates were clean.

"So, I wanted to cook for you tonight because you mean the world to me, Aeries, and I want you to know how loved you are." I started the conversation, lacing my fingers together and resting my hands on the table before me as I looked into her eyes.

Aeries placed her hand on her heart. "Aww, babes, you're so sweet. I love both of you so much."

I looked at Mahant and smiled, then back at Aeries. "We both love you, too. I've grown to love you and you've brought so much joy to my life, so thank you."

Aeries stood up and walked over to me, hugging me, not letting go. We pulled away from each other and gave one another a sweet kiss. Aeries then returned to her seat.

"Look, I know we are soul-tied for life. But I want to ask," I got nervous and my voice cracked. "I'd like to make us official."

Aeries' eyes widened, and a huge smile formed on her face. "Official?"

"Mmm," I responded, then waited for her response.

"Umm, you've been mine girl, of course. We are official." Aeries playfully confirmed.

I lit up, and my aura glowed with extraordinary power. I looked at Mahant, who looked proud to witness this moment, his smile big and beautiful.

"This makes me so happy." My eyes watered, and I attempted to hold back tears. "I have one more question for you."

Aeries leaned forward and placed her chin in her hands, smiling at me and Mahant, waiting for me to continue as if she already knew her answer.

I gestured with my hands as I explained the next part. "You're almost always here anyway, and we think it would be best for everyone if you moved in."

"Oh! Move in?" Aeries leaned back, surprised. "Are you sure you want me to move in?"

"Absolutely." Mahant finally spoke up, and I nodded.

"You or Mahant wouldn't have to go back and forth to see each other or me. We'd all live under the same roof, chipping in when necessary. There is more than enough space here for the three of us. What do you say?"

Aeries thought long and hard for a moment, then smiled. "I say... yes."

Mahant jumped up and ran over to her, picking her up and swinging her around in the air, while I stood up and went to the fridge to get the wine. I returned with the wine and three glasses, pouring into each one until it was halfway full. I handed each of them a glass, and before Mahant could say he didn't drink, I gave him a look.

"It's just one celebratory glass." I held the glass in the air.

Mahant shrugged and then clinked his glass with mine, and Aeries did the same. We then drank our wine, and I went in for another kiss, pressing my lips into Aeries and wrapping my arms around her waist. I then took her hand and led her into the bedroom and to the walk-in closet, revealing a section of the closet that Mahant had cleared out for her space. In the space was also a giant stuffed teddy bear for Aeries, with a card that said 'welcome home.'

"Your very own space!" I did a cute pose, showcasing the space before me.

Aeries laughed and shook her head. "You're so adorable, thank you."

For the rest of the night, we discussed moving plans to get what Aeries wanted for the condo. After we scheduled the movers and made the plans, we spent some of the night cuddling on the sofa and watching movies. The rain coming down dramatically created a comforting space, setting the mood perfectly. After a while, we turned off the TV and all the lights, lit some candles, and enjoyed the ambiance of nature. It was thundering and lightning, lighting up the entire apartment since the blinds were open.

Eventually, Aeries and Mahant fell asleep on the sofa, leaving me to my thoughts. I was happier in these moments and truly loved Aeries. And even though Mahant created a new soul tie, I was finally working through it. A lot of the anxiety within me resided, and I felt myself clinging to the anticipation of being around Aeries and Mahant daily. However, I would be lying if I said the plan I conceived in my head regarding my wish with the universe had subsided. It was still there, very much present and embedded into my mind's deepest, darkest crevices.

Even though we were in sync, in perfect harmony, I still questioned what I truly wanted for myself.

What did Imani want?

I knew what I wanted, and it was a hard pill to swallow.

So, I promised myself that this would be the timeline I explored with my loved ones, building everlasting memories to take into the future. And as the years pass, teach Aeries all that I know about existing with memories from your past, being okay with it, and practicing meditation.

Knowing where my path led helped me calm the fire that Mahant had lit within me. Finally, I could relax, allowing the storm outside to take over and guide me to an uninterrupted sleep.

The next morning, we meditated together to see if we could reach Troterion. We could only jump to Troterion if the universe created a Troke for Aeries, so we wanted to see if that was the case.

We sat on our yoga mats on the living room floor, forming a circle. First, we practiced breathing exercises to ground us in the present moment.

As we breathed, I calmly spoke. "This is about opening your crown chakra. Now, the way to do that is to connect to something greater than yourself. In this case, that would be Planet Troterion."

With their eyes closed, Aeries and Mahant continued to breathe in through their nose and out through their mouths. So I continued, "So, since you have never been to Troterion. I will explain in great detail what you will need to envision. You will hold on to this, believe everything I say is possible, and find Planet Troterion."

Aeries nodded, her posture and mudra beautifully crafted by her alone.

"How will I know if I've done it right?" Aeries remained unmoved, her eyes still closed as she focused on her breathing.

I finally closed my eyes and began connecting with Troterion. "You will enter a scary space called the void, where darkness will consume you. That's when you know you're halfway there. Once you're there, don't break your focus. Hold on to Troterion and allow your third eye to open all the way."

Aeries spoke softly, "Okay, I can do this."

I started linking my mind to Troterion, picturing the beautiful planet with its different colorful blue, red, and green trees. I envisioned giant islands that floated in the sky, with water slowly falling from the vast lands and then floating in mid-air. The mountains stretched as far as the eye could see. Not only did I picture Troterion through my mind, but I could taste and smell the serene landscape. I wanted to take Aeries to Troterion Meadows—the most powerful sacred grounds in Troterion. So, I pulled Troterion Meadows to the forefront of my mind, and since it was an easier place to envision, it would be an excellent start for Aeries.

"Picture you are in a meadow stretching as far as the eye can see. For miles and miles away, all you can see are beautiful blue and yellow flowers that are sweet, citrusy, warm, and inviting. The meadow is full of these flowers, some planted in the ground and some floating." I inhaled deeply and then exhaled as I continued to picture our destination. "The pollen is whisking away in the wind all around you, and all your aches and pains are slowly disappearing because of its powerful healing properties. It feels like what most people would describe as heaven—peace, serenity, and comfort. This place is real Aeries. Hold on to it and tell yourself to go there."

Aeries continued her breathing exercise as I painted the picture of Troterion, whispering gently and feeling myself transition between realms at this very moment. "Overhead are giant pieces of land, floating in the sky with droplets of rain floating around them. In the distance, you can see giant mothering planets, suns, and moons orbiting around because your eyesight is one thousand times more advanced than a human's. And finally, the air in this meadow is reminiscent of honeysuckles, crisp and sweet like apples, but very thick. You must slow down your breathing to match Troterion's atmosphere."

Suddenly, Aeries choked., Her breathing interrupted as her body convulsed forward. I could tell Mahant had already shifted to Troterion because he didn't move a muscle when Aeries moved, so I scooted forward to hold her up. Her body's response, like this, was a clear sign she had a Troke and was jumping timelines. However, this was when things got incredibly scary. This transition was the most dangerous part of jumping, where you don't want to get stuck in the void. I hoped and prayed that Aeries had the strength to make it through.

I continued to speak to her as she transitioned between realms, hoping my voice reached her. "Breathe through this part and do not let go of seeing Troterion, Aeries. Once you reach the void, continue to focus on your meditation and breathing exercises."

Eventually, Aeries stopped convulsing, and she sat up straight, breathing slowly in and out. I sat back on my yoga mat and started my meditation to open my crown chakra and jump to Troterion. It didn't take long before I made it to Troterion and into the meadow.

Mahant was lying on his back, waiting for us as he twirled a flower between his fingers. His long, purplish-blue tail thudded slowly on the ground.

I approached and stood over him. My dialect switched to Trosthu. "Eka'ra shi'lo, Mahant. No Aeries yet?"

"Eka'ra shi'lo, babe." Mahant sat up and looked around, then up at me. "No, she has not arrived yet."

I got nervous and approached Mahant, sitting next to him as I basked in the sun and allowed my body to absorb into the planet. "I hope she makes it."

Finally, after about five minutes of nervously waiting, Aeries appeared in front of us, sitting Indian style. Mahant and I both jumped up and tackled her. Aeries' eyes were wide, and she laughed as we landed on the flowers and rolled around.

"Okay, okay! Let me get my bearings!" Aeries pushed us off of her and then sat up. "The air feels so different here. Oh my gosh, look at my hands!" She maneuvered her hands around in front of her face, examining them. Her tail then slapped her side, and she jumped. "I have a tail?!"

Mahant and I laughed as she realized she was not a human being. Aeries attempted to stand up and stumbled. Mahant jumped to his feet and grabbed her arms, helping her to her feet.

"Easy now, gravity here is different, so you must adjust." Mahant was delicate with her, like a baby, teaching her how to take her first steps.

I smiled at his attentiveness and then stood up as well.

"Eka'ra mok'du, Aeries." I touched her arm, and she turned around to look at me.

Aeries spoke in Trosthu, "Eka'ra Mok'du? You said, 'welcome home', and I can understand what you're saying and speak this language. What is it?"

I hugged her, pressing my shoulder into hers as I touched the back of her head. "It's Trosthu, the language of the Troke people."

Eka'ra shi'lo was a greeting, used for people who had been to Troterion before and could transition back wherever they came from. Eka'ra Mok'du was for those new to Troterion, who were visiting for the first time.

"We are Troke people," Mahant added as he hugged her as well.

"Fascinating, truly remarkable." Aeries continued to examine herself. She touched her tail, allowing it to slide over her palms and drop back behind her. She then tried to take another step forward, balancing against the gravity—or lack thereof. At every step, pollen dispersed around her, and she inhaled the particles that floated around her, healing her inner being. Aeries inhaled deeply, then exhaled, taking in the fresh air. She crouched down to smell the flowers and fell into the meadow, rolling around.

Mahant and I looked at each other and chuckled, then turned our attention back to Aeries, who was enjoying herself.

Mahant then pointed in a direction. "Kaelun's village is that way. The cave is in the opposite direction. The mountains are over there, and there's just an endless meadow that way. Where do you want to go?"

Aeries stood up and thought for a moment. We allowed her to choose, since she was new to Troterion. "Kaelun's village sounds fun!"

We walked towards Kaelun's village. It was a long walk, but before we knew it, we reached a lake, and Mahant was extremely excited.

"I love this spring," Mahant admitted as he walked into the water, lay on his back, and floated. "It's so refreshing, warming, and relaxing."

Aeries entered the water after him and floated on her back as well. Then I followed. We swam around in the lake for a while before continuing our journey to Kaelun's village. The water felt like a hot spring, soothing every muscle as you immersed yourself in it. Rain came down from the islands above a little harder, then once reaching the lake, floated slightly above it—as if gravity wouldn't allow it to touch any solid object, but bounce between them like a magnet's repellent. Some droplets were raining on us, while others danced around us in harmony, like a symphony of music. Swimming in the rain was enjoyable, and smelling it always took me by surprise—the aroma was like a mix of freshly cut grass and laundry.

We finally finished basking in the sun, continuing our way to the village. It was a walk through the woods, where giant trees nestled firmly into the ground, and grew larger the further we walked. Mahant led us through the forest until we finally came across a path that led directly into the heart of the village.

Domesticated Amilo grazed in the farm pens as we walked by several homes. Above us were rope ladders, stretching from one tree to the next, allowing people to walk across them. People were bartering and mingling as we walked through the village. I'd never been to this village before and assumed this part was the market. Trinkets and shops were on both sides of the dirt road, and Troke people were sitting on the ground, weaving baskets and crafting hunting gear. My eyes met Aeries as she looked around, completely enchanted by everything. She made her way to one shop selling mesmers—jewelry or body art for the Troke people.

"They're called mesmers. They're like spiritual pieces of jewelry that you wear. Kind of like adornments." Before I could finish explaining, Aeries' eyes focused in on one, and she touched it. It resembled a fiery, crescent-shaped crystal bracelet. "The way these work, they all have meaning, and they choose you, not the other way around. So that one called to you."

An older, raspier voice came from behind the booth, speaking Trosthu. "She's right... And that is the solus crescent, representing passion and love but from within. When you get chosen by the solus crystal, it means you are the bridge to solidarity. You hold the power to restore and reunite." The woman picked up the bracelet, reached forward, and grabbed Aeries' wrist. She then tied it around Aeries' wrist and smiled at her.

Aeries stepped back a bit. "No, I have nothing to pay for this, please. It's beautiful, but—"

"Nonsense." The lady interrupted as she let go of Aeries' hand. "It is yours. I give them away for free. Now I am your seer, Cofè, and Keetsi ak'lo a toru."

"What's mine is yours," I repeated that last part, while smiling at Aeries. Aeries looked at both me and Mahant, happier than ever.

"Thank you, Cofè." Aeries returned her gratitude before we walked away.

Mahant and I both had mesmers, and we got them hundreds of years ago when we visited Troterion together. My mesmer was a star crystal bracelet, and the lady who gave it to me was named Marlo—a wise woman and seer, just like the lady who gave the bracelet to Aeries. Only seers could distribute these kinds of powerful relics. The bracelet featured multiple stars lined along the leather fabric, representing beauty and intelligence. Marlo explained the bracelet chose me because I was divine and worldly, just like every star in the universe—a compelling recognition of how the universe flowed through me and channeled everything. I had the power to move energy, ignite love, and weave my web into anyone in the universe.

Mahant's mesmer was the sun—explosive, powerful, and instantaneous. The power to change people, rebalance, and ignite passion in them nestled into the deepest parts of his spirit.

As we walked through the market, Aeries was drawn to every shop. She would stop, speak in Trosthu, and ask what things were. She was very inquisitive and excited when she met everyone and saw their shops. It was fun introducing her to everything—from the animals to eating; everything was new to her and a riveting experience. We pointed out the Doxtails we saw swimming in the lake, now grilled at some shops. Most things were either bartered or given away for free. If we received something for free from one shop, we would trade it for food, a drink, or a trinket at the next shop. Aeries tasted Doxtails and Umni fruit, weaved baskets, and conversed with Troke, some of whom stayed on Troterion, and Troke who jumped to other timelines, like us.

We eventually left the market and made our way to the community center in the village, where there was a massive bonfire, music, dancing, and a variety of food. There were Troke people playing Parchellos–a flute-like instrument that plays beautifully crafted, melodic sounds. Many Troke also banged on drums, creating a symphonic groove to the beat. Music was universal, and I loved that about every timeline or planet we were blessed to be on. We danced, taught Aeries some of the native songs, and enjoyed the rest of our time on Planet Troterion.

Eventually, Kaelun showed up, and we greeted him as he dropped off baskets full of Doxtails and Umni. It was hours after we arrived that he finally showed up, just as we were about to get back to our timeline.

Mahant ran up to Kaelun and hugged him. "Eka'ra shi'lo, Kaelun!"

"Eka'ra shi'lo, Mahant. I see you are in good spirits, with no memory fog." Kaelun immediately saw Mahant's improvement and voiced his happiness.

Mahant nodded and then looked at me and Aeries. "Yeah, thanks to these two. I feel better than ever."

Kaelun turned to me, and I half-knelt before him, greeting him. "Oh, don't be so formal." Kaelun laughed, then pulled me in for a less formal hug with our shoulders. He then let go and looked at Aeries. "And who might this beauty be?"

Mahant turned to Aeries. "This is Aeries, our soul tie. We just found out the universe created a Troke for her. She's new to the universe."

"Eka'ra Mok'du, Aeries." Kaelun went in for a hug, and Aeries tried her best to hug him back.

I chuckled and then touched Aeries' shoulder. "You'll get the hang of it."

After a few hours of hanging out, we headed back home. Kaelun offered his home so we could transition back to our timeline. His home was gorgeous—tucked away inside the village's largest tree. There was a makeshift bed with lots of fur and bedding on top, creating a cozy atmosphere. He had hunting gear tucked away in a corner, and a rope ladder that led up the hollowed-out tree and outside. It was very homey and smelled of fresh pine mixed with maple. We sat in a circle on the floor and began our meditation to return home.

I sighed deeply and locked my eyes onto Aeries' eyes. "The return home should be easy. All you have to do is concentrate on my condo—the space, the smells, imagine what it looks like, even tastes like."

Aeries nodded her head and then closed her eyes. She sat Indian style and formed her hands into a mudra. Her breathing exercises started without me saying anything, and I could tell she was getting the hang of it.

"There you go, feel the transition and accept it, welcome it." I closed my eyes after she closed hers and focused on my breathing.

We all sat in silence, meditating peacefully in the serene escape of Kaelun's home. Finally, I felt my body shift, a surreal sensation that remains with me to this day. Feeling the energy leave one's body, transform into a metaphysical state, and then shift realms was an intense experience. Like a sudden rush of adrenaline coursing through your body, giving you a high you can't get outside of jumping. Then your body lands back into its physical state, in another timeline.

We were back home, Aeries, Mahant, and I, slowly opening our eyes and smiling big at each other. Aeries exhaled deeply, and I shook my hands, releasing energy from me.

"You did it, babes. You mastered jumping to and from Troterion." I gloated, knowing that I was a great teacher. "How do you feel?"

Aeries leaned back and held herself up with her hands pressed flat against the floor. "I feel amazing, truly amazing."

"I'm proud of you," Mahant added as he stood up and grabbed water from the fridge for us all. He came back, handed us the bottles, twisted his bottle cap off, and took a drink. We were all parched, following right behind Mahant, and drinking our water.

Aeries spoke after she finished drinking. "Thank you, babe. I'm so happy I could get to Troterion. I'm glad the universe created a Troke for me."

"Me too! Now you can jump to Troterion whenever you please. Through meditation, at night when you sleep." I stood up from the floor and rolled up my yoga mat. Aeries and Mahant both did the same, and then we put the mats into the closet. It was very late, so we called it a night and got ready for bed.

I was so happy that Aeries had a Troke and would be able to visit Troterion with us whenever Mahant and I went. After we all took showers, we climbed into bed and cuddled up next to each other.

All I could think of was how successful today was, and how I wanted many more of these days to come.

Chapter 22

A few years had passed, and we were getting ready to attend Stacy and KJ's wedding. They invited all of us, including Soja and Kat. The beautiful wedding was on the beach, with white chairs in the sand and flowers attached to them. There was an archway for the bridal party to stand under. It was a small and intimate wedding ceremony. Stacy had her best friend as the maid of honor, with one sister as her bridesmaid and the other as a flower girl. KJ had his brother as his best man and Mahant as the groomsman.

After the ceremony, we went to a venue right off the beach for the wedding reception, where the DJ played hit music with a nerdy twist, featuring anime theme songs—a perfect blend of both KJ and Stacy's styles. It also piqued Mahant's interest because he was an anime lover. I found him talking to KJ's brother, Nick, about anime.

"Hey, Demon School is the best anime ever. Hands down." Nick says to Mahant in a dramatically expressive way.

Mahant nods his head with approval. "Oh, absolutely. Demon School is riveting and bold. It's different. C'mon, the first black anime. Who's your favorite character?"

"Hakinara Takashi, easily." Nick crossed his arms, responding immediately.

"Yoo, sameee!" Mahant agreed. "His ability to go through each battle, then rewind time so that he knows each attack move is unmatched. Nobody can ever beat him."

Nick nodded his head, agreeing and holding onto every word Mahant said. "But they still make it interesting enough to where we believe he's actually losing a fight, and then in the end he comes out victorious."

"What do you think about Sokan?" Mahant asked Nick while smirking.

"Oh, Sokan is head over heels in love with Hakinara. It's so obvious. They tease each other constantly, but the moment Hakinara is under pressure, Sokan loses his shit."

I continued to listen to them go back and forth, enjoying seeing their auras illuminate around them. Nick was tall like Mahant, with a thick beard and jet-black hair. He was handsome and had a nerdy quality, just like Mahant and KJ. It was cute.

"The show received a lot of backlash, but the community loves it. I mean, a black boy-love anime is different. But I fucks with it." Nick admitted.

Mahant touched Nick's shoulder. "Me too, man. Nothing wrong with a little representation for my black and gay community."

Nick looked at Mahant and nodded. "I knew it! But I didn't want to be so forward."

I chuckled at Nick's response.

"Wait, you knew it? Do I scream gay to you?" Mahant looked at Nick.

Nick threw his hands up. "Don't mean to offend if you're not. I don't think I've met anyone ever that watches Demon School and isn't gay."

Mahant laughed and then stopped being so serious. "I don't like labels. I just like what I like. Plus, you watch Demon School too. What's your excuse?"

"No excuse, I'm simply bisexual. There's no hiding that." Nick shrugged as he spoke.

I winked at Nick and he smiled at me. Nick seemed sure of himself, without a doubt. It was interesting yet refreshing to see these alpha men discussing their sexualities openly.

Mahant and I have shared our many experiences with different sexes and beings, so this was nothing new for us. I could already sense in Nick's aura that he was fluid; it just was not in me to pose questions. If it were for me to know, I would know, and now I do.

"That's cool." Mahant nodded and then turned to look at me. "This is my girlfriend, Imani, by the way. Imani, not sure if you met Nick yet."

I placed my handbag underneath my arm and then held my hand out to greet him. "I haven't. Nice to meet you."

"The pleasure is mine." Nick grabbed my hand and gently shook it while giving me a warm, friendly smile. His teeth were beautiful and perfectly white. His aura was radiant, with a yellow hue surrounding him.

Nick turned his gaze back towards Mahant and nodded. "Great talk, man. Maybe we can do it again sometime."

"For sure, we will." Mahant promised.

Nick then walked away, leaving us alone.

I grinned at Mahant. "I'm sorry I interrupted. You two seem like you were hitting it off."

Mahant smirked again and looked at me, then leaned in and kissed my lips. I kissed him back and rested my hand on his chest, rubbing his heart through his suit. As Mahant kissed me, he spoke. "You look so good in that dress."

I pulled away from his kiss and looked down at my dress. "Thank you, you look handsome yourself."

Mahant wrapped his arms around me, and we danced to the beat of the music slowly. As we danced, I looked around, watching everyone mingling or dancing. KJ and Stacy were on cloud nine, dancing in the center of the venue, gazing into each other's eyes longingly.

I was so happy for them.

Kat and Soja were dancing together as well on the dance floor, and Aeries and Nick were talking by the bar. More guests, including other family members, came to support KJ and Stacy.

A few minutes later, Soja and Kat made their way over to us.

"I love you guys. You two make me sick because you're so stinking cute!" Kat drunkenly yelled as Soja held her hand.

I laughed and rubbed Kat's shoulder. "And you two are adorable as well. Listen, you both are our next wedding couple."

Kat looked at Soja surprised, then she turned red.

"We will see." Soja gave me a look. "What about you and Mahant, marriage in your future?"

I patted Mahant's chest and then looked at him. "It's not really our thing in any timeline, but who knows?"

Kat and Soja smiled at us, then we all danced together, enjoying each other's company. As the hours passed and the night drew to a close, people exited the venue and headed home. The entire gang found ourselves back down by the beach.

"Alright, listen!" Mahant yelled as we were all laughing from the excessive number of drinks we had. "We are all going to run into the water, but first, I have to say this. You are all wonderful people that I love so much. Let's promise to remain close friends for as long as we live and share moments like these going forward. Congratulations again to the married couple, Stacy and KJ! I've seen so much growth from both of you, and so much love. I can't wait to witness the next chapter in your lives!"

Everyone cheered, then Nick spoke next. "I love you, little brother! I wish you and sis-in-law happiness for many years to come. I'm also thankful for new friends!"

"Thanks for having us, and I'm so excited to be a part of such a wholesome wedding ceremony!" Soja added to what appeared to be speeches by everyone.

Kat piggybacked on what Soja said. "Yeah, thanks so much for the invitation and just being really great friends these past few years. You two embody what love truly is, and I can't wait to see where your journey takes you as well."

Aeries looked around as everyone turned their attention towards her. "Well, I love all of you and enjoy bonding and spending quality time. It's been hard for me to make friends, but you all are the best friends anyone could ask for."

I held onto Aeries' hand, squeezing it tightly as she spoke. "I guess I'll wrap up the speech by saying you two are beautiful and so very blessed to find each other. I know you both love one another so deeply, I can see it, and it's beautiful. I love all of you and thank you for all the time spent and memories built."

Nick had his hand on Mahant's shoulder as we all huddled around each other.

"Okay, are we ready? On three!" Nick yelled, looking deep into Mahant's eyes. "One! Two!"

And before he could get to three, everyone started running. Kat tripped and fell to the ground, and Soja tried to pick her up. We all continued running, laughing as we entered the water and dove in. Considering it was a late-fall wedding, the water was freezing, so we all screamed in shock. Luckily, there weren't many people on the beach to create a disturbance.

We splashed each other as the moonlight shone brightly down upon us, casting a beautiful glow across the water, rippling at the disruption of us horsing around.

There were many nights like these from that night on. We spent a lot of time with family and friends, creating memories we could cherish. My mom and dad met Aeries and Mahant and approved of both. One of my father's remarks was that I was a fascinating, carefree spirit he envied, because I always seemed to live my life the way I wanted. How far from the truth was that? Ironically, it resonated with me because I told myself that would be the new Imani one day.

We made it a point to take at least two big trips a year. One of us would pick a destination, plan it, and we would go together as friends to bond. And every single year, we kept that promise and explored beaches, went camping, went on cruises, and rented lake houses. Nick even came along for a few trips, and Mahant and he were always a handful whenever Nick was present. All in good company.

Stacy and KJ stayed together and had so many kids. It was hard keeping in touch with them after a while, but we would see them here and there.

Soja and Kat eventually got married, and their wedding was considered the wedding of the century because of the connections Kat had built with people. Years later, they moved out of the city into a more suburban neighborhood. Kat underwent fertility treatments and had their first child, making me an auntie of a beautiful baby boy named Swali. We stayed in touch and continued our friends giving dates.

The years passed, and we grew old. My favorite parts were Mahant's confidence and the evolution of Aeries. Mahant's mind was a force—sharp, relentless, and deeply tied to his past. He infused our relationship with an intensity and spontaneity that I hadn't seen since Utopia. There was an undeniable allure to him—a magnetic quality stemming from the vast knowledge he possessed. It was as if his memory operated on an entirely different level, capturing details with a clarity that made every moment with him last forever.

Now, Aeries was a completely different person. She was still very emotional, but with more passion and love. Her unmistakably raw, nurturing nature sometimes reached a level beyond even mine. None of us ever fought, and I had the pleasure of seeing all our love blossom even stronger. Aeries catered to us as we did to her, loving us with everything that she was. We continued our meditation practices and often jumped to Troterion.

Even though things were copasetic on the outside, I fought through the years while being with Mahant and Aeries. They couldn't see my depression breaking me down to nothing from within, and it wasn't their fault they couldn't see it because I wore the mask perfectly to give them the best years of their lives with me in it. And it wasn't all bad—there were good moments, ones that made me happy and almost convinced me to reconsider the wish I wanted to ask the universe. Ultimately, I stood ten toes down, knowing that eventually there would be an end to all this pain.

Eventually, we grew old and ended the timeline as one I'm sure they would never forget. However, that was my goal.

CHAPTER 23

This feeling was all too familiar—death. A bright white light transitioned into the stars, and the planets aligned. I emptied into a space where I floated around, waiting for that voice to say something.

Once again, a vast, boundless space welcomed me—a realm that stretched far beyond the constraints of man, time, or comprehension. I looked down at my hands, which were changing into different beings. Each transformation was a fleeting glimpse into the vast array of beings I had been, or could be. It was a breathtaking reminder of life's beauty and all the paths existence offered.

"Hello again," I called out into the universe.

The universe spoke. "Hello, my beautiful child."

This conversation with the universe was my chance to get answers, and I did not want to waste a single minute.

I had so many questions for the universe, and I knew they would answer whatever question I asked.

"How come you soul-tied me and Aeries?" I asked my first question, my curiosity gleaming.

"Ah, Tri Flames." The universe vibrated around me, then continued. "You, Mahant, and Aeries are the first of its creation. I mended your souls into one, then split them into three. Thus, creating one of a kind. This bond is much more powerful than a soul tie or Twin Flame and I cannot reverse it."

I couldn't believe that we were the first of its creation, with our connection being more powerful than a twin flame. No wonder our connection was so intense in our physical bodies back in Bluepoint City.

I was confused, but asked another question, "Did I fix Mahant, or was that Aeries doing?"

The surrounding universe released an energy like no other. A feeling I've never felt before. It was a sensation beyond words, as though every particle in the air brushed against my soul and ignited something dormant within me. The energy was alive, pulsating with a rhythm that felt inexplicably familiar, yet entirely new. I could feel the emotions of this vast space. We were one, the universe and me. For a moment, I could sense something more than knowledge and power—raw, unfiltered emotions.

"You both fixed Mahant together, Imani. Your energy is the most powerful in the universe. Alone, you both mended his broken mind for good." The universe explained, its tone more cheerful than ever before.

I couldn't believe I helped fix him. I finally understood Aeries and my power together. All this time, I doubted my power and will to fix Mahant. After seeing Aeries and Mahant at Dustin's, I let my mind cloud my judgment, a fog of doubt and emotion creeping in until I could no longer see the truth clearly. It wasn't just a fleeting moment of uncertainty—it was a complete takeover, as if my thoughts had spiraled out of control, forming a storm I couldn't escape.

In the chaos, I lost a sense of myself. The person I thought I was—the steady, intuitive, grounded version of me—was nowhere to be found. My intuition, once my guiding light, faltered. The voice inside me that had always offered wisdom and balance went silent, drowned out by doubt and confusion.

On top of battling those wicked thoughts, in the pit of my stomach was jealousy that, alone, this task would have never been possible without Aeries, which still bothered me. The universe had given me an impossible task through the countless timelines, and now gloats in its new Tri Flame creation. I couldn't believe how apathetic the universe was at this moment, not realizing the torture I put myself through this timeline, simply because of a tie I didn't ask for.

"For hundreds of years, I've been trying to fix Mahant. Then you grant his wish, binding me to someone I had never met. Forsaking me, not allowing me to fix him solely, because clearly you believed I needed help!" I yelled, frustrated and within my rights. I have never been upset with the universe or elevated my voice to it.

I paused.

I then remembered the universe's promise—if I could fix Mahant, the universe would grant me one wish. "You made me a promise if I fixed Mahant."

The universe responded, "Yes, my child. I did. You wanted to be in the same timeline as Mahant?"

"No!" I yelled, then got quiet, thinking about what I was about to ask. "You said you would grant me a wish, and yes, that was to be in the same timeline as him going forward, but I have changed my mind. I wish to not remember. I want a fresh start and to be as far away from Aeries and Mahant as possible."

There was an eerie silence between us briefly. The stars pulsated around me, and I waited for a response.

"You don't want to remember?" The universe seemed saddened, a new emotion I'd never witnessed before. "That is a gift, my child."

"It's not a gift, it's a curse! Remembering that I'm not good enough, remembering that I'm not Mahant's only soul tie anymore. Why would I want to feel the way I felt in Bluepoint City forever?"

The stars around me shimmered as the universe spoke again. "Your love for both Aeries and Mahant is not a curse."

I sighed and shook my head. "I love them, but I need to learn to love myself again. I don't want to live for anyone else's happiness any longer. I want to be free, universe."

"As you wish, Imani—a fresh start and new beginnings. You will not remember." The universe explained and continued, "Your story does not end here, Imani. You will be free, but soon you will realize that those bonds exist only because you exist."

For the first time, I wasn't hanging on to every word that the universe spoke, only the ones where it granted me my wish.

"But Mahant and Aeries can find me and restore my memories?" I questioned, my tone heavy with concern.

The stars continued to glow around me as the universe spoke, "Yes, I cannot and will not fully break the thread to your Recollections Contract. But I will hide you in the vast universe for you, my child, so that they cannot find you. I will shield your mind, and you will start over. However, when you are reborn, you will not remember. You will not get to meet me again beyond the stars. Your life will be normal as a human for as long as you live—no more different species, that I can do."

I thought long and hard about what the universe was saying. "What about my Cosmic Stipulation? What about the synced death?"

"Cosmic Stipulations, I can remove or create. What does Imani want, my child?"

"I don't want a synced death. I don't want to remember them. I just want to be free. Please hide me, Universe." I held my arms close to my heart as I made my wish.

The thought of repeating this cycle or being tethered to the same path felt suffocating. It's like being trapped in a story I no longer want to tell, where every chapter leads to the same inevitable conclusion.

What I wanted was true freedom.

I wanted to be unbound, to step into a life where I am whole on my own, not a fragment of two other people. I wanted to feel the wind in my hair and the ground beneath my feet and know my choices were mine alone. And now, more than anything, I want to break free from it all, to find a space where I can truly be without the burden of what came before. I told myself repeatedly that Mahant would be okay without me. I convinced myself that his life would be better because he had Aeries. Most importantly, I said to myself that, for once, I wouldn't put anyone else's happiness before mine. I also wanted the loud, nauseating, and relentlessly suffocating turmoil that brewed in my mind to stop.

"No more synced death, my child. No more memories," the universe finally spoke again. Its tone had a subtle, almost scary shift—something akin to regret or perhaps reluctant acceptance. For the first time, it felt as though even the universe itself carried the weight of its own choices, as if the grand design it had so carefully woven had unraveled in ways it had not foreseen.

Or maybe it wasn't grieving its decisions at all. Perhaps it was mourning mine.

For a moment, I felt guilty, even knowing I shouldn't have. "Your energy has shifted, universe. How come?"

Light from the stars and planets around me glowed. It got quiet again. The universe was thinking, and I waited patiently. The surrounding energy phased from this intensely pulsating vibration to a more relaxed version. Coming into this space, I felt elevated—now I was calm. My energy was now in sync with the universe again.

The universe spoke, "My child, I have only ever wanted you to experience love and life. Even while short-lived, you, Mahant, and Aeries will be a song and dance stretched far across the universe. Deep down, you believe my doings were a burden, but because of those doings, you are now stronger."

"I don't want to be stronger." I sighed and shook my head. "All I ever wanted was to love Mahant, but now I need to love myself. You said it yourself, universe, Mahant's mind is no longer broken. He will be okay. Now I must find my path, create and solve my own burdens if necessary."

Monotone, the universe, responded. "I understand, my child."

If the universe could breathe, it would paint breast-strokes across my heart in agony, in pain. I could feel the internal cries of the universe etched inside me, but they remained monotone. The universe thought it delivered, but I came crashing down hard on it, fleeing the hell it placed upon me. I was happy that the universe would hide me beyond the stars, and all my memories would cease to exist.

I had told myself in Bluepoint City that I would leave them with positive memories of me as a gift for when I left this world and left them behind. I hope those sentiments were enough, but either way, I needed this. I had to live for myself now and stop worrying about Mahant and Aeries. I wished them a good forever after, without me.

Those were the last words spoken from the universe, their final words lingering in the vast silence around me like echoes from a place beyond time.

I turned and saw the swirling of a nearby black hole, its immense gravity reaching out to me. It wasn't as threatening or cold. Instead, it was calm, deliberate, and sure, as though it knew I belonged within its deep, dark depths.

I surrendered to the pull, letting it reel me in. The sensation was surreal—weightless yet all-encompassing, as though I were being unmade and remade with every passing moment. The edges of my being blurred, merging with the darkness.

And then, amidst the overwhelming blackness, I saw a light. It was faint at first—a distant glow at the far end of the abyss—but it grew steadily brighter, warmer, and more inviting.

Without hesitation, I entered the light, my energy merging with it in perfect harmony. It was more than an arrival; it was a transformation, a release from the weight of the past, and an invitation to begin anew.

At that moment, I was reborn. Not just in body, but in essence. Everything I had been and everything I could become merged into a single radiant truth. I wasn't returning to life—I was becoming something more. Something whole. Something free.

This time, I was reborn again, for me.